Spare Me

PARKER BLYTHE

Cover Design by Kelsey Bowman, Let's Get Lit Studio

Edited by Sarah Pesce, Lopt and Cropt Editing

Print ISBN: 979-8-9919083-0-6 / Ebook ISBN: 979-8-9919083-1-3

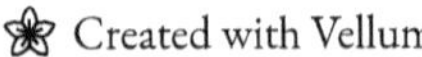 Created with Vellum

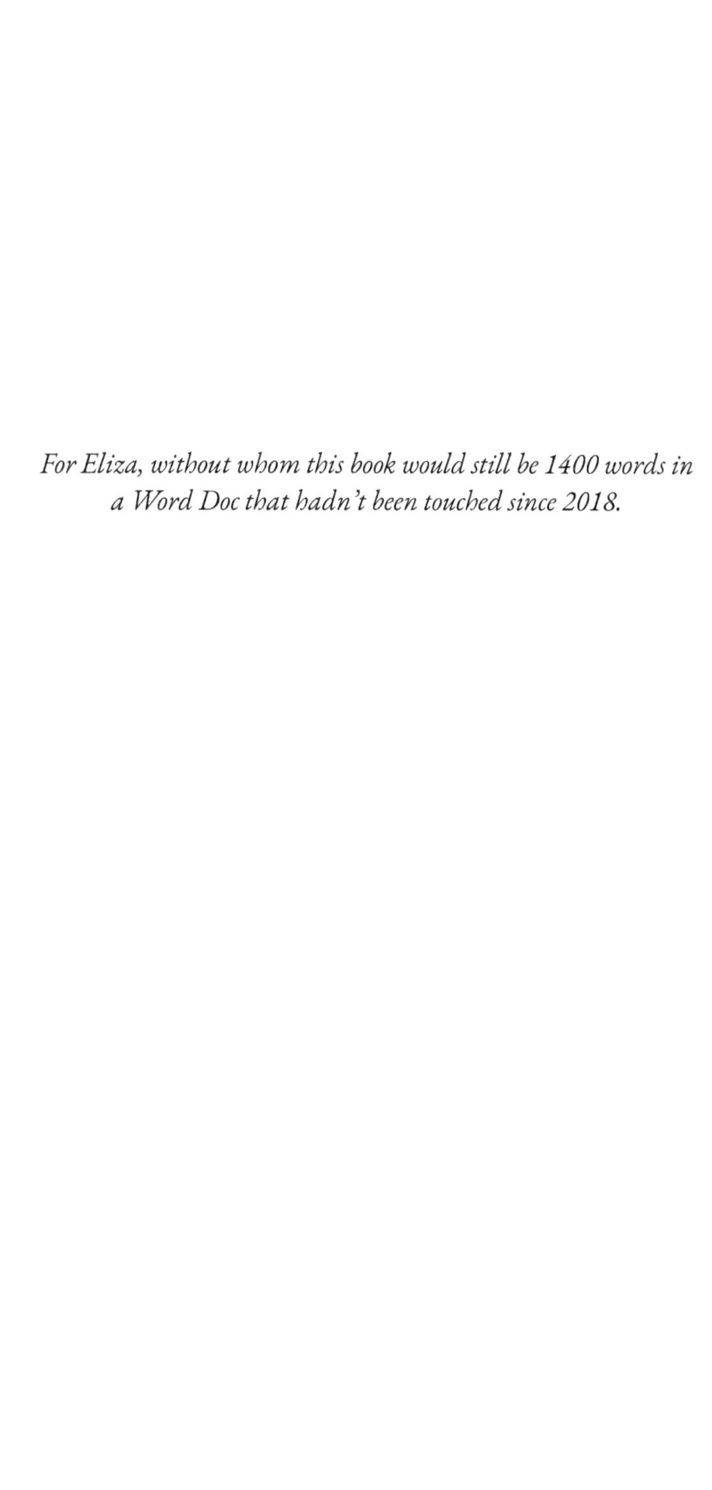

For Eliza, without whom this book would still be 1400 words in a Word Doc that hadn't been touched since 2018.

Dear Reader,

Thank you so much for choosing to read *Spare Me*! I'm so excited for you to meet Alex and Maddy and get to know their world. Although this book takes place in a time and reality that is, for all intents and purposes, identical to our own, it's important to know that the British Royal Family I've created in this book is based in no way on any living members of the actual British Royal Family. I've been a royals watcher for years, so I tried to include details that seem plausible given what I know of the real life Royal Family where they seemed appropriate, but those are sprinkled amongst lashings of creative liberties. None of the characters are based on real life members of the British Royal Family and any similarities are fully coincidental.

Spare Me, is at its heart, a love story. But some parts of the love story do mention topics that may be difficult for some readers. Please be aware of the following content warnings and proceed accordingly. This book contains:

• Graphic sexual content

- Alcohol consumption
- Death of a spouse (off page and before the events of the story)
- Panic attacks

And without further ado, I hope you enjoy *Spare Me*!

Chapter 1

At least it was gin.

Her martini assailant could have just as easily spilled an entire piña colada on her and left her smelling like coconut for the rest of the evening. Okay, maybe not piña colada. The likelihood of a bartender at a royal engagement party making something like a piña colada seemed slim. But a lemon drop would have been sticky, and whiskey smelled terrible, so at least it had been a classic gin martini, and, better still, it had been up, not on the rocks, so she had been spared the added awkwardness of having to fish ice cubes out of the top of her black evening gown.

Yes, Maddy reflected ruefully, if one had to have an entire drink dumped down one's front at a black-tie event at Buckingham Palace, a gin martini was about the best-case scenario.

She'd been standing in line at the bar when it happened. The cocktail hour at the engagement party for Prince Benjamin and Hannah Cromwell was in full swing. She'd checked to be sure that her "charges," the fourteen-year-old twin daughters of the American ambassador and his wife, were safely ensconced in conversation with their parents and a group of other dignitaries, and then slipped away to snag a desperately needed drink. Contrary to appearances, she was *not* the au pair or the nanny, but the "other duties as assigned" section of her job description as the ambassador's cultural attaché seemed to be rapidly expanding to include "teenager wrangling" and "assistant to the ambassador's wife" on an alarmingly frequent basis.

She was lost in thought in the line for the bar, her brain ranging from reviewing the details of Mrs. Stewart's schedule for the next day to wondering whether she looked as out of place as she felt at the swanky event. The room was crowded and she had been gradually pushed forward to stand a bit closer to the tuxedoed back in front of her as she waited. Suddenly, the tuxedoed back became a tuxedoed front and Maddy's thoughts were wrenched back to the present as her neighbor in line turned, bumped into her, and dumped his martini squarely down the front of her dress. Frigid liquid ran down her cleavage toward her stomach. Her cheeks were on fire, and she knew intuitively that she had to resemble a tomato in a gown. Despite a sudden and overwhelming instinct to burst into humiliated tears, Maddy closed her eyes, took a deep, intentional breath, and tried to recenter herself. She absolutely was not allowed to make a scene. Not here. Not now. She hadn't had time to go shopping, so if her dress was ruined, at least she'd already gotten her money's worth.

"Oh, Christ, terribly sorry," her martini assailant blustered, as a bartender rushed over with a towel and then obviously confronted his inner conflict over how to best help her when to blot her dress would involve some decidedly inappropriate touching. She gratefully accepted the towel, and taking one more steadying breath, she prepared to face the man who had just drenched her. Plucking the spear of olives that was dangling from the boatneck of her gown, she handed it back to the drink-spiller. "I believe this is yours?" she said wryly.

"Ugh, yes," he groaned, taking it and dropping the offending fruit back into his now-empty martini glass. "Really, I'm sorry. That was positively idiotic of me."

Maddy finished blotting as much of the gin from her dress as she could and handed the towel back to the bartender, who was already handing a new drink to her assailant. Deciding not to waste her turn at the front of the line, she turned to the bartender. "I guess to keep with the theme, I should have one of those too." Might as well try to make light of the situation, even as she mentally panicked about the impropriety of spending an evening reeking of gin. "But make mine dirty."

The drink-spiller grinned cheekily. "A girl with good taste."

Maddy managed to force herself to focus on his person rather than his klutziness or choice of drink for the first time. He looked to be in his early thirties, brown hair, blue eyes. His smile was cheeky, but even as he seemed to focus on her, she noticed that he was keeping a keen lookout on the rest of the room. Maddy had just decided to try to further quell the awkwardness by introducing herself when a shorter Black man with a cell phone and a harried look hurried up to Mr. Martini, and breathlessly said, "Sir, they're looking for you!"

Maddy found herself wondering who "they" were. Other people at the party? The mob? Interpol? She was almost too busy pondering this thought to notice that Mr. Martini was apologizing again and telling her to send him her dry cleaning bill. By the time she had the presence of mind to wonder how she was supposed to know where to send the bill—not that she'd even consider doing so—the two men had disappeared into the crowd.

She made her way away from the bar to a quieter corner to sip her drink—extra dirty, just the way she liked it, with what she assumed had to be extra pity olives—and survey the damage. She thanked her lucky stars that her dress was black, which meant that the impact of the spilled drink was almost entirely olfactory rather than visual. She'd been in a hurry to get ready after supervising the twins' primping, so she'd grabbed the first unwrinkled vaguely formal-looking item she could find in her wardrobe, an older dress from college. It was black satin column dress that had a high boatneck and spaghetti straps.

As Maddy tried to decide whether the scent of Tanqueray was really as overpowering to those around her as she thought it was, Delia Stewart swept up to her. From the look on her face, it was readily apparent that, yes, she did smell like a distillery. *Great.* "Madeleine, *what* is that smell? Did you bathe in gin?"

"Ha, good one, ma'am. Someone spilled a drink on me while I was waiting in line at the bar."

"Hmm. Well, I guess it's a good thing you weren't planning to stay for dinner, anyway."

Much as Maddy would have liked to stay to witness the lavish dinner and dancing that was to follow, she'd been tasked with escorting the twins, Amelia and Audrey, back to the embassy after the cocktail hour. Not to mention she hadn't been invited.

"Did the prince's private secretary reply about the meeting Monday morning? We need to get the program for the gala concert ironed out and solidify the guest list for the champagne reception with the musicians for after the performance."

Maddy silently mused that the royal family's staff was probably otherwise occupied with the planning of the current party celebrating the engagement of King Albert of England's oldest son to his longtime girlfriend, but only pulled out her phone from her small evening bag and checked Mrs. Stewart's email. "No, ma'am, nothing yet. If I haven't heard from them by the middle of the day tomorrow, I'll follow up to confirm."

"Okay, thank you. What's my first meeting tomorrow?"

"You have an eleven a.m. coffee with the head of the children's hospital gala committee, followed by a twelve-thirty lunch with the new Canadian ambassador's wife, your two-thirty hair appointment, and then dinner with Ambassador Stewart at seven at Claridge's."

"Thank you, Madeleine." Mrs. Stewart paused and gave her an appraising look and said, not unkindly, "At least black doesn't show the stain too much."

Maddy smiled resignedly. "That's true."

Her boss barreled on, "And really, nobody has any reason to notice you, anyway."

There it was. Delia Stewart was not intentionally unkind, but she had the kind of laser focus on her husband's career—and, by extension, her own—that made her somewhat oblivious to the minor details around her, including other people's feelings, needs, and schedules. Andrew Stewart had political aspirations much grander than the American ambassador to the Court of St. James, and Maddy often thought to herself that, once Mr. Stewart became a bit more prominent, she could see his wife trying to attain her own political post.

Mrs. Stewart spared her the awkwardness of trying to respond to her last remark by saying, "Okay, well, the cocktail hour should be over soon. The driver will be waiting outside for you to take the girls back to Winfield House. Try to see that they eat something besides potato chips for dinner and be sure that they're in their rooms by ten."

Maddy sighed. All she wanted to do when she got back to the residence was to get out of her heels and curl up with the most recent season of *The Real Housewives of Salt Lake City* on her VPN, but she'd smile, nod, and do what she was told. "Yes, ma'am," she said to Mrs. Stewart. "I'll see what I can do."

Just then a gong echoed throughout the room—yes, like an actual gong—and a uniformed staff member announced dinner. *Do they own that? Or do they borrow it from the London Symphony for fancy events?* As Mrs. Stewart turned to look for the ambassador and the girls, Maddy quickly bolted as much of the rest of her cocktail as she could in one gulp and found a spot to ditch her glass. Seeing the twins standing with their father a little ways away, Maddy wished Mrs. Stewart an enjoyable rest of the evening and herded the two teenage girls towards the grand staircase that would return them to the car bringing them back to the ambassador's residence at Winfield House.

Chapter 2

Having just attended a royal engagement party at Buckingham Palace should push one firmly into the "thriving" column of life. Maddy Cartwright, however, definitely wasn't there. Yet. Three months earlier, her parents had sat her down, told her they loved her but it was time for her to figure out her next move, and put her on a plane to London to work for one of her father's closest Army buddies, who happened to be the US Ambassador to the United Kingdom. And while she hadn't exactly made the independent choice to uproot her life and move across an ocean, she'd determined, upon arriving, that she was going to pull herself out of her guilt-laced grief swamp, and become Maddy 2.0. She'd made herself a list and everything.

Maddy 2.0:

- Go to London and live like an independent single lady for at least a year
- Finally apply to master's programs

- Have a casual fling
- Learn to bake

As she stood up in the Winfield House pastry kitchen, having just slid a tray of millionaire shortbread into the oven, she could at least check off that last one. Sort of. Nadia Chatterjee, the pastry chef at the ambassador's residence, had immediately latched on to Maddy and forcibly become her friend, chipping away at the chain mail Maddy had wrapped herself in over the last year and a half. Even though Maddy wasn't entirely convinced she was in a good place to be someone's friend at the moment, she'd appreciated the effort and seen it for the opportunity that it was: she'd at least be able to check off one thing on The Maddy 2.0 List. Sure, she wasn't making the caramel herself yet, and Nadia had saved her chocolate from being over-tempered at the last possible second, but the shortbread part? Maddy more or less had that down.

Besides that, she really hadn't made any progress on her goals. Was she living in London? She was. But she'd been there for six months, and besides jogging the ring around Regent's Park and the occasional happy hour with some of the other attachés, she still hadn't really managed to make herself leave Winfield House. Which made item three, "have a casual fling," significantly more difficult. She also had a number of tabs open on her personal laptop with information about various master's degrees in foreign service and international affairs, but she hadn't gotten further than starting a list of prospective programs on a yellow-lined notepad on her coffee table.

"Okay, so next time, we're going to do what?" Nadia asked, expectantly looking at Maddy, her crisp white chef's coat and pristine sage green headscarf a stark contrast to Maddy's flour-streaked black apron..

"Not get lost in thought while we're stirring the chocolate," Maddy said, simultaneously chastised and annoyed. This wasn't the first time she'd nearly ruined one of Nadia's desserts for an event.

"Right," Nadia said. It seemed like she was about to say something else when they were interrupted.

"Pardon me, girls!" The cozy British-accented words came from behind a veritable flotilla of flowers.

"Eddie, what in the world is that?" Maddy asked, quickly making space on a counter for her favorite of the Winfield House butlers to put down his load.

"They were just delivered for you, Ms. Cartwright," he said, his ruddy face finally emerging from behind the giant floral arrangement as he set it down.

"Those can't be for me," Maddy said dismissively. "They have to be for Mrs. Stewart. Or the ambassador. And where did they find ranunculus in October?"

"It says right here, Madeleine Cartwright," Nadia told her, peering at the card sticking out of the aromatic riot of pinks and whites. "Have you been hiding a secret lover from me?" she demanded, looking up at Maddy with intense curiosity.

"Of course not!" She reached over and took the card from Nadia. "This has to be a mistake."

The card was indeed addressed to her, so she opened it and started to read. *Dear Madeleine*, it began—only Mrs. Stewart called her that, and these definitely weren't from her—*Allow me to apologize again for my clumsiness last night. I hope your dress isn't ruined. Please do send the dry cleaning bill to my secretary.* A phone number and address followed. "*Warmest regards, A.W.*"

"Well?" Nadia demanded, the intense desire for the gossip sparkling in her brown eyes.

"Uh, it's from Mr. Martini."

"Who?"

"Okay, that's not his real name. I don't know his real

name, although apparently his initials are A.W. Last night at the party this guy accidentally spilled an entire cocktail down my dress. He apologized all over himself and told me to send him my dry cleaning bill, but then he disappeared before I could get his name. Not that I'd send him the bill, anyway." She paused for a second. "But he also didn't get my name... so how the heck did he know where to send me a full greenhouse of flowers? Should I be creeped out?"

"Oh my god, that is like something out of a rom-com!" Nadia gushed. "Let me see the card!" Maddy obligingly handed it over, and Nadia scanned it quickly. "Damn, Maddy, this is some next-level romantic shit."

"Or some next-level stalker shit."

"Nah, there were so many important people there last night. I'm sure all he had to do was tip someone from the secretary's office to get the guest list. How many Americans could have possibly been there?"

It was a fair point and, Maddy admitted, kind of a relief. She had come here precisely to escape everyone recognizing her, and so far it had worked. She wasn't ready to dive back into being under a microscope constantly.

"I'm going to take these downstairs before anyone else sees them and starts asking questions," Maddy said, hoisting the vast arrangement into her arms. "Can you get the door for me?" She peered around the side towards the door to her rooms. "And any chance there's any lunch left?"

The embassy staff usually ate lunch at the cafeteria in the gigantic modern embassy in Nine Elms London, but the fancy LEED-certified building had sprung a number of fancy LEED-certified leaks, which meant that most of them were now working out of spare offices in Winfield House, the sprawling mansion nestled in Regent's Park that had been home to every American ambassador in London since the 1950s. Nadia and Pierre, the main chef, had teamed up with the chefs from the embassy to start churning out lunch for the hundred or so attachés, clerks, and various other staff, serving in the vast state dining room that was normally only used for state visits and large events. Maddy had missed lunch service that day, though.

"Definitely," Nadia said, reaching around the flowers to open the door for her friend. "How does soup and a salad sound?"

"Heavenly," she said from behind the fragrant wall of ranunculus. "You're the best. I'll be right back."

She descended the wooden stairs carefully, wondering where on earth she was going to find space for such a large arrangement. The average cultural attaché didn't live in the embassy with the family, but then again, the average cultural attaché had to undergo a series of interviews and navigate miles of bureaucratic red tape before being assigned a duty station, whereas Maddy's father had made a phone call to an old Army buddy.

Her rooms had once been part of the scullery, but had been retrofitted at some point during the multiple expansions and renovations of the mansion. As a result, Maddy descended an exposed stairway into her living area. It was small, and somewhat hilariously furnished with assorted pieces that had overstayed their welcome in various parts of the main house. There was a cozy sitting area at the bottom of the stairs with an overstuffed couch and an armchair circling a comically fancy coffee table juxtaposed with an oval rag rug. Beyond the living area was a small dining table with two chairs and a tiny kitchenette with a mini fridge, kettle, and microwave, as well as a microscopic bathroom with a shower and toilet. Then, opposite the entry staircase was another small staircase that led to a lofted bedroom. One entire far wall of the loft space was a soaring, arched wall of windows. It filled the room with near-blinding light when the sun was out, gave her the vague feeling of being in the dining area of a fast food restaurant circa 1992, and, she feared, would probably be chilly in the winter, but she appreciated having her own space and the fact that she didn't have to find her own apartment on short notice in a foreign country.

After quickly assessing her options for placement of the flowers, she landed on the small table in the kitchenette since she never sat there and if she left it on the coffee table she wouldn't be able to see the TV. As she stood back, looking at it, dwarfing everything else in her small living space, she pushed back the feelings that threatened to bubble up.

The last time anyone had sent her flowers they had been under much different circumstances. At that point she wasn't sure if she'd ever be able to see a rose without feeling deep grief and gnawing guilt. She found herself idly fingering the chain that hung beneath her ivory silk boatneck shirt. This wasn't like that. This was just a friendly, if over-the-top, gesture from a random stranger she'd probably never see again. The flowers really were pretty. She allowed herself a quick sniff of the nearest ranunculus, wondering again where Mr. Martini had sourced the flowers so far outside of their typical growing season. She let her mind wander briefly back to Nadia's assumption that they were from a lover. The last thing she needed was to entangle herself in another relationship.

Just then, the door to the main kitchen opened and Nadia's voice echoed down. "Come on, love! Before your soup gets cold!"

Maddy jumped, pulled from the memories of the past. She drew her hand back from the front of the blouse where, despite its existential weight, the chain made only a faint disturbance. Taking a deep breath, she smoothed her navy-blue pencil skirt, and headed back to Nadia and her lunch.

When Maddy got back to the kitchen, Nadia had set a place for one with a steaming bowl of cream of roasted red pepper soup and a small garden salad. A can of Maddy's favorite sparkling water stood next to it, and Nadia had taken the bar stool next to Maddy's.

"So! Tell me everything about the party!" Nadia urged, leaning in expectantly.

Maddy thought back to the night before. "I mean, it was a very fancy cocktail reception," she said. *Fancy people nonsense*, a familiar voice echoed in her brain. She knew her lack of enthusiasm was going to be disappointing to her friend, so she tried to dredge up some enthusiasm or interesting details. "The most exciting part was definitely getting doused with a full martini," she said, reliving the cringeworthy moment, "and then having Mrs. Stewart ask me if I'd bathed in gin." Nadia winced, obviously clearly imagining how that interaction must have gone. "Oh, and they had a full-on dinner gong. Like something out of a symphony hall!"

"I mean, it's a palace. I'm sure they have a few of those just laying around. Did you see Ben and his fiancée?"

"Are we on a first-name basis with the heir to the British throne now?"

"I mean, his family colonized my country, and my taxes pay to heat his country homes and fuel his private helicopter. I think I've earned it."

"Fair enough," Maddy replied wryly, pausing to drizzle Caesar dressing over her salad. "Well, I heard the ruckus when they made their entry and sort of saw their heads over the crowd. I could see she had on a blue dress, but that was about it."

Nadia sighed. "Next time you have to find an excuse to get closer!"

"Oh yes, I'm sure there will be many more occasions on which I get to share air with the heir."

"Okay, well what about Prince Alex? The tabloids are all saying he's back for good this time."

"Sorry, Nadia." Maddy sighed, knowing she was disappointing her friend. "I wouldn't be able to pick that guy out of a lineup if I had to." She paused for a moment. "But I probably actually should Google him. Supposedly he's coming to the planning meeting for the Armistice Day concert on Monday."

"You think?! You definitely better Google him or you might wind up curtsying to the wrong person!"

Chapter 3

Monday morning found Winfield House in a tizzy. Embassy staff were scurrying about their business and Mrs. Stewart was pacing her office, a cup of coffee threatening to splash onto her perfectly crisp white collared shirt in one hand, a half-eaten cranberry scone in the other, and two large hot rollers still tucked into her ash blond hair.

"It has to be perfect, Madeleine," she was saying, as Maddy tried to offer her a napkin.

"Ma'am, it's just the intro meeting," Maddy said, attempting to placate her unusually flustered employer. "It's our chance to meet his staff, start going over logistics, and get a schedule worked out for the rest of the meetings before the concert."

Although she understood why Mrs. Stewart was stressed, Maddy also had to inwardly roll her eyes a bit. Yes, the ambassador's wife was the face of the Armistice Day concert she was co-hosting with Prince Alexander, but the two of them wouldn't really be doing most of the legwork. That would be left to Maddy, the other cultural staff, and the prince's people.

Really, if anyone should be stressed, it was Maddy herself. She finally had a real job to do, with responsibilities that had nothing to do with fourteen-year-old girls or maintaining Mrs. Stewart's schedule.

"Yes, but nobody's seen the prince in years! He's practically a recluse!" Mrs. Stewart exclaimed.

It was hyperbole, but not entirely untrue. The younger son of King Albert and Queen Sarah had left England to work on restoration after a catastrophic typhoon in New Zealand several years earlier and had only rarely returned home, mostly to join the family at their private retreat in Scotland. He had appeared briefly on the balcony at Buckingham Palace on the occasion of his father's silver jubilee, but there had been so many royals crowding the small space, and Prince Alexander had managed to position himself half behind a pillar and half behind his elder brother who was sporting the tall hat associated with his military regiment's formal uniform, and had been mostly hidden from public view. The British tabloids speculated regularly about the prince's notable absence, hinting at everything from substance abuse problems to mental health issues to the Daily Mail's comical suggestion that Prince Alexander had had botched plastic surgery and was too embarrassed to face his country. Regardless of the reason for his long absence, though, Prince Alexander had certainly made himself something of an enigma. His return to London in advance of his brother's wedding and, presumably, to take up more of a public-facing role had the UK's royalists slobbering for news, photos, anything. Maddy didn't really get the fuss, but she did understand why Mrs. Stewart considered this collaboration such a big deal.

Prior to moving to London, Maddy had never really considered the British royal family. She'd never been one of the girls who had posters of the young princes in her dorm room or bought the special editions of *People* dedicated to them.

The princes were both undeniably attractive, but they'd never taken up any space in her mind. Until now. Mrs. Stewart had been obsessing over the impending royal visit to Winfield House for days, agonizing over everything from what to include for refreshments to driving Maddy up the wall nitpicking the font she'd selected for the meeting agendas.

"Ma'am, as my father always says, 'He puts his pants on one leg at a time just like the rest of us,'" Maddy reassured her, rescuing the half-full coffee cup and the scone from Mrs. Stewart's precariously distracted grasp. "Now why don't you go finish your hair, put on some fresh lipstick, and I'll meet you in the family dining room in ten minutes."

Mrs. Stewart took a deep breath. "You're right. Your daddy always has his head on straight." One would hope so, given that over the course of a thirty-five-year career in the Army culminating as a three-star general, he'd been responsible for the lives of hundreds of thousands of soldiers, many of them eighteen-year-old boys with as much sense as a cotton ball. She glanced at Maddy. "Is that what you're wearing? To meet the prince?"

Maddy looked down at her outfit. She was wearing tan pants with a pale blue silk shell and light brown Tory Burch flats. "This? Oh, no, of course not," she said. *At least, not anymore.* "I'll just run down and throw on my actual outfit."

"Good." Mrs. Stewart nodded. "We have to make a good first impression. He's a *prince*, after all!" Maddy sighed as Mrs. Stewart left to go finish putting herself together and headed towards her own room to find something more appropriate for meeting a prince.

Fifteen minutes later Maddy speed-walked toward the family dining room. It had taken her longer than she'd anticipated, having realized that despite having a reasonable wardrobe for government work, she apparently did not own anything that she thought Mrs. Stewart would deem appropriate for meeting a prince. Prior to Mrs. Stewart's comment, it hadn't really dawned on Maddy that the prince would even notice she was there. Maddy had thoroughly briefed Mrs. Stewart on the preliminary arrangements for the concert, which would feature military bands from both countries and welcome a number of active-duty service members in addition to a selection of military families whose service members were deployed. She had planned to station herself somewhere discreet where she could fill in any information that slipped Mrs. Stewart's mind and ideally also be close enough to the refreshments to snag one of Nadia's amazing brownies before everyone else ate them.

Now, as Maddy rushed towards the meeting, freshly attired in a navy-blue sheath dress, a pale pink cardigan, and her black patent leather slingback heels, she realized that she hoped the curtsey she'd learned as a four-year-old at the ballet classes she'd briefly taken while her father was stationed at Fort Bragg was the same curtsey one gave to a prince. She was grateful that she'd taken time to reread the briefing that the Kensington Palace protocol office had sent over that reminded her to call the prince "Your Royal Highness," but in that moment, she realized she'd never gotten around to trawling the internet for recent pictures of their royal guest. She hoped it would be obvious when the time came. It had to be, right?

As she approached the family dining room, she realized that her plan to be stationed in the room before the royal delegation arrived had been foiled, as she heard Mrs. Stewart ushering a small handful of people ahead of her toward the meeting.

Maddy slipped in behind them as Mrs. Stewart invited the prince and his small entourage to help themselves to tea and pastries. "I hope you'll enjoy, Your Royal Highness," she was saying, her lush Alabama drawl even more pronounced than usual. The prince had his back to Maddy, so all she could see was a navy-blue suit jacket and medium-brown hair. He had three staff members with him. Maddy knew from reading the briefing that the tall white man in a black suit must be his security guard, while the shorter Black man was his personal secretary, Eric Okonkwo, and the other woman was Maddy's counterpart, Sloane Travers, with whom she'd been in periodic email contact over the last month to confirm initial details and schedule the meeting.

A sudden sneeze escaped from Maddy's mouth, and her hopes of going unnoticed flew out the window. "Oh, good, *there* you are, Madeleine," said Mrs. Stewart. "Your Royal Highness, please let me introduce Madeleine Cartwright, my right hand on this project."

Prince Alexander pushed back his chair and turned to face Maddy, who just barely managed to keep her jaw from hitting her chest.

Oh shit.

It was him. Mr. Martini was Prince Alexander.

A.W. was Alexander Windsor.

Chapter 4

As Alex turned to face Madeleine Cartwright, he tried to suppress the delighted smile that threatened to overtake his face at the shock written across hers. He'd been practically giddy when Eric told him that the enchanting woman he'd doused with gin was the same person organizing the Armistice Day concert for the American delegation. He hadn't had much time to process her appearance when he saw her up close at the engagement party, but now that he was standing in front of her, shaking her hand, he had a chance to really absorb her. He'd caught a glimpse of her chocolatey brown eyes before she'd lowered them deferentially and bobbed a curtsey. She had mahogany hair tied back in a low bun at the nape of her neck. Out of nowhere, he found himself imagining what it would feel like to slide his hands through her hair. It looked thick and luscious. He wondered what it would look like fanned out across his pillow.

"Your Royal Highness?" Delia Stewart's southern accent burst into his daydreaming, which was a good thing, seeing as it had been headed in a decidedly not-safe-for-work direction. He coughed, mentally shaking himself and refocusing on the meeting. Luckily he was quickly able to ascertain that the ambassador's wife had been offering him a plate of appetizing baked goods and helped himself to a fudgy-looking brownie with a word of thanks. He'd been trained to eat little, if anything, in situations like this. Accepting a cup of tea or coffee was fine, but food in a meeting situation could lead to too many awkward or impolite situations that the royals didn't want to find themselves in. But the brownie looked too enticing to pass up.

He broke off a corner and resisted the urge to make an obscene noise as he slipped it into his mouth, forcing his face to look engaged in what Sloane was saying as moist, fudgy goodness exploded across his tongue. As he reached down to break off another bite, he caught Madeleine Cartwright looking at him. She seemed to be trying to hide a small smile, as if she could see his inner battle between professional behavior and giving in to his reaction to the decadent pastry. He realized that she, too, was breaking off the corner of a brownie, and she cocked an eyebrow in his direction, almost as if she was toasting him, before popping her own bite in her mouth and returning her attention to the meeting.

Alex tried valiantly not to focus on her mouth as he tried to tune in to what Mrs. Stewart was saying about American service members and their families—an important and meaningful cause, to be sure—and he might have succeeded, if he hadn't noticed, out of the corner of his eye, Madeleine surreptitiously licking a crumb of brownie off the tip of her finger. His thoughts immediately slammed back to X-rated territory, imagining what he could do with that mouth, her pink lips...

Get a grip, man, he chided himself. This was not at all like him. He kept his sex life in the bedroom—and very casual. He needed to get laid. Surely, if one brief, disastrous meeting at a party and watching the same woman take two bites of a brownie were sending his mind straight to the gutter, he needed to do something.

* * *

After the biological imperative to breathe forced Maddy past her momentary shock (*Breathe, Cartwright*, she'd heard that familiar voice in her head say), she'd made an awkward curtsey while shaking his hand and trying to keep a neutral face. She was decidedly ambivalent about the need to show deference to this man who, solely by dint of his genetic material, had apparently earned a higher station in life than everyone else, but in that moment she'd been very glad that the occasion didn't call for eye contact. She'd tried to keep her eyes firmly glued to the top button on his blazer – below his face, above his crotch, obviously – but at the last second before their hands separated, she had glanced up.

He had kept a completely neutral expression except for his eyes. If one didn't look closely, they would have had no idea that the two had ever interacted before, but Maddy saw the merest glimmer of a twinkle in his eye as he released her hand and said, "A pleasure to meet you, Ms. Cartwright."

"Your Royal Highness," she murmured, quickly looking down again and scurrying to the seat Mrs. Stewart indicated at the large table.

As Mrs. Stewart opened the meeting with a borderline obsequious welcome to their royal guests, Maddy had tried to get a hold of herself. She shouldn't have been so unnerved by seeing Mr. Martini—that is, the prince—again. If anyone should have felt awkward, it was the person who had summarily dumped ice-cold gin and olives down her dress. Yet somehow the suddenness of seeing him so unexpectedly, combined with the twinkle in his eye that told her he remembered her had been unsettling. He hadn't seemed surprised to see her at all. Then again, Maddy reflected one of the many times she'd replayed the scene in her head, he wouldn't have been. He had figured out exactly who she was and, by extension, would have been expecting to see her, whereas she had barely given a second thought to encountering the second in line to the British throne, let alone imagined that he wouldn't be a total stranger.

As the meeting proceeded, Maddy gradually found her footing again. As Prince Alexander's staffer Sloane discussed the seating arrangements in the Royal Albert Hall and went over what would be needed in the musicians' green rooms, Maddy found herself sneaking glances at the prince. She'd barely processed what he looked like at the party, too busy trying to alleviate the awkwardness of the moment and liberate her dress from the Union Jack-topped party pick of olives stuck in her cleavage. In the meeting, however, she had time to really take him in. His close-cropped hair was brown with some red tones that the light caught when he turned his head. His eyes were gray-blue, fringed with annoyingly lush lashes. His high, chiseled cheekbones would have made his face almost too sculptural, except the slightest hint of a dimple graced one cheek and a cleft of his chin, which softened his visage.

She hadn't known what to expect from him at this meeting. The fact that he'd come in person rather than just sending staff told her that it was at least of passing interest to him, but it became quickly apparent once the meeting began that he was clearly invested in the success of the event. Whether out of his own interest or because his family told him he needed to be interested, Maddy wasn't sure, but it was clear he'd read the materials he'd been given, and he didn't hesitate to express his opinions.

The meeting wrapped up after about an hour, and they all stood to begin the obligatory round of farewells. Somehow

Maddy had found herself leaving the room last, just behind Prince Alexander. "Ms. Cartwright," he said, extending his hand. When he held her hand a fraction of a second longer than was customary, her eyes had shot up to find him grinning down into hers. "A pleasure," he said, before releasing her hand and sweeping back to his car with his staff.

Chapter 5

"Come in!" Alex called, responding to the light knock on the door of his office at Kensington Palace. Prior to this trip home, he had rarely been given any official duties, so there were absolutely no personal touches in this space—yet it had somehow been decorated to the gills. A strangely imposing portrait of his parents hung on the wall next to the door, framed photos of him and his brother posing stiffly arrayed across the mantle, and a shelf crammed full of books that he'd never seen before.

Eric stuck his head around the door, and Alex smiled in relief that someone had come to disrupt the stultifying briefing he was reading. Eric Okonkwo had been one of Alex's first friends at Cambridge. They'd bonded over finding the best quiet sunny corner of the library during marathon studying sessions for their first-year literature seminar and had become fast friends when Alex realized that Eric didn't give two shits about who his family was and Eric realized that Alex was deeply conflicted about his family's wealth and the way they'd acquired most of it: namely, off the back of Eric's enslaved ancestors. He was absurdly smart, took no bullshit from anyone, and was one of the most organized and efficient people Alex had ever met, so when Alex had been summoned home from New Zealand, Eric had been his first call.

"Thank god," Alex said, leaning back in the leather desk chair and shoving his reading glasses up into his hair. Alex truly wanted to be involved in the family business, but having missed out on all the "memo reading" lessons that Ben had had as a child, he was going to have to insist that someone start sending him things that were less incomprehensible if they actually wanted him to be of any real use. "If I have to try to read this for any longer, I think my eyeballs might actually fall out."

Eric cracked a smile, but it didn't go all the way to his eyes. "Do you have a minute?" he asked, the serious tone in his voice reinforcing what Alex had already deduced. Something was wrong.

"Of course, mate, come in." Alex gestured to one of the leather club chairs in front of the fireplace and stood to join his friend in the opposite chair. Eric took the seat Alex had indicated. His hands were grasped in his lap, fidgeting in a way that Alex hadn't seen since the moments before their last finals at Cambridge. His dark eyes were focused on his hands, avoiding looking Alex in the face. "Eric," Alex said gently, trying to tamp down the alarm that was rapidly causing his chest to feel like it was being filled with lead. "What's wrong? Is it Marco? One of the kids?"

Eric's eyes flew up. "No, no, it's nothing like that. They're fine." He took a deep breath, pressed his lips together, and leveled Alex with A Look. "But I don't think I can keep working here."

Relief coursed through him at the news that nobody was seriously ill or dying, followed immediately by the emotional whiplash of sheer panic of the knowledge that there was no way he could be a working royal without Eric's brilliant mind and even-keeled competence on his team. He opened his mouth to speak, but Eric barged onward, clearly trying to get through what he had come to say as quickly as possible.

"You know I love you like a brother," Eric said, "and I know you don't stand for everything that this... this institution stands for. But I just can't continue working somewhere where the priority is so clearly on maintaining this obscene wealth that was built on generations of oppression without any acknowledgement of that. Not even an indication that anyone other than you recognizes that. I can't do it, Alex."

Alex swallowed, his heart sinking, as he tried to process what Eric was saying. He knew the next thing he said had the potential to dramatically impact the way the rest of the conversation went, so he took a deep breath and tried to curb his immediate instinct: to beg his friend not to leave. " Thank you for telling me. That can't have been easy to say to my face, even after a decade of friendship."

Eric's face was inscrutable, a combination of resignation, confusion, and maybe even fear. He nodded awkwardly, muttering, "You're welcome."

Alex took another deep breath, wracking his brains for how to proceed in the conversation. He desperately wanted Eric to stay. He needed him, not only for his competence and smarts, but also for the exact perspective he was bringing to this conversation that was so sorely lacking in every other corner of Kensington Palace. And Alex needed Eric to know that he deeply valued that perspective without tokenizing him.

"If it's truly what you want, I will—extremely begrudgingly—accept your resignation," Alex began, and he saw some of the tension leave Eric's shoulders. "I recognize I have no right to ask this, but I have to ask... what would it take to convince you to stay?" He saw the surprise register on his friend's dark features, but when an immediate rejection wasn't forthcoming, he pushed forward. "Because you're absolutely right, it's disgraceful that there hasn't been more acknowledgement of my family's history. Inexcusable, really. It should have been among the first things I tried to make happen when I came back." He paused for breath, and when Eric still didn't say anything, he dove back in. "But the thing is, I think we could do it. I think I could make it one of my patronages. But I can't do it alone. There's no way a privileged white bloke should be leading this charge. Even I know that. So if you'd be willing to stay, I think we could at least start to dismantle some of the bullshit from within." He paused again, suddenly worried he might be pushing too far or could have said the wrong thing. "If that's of any interest to you, of course."

Eric sat back in his chair, looking into the empty fireplace pensively. He sighed. "I don't know, Alex."

"And that's okay!" Alex rushed to reassure him. "You clearly thought a lot about this before coming here to talk to me. I don't expect you to reverse course without giving it similarly serious thought. How about this: what if I start by talking to my parents about how much we might be able to get from crown funds for this, and take their temperature on the idea of it as a project? While I do that, you take some time to think about it. Decide if it would change your mind about leaving. Do some dreaming about what you might want it to look like. And then we can talk again in a few days. And if you tell me then that you still want to leave, I'll accept it, no questions asked, and we go back to being just friends."

Eric took a breath and then gave a brisk nod, a decision clearly made. "Okay," he said. "I'll think about it."

"Good," Alex said with a relieved smile. "And Eric?"

"Yeah?"

"Really, thank you for talking to me about this. I hope I won't let you down."

Eric didn't say anything, but gave him a small smile as he walked out of Alex's office.

That Sunday Alex, Ben, his fiancée Hannah, and the king and queen sat around the table in the private dining room at Buckingham Palace. As usual, it was a boisterous gathering with Ben and his father arguing jovially about something or other —Alex had lost track of what—Hannah and his mother having an earnest discussion about the wedding, and Alex just sitting back, the quiet one, as ever. He'd been trying to figure out how to bring up his conversation with Eric for the whole evening. Cocktails had started with Ben and Hannah bursting in with an ebullient story about something they'd seen on their drive back from visiting Hannah's parents in the Cotswolds for the weekend. Then, as that conversation had died down, they'd been called to the table. And then, and then, and then... the dessert dishes were being cleared and Alex still hadn't managed to force his way into the conversation. He'd wanted to be graceful about it. But he was starting to see that, as usual, the only way he was going to be able to make his voice heard was to bulldoze into the maelstrom of extroverts.

"So Eric threatened to quit this week," he interjected loudly, apropos of exactly nothing.

The startling revelation had the intended result—the rest of his family all stopped what they were saying and turned to look at Alex with total shock on each of their faces. Even his mother's cat, Anne of Cleves, stopped attempting to demolish a stuffed mouse on the carpet between the antique sideboard and the door to look at the humans.

"Why in God's name would he do that?" Alex's father finally asked.

"Did you two have a falling-out, dear?" His mother looked concerned. She loved Eric, and Alex wasn't actually sure that if they *had* had a falling-out that she would have sided with him, her own flesh and blood.

"No," Alex said, taking a deep breath before launching into his prepared speech. *This must have been how Eric felt before he talked to me. Bloody awful.* "He feels like he can't keep working for an institution that isn't willing to own up to the significant role it played and continues to play in upholding white supremacy."

Out of the corner of his eye, Alex saw Ben's eyebrows shoot up and noticed a look crossing Hannah's face that seemed to be saying, *Right on, mate.*

"And I certainly can't fault him," Alex said, in a voice that he hoped sounded more self-assured than he felt. "So both because I don't want to lose the most important—and really, only—member of my staff, and because he's exactly right, I think we need to do something about it."

His father rested his elbows on the table, steepling his fingers under his chin. "What are you proposing, son?" he asked, his thoughts on the matter wholly inscrutable. *Damn decades of diplomatic training.*

"I think we start a reparations fund," Alex said simply.

"Well, we certainly can't call it that," his father responded, as if on reflex.

"Why the hell not?" Alex asked, trying not to get defensive.

"I, it, we..." He'd rarely seen the king stumble over words like this, which was how Alex could tell he'd really stymied him. "We just... we can put some money toward it. But we can't call it reparations. That's like admitting we committed a crime!"

"I mean, *we* didn't, but our ancestors did, and we certainly haven't done anything to make it right," Alex volleyed back, hackles rising.

"I think what your father is trying to say, dear," his mother broke in, clearly donning her peacemaker hat, "is that it's a very worthy idea. I think we just need to workshop some of the language."

Alex pursed his lips. He knew he couldn't expect to get absolutely everything he wanted on the first shot, but he wasn't going down without a fight.

"I mean, frankly, what we think doesn't really matter that much."

"It's our money," his father replied.

"Yes, but the other important part of this is that we're going to give the money, we're going to use our positionality to bring awareness, and we're going to give Eric a staff to do the actual work here. They'll be the ones setting the parameters, figuring out what's appropriate."

"Now, son, Eric is wonderful—"

"Dad, that part is nonnegotiable."

"He's actually right," Ben spoke up for the first time. "If nothing else, think of the optics of an old white chap telling a bunch of people his family had oppressed for years how to spend the money he was giving them."

"Exactly," Hannah added. "And you should make sure it's not just crown funds. I mean, it should be that too. But since a lot of that comes from taxpayer dollars—including the people who will be receiving this funding—it means they'd just be getting back money they already paid. You're going to have to open up your own pockets."

Alex beamed at her, attempting to telegraph his gratitude with his eyes. "That's a brilliant idea."

The king shifted in his seat. "I... you may be right," he conceded. "Why don't you get a meeting on the calendar with me and my chief of finance, and we can start to think about it?"

"I want Eric there too," Alex insisted.

"Eric too," his father agreed.

"Done."

Alex relaxed back into his seat, satisfied and relieved. It wasn't often that he burst into the family scene, and for once, he was doing it to help someone else.

Chapter 6

The weeks leading up to the Armistice Day concert flew by, the slight crispness of October giving way to the decidedly overcast chill of November. Maddy had been surprised when the city was fully decorated for Christmas in early November, but she supposed that in the absence of Thanksgiving, there was no reason to delay merriment, and the festive lights brightened things noticeably as the sun set earlier and earlier.

She hadn't seen Prince Alexander since the day of the meeting at Winfield House ten days earlier. She'd been in frequent correspondence with his staffer Sloane, who was incredibly competent and very witty, but the prince hadn't been involved further. She found herself thinking about that day at Winfield house more often than she wanted to, though.

The day of the concert, Maddy arrived at the Royal Albert Hall early to ensure that everything was set up the way it was supposed to be. Mrs. Stewart had insisted that she needed "glam," as she called it, and so Maddy had reluctantly allowed the stylist Mrs. Stewart hired for herself to sweep her brown hair into a low, curling style. "I'll be working all night—it can't be anything too fussy," Maddy had cautioned before sitting down. Maddy still wasn't sure that all the extra fuss was worth it, considering she'd be behind the scenes all evening.

"Absolutely, doll," Charlie said, ushering her into a chair he'd situated in Mrs. Stewart's sitting room. He was wearing a vibrantly patterned, extremely slim-fit button-up shirt, which was open at the neck to reveal what looked to be four or five gold chains and a smattering of dark chest hair. Her stomach was in knots as she ran through the plans for the evening in her head, half listening to Charlie's animated chatter about this and that. Thankfully, he was the type of extrovert who required very little from other participants in the conversation. She tried to keep her hands calm in her lap as he curled and pinned, and mentally rehearsed all the things that could go wrong and how those catastrophes could be either averted or remedied. Of course all of her anxieties were strictly event planning-related. None of the swirl of thoughts in her head or the flock of butterflies in her stomach were at all consumed by thoughts of Prince Alexander. Not even one.

Maddy had to admit that even though she'd spent years doing her own hair for Army balls, this looked miles better than anything she could have done herself. Over her protests, Charlie had left a few curling tendrils around her face before pinning the rest back at the nape of her neck. After emerging from a typhoon of hairspray that she almost believed might make her hair last the whole evening if the fumes didn't suffocate her first, Maddy grabbed the garment bag with her dress and shoes and shoved some jewelry and a lipstick along with her phone into her clutch and rushed to the embassy car waiting at the front to take her to the venue.

When she arrived backstage, Sloane was also there, racing around. "I've put the teddies for the kids in the reception room, but the conductor's special soda isn't in the green room!" she blurted out as Maddy entered.

Maddy sighed and rolled her eyes. "I knew we should have just used the conductors from the military groups instead of bringing in this Venezuelan hotshot." She took a deep breath. *It's the people like us who get things done,* the voice she couldn't shake echoed in her head. *And celebrities are not like us.* "Okay, you make sure everything is ready for the reception, and I'll go find the stage manager to ask about the drinks."

"Thanks, Maddy," Sloane said. They made a quick stop at the room backstage where they'd change before Sloane pointed Maddy toward the stage manager's office to sort out the soda snafu. *Always saving the day, Cartwright,* she heard, reverberating between her ears with the familiar chuckle she knew she'd never hear again.

Two hours later, the South American soft drink had been located, the reception was set up, and everything was just about ready. Sloane walked up to Maddy, looking fierce in a slim forest-green pantsuit and killer gold heels. "Oh my gosh, you look *fabulous*!" Maddy exclaimed. "I wish I'd known pants were an option!"

"Do you like?" Sloane asked, giving a small twirl. "My wife's a stylist, and she says if Hannah Cromwell, she who will be queen, can wear pants, I can too!" She looked at Maddy's boyfriend jeans and relaxed button-up shirt. "You'd better go change. Eric just texted that he and the prince are fifteen minutes out."

Maddy nodded. "The Stewarts are on their way too. I figure it'll take them a few minutes to get through the throngs outside, but I'll go get ready so I'm here when they get in."

Maddy headed back to the small room where Sloane had told her to put her things. Slipping quickly out of her casual clothes, she stepped into the dress she'd brought. It was sleeveless navy-blue silk with a high neck and a delicate metallic pattern woven through the fabric. It wasn't skintight, but hugged her hourglass figure before ending mid-calf. *Classic and understated,* Maddy thought, looking at herself in the small mirror on the back of the door. *Just like I'm supposed to be.* Her eyes caught on the chain that hung around her neck. *You would have loved this,* she thought to herself as she grasped the dog tags in her hand and swiftly deposited them beneath the neckline of her dress, where they'd be unseen.

"Maddy, are you ready?" Sloane's voice came around the door a second before she appeared.

"Yup!" she said, a chipper tone in her voice that she didn't really feel. "Just tossing on some jewelry!" She jammed a pair of small pearl drop earrings through her earlobes, swiped on a fresh coat of berry-colored lipstick, and slipped her feet into navy-blue strappy heels before grabbing her phone and her clutch and following Sloane through the backstage door and into the rapidly filling house.

* * *

MUM

Are you ready for the concert this evening?
I hate that we can't be there, darling!

DAD

Don't forget to just take a few deep breaths
and smile before you go out. You're going
to be great, Alex.

BJ

*gif of Leslie Knope giving thumbs-up and
saying "You've got this!"*

Alex sighed, shaking his head as he closed the family text thread, which Ben had drunkenly renamed "Royal Flush." His parents hated it, but also weren't tech savvy enough to figure out how to change it back, and Alex and Ben had both been bribing their staffers for about five months not to show them. He slipped his phone back into the inner pocket of his tuxedo jacket and looked out the heavily tinted window of the Range Rover at London traffic. His family meant well. They wanted him to do well. He should be grateful for their encouragement. But he couldn't help but feel a little resentful. He had worked hard to overcome the stage fright that had defined his life when he was a child. The moment that he froze giving his one big line in his father's coronation had been more than twenty years ago. And yes, he'd been moderately traumatized by choking on international television with the world watching. And yes, his parents had tried to do right by him by thoroughly sheltering him from the press ever since. But in the intervening two decades, he'd managed to work through both the trauma and the reticence that had caused it. So while he appreciated his family's care, he wished they'd stopped to notice that he no longer needed it. Or at least, no longer needed it in the same way that he once had. He just wished they saw him for who he was in the present, not who he had been in the past.

Alex heard Eric clear his throat quietly from the other side of the back seat. "Alex," he said quietly.

"Yup." Alex sighed and turned to face his friend as they crept toward the concert hall.

"You alright, sir?"

"Eric, I've told you time and time again, you have to stop calling me sir. It makes me feel weird."

"I'm worried your father's secretary will sack me if I don't call you 'Your Royal Highness,'" Eric said dryly. "'Sir' was the compromise."

"Well, I'll sack you if you don't just call me Alex, you big weirdo. Malcolm doesn't make my HR decisions, and if he gives you any trouble he can answer to me."

Eric nodded tightly and moved on. "So when we get there, there will be press. Smile and nod, no need to talk to anyone. Just be your pretty self for a few minutes, and then we'll get you inside and seated for the performance." Eric glanced at his phone. "The Stewarts just pulled up, so we'll be about three minutes behind them."

"Right, good," Alex said. As much as he hated to admit it, he did close his eyes and briefly take a few deep breaths as he mentally prepared for the paparazzi's onslaught—not because his father had told him to, but because it felt good. He didn't freeze up in front of large audiences anymore, but it didn't mean he enjoyed the frenetic chaos of flashing lights and near frantic voices calling his name and asking for comment. But he could do it.

They pulled up to the curb and Alex sat up a little straighter, readying himself to go in. He opened his own door —a thing that his chauffeurs hated—and plastered on his public-facing smile as he buttoned his tuxedo jacket and headed for the red carpet, smiling and waving to the crowds of photographers and supporters who were calling his name. He strode to the first mark and smiled broadly, trying to think of something that might actually make his smile seem genuine. His mind lit on the fact that he was going to see Madeleine Cartwright soon, and he could feel the smile immediately actually reaching his eyes. He wondered what she would be wearing. He knew she'd looked professional and pretty in their meeting, but from what he remembered of their brief encounter at the party, she looked stellar in a dress. He shifted a bit so he was looking at a different group of photographers and wondered if he might have a chance to actually talk with her tonight. He'd spent a fair bit of time over the past days trying to unpack why this one woman that he'd met twice and talked to one-on-one for a grand total of, generously, two and a half minutes, was taking up so much of his headspace. Why he couldn't stop thinking about her and what she might be like, and fighting off the mental urge to imagine other things. Things he definitely needed to not be thinking about while on a red carpet in front of a throng of press.

He took a few steps further down the carpet to a second mark and smiled again, trying to stay loose, to keep it genuine-looking. There was a small stir by the far side of the carpet, near the entrance to the theater, and suddenly Ambassador and Mrs. Stewart re-emerged. He walked toward them, smiling broadly, shaking their hands warmly, trying to remember his media training so that the photographers would get the best angle of their greeting and not the inside of his ear or something. The photographers called for the trio to pose together, so he gamely stood with his shoulder just behind Mrs. Stewart to give the impression of touching her without looking like he was getting handsy. After several moments, the Stewart twins were shepherded out, and after a few photos with the girls, one of whom couldn't stop giggling and blushing when she made eye contact and one of whom looked wholly over the whole scene—*same,* he thought to himself— all five of them waved once more and then headed toward the entrance to the theater.

Eric met him at the end of the step-and-repeat and guided him toward the door to the theater. "Good job, mate," he muttered under his breath.

"Thanks," Alex responded. His eyes were roving across the growing crowd milling about. *Just looking around. Not for anyone in particular. Identifying the emergency exits and such.* He knew it was a lie, but he had to keep telling himself that. "It's hard work, you know," he added sarcastically. Eric gave him A Look, but remained quiet, clearly knowing that any response to his asinine comment was likely to be the wrong one. Alex sighed and aborted an attempt to rake his hands through his hair just in time to avoid totally mussing it before he was about to be on stage. "Sorry." He sighed, looking down at Eric. "How much time do we have?"

"The concert starts in twenty minutes."

"Shall we see if we can snag a glass of that?" he asked, motioning with his head toward a group of people holding flutes of champagne.

"Trying to loosen up before your speech?" Eric asked teasingly.

"You wouldn't want me to freeze up again and embarrass myself. Or would you? Are you getting bored at work?" Alex ribbed.

Eric snagged two glasses from a passing server, handing one to Alex before clinking the rims together. "No, but really, are you feeling okay about tonight? You like the speech and everything?"

As irritating as Alex found the constant references to his childhood blunder, he knew that Eric was genuinely checking in. "Yeah, it's fine, mate. Thanks." And then, to reassure Eric, he stressed, "I'll really be fine."

"I know. I know that's not a problem for you anymore. Just checking—it *is* your first big appearance since you've been back."

"Thanks," Alex said, nudging Eric's shoulder with his own as a gesture of affection. Wouldn't do to have someone seeing them hug and then assume that Alex was playing for the other team. Not that there was anything wrong with that. Other than that Eric's very handsome and very muscular rugby player husband might have something to say about it.

After he'd talked with his family, Alex and Eric had talked again, and Eric had agreed to stay on, providing they actually moved forward with the reparations project. They were meeting with the king's office the following week, and Alex had already asked the palace HR office to start looking for another staffer to pick up some of Eric's low-level work to give him more capacity to take the lead on their new initiative.

Alex was just about to open his mouth to say something else when Mrs. Stewart bustled up to him. "Now, Your Royal Highness, won't you come meet…" she said, towing him away towards the center of the room where a crowd was growing. He pasted his public smile back on, hastily handing his champagne flute to Eric, and followed her once more unto the breach.

Twenty minutes later, the lobby lights started to flicker to indicate it was time for the audience members to take their seats. Alex finished up his conversation with a young pilot from the RAF, shaking hands with the woman who looked younger than him and turned to find Eric at his elbow. "Ready to go up?" he asked, leading Alex towards the staircase that would lead to the Royal Box where he'd be sitting with the Stewarts.

"Yup," Alex responded, once again, trying to take in the scene without appearing to be looking around. After a brief delay that seemed to be related to the fact that the ambassador had seemingly never met a stranger, the Stewarts joined him at the bottom of the stairs and they started up, Ambassador and Mrs. Stewart arm in arm, with the twins behind them with a staffer who was not Madeleine Cartwright. Ambassador Stewart, a gregarious man who was impossible not to like, was regaling Alex with a story he was only half paying attention to about having drunkenly stumbled into a tuba during a military event in his youth.

When they arrived at the top of the stairs, Alex turned left, leading the Stewarts toward their box, and barely managed to avoid tripping over his own feet. Madeleine Cartwright was standing about ten feet away, her head leaning close to Sloane's, conferring about something on Sloane's phone. As Sloane nodded and walked into the box, Madeleine looked up, and Alex fought the urge to stop and stare. She was wearing a sleeveless navy-blue dress with a high neck and a skirt that fell to just below her knees. It might have been plain except it had a subtle iridescent pattern woven into the fabric that made her shimmer. Her hair had been pulled back and slightly to the side so a knot and small cascade of curls were visible just over her right shoulder. Silver earrings with a pearl drop hung from her ears, a narrow silver bangle adorned her left wrist, and a silver chain had been tucked beneath the neck of her dress, concealing anything that might have hung from it.

Somehow, Alex managed to keep walking and breathe normally. As their group approached, Madeleine stepped up to them and dropped a small curtsey in Alex's direction. Normally the outdated act of deference didn't impact him. People had been bowing or curtseying in his general direction since he was a child, and he was as used to it as one can be used to an archaic show of obeisance. But somehow when Madeleine Cartwright curtseyed to him, he wanted to stop her, to take her chin in his hand and make her look into his eyes. To tell her that it was an obsolete recognition of his birthright that didn't make him any different than her other than where he lived and absurd generational wealth. But, of course, he didn't do any of those things. The moment passed in seconds, and all he could do was shake her hand and give her a warm smile and a quiet "Good evening" as she ushered him and the Stewarts ahead of her into the Royal Box.

Chapter 7

The evening progressed more or less as well as anyone could have expected. A baby started crying loudly midway through *Appalachian Spring*, but really, Maddy thought, that was on them for inviting children to an orchestra concert.

Maddy was fighting a very uncharacteristic impulse to beam with pride. *Of course you should be proud, Maddypants,* the voice she couldn't seem to shake echoed in her mind. It was moving to see members of both countries' military bands alongside musicians from the London Philharmonic playing together. The repertoire was a nice mix of patriotic numbers, a smidgen of film music, as well as classical pieces from both sides of the Atlantic. They were pulling this off, and people seemed really pleased, which, in turn, made Maddy feel pleased. As a military family member herself, she knew what these families went through, and to see them waving the small flags they'd been handed when they entered and smiling with each other buoyed her. It had been eighteen months since she'd really felt useful like this and, as much as she was glad to have found a new life for herself with the embassy, it also felt good to be giving back to the military community again.

After a brief intermission, Maddy had allowed her mind to wander just a bit. Mostly thinking of how to circumvent anything that could possibly go wrong at the champagne reception following the concert, but also glancing around the Royal Box. Ambassador and Mrs. Stewart sat with the twins between them in the front row of the box, Prince Alexander at Mrs. Stewart's left. Sloane and Eric sat just behind the prince. Eric seemed genuinely interested in the music, his dark fingers tapping against his knees and his brown eyes watching the musicians keenly. Sloane was surreptitiously checking her phone. Maddy stood at the back of the box, near the door. There was a seat for her next to Eric, but she had been too full of anxious energy to sit quietly after the first half of the concert, so she had taken a spot next to the prince's security guard.

They were about halfway through Gustav Holst's *The Planets* when it happened. The slow section of "Jupiter" started, and Maddy was suddenly transported to another place and a very different time.

"Jupiter" burst from the organ pipes, and she peered around a corner. Evan stood there, his ornamental saber shining, his shoulders square and at attention, with a huge smile on his face. Maddy beamed, hiding behind the wall where she waited for her own entrance music to begin, the white lace dress cascading behind her as she grasped her bouquet of white flowers tightly. The wedding coordinator threw open the doors to West Point's Cadet Chapel, and Maddy saw Evan stride forward, grinning ear to ear as he headed toward the altar. She looked up at her father, smiling through happy tears. "Are you ready, sweet pea?" he asked, offering her his arm. She nodded as the organ crescendoed through the climax of the music, and she took her place at the back of the chapel, ready to take her own walk.

In Royal Albert Hall, Maddy found her vision unexpectedly clouded and felt a lump in her throat. She silently started to panic. She wasn't a crier. This wasn't about her. But the music soared on and she was suddenly afraid she was going to start sobbing. Glancing quickly at the front row to ascertain that nobody would notice, she slipped through the doorway to the hall outside the boxes, thanking every deity she could remember that the box was separated by a curtain rather than a door, making her exit nearly silent.

As she rushed a few feet down the hall, her back to the box, she gasped for air, trying to regain her composure. *How is this happening,* she thought, infuriated. *You* cannot *be doing this right now, Maddy. The time for crying was eighteen months ago and you didn't do it then, so you sure as shit don't get to do it now.* For once, the voice was silent. The one time she might have actually appreciated it, it wasn't there. *He* wasn't there.

"Are you well?" a quiet voice broke into her thoughts. Not the voice of the ghost that haunted her daily. An actual, corporeal voice. One with a posh British accent. She froze. "Ms. Cartwright?"

"I'm fine," she responded in a stage whisper from around the lump still choking her, still trying to force oxygen into her chest.

"I'm pretty sure that's demonstrably untrue," the voice said, nearing. A pair of black patent leather dress shoes and the hem of a pair of black tuxedo pants strode into her field of vision, and she realized that the voice belonged to Prince Alexander.

"Your Royal Highness!" Maddy exclaimed, horrified. "What are you doing here? You have to be in there!"

"I'm a prince," he said simply. "I can really do pretty much what I want to." The way he said it wasn't conceited sounding, merely just a statement of fact, even if it was offered with a hint of a smirk. His expression went serious. "But you are definitely not well. What's wrong? Are you ill? Can I call someone?"

Maddy finally managed to take a normal breath and steady herself. "No, I'm not sick. I just..." She groped for words. "I just needed a moment. But you really need to be back inside. If someone notices you're gone..."

"Madeleine," he ventured, as if testing out the use of her first name.

"It's Maddy," she blurted. "Nobody calls me Madeleine. Well, nobody except Mrs. Stewart."

"Okay, Maddy," the prince corrected. "How can I help? What's upset you?"

She took another calming breath, looked at the ceiling, and used her fingers to wipe away the slight dampness that had collected beneath her eyes. "Really, I'm fine," she said, managing to make eye contact with him for the first time. His eyes were full of concern and a healthy dose of skepticism.

"You're sure?" he prodded.

"Yes, that piece just brings back some memories," she added.

The prince looked like he was about to ask another question when applause started to waft out from around the curtain to the box. Just then Sloane stuck her head out. "Your Royal Highness? It's time for you and Mrs. Stewart to go down to make your speeches."

"Go," Maddy prompted, resisting the urge to give him a small shove. She didn't know much about royal protocol, but assumed shoving the Spare was squarely on the "no fly" list.

The prince gave her one last searching look and then stepped back into the box to collect Mrs. Stewart and escort her to the stage where they'd be making some brief remarks before the final set on the concert, a medley of the anthems of the two countries' various military branches. Maddy stepped a little further down the hallway to avoid crossing paths with Mrs. Stewart, and then, when she heard the riotous applause that signaled their appearance on stage, slipped quietly back into the box.

She resumed her seat behind the twins as she heard the prince say, "And although I haven't served myself, I certainly know a thing or two about duty to one's country." The crowd cheered wildly, and he smiled broadly. "We are so thrilled to welcome so many members of the armed forces of our two great nations this evening. It is a privilege to honor you all and your families. And so, as we close the concert we ask you to stand and be recognized when you hear your branch's anthem. And that includes you too, family members. Our service members couldn't do what they do without you."

The audience applauded as the prince and Mrs. Stewart stepped to the side and the conductor struck up the orchestra. Maddy's heart stuttered a bit as she heard the snare drum begin and saw uniformed soldiers march to the floor in front of the stage, each holding their military flag. The music washed over her as the Royal Navy March began and she saw sailors standing at attention in the seats below, and families scattered around, including one little girl saluting in an adorable sailor dress.

As "The Army Goes Rolling Along" began, though, Maddy froze. Out of the corner of her eye, she saw Ambassador Stewart stand, his military medals gleaming on the front of his dress uniform. As the twins rose next to him, Maddy slowly managed to get to her feet, feeling a bit wobbly. *Pull it together, Cartwright,* she told herself, *You've been doing this for almost thirty years.* As she took a steadying breath, she suddenly felt a small hand sliding into hers and looked down to see Amelia Stewart reaching a hand back and smiling up at her reassuringly. Maddy stepped forward into the place that Mrs. Stewart had vacated, to stand next to the teen. The girls knew as much as anyone did about Maddy's past, and when Amelia squeezed her hand, Maddy squeezed back, taking another deep breath and willing her lip to stop quivering.

Looking around the crowded hall, she saw a handful of other US Army members and their families. And then her eyes landed on the stage and met Prince Alexander's. He was looking directly at her, his gaze steady with a hint of a question. She nodded at him slightly, and he tipped his chin in return.

As the Army anthem ended and the RAF's hymn began, Maddy and the Stewarts all sat. Ambassador Stewart reached around the twins' shoulders to find Maddy's arm and gave it a quick squeeze. Of anyone, the ambassador probably understood her situation best, and the small gesture was more comforting than she would have expected. Although she didn't spend much time with him, even living under the same roof, Ambassador Stewart, or Colonel Stewart as he'd been when she'd first known him, had always been her favorite of her father's friends. When the unthinkable had happened and she'd needed to get away, there were few she would have trusted to help her, but Andrew Stewart was one. His small sign of his support helped her pull herself together and refocus on the reception.

Thirty minutes later, the champagne reception was in full swing. The large room was full of service members and their families. Members of the orchestra mingled with other embassy staff. A few children zoomed around the room, weaving amongst adult legs, hyped up on too many Shirley Temples. Maddy had a large wicker basket filled with small plush bears that she was handing out to the children. She saw the little girl in the sailor dress she'd noticed during the concert and made her way over. The girl was probably four or five years old and had blonde hair in an adorable crown of braids.

"Would you look after this bear?" Maddy asked, crouching to her level to offer her one of the stuffed bears wearing a yellow hat and a blue duffle coat.

The girl shyly accepted the toy, and thanked Maddy at her mother's prompting.

"My name's Maddy. What's yours?" she asked, smiling at the little girl.

"Emma," she whispered shyly.

"Did you enjoy the concert, Emma?"

"Yes," she lisped, then added, "I liked it when they played my daddy's song."

"Is your daddy a sailor?" Maddy asked gently.

"Yes, he's on a boat in the ocean far away because he's super brave," Emma announced proudly.

"Do you know who else is super brave?" Maddy asked. When Emma shook her head, Maddy pointed at her. "You."

"Me?" Emma asked incredulously. "But I'm 'fraid of everything!"

"But being brave doesn't mean that you aren't scared. It means that you do scary things even though you *are* scared. And sending your daddy off to go do a really important job is about the bravest thing I can think of." Emma beamed with pride. "And I know he's really proud of you." She looked up from where she was crouching to see Emma's mother blinking back tears and stood to put a comforting hand on her arm. "And he's proud of you too," Maddy added, swallowing the lump that was rapidly forming in her own throat as she comforted the military spouse who couldn't have been much older than Maddy herself. The woman thanked her before following her daughter away toward a large table laden with hundreds of cookies.

Maddy turned to find another family to talk with and ran

straight into a firm, warm, masculine body, smacking it with her basket and sending bears tumbling to the floor.

"I'm so sorry!" She gasped out, mortified.

"It's alright," a now-familiar deep voice chuckled. "It would seem that turnabout is fair play."

Maddy scrunched her eyes in humiliation, knowing that her face was turning beet red. It was the first time in their brief relationship that either of them had acknowledged martini-gate.

"At least it wasn't gin," she answered wryly. "But I'm still sorry."

She dropped to her knees and started piling bears back in her basket. To her surprise, the prince joined her on the floor, helping to corral the errant toys. "You were so good with her," he said, placing a few stuffies carefully back in her basket.

"I was only saying what I know I would have wanted to hear." Maddy said, deflecting his compliment. "I've got this, Your Royal Highness. You should be talking with your guests, not on your knees with me." She regretted her word choice as soon as she said it and felt her cheeks turning red again.

Mercifully, he didn't respond beyond cocking one eyebrow at her and continued to collect bears. "Was your father in the military too?"

"He still is. He's a three-star general," she replied. "Until I moved to London, being an Army brat was basically my entire identity."

"And now?" he asked, seeming to surprise them both with his question. But Maddy was saved from having to figure out how to answer by Eric coming to the prince and whispering something in his ear. "Please excuse me," he said to Maddy, almost regretfully.

"Not at all, Your Royal Highness." Maddy smiled at him as he stood and followed Eric to the other side of the room.

The rest of the event passed in a blur. Toasts were made,

sponsors were thanked, and Maddy passed out more stuffed bears, squeezed more hands, tried to connect. By 11:30 p.m., the final guests were leaving. Maddy exhaled, looking around at the familiar party carnage that waitstaff were already tidying away.

"We did good, Cartwright," came Sloane's voice from beside her.

"We sure did," Maddy replied. "Thanks for everything. Y'all are a well-oiled machine."

The Stewarts came up to them just then, the girls trailing behind their parents looking bored and sleepy. "Maddy, you did great tonight. Your mama would be proud," said Ambassador Stewart, patting her on the shoulder.

"Thank you, sir. I did learn how to throw a party from the best. I just have a few more things to square away here," Maddy said, turning to Mrs. Stewart. "Y'all can take the car home. I'll grab an Uber."

"We can wait—" the ambassador started to say, but his wife interrupted him with A Look.

"Andrew, the girls are exhausted."

"It's been a long night. Y'all go ahead, and I'll see you in the morning." Maddy said, ushering them toward the door.

When she'd seen them out of the reception room and heading down the staircase towards the side door where their chauffeured car waited for them, Maddy turned back toward the reception room. Glancing around to be sure nobody was in sight, she slipped off her heels and sighed in relief.

Hooking the straps of her shoes around two of her fingers, she headed back towards the room where she'd left her street clothes. The door was slightly ajar, but she didn't register until she was walking in that someone was inside. "Mum, I'm *fine*. It's like you—" the prince was saying impatiently, cell phone pressed to his face. She turned to rush out of the room again, but Prince Alexander waved her back in. "Mum, I have to go.

We'll continue this conversation tomorrow... yes. Love you too. Goodnight."

He hung up the phone, raking a hand through his hair.

"I'm so sorry, Your Royal Highness, I didn't realize—" Maddy began, but he cut her off.

"Alex," he said quietly. "My friends call me Alex."

She hoped her shock didn't show on her face as she slowly said, "Okay then... Alex." She fought off the urge to look over her shoulder as if she might find a beefeater there, waiting to haul her away for calling the king's son by his first name. "I didn't mean to intrude," she said, returning to her previous line of apology. "I just—"

He interrupted her again, as if he hadn't heard her. "Do you ever feel like you don't know who you truly are? Like, as if your identity was purely dictated by one thing that everyone knows about you and only that?"

Maddy froze, wondering if he knew. *Only literally every day of my life and especially the last eighteen months.* "Yes, I think I understand what you mean."

"It's fucking exhausting." He sighed, shoving both hands through his hair, giving him a slightly disheveled look that was totally out of line with his princely demeanor and definitely not at all sexy. Not in the least.

"Being reduced to one aspect of who you are? Yup, it sure is." Maddy said, exhaustion creeping into her voice. "Feeling like you aren't allowed to express any of the other facets of who you are? Always having to live up to that one thing and be examined under a microscope for it?"

The prince—Alex—finally looked up at her. "You do get it," he said, looking at her as if he was seeing her in a different way. She shrugged, suddenly feeling like the room was too warm, too small. She found herself acutely aware that she was barefoot in a cocktail dress, and she noticed Alex looking at her, something that almost looked like interest in his gaze.

They were standing close enough that she could smell his unique, masculine scent—sandalwood mixed with something she couldn't pinpoint that was probably a fiendishly expensive cologne. The air sizzled with something, a sensation she didn't want to give too much attention to, and so Maddy started gathering the things she'd left in the small room before the event.

"This was a really lovely event, Maddy. You did a brilliant job."

"Thank you, sir," she replied, feeling her cheeks go red.

"Alex," he corrected.

"Alex," she repeated, daring to look at him.

His gray eyes were piercing, as if he was really seeing her. The way he was looking at her made her stomach squirm in an unfamiliar way, heat pooling between her legs as his eyes moved slowly down to her lips. *Nope, this isn't happening. I'm not allowed to have a crush, and I'm definitely not allowed to have a crush on the freaking prince of England.*

"I should go," she said awkwardly, cooling the temperature in the room and killing the mood instantly.

"Yes, of course, I'm sorry to have kept you," he replied, almost visibly shaking himself, fidgeting with the button on his suit jacket.

"Good night, Your Ro– Alex," she said, conjuring a smile that she hoped was believable.

Their hands brushed as she almost ran past him to escape the tiny room, an electric sensation shooting up her arm at the slight contact. "Good night, Maddy." She heard him say behind her as she made her way quickly past Sloane and Eric and out into the night.

Chapter 8

Who is this?

Maddy snorted. She wouldn't have expected the prince to have a sense of humor. In their limited interactions so far he'd been serious, confident verging on cocky, at times shy, but never particularly light-hearted.

How did you get my number?

Wow, stalker much?

> They were beautiful, by the way. Thank you.
> That was very kind and very unnecessary.

MR. MARTINI

It was nothing. I'm guessing by the fact that
you're responding to my SMS that you did,
in fact, get home last night?

> Nope, this is my ghost. Hello from the other
> side 👻
>
> Yes, I got home fine. Call off the
> constabulary, London's cabbies are still
> passing muster

MR. MARTINI

Why didn't you ride back with the
Stewarts? Didn't they have a car there?

> They were ready to leave before me, so I
> sent them on. It wasn't a big deal.

MR. MARTINI

If you were mine, you would never be
finding your own ride at half midnight.

"If I was *his*?" Maddy was about to unleash a feminist screed by text when Alex's next message came through.

MR. MARTINI

My employee, I mean

> I see...

The typing bubbles appeared then disappeared several times before his next message came through.

MR. MARTINI

I'd like to get to know you better.

Have dinner with me?

Maddy's jaw dropped. "Did the prince of England really just ask me on a date?" she asked the empty room, her voice rising an octave, nearly squeaking the word "date."

MR. MARTINI

I mean, if you'd like to. I won't send Scotland Yard if you say no.

Maddy chewed her bottom lip. The fact of the matter was that yes, of course, she did want to go. But where royals went, so did the paparazzi. She'd had her fair share of photographers in the last two years and had no desire to be thrust back into the media melee. And, of course, the idea of a new relationship was out of the question. She was done being connected to men whose careers came with a spotlight. Maddy 2.0 had no business getting involved with anyone, least of all the second in line to the throne. If anything, she should be looking for forgettably attractive men to have casual flings with, not a literal celebrity.

I'm flattered, really. But I'm super busy with work right now.

It was partially true. As the autumn deepened, there were more and more events she'd need to help prep the Stewarts for and attend. But mostly, it was just better that way.

MR. MARTINI

Okay, what about coffee?

Maddy's eyebrows raised. She hadn't expected him to counter. Then again, he probably wasn't used to people turning him down.

Alex, I really can't.

There was a longer pause before his next response.

MR. MARTINI

If you're seeing someone else, it could just be platonic.

Maddy huffed out a laugh. The idea of anyone else was borderline ludicrous to her.

It's not that.

She paused, trying to figure out how to compose the rest of the message in a way that was both truthful and also completely devoid of information.

I'm just trying to work on myself. I'm still getting settled in London, still trying to get acclimated to this job.

The typing bubbles appeared, disappeared, and reappeared a few times before his next message came in.

MR. MARTINI

Understood. Well, if you want someone to show you around town, you know who to ask. My family's lived here for quite a while.

> LOL. Understatement of the century.
> Thanks, Alex. Appreciate the offer.

Maddy sighed and laid her phone face down on her desk next to her keyboard and tried to get back to working her way through her inbox, which had gotten out of hand in the frantic run-up to the Armistice Day concert. A big part of her had wanted to say yes to Alex's invitation. Had wanted to see what it would be like to spend time with a prince. What girl wouldn't? But she also knew that after a lifetime of being in someone's shadow, the only way to change the trajectory of her own life, to take things by the reins, would be to make choices that would put her on that new trajectory. And she knew without more than a moment's thought that dating the spare to the British throne was the pinnacle of playing second fiddle.

Maddy didn't hear from Alex again that day. Or at all over the weekend. But the following Monday, midway through the morning, she got another text.

MR. MARTINI

> This wasn't you, was it?

His message was followed by a link to an article about an American tourist who had accidentally wound up in Dover after falling asleep on a commuter train and then gotten lost in the warren of decommissioned military tunnels in the famed white cliffs before someone had rescued her.

Maddy giggled, as she typed out a response.

> Thankfully, no. Glad to know you think so
> highly of my intelligence, though!

MR. MARTINI

I mean, you said you hadn't had much time
to get to know the city. I was mostly joking!

Maddy could practically hear him sputtering as he tripped over himself to apologize.

> I know you were just teasing me. It's fine.
> That's hilarious.
>
> As was this. Did this happen to you too?

She linked to an article she'd seen a few days earlier where a celebrity was asked about going to school with Prince Benjamin and had said he liked standing near him on the rugby team because everyone wanted to be able to say they'd tackled a prince.

MR. MARTINI

Thankfully, no. They knew better than to put
me on a rugby pitch. Definitely had a few
kids at school try to befriend me for less
than genuine reasons, but nothing like that.

Maddy paused. She hadn't meant to take the conversation deeper.

> I'm sorry, Alex. That's awful.

There was a longer pause before he replied again.

MR. MARTINI

Comes with the territory. I'm fine.

> Now will you have dinner with me? Coffee? Lunch?

Maddy smiled ruefully as she started typing.

> Nice try, but still no.

They went on like that for another week. Intermittent lighthearted texting banter, always ending with him trying to get her to go out with him and her demurring. She had to admit that it got harder to say no each time. But she just kept reminding herself that this new chapter was supposed to be about putting herself first. About making the most of her independence. About trying new things. Not about diving back into a relationship with someone whose career would force her back into the public eye.

One night Maddy was lazing on her couch, scrolling aimlessly on her phone with an episode of a mindless reality show about rich women behaving badly streaming on her laptop when her phone rang. It was Alex.

"Hello?" He'd never called her before, and she found herself curious about why he was calling now.

"Hi, Maddy," he said. There was a slight pause. "Is this a bad time?"

"No, this is fine," she said, reaching forward to pause her show. "How are you?"

She heard him sigh quietly through the phone. "I just... at the risk of sounding like an ungrateful prick, sometimes I wish I had a different life. One with more agency. The ability to make decisions without having to get my father and a committee of his staff to agree to things." A beat. "Do... do you ever feel that way?"

She let out a shaky laugh. "I think I know how you feel," she said carefully. "I mean, I can imagine what would make you feel that way, but is there something specific that's happening right now to make you feel like that?"

He sighed deeply. "Yeah, I just... sorry. You're probably super busy, and I'm just calling you randomly. I just wasn't sure who else I could call who might understand. And after the conversation we had after the Armistice Day concert, I sort of thought you might."

"Alex, I'm literally sitting here watching a big screen while scrolling aimlessly on a little screen. This is fine. What's up?"

"I don't know if you met Eric, my private secretary?"

"Yeah, he seemed great. Really easy to work with. Why?"

"He threatened to quit because my family are basically the poster children for unearned white privilege and he can't stand working for us anymore, which, fair. So I went to my parents and asked what we could do about it and my father seemed... about as open to it as I could have expected. But we met with his staff today to talk more about it, and they were just... ugh. I should be used to this by now, but they were simultaneously so brownnosing to me and almost condescending to Eric, and I felt terrible for bringing him there and subjecting him to these elitist pricks and also... just so mad about it."

Maddy let out a long exhale. "Yeah, that sounds rough. Change can't come easy to an institution like your family. What did Eric say afterwards?"

Alex sighed. "Not much. I mean, he still hasn't formally quit—I asked him to wait until we could see what we might be able to do about setting up this reparations fund and putting him in charge of it, so he hasn't said no. But he also hasn't said yes."

"But did your father's people say no?"

"Not in so many words. I just—" He broke off, clearly searching for the right words. "I knew that I had no idea what his lived experience was like. But I didn't realize the extent to which I didn't know until this conversation. It's like they thought he wasn't smart enough to realize that they were talking down to him. The man did better at Cambridge than I did. And any idiot could have seen that. It was gross."

"And what did you do about it?"

Another heavy sigh. "Not enough." He sounded defeated. "I apologized to him afterwards, but I should have spoken up more in the meeting."

"It's hard," she said. "Standing up for the right thing is hard, and you're trying to start these conversations in a space where nobody has ever even considered doing that. So maybe today wasn't perfect, but the fact that you recognize that you could do more is a good step. Is there another meeting?"

"Yeah, we're supposed to meet again next week."

"Well, good," she said. "You've got another chance. What do you think you want to do differently next time?"

He was quiet for a moment. "I think I want to talk to Eric first, see if he wants me to speak up for him... but I want to shut them down."

"I think that's a good idea."

"Thanks, Maddy," he said. "Sorry, I know this is kind of heavy. I just feel like I can't talk to Eric about this part, and my brother is all wrapped up with the wedding and also only kind of gets it."

"Don't apologize. I'm honored that you trusted me with this."

"Now will you *please* go to dinner with me?"

"You really aren't used to people telling you no, are you?" She responded with snark, hoping to avoid the heart of the conversation.

"Well, come to think of it, no, but that's not it. I just... even though we come from such different places, I feel like we have a lot of things in common. I don't have a lot of people I can talk to and who will actually be straight with me instead of just telling me what I want to hear. I'd really like to get to know you better. Please, Maddy?"

Now it was her turn to sigh. "Alex, I just really don't think that's a good idea. Surely you can understand why." If Alex had her address and phone number, there was no chance he didn't have a full dossier on her and her history. He was clearly not stupid and would have to understand that being seen publicly with her wouldn't be good for either of them.

"Look, I know I'm a liability in a relationship. But in case you hadn't heard I'm new back in town and could use a few friends. And," he went on, "it seems like you could too."

Maddy wished she had someone she could talk this through with. The truth was that she was intrigued by Alex. She had, admittedly, never spent much time considering what a prince would be like, but the reality of him definitely wasn't what she would have expected. Nadia had worked hard to befriend her, and Maddy liked her a lot. But they weren't close enough for Maddy to tell her about everything that had happened before she came to London. The only people in London who knew about her past were the Stewarts, and she definitely couldn't talk to them about the fact that Prince Alex was texting her. So maybe she needed some friends too. She couldn't believe she was even considering this. It seemed like a supremely stupid idea. And yet, he'd worn down her resistance thoroughly.

"So, we're going to have to unpack that 'I'm a liability in a relationship' line, but I guess there's a chance that I could use a friend in London. Dinner. On the DL. As friends."

"I promise we'll keep it discreet," he said. She could hear the victory in his voice. "I'll text you with the details."

· · ·

Maddy started to question her decision almost immediately, but she'd made a commitment and wasn't going to back down from it, so the next night just after seven, she slipped out of Winfield House and walked toward the Tube. She didn't seriously think anyone was following or taking note of her movements about town, but she figured that on the off chance that the paparazzi were watching, she was less likely to be followed in the Underground than she was in a cab.

She'd agonized over her outfit in a way she never would have if she was going to meet any other "friend." *You never thought about what you were going to wear when we hung out as friends*, Evan's ribbing voice resounded. After scouring the restaurant's Instagram to see that it was a low-key upscale gastropub, she'd decided that her work clothes would be too much and make it seem like a business meeting. She'd never seen the prince in anything less formal than a suit, so jeans felt too casual. She finally settled on a maroon turtleneck sweater dress, black tights, and black booties.

Maddy walked up to the restaurant at 7:32. She paused for a moment outside, gathering her composure and trying to settle her nerves. *It's just dinner*, she kept repeating. *A friendly dinner among friends. Friends are allowed to have dinner together. This is casual. A casual, friendly dinner.* With one more stabilizing breath, she approached the entrance and went in.

It was amazing how much quieter it was inside, even for a relatively popular bistro on a Thursday night. The bustle of the street outside faded away almost instantly to a quiet hush of conversations and the clinks of glassware and utensils on plates. The smell of high-class fried food wafted over her, and she inhaled appreciatively.

She approached the hostess desk and gave the name that Alex had texted her. The staff member nodded as if they had the prince in for dinner every night and asked Maddy to follow them. They led Maddy back through a dark hallway to a door, which they knocked on twice and then opened.

Inside, Alex sat at a table for two. The room was a small private dining room, clearly intended for small gatherings, but theirs was the only table set for dinner. Although she certainly understood why they would be dining in private, Maddy found it a little odd.

As Maddy entered, Alex stood, as if on reflex. He was more casual than Maddy had ever seen him—dark jeans paired with a soft looking green V-neck sweater under a blue blazer. He nodded his thanks to the host before coming to Maddy and kissing her casually on the cheek. She tried to ignore the niggling fear that her cheeks might have flushed at the gesture, which absolutely didn't mean anything.

"Thanks for coming," he said, joining her at the table. "I have to admit, I was a little afraid you'd change your mind."

She smiled uncomfortably, wondering how open she could afford to be with him. "I have to admit, the thought crossed my mind." *Apparently that open.*

"Why *did* you come?" he asked, looking at her intently, as if she was the only thing in the room, which she supposed she was, given that they were sitting in a near-empty private dining room.

"Honestly? I'm not sure." She huffed out a sardonic laugh. "I probably shouldn't have. If anyone finds out I'm here with you, we'll both be in big trouble." He was still gazing at her, his eyes telling her that he was waiting for more of an answer than the non-answer she'd given him. She sighed. "The real answer? I think part of me knew I'd never forgive myself if I turned down dinner with the prince of England." He inclined his head in a way that told her he wasn't too surprised. "And also, you intrigue me," she said honestly. "You're not what I expected, whatever that was, and I wanted to find out more."

She swallowed. "Why me? Why would you try to befriend me, of all people?"

"Well, you're kind, you're smart, you're witty, and I think we have some things in common. The way we feel about family and loyalty." He smirked a little. "And I'd be lying if it wasn't damned appealing that you clearly had no idea who I was until I showed up in that first meeting at Winfield House."

She laughed ruefully and put a hand to her forehead, hiding her eyes. "I suppose that's valid. Although to be fair, you've done a pretty good job of hiding yourself. I bet there are plenty of your own countrymen who couldn't pick you out of a lineup of guys in a tuxedo."

They were interrupted when their server came to take their drink orders and the slight awkwardness dissipated as they perused the menu.

"So tell me," she said, when the server had left with their menus, "what were you doing Down Under?"

"Well, for one thing," he began, "'Down Under' refers to Australia, and I was in New Zealand."

"Avoiding the question," she said into her glass of water.

"What was I doing?" he asked. "I was trying to be useful. I have a degree in the history of art and architecture from Cambridge. I did an internship with a restoration firm. At first they sent me down there as a gesture of goodwill after that bad typhoon to show that The Family cared." Maddy could almost hear the capitalization in the way he said "The Family." "But when I got there and saw the devastation and realized what a huge project it was going to be, I asked to stay." Their server returned with their drinks. When they were alone again he continued. "I could use what I'd learned in combination with this absurd privilege I have, my connections and resources, to try to help. At first I think the people expected me to stay for a photo op and a PR boost and then leave with the photographers. And really, that's what I was originally supposed to do. But then I started building relationships, talking with the folks who lived there. And I don't know." He trailed off. "It's not like I was anonymous there, but the press there doesn't care about me the way the press here does. The people there were just trying to figure out how to rebuild a sense of normalcy, and they didn't care who I was as long as I was there showing up and trying to help. So I just stayed. And a two-week trip turned into a month turned into three months turned into years."

"So why did you come back?" Maddy asked, hoping that if she got him talking about himself he'd be distracted from asking her questions about herself.

"Duty called," he said wryly, taking another sip of his beer. He sighed, gave Maddy a searching look, and, seemingly having made a decision, went on. "And with the wedding coming up, my family is going to be in the press more and more. It was going to look weird if I didn't start showing up for things. So my father called and told me it was time to come back. And that was that. I'd had a good run, shirking my duty to the family business and playing at being a commoner"—the sarcasm dripped from his voice—"but playtime was over, and it was time for me to grow up and come home."

"What would have happened if you had just said no? Refused to get on the plane? Fed your passport to a platypus? Taken refuge in a hobbit hole?"

He chuckled. "Platypuses are Australia." Maddy raised her eyebrows at him, clearly waiting for the rest of his answer. "Pretty sure MI-6 would have gotten involved. And they have their ways," he said, with an air of dark humor. "And really my parents can be like dogs with a bone. When they want me to do something, they're not going to let go until it's done. It was either stay there and wake up to increasingly nagging voicemails every morning until I gave in, or just come when they asked and save myself the hassle."

"And how does it feel to be back?" she asked.

"Well, it's reassuring to have the water in the toilet bowl going the right way again," he quipped. "Right unnerving that is." She laughed and then waited for him to go on. "I mean, it's fine? As much as this conversation might not make it seem like it, my parents and I actually have a pretty good relationship, so it's nice to be able to see them more often and spend more time together. And of course, I'm glad to be here for Ben and Hannah." He stopped for another sip of beer. "But I guess even though I've been back for three months I'm still trying to find my footing. Figure out where I belong in the new family order. Find the things that give my life here meaning." A pause. "How do you get me to just spill all of my feelings?" he burst out, laughing. "Are you secretly a therapist?"

"Tell me about your childhood," she deadpanned with a quirked eyebrow.

They were interrupted then by the arrival of their food, and the conversation drifted to inane small talk for a few minutes as they tucked in.

"Ohh my god," Maddy mumbled around the cheeseburger. "It's a good thing this isn't a date because this is *so* not a first-date food, but *damn* is it delicious."

"What in heaven's name is a 'first-date food'?"

"It's something the girls at college used to talk about," she explained. "*Apparently* on a first date you're supposed to find something that isn't too messy, won't get stuck in your teeth, and won't risk giving you bad breath." She paused to take another bite. "It's honestly shockingly hard to find something besides salad that meets all three of those criteria."

He cocked his head to the side, "Yes, I suppose if those are prerequisites, it does seem kind of limiting." He paused, thoughtful. "I have to confess, I sincerely doubt the dates on the other side of the table were putting that much thought into what they were ordering."

Maddy smiled ruefully. "You're probably right."

"So how do you like London?" he asked, turning the conversation in her direction. "What brought you here?"

"It's great!" she said, hoping she sounded suitably enthusiastic and simultaneously steeling herself for more questions. "I mean, of course, I work a lot, so I haven't had much time to really explore. But I love the architecture and the history." At least that was something she could say honestly.

"What's your job like?" he asked. "How did you end up working for the ambassador?"

"It's good," she said, mentally searching for what she could say without going too deep. "I like my coworkers, and it's nice to finally feel like I'm using my degree at least a little bit."

She intentionally hadn't answered the second question and was relieved when he followed up with "What's your degree in?"

"I got a bachelor's degree in American Studies from Vassar," she replied.

"You Americans," he teased. "Only you would decide you needed to study your own country. You don't hear about us taking degrees in British studies or Kiwi Studies."

"Yeah," she snorted, "because if you tried to research British Studies it would be a whole lot of 'and then we colonized this foreign land and then we stole that priceless artifact with the excuse that the people who created it certainly couldn't be responsible for it.'"

"And that's different than your beloved melting pot, how?" he asked.

"Touché."

"And how did you wind up working for the ambassador?" he said, coming back to his original question.

"Actually, he's an old friend of the family. You know how that goes." Alex chuckled wryly and tilted his head slightly in acknowledgement. "What do you miss most about New Zealand?"

He looked at her a bit oddly, but politely refrained from commenting on her abrupt change of topic. He thought for a second. "The anonymity. After I'd been there a few weeks, the people got used to me and stopped paying attention. I've never had that kind of freedom to go about my day-to-day life without feeling like I'm constantly being watched or worrying that by showing up somewhere I'm going to cause problems for other people or create a disturbance. I mean, I still had a guard with me, but I could do my own grocery shopping, go on hikes, eat out without having to reserve a private room under an assumed name."

"I can certainly see how that would feel liberating." Maddy said, swallowing the last of her burger and wiping her mouth with her napkin. "And what's your plan now that you're back here under your microscope?"

"Still trying to figure that out." He stole one of her fries and ran it through a puddle of gravy on his own empty plate. "For now I'm just going where I'm told, shaking hands and trying to be a good son. One of these days I'll need to make a plan, though, or I'll start going mental."

"It's an inflection point," she said.

"Hm," he mused. "I suppose it is. I guess I'm at a bit of a fork in the road."

"Scary," she said. "But also kind of exciting."

He smiled at her. "That it is."

The sound of voices passing in the hallway filtered into the silence and before Maddy could stop herself she blurted, "So what did you mean when you said you were a liability in a relationship?" she asked, referring to his texts on the morning after the concert.

He sighed. "Wow, you really don't do small talk, do you?"

"I mean, who knows if I'll ever share a meal with a prince again. I need to be sure I get all of my questions answered!"

"Well, you've been in London long enough to see that the paparazzi can be vicious to royals. There's no anonymity, very little of what the average person would consider normalcy, and almost everything we do is scrutinized by the press. Most people are decidedly disinterested in all of that baggage, and the ones that like the attention don't tend to be my type."

She nodded. "That makes sense."

There was a beat of silence. "But I suspect you knew that already. You're clearly very bright, and you said yourself that spending time together wasn't going to be good for either of us." It wasn't a question, but he seemed to be waiting for her to say something.

Maddy fidgeted, the outward sign of her interior panic as she tried to decide how to answer him. Part of her just wanted to tell him everything. It would be such a relief to be totally open about her past. But she couldn't. Whatever "this" was with Alex, it couldn't become anything more than a superficial friendship. To do anything else would be in direct contravention of the plan for Maddy 2.0. And she had to stick to the plan. Even if it was going to sting to do it. She decided she had to rip off the bandage. This whole evening had probably been a mistake. "I should get going," she said. "I have an early meeting tomorrow." She started to push back her chair.

"Maddy, wait. I didn't mean to make you uncomfortable." Alex said, reaching across the table to put a hand on her arm. "I'm sorry. You're just kind of an enigma to me. You're so good at drawing out other people—that woman and her daughter at the concert, my staff, hell, *me*—but you're a little sphinx-like yourself. I just wanted to know you better, but I can see you're a private person. I'm sorry for prying."

She looked at him searchingly. "I think I'm just confused.

You clearly have a report on me. You're right, I'm *not* stupid. I'm confident your people did a thorough background check on me before you walked into Winfield for the first time, and my story is not at all hard to find. Anyone with access to Google could pretty much find my entire life story with two clicks. I guess I just don't understand why you're asking when you clearly already know."

"Maddy, my *staff* have a file on you. I'm sure Eric knows not only where you live and your life story, but how you take your coffee, and what's in the darkest recesses of your internet search history." Maddy flushed, but he barreled on, seemingly oblivious. "I have no interest in getting to know you from a security report. I want to get to know you from *you*. I asked him for your contact information, but I haven't seen the report myself, and I'm not planning on reading it. I don't know anything about you that didn't come directly from you or my own observations."

Her body relaxed, a surge of nerves and adrenaline that she hadn't even been aware of experiencing vanishing rapidly.

"Eric knows I'm here with you, and I trust him like a brother. Actually, probably more than my own brother, who has been known to make some shockingly bad decisions in his day. Eric wouldn't let me be here and you wouldn't have been hired to work for the embassy if you were a criminal or a sociopath."

Realizing Maddy wasn't going to bolt imminently, Alex removed his hand from her arm. "Like I said, I'd like to get to know you better. As a friend. But I want to earn your trust. You clearly haven't Googled me, despite the full knowledge that there was ample information about me out there, and even though I had no idea your life was so easily accessible, I wanted to grant you the same courtesy."

She sighed and dropped her head. "I'm sorry. You're right. I have a hard time opening up to people, especially lately. It's been…" She fought past the tightening in her throat. "It's been a long couple of years. But I think you're right that we probably have some things in common and it seems like we *could* both use some friends." She was startled to discover that she actually could imagine telling him her story. Someday. But not yet.

"It's late," she said, stifling a yawn. "We should ask for the check." She reached for her purse and looked around, realizing that the server hadn't been in recently.

He scoffed at her. "You don't actually think I'm going to let you pay, do you?"

"This isn't a date, for one thing," she began indignantly. "And for another thing, even if it was, don't tell me you buy into that kind of patriarchal nonsense."

He held up both hands in a placating gesture. "It's not a date, you're right. But last I checked, the attachés at the American embassy don't get the best pay, and my family" —he paused for a moment in mock thought—"oh, that's right, my family basically owns this country. So I think I can get this one."

She rolled her eyes, but backed down.

"Well, thank you for a very interesting evening, Alex," she said, still faltering slightly at using his first name.

"And thank *you*," he said, smiling at her warmly. "I can't remember the last time I've enjoyed talking with someone this much."

Maddy shrugged into her coat and hefted her Liberty tote —her sole splurge purchase since accepting the position at the embassy—over her shoulder. "So, how does this work?" she asked. "Do I go out the front, and you wait five minutes before sneaking out the back?"

"Actually, it works pretty much exactly like that."

She shifted somewhat awkwardly, unsure of how to leave

things, then turned to him and extended her hand. "Good night, Alex."

He clasped her hand warmly. "Good night, Maddy."

She tried to ignore the electric surge that shot up her arm when they touched, and she quickly turned and left the room, heading back through the main dining room of the restaurant and out into the cold November night.

Chapter 9

Having dinner with Maddy was a revelation for Alex. He couldn't remember the last time someone had challenged him like she had. She wasn't reverent, she didn't try to suck up to him, and she was clearly not attempting to say only what he wanted to hear. He hadn't spent much time with many Americans, so he wasn't sure if it was her country's famed directness or just who Maddy was as a person, but he found himself fascinated by it.

In the days after their evening together, Alex kept finding himself replaying portions of their conversation in his head. The things she had said. The things she pointedly hadn't said. The way her eyes rolled back in her head when she'd first tasted her burger... He made valiant efforts towards keeping his mind firmly on the sidewalk and out of the gutter. She was beautiful, there was no denying that. But truth be told, he knew a lot of beautiful women, and none of them captivated him the way Madeleine Cartwright did.

He'd rarely been tempted to Google new acquaintances—although, to be fair, most of the people he socialized with had known him since one of them had been in nappies—but several times he'd had to stop himself from opening a new browser window on his phone and typing in her name. The knowledge that Eric had her full dossier in his office floated in and out of the recesses of his brain at least once a day, and he almost had to physically shake himself to remind him of his commitment to himself not to look. He had meant what he said to Maddy: he wanted to get to know her the way any normal person did, not by reading about her in the press or in a security file. He, of all people, knew firsthand what it was like when someone entered a situation thinking they knew a person based on what they'd read about them, and he never wanted to do that to anybody else. But he'd be lying if he said that he wasn't extremely tempted.

He found himself wondering what had transpired that would make her story so easy to find. The way she skirted the topic wasn't an attempt at any kind of modesty, real or feigned. It was true avoidance. He flashed back to the night of the Armistice Day concert. Of noticing someone exiting the Royal Box out of the corner of his eye and realizing it had been her. He wasn't sure what had made him follow her, but it had been instinctual. Something had just told him he needed to. And then he'd found her in the hallway, fighting back tears. Even though they still hadn't known each other well, in that moment he'd had an almost visceral urge to pull her into his arms and make it all better. To erase whatever was causing her pain. Something told him the two puzzling moments were connected. And he was fairly certain he wasn't going to like the reason.

He'd been ready to ask Maddy to get together again almost as soon as she'd walked out of their first dinner, but he also intuited that if he pushed too hard she would bolt, so he made himself wait a few days before he texted her again.

Hey, do you want to do something this
weekend? Hang out or something?

THE HOT AMERICAN

How does one "hang out" when one is the
prince of England?

Well, you could come over and watch a
movie? I know it's kind of boring, but
staying here is the easiest way to not be
seen.

THE HOT AMERICAN

That works for me.

You should know that I don't do war films
and despite my utter distaste for society's
obsession with the gender binary, my taste
in movies skews decidedly towards what
most people would consider "girly."

Alex laughed to himself before setting about finding the
perfect response and settling on a gif of Kristin Wiig shim-
mying down the aisle of a plane in *Bridesmaids* and sending it
to her

THE HOT AMERICAN

He knows how to use a gif, folks! Who
would have thought?!

I contain multitudes

THE HOT AMERICAN

I can see that you do

Alex typed out his standard slate of instructions for someone visiting him at his apartment on the grounds of Kensington Palace for the first time and agreed on Saturday afternoon for their movie date.

Not date, Alex reminded himself. *Definitely not a date.*

THE HOT AMERICAN

I feel like hanging out with you requires a scavenger hunt. Or at the very least, very strong reading comprehension skills.

So what I'm hearing is that you think I'm a treasure?

THE HOT AMERICAN

You might need to get your hearing checked.

Nobody other than his brother had ever been this sassy with Alex, and he couldn't deny that he loved it. This whole "hanging out platonically" thing was proving to be a serious challenge. And yet Saturday afternoon couldn't come soon enough.

When he finally heard Maddy's soft knock on his front door Saturday afternoon, Alex had to pretend that he hadn't been pacing the entryway waiting for her to arrive. He waited a beat, took a breath, and walked toward the door, grabbing his corgi puppy, Bertie, on the way.

He opened the door and smiled at Maddy, cradling Bertie in one arm as he held the door open with the other. "Hi," he said, "Sorry, I hope you're okay with dogs."

"Of course!" Maddy cooed, holding out a hand to let Bertie sniff, his stubby legs flailing as he tried to escape Alex to smother her with puppyish affection. "We never had dogs when I was a kid because we moved too often, but I always kind of wanted one." She turned her attention to the small bundle of brown and white energy. "Hi, buddy!" Smiling up at Alex, she asked, "What's his name?"

"Bertie," Alex said, closing the door behind her.

"What a good boy, Bertie!" she said in a tone of voice that people only used with dogs and Alex generally found annoying (and insulting to the dogs). He somehow found it entirely charming when Maddy did it.

"Did you have any trouble finding us?" He put Bertie down, silently begging the little menace to be polite for once in his short life.

"Well, there was no X marking the spot the way you said there would be," she said with a cheeky smile, "but your instructions were very clear otherwise, so I did manage to find my way."

"Good. Can I take your coat?"

She shrugged out of her jacket, and he hung it on the coat rack in the entryway as she stepped out of her shoes. She was wearing jeans and a black sweater that looked very soft. Unlike the other times he'd seen her, it didn't look like she was wearing makeup, and her hair was in what he was pretty sure he was safely allowed to call "a messy bun." In short, she looked comfortable and refreshingly casual.

"I have to admit," she said, taking in the tiled foyer of his apartment, "that you calling this an 'apartment' feels a little misleading."

He flushed. "Yeah, the term is a bit outdated." His "apartment" was really a row house of sorts, one of several reserved for various members of the extended family. He had a kitchen that he barely knew how to use and a home gym on the ground floor, and then an office, his sitting room, his own bedroom, and a guest room on the second floor. Compared to other royal residences, it truly was modest, but he could also easily see how, to a normal citizen, calling it an apartment was almost farcical.

"And you, like, don't have a butler or anything?"

"Sorry to disappoint you, but no. I have a housekeeper who comes in to clean and bring in meals a few days a week, but with it just being me and Bertie, I don't really need more than that."

"How positively sensible," she said wryly. There was a slightly awkward pause before Maddy said, "So where's the movie theater?"

Alex laughed. "Let me give you a tour," he said, leading her towards the steps to the second floor. "Although I'm afraid you may be disappointed in the lack of cinema."

"Oh yes, of course, it's a 'cinema' here," she said with light mocking in her voice. "Although really, that's such a classier name for it than 'movie theater.' I guess y'all do get some things right sometimes."

"'Y'all'? Are you Southern?"

"I'm from all over," she said with a sigh as they reached the top of the stairs and he led her into his sitting room. "My parents live in Kansas now, but we spent time all over when I was a kid: North Carolina, Germany, Arizona, Alaska... we've hit most of the major US Army bases. But my dad's from Texas originally, and really, if you think about it, 'y'all' is an incredibly useful word. Most other languages have a word that means 'you guys.' For some reason because ours is so dialectical it just gets made fun of."

"I suppose you're right," he said. "I never thought about that before." Not for the first time Alex found himself impressed by how intelligent and incisive Maddy was.

"So this is the sitting room," he said, feeling a bit uncertain in a way that was alien to him. He wondered what she saw when she looked around his space: the dark brick fireplace on the wall next to the door; a flatscreen TV mounted above it; the window seats along the right wall, piled with pillows; the bookshelves against the far wall; dark green rugs; a brown leather couch, and a matching overstuffed armchair.

"Nice," she said, smiling and tucking herself into the corner of the sofa. Bertie immediately leaped up next to her and settled down. Alex saw he'd have to fight for this woman if he didn't want to lose her to his dog.

She stroked Bertie's ears absentmindedly as she looked around. "This seems cozy," she said.

"It works for us," he said, uncertain of how to respond. It wasn't like he could take credit for the way his apartment looked. Before his return from New Zealand, someone from his father's staff had called about how he wanted his space furnished, and when he'd arrived, it had been like this. He'd added a few framed family photos and some art from his travels, but otherwise, it could have been a living room in a catalog.

"Can I get you a drink?" he asked, changing the subject. "Beer? Wine? Water? Tea?"

"Water would be great," she said, smiling up at him.

"I'll be right back," he said.

He descended to the kitchen on the ground floor and grabbed a few bottles of flat water along with some cans of flavored sparkling water. It occurred to him that they didn't have any popcorn to have with a movie, but opening his pantry he found a few bags of different flavored crisps and brought them along as he returned to the second floor.

Maddy was examining the books on his shelf when he returned. "See anything you like?" he asked as he put the snacks and drinks on the coffee table.

"I'm so nosy about people's bookshelves," she said,

walking back to retake her place on the sofa. "I always feel like you can tell a lot about people from what they read." She examined the selection of beverages he'd brought up and selected a lemon-flavored sparkling water.

"And what can you tell about me from my books?"

"You like dude books," she said directly.

He laughed. "I suppose I do," he allowed. "In my defense, some of those are mine, and then a lot of them are things that the decorators brought over from some other library so that those shelves wouldn't look empty."

"Of course, as one does," she said with a sarcastic nod.

He laughed and picked up the remote before flopping onto the opposite end of his sofa. "So we've established that war movies are bad, girl movies are good."

"I mean, movies don't have genders, but yes, correct."

"Okay," he said, clicking into the first streaming service on his television without looking. When the first sound he heard was a quiet moan his eyes flew to the screen in horror when he realized he'd unwittingly clicked into an app that featured high-quality pornography. "Oh fuck!" he said, slapping frantically at the remote to get the image off the screen.

"Indeed," Maddy said. She was blushing furiously, but there were also tears of mirth in her eyes. "That's not *exactly* what I meant when I said I liked 'girly movies,' Alex."

"Maddy, I'm so sorry, I can explain—"

"Explain what?" she said matter-of-factly. "You watch porn, I read smutty novels. We all have to get our yayas out some way or another."

"So you read smutty novels?" he asked, distracted from his humiliation by her revelation.

"Focus, Windsor!"

"Right, so not that," he said, refocusing his full attention on the screen so that when he pushed the button again he was positive he was going into a normal movies app.

After several moments of debate peppered with banter about what to watch, they settled on *When Harry Met Sally,* a movie he'd seen a million times, which was convenient, because it meant if he got distracted watching Maddy watch the movie, it wouldn't matter. At that moment, Bertie looked at him with a face that said, *You are completely screwed.* The timing was so uncanny it almost seemed like the dog could read his mind. Which was obviously impossible.

After the opening scene of the old people talking about their romances, Maddy reached forward and examined the packets of crisps he'd brought up. "I'll definitely give you this: your chip flavors are so much better than ours." She picked the smoked paprika flavor and opened it, tossing a few into her mouth. "*Why* don't they have these in the States?" she asked around the mouthful of crisps. "It's so unfair!"

Alex laughed and took the proffered bag, helping himself to a few. "What can I say?" he answered cheekily. "You can't top the original?" She gave him a sassy look and snatched the crisps back from him, refocusing on the movie.

Several minutes later as Harry and Sally were embarking on their road trip from Chicago to New York, Alex groaned internally as Harry began a monologue about how men and women couldn't be friends because someone always wanted sex. He sensed, rather than saw, Maddy fidget uncomfortably, and he wracked his brain for something witty to say to diffuse the awkward moment. Because the truth was that he *did* want to have sex with Maddy. Badly. In a way he hadn't wanted a woman in a long time. He'd slept with a few women since he'd been back from New Zealand, but it had been a purely phys-ical act. And he'd realized each time that the purely physical sexual encounters that he'd grown used to engaging in weren't satisfying him the way they used to. He wanted Maddy in a way that transcended the physical. But, he had to remind himself sternly, that was explicitly *not* what she wanted. Even if

Harry was right. And so he forced himself to think about anodyne things—mentally reviewing his schedule for next week, planning out when and where he would make time to take Bertie on longer walks, how many socks were left in his drawers—until he could return his focus to the movie.

It worked, too, until the scene where Harry and Sally were at Katz's Deli and Harry boldly proclaimed that he'd know if a woman had ever faked an orgasm. Alex glanced at Maddy out of the corner of his eye and saw a smirk on her face. "What?" he asked, nudging her with his toe.

"Hm?" she looked at him.

"What's that look on your face?"

"I mean..." She flushed. "Statistically, if you've been with more than a few women, someone's faked it with you. She's right about that math."

"Oh, is she?" he asked, shifting so he was facing her.

"Oh, come on, you know she is."

"No, I don't," he said, taking on an affronted tone. "The women I've been with are all very well satisfied, thank you very much."

"You know you sound just like him, right?" She nodded towards the screen where Billy Crystal's Harry was looking increasingly uncomfortable as Meg Ryan's Sally was now giving the performance of a lifetime, faking an orgasm in the middle of the crowded deli.

He fumbled for a smart comeback and, not finding one, turned the tables towards her. "So you've done that?"

"What? Had a loud fake orgasm in the middle of lunch? No, of course not." He gave her a look that she looked like she wanted to ignore. After a long pause, she reluctantly answered, "Yes. I have."

He found himself resisting a totally bizarre urge to growl. "That's criminal."

"To fake it?"

"Well, I mean, that part's kind of dishonest. But a man who knows what he's doing doesn't have this problem."

"Oh, and you're the prince of orgasms in addition to being the prince of England?"

"I mean…"

She rolled her eyes dramatically. "Oh my god, Alex."

"What?"

"Did it ever occur to you that women probably want you to like them and, as such, might"—she paused, as if searching for a word—"exaggerate to make you feel good about yourself?"

He blinked. He genuinely hadn't ever considered that. He didn't *think* the women he'd been with would have spontaneously heaped quite as much praise on him as they did after their encounters if he wasn't actually good at pleasing them. But now he wondered.

"Mm-hmm." Maddy hummed as the woman in the booth next to Harry and Sally asked for "what she's having." She shifted, seeming uncomfortable, and tried to refocus on the movie, but Alex couldn't let the topic drop that easily.

"Look, Maddy, I'm willing to allow that maybe it's happened to me. But in a real relationship, there's no room for that. You deserve to be with someone who you feel comfortable being honest with. Who knows you well enough—knows your body well enough—to know what to do with it."

Her cheeks flushed and she wouldn't look at him.

"Let's not talk about it," she said, her voice almost a whisper. He could almost see her withdrawing into a shell, like a scared snail.

He desperately wanted to push. To find out who the guy was who had disappointed her, who hadn't taken the time to understand how to make her feel genuine pleasure. But he could tell he wasn't going to get much further, and he didn't want to risk scaring her away completely. So he dropped it.

But he didn't stop thinking about it. Not while they finished the movie, not while they chatted about inane topics while eating Indian takeout, not when he walked her to the door and watched her head back towards the gate. He knew it probably wasn't a good idea to let himself think about it, but he did. He thought about how she'd been unsatisfied and how he wanted to be the one to make it right.

Chapter 10

MR. MARTINI

Bad news bears

> Who in their right mind says 'bad news bears'? Is this a cry for help? Have you been kidnapped?

MR. MARTINI

I need to cancel.

> Oh, that's ok. Everything alright?

MR. MARTINI

Yeah, it's fine, I'm just a little under the weather.

> Define "under the weather"

MR. MARTINI

It's just a mild flu. Eric had it last week. His kids brought it home from nursery.

> "A mild flu"?

Have you seen a doctor? Do you have a fever?

MR. MARTINI

I'll be fine, I just need some time to lie around.

Is Eric there with you?

MR. MARTINI

No, it's Saturday. He's home with his absurdly attractive husband and their two ridiculously cute kids.

What about the rest of your staff? Your family?

MR. MARTINI

My housekeeper only comes during the week, my parents are at Windsor for the weekend, and god knows where Ben and Hannah are.

Maddy rolled her eyes. Really, what was the point of having basically limitless generational wealth if not to use it for sensible things like hiring help?

But you have enough medicine and Powerade and stuff, right?

There was a long pause. She saw the bubbles indicating that Alex was typing appear and disappear a few times before she finally gave up and called him.

"Mads, I'm really fine," he said, in lieu of a more standard greeting. But his voice was raspy and as soon as he got that one sentence out he was overtaken by a hacking cough that ended with a frankly pitiful sounding groan.

"Tell me again how you're fine," she said drily. When no response came she went on. "Are you at least hydrating? Have you taken anything?"

She heard him sigh and a rustling of fabric that made her think he was trying to get more comfortable wherever he was lying. "It's just a little flu."

She frowned. "So no and no. How long have you been sick?"

"A few days," he said quietly. "And I ran out of paracetamol yesterday."

"Alex," she said, gentle chastisement in her voice. "Why didn't you order more? Certainly they have UberEats at Kensington, if you refuse to ask anyone else to help."

"I didn't want to be a bother."

Maddy sighed. She didn't have plans for the day since she and Alex had planned to watch a movie and order takeout again. Showing up at his house with supplies was taking their friendship a step further than she really intended to. But she was also worried that he wasn't taking care of himself, which was pretty much her kryptonite.

"I'm coming over. I'll be there in an hour with more medicine and some Powerade."

"Mads, really, I'm fine. I don't want to get you sick." She noted that his protests were getting weaker and weaker. He seemed to have picked up on the fact that she wasn't going to give up.

"We'll see about that," she grumbled, getting to her feet and slipping into her shoes. "Text me the code to get into your door."

An hour later, Maddy let herself into Alex's apartment, opening the door the smallest possible amount to prevent letting Bertie out. She was surprised to find that he wasn't there, waiting to attack her ankles. "Alex?" she called out, toeing off her shoes in the entryway.

She heard a cough, followed by "I told you I was fine,"

wafting down from the second-floor sitting room in a voice that was clearly anything but fine.

She followed the sound of Alex's wracking cough to find him lying on his side on the couch, huddling under a navy-blue chenille blanket. He was wearing a gray hooded sweatshirt, and his cheeks were flushed, eyes glassy. Bertie lay in the crook of his bent knees, his small head and paws resting on Alex's hips. "Good boy," she said to the dog, whose face wore what could only be described as a look of concern. She scratched him absentmindedly behind his ears as she turned to his person.

"Fine, eh?" she said, putting down the shopping bag she carried and leaning over to feel his forehead. His skin burned beneath her cool hands and her brow creased with concern. "Have you taken your temperature?"

He sighed. "Not today. Maddy, it's just a flu. I'll be fine, really. I don't want you to catch this."

"I really thought royals were supposed to have staff to dote on you 24/7," she grumbled. He coughed again and groaned. She softened her tone. "Where's the thermometer?"

"In my bathroom, in the cabinet behind the mirror," he said, sounding exhausted and resigned to his fate as her patient.

"OK, I'll be right back," she said heading towards the hall.

From her previous visit to his apartment she had a vague idea of where his room was, but she hadn't actually been in it. She pushed open the door and took in his space. It was large with cream walls and light carpet. Just to the right of the door, a towering armoire stood against the wall. A window seat piled with throw pillows was centered on the wall to the right, overlooking the rest of Kensington Palace. There was a small sitting area anchored by a plush forest-green circular carpet, patterned in elaborately creeping white flowers. His bed was to the left. Medium-brown wood with posts that soared toward the ceiling, it was less ornate than she would have imagined a prince's bed would be. Not that she'd imagined his bed. Covered in mountains of snowy pillows and a white duvet, it looked surprisingly cozy and inviting. Maddy found herself wondering what it would be like to launch herself at it and sprawl across the large mattress. Or to be thrown onto it from strong, muscular arms…

Realizing she'd been standing there staring, Maddy headed across the room toward a door that obviously led to an en suite bathroom. Making a conscious effort not to be too nosy, she went straight to the medicine cabinet, located the thermometer, and returned to the sitting room.

"Where's your water?" she asked, pulling a bottle of pills from her bag and shoving the thermometer under his tongue.

"Um…" Alex looked around blearily, his voice garbled by the thermometer. "In the faucet?"

"Doesn't even have a water bottle," she grumbled under her breath, as she reached into the bag of supplies she'd brought with her and handed him a red Powerade as the thermometer beeped. "Thirty-eight point six… I have no idea what that number really means, but you're burning up, so you're going to take some of these." He heaved himself up to a half-sitting position so he could crack the seal as she handed him two white pills.

"What have you eaten today?" she asked, looking around and noting a lack of dishes nearby.

"Uhm…" Thinking seemed to be hard for him. "I had a protein bar when I woke up."

"Oh, Alex." She sighed. "If I heat up some soup, will you eat it?"

"I don't have any soup," he mumbled, snuggling back down into the couch, Bertie resettling himself around Alex's legs as he shifted.

"Then it's a good thing I brought some," she said, pulling a clear plastic takeout container out of her bag.

"Mads, I don't want any," he said, almost whining. "I really don't feel well."

"'Mads,' huh?" she said, smiling at him with amusement.

"You're so good to me, Mads." He gave her a loopy smile.

She rolled her eyes. "Ok, I'm going to put this in the fridge. Don't go anywhere. I'll be right back."

"Okay," he mumbled, miserably.

Maddy found her way down to the small but lavishly appointed kitchen on the first floor. She put a second bottle of Powerade and two containers of soup in his fridge, noting that there was also something in there that looked like shepherd's pie.

She stopped for a moment, thinking. If she was smart, she'd leave. She'd checked on him, made sure he was hydrating, and brought him food, medicine, and electrolytes. Technically, she'd fulfilled her duties as a friend. But he seemed so pathetic and sick, and he clearly wasn't going to call anyone else to come take care of him. Against her better judgment she sighed and headed back up to the sitting room, preparing for the long haul.

The medication helped his fever a little, and Alex drifted in and out of sleep for much of the afternoon. She sat in a surprisingly cozy armchair and read a book on her phone, prompting him to drink when he woke and coaxing him to eat a few crackers and even a bit of soup at one point.

As evening fell, though, his fever returned. "Maddy, I don't feel good," he whined, thrashing his legs on the couch as he tried to get comfortable and dislodging a disgruntled Bertie in the process.

"I know, Alex," she said placatingly, coming over to feel his forehead. He was burning up again, but it was too soon for him to take more medicine.

"That feels nice," he said. She hesitated for a second before drawing a hassock closer to where he lay so she could gently stroke her hand through his hair. He sighed contentedly and quieted a bit. "You're so good at this," he said. "I don't know how some lucky bastard hasn't snatched you up yet. You'd be such a good wife. Such a good mum."

She froze. She knew it was the fever talking and he probably wouldn't remember any of the conversation, but all of a sudden she was tempted to tell him everything. She shook herself a bit and went back to running her fingers lightly through his hair. "That's sweet, Alex," was all she said. "But it's not true." *Maybe someday you'll understand why.*

She almost thought he had fallen back to sleep when she heard him ask, "Did your mum take care of you when you were sick as a little girl?"

"Yes," she said. "Where do you think I learned how?" She paused for a second, still calming his forehead with gentle caresses. "I was barely ever allowed to watch TV when I was a kid, but when I was sick, I could watch as much as I wanted. She'd bring me meals on the couch and sit at the other end reading her book while I watched TV." Another pause. "Did your mother take care of you?" she asked, tentatively, almost afraid to hear the answer.

"Well, sort of," he said, his eyes closed. "She had so many appearances to make so she was busy. It was mostly our nanny, but if Mum didn't have to go out, she always put us to bed, and when we were sick, she'd usually come to sit with us at least a little during the day. She used to read to me..." he trailed off.

She'd noticed a book earlier, lying face down on the coffee table, open to a page part way through. "Do you want me to read to you?" she asked.

"Would you?" He looked up at her, surprised.

"Sure," she said and reached for the book. It was a mystery

by an author she wasn't familiar with, but she just opened the book to where he'd stopped and started reading.

At some point she must have fallen asleep, because when she woke up, the book was lying open in her lap and her arm was asleep from where she had rested her head on the arm of the sofa, her elbow a somewhat bony pillow.

She shook herself and quietly reached for her phone to realize it was almost one a.m. She had a brief inner debate about just going back to sleep, but decided that it was going to be odd enough if anyone saw her sneaking out of Kensington Palace at one a.m., let alone seeing what would certainly look like the walk of shame the next morning. Gently, being careful not to disturb Alex, she straightened his blanket and brushed her hand across his forehead again. It was much cooler. His fever had broken. Hopefully with a good night's sleep he'd wake up feeling much better the next morning.

As she crept over to pick up her bag, Bertie woke and jumped from the sofa, looking at her expectantly. Realizing he hadn't been outside in hours, Maddy allowed him to follow her downstairs, located his leash near the backdoor, and quickly let him out to do his business. When he was done, Bertie immediately vaulted back up the stairs to resume his position nestled in the crook of Alex's legs. Maddy followed the small dog up the stairs and took one final peek at Alex's sleeping form. She resisted a sudden strange urge to drop a kiss on his forehead. Shaking herself, she turned resolutely toward the door, crept down the stairs, stepped into her shoes, shrugged on her coat, and slipped out into the cold night, pulling a bulky scarf up around her ears as she headed toward the gate.

* * *

When Alex opened his eyes the next morning, it took him a second to figure out where he was. He was slightly clammy, there was drool crusting one side of his chin, and Bertie was standing on his hips, nudging Alex's shoulder with his snout, gently but insistently. And then it came to him. His den. He'd been sick. Maddy had taken care of him. Running his hand across his face, he gingerly sat up. "Do you need to go out, boy?" he asked, looking at Bertie, who quickly jumped down and sat in the doorway to the stairs.

He stood up slowly, realizing that he was sore, but that it was from sleeping curled up on his couch, not from the fever, and that he was tired, but not the bone-deep exhaustion he'd felt the day before. Whatever fresh hell that had taken him down for the last few days seemed to have passed. Bertie yipped impatiently and Alex finally started moving, following the corgi down the stairs and toward the back door of the apartment, where Bertie's leash hung on a hook. Alex shrugged into the barn coat next to it and slid into the hideous but serviceable athletic shoes that rested next to the mat inside the back door before clipping Bertie's leash to his collar and shuffling outside blearily.

The cold was bracing, the early morning air cleansing his lungs as he took some deep breaths and walked a ways into the park that extended behind his apartment so that Bertie could relieve himself. As Bertie wandered around, sniffing and marking every rock that he saw as his, Alex recalled the previous day.

When he'd texted Maddy to cancel, he never in a million years expected her to show up. Yes, if he'd texted his family someone would have dropped off a care package or sent a doctor to look in on him, but it had been years since anyone had truly taken care of him. He remembered her unique blend of pushiness and gentleness, forcing him to drink some Power-ade, coaxing him to eat crackers, chiding him for not having been hydrating or feeding himself before she got there. And the way she'd sat with him, stroking his hair so tenderly it had been like... he suddenly remembered commenting on the fact that she wasn't married, and groaned. What a stupid, insensitive thing to say. But her answer had been puzzling. *That's sweet, but it's not true, Alex.* What had she meant by that? As idiotic as it had been to hint at the question, he sort of understood why he had—the more time he spent with her, the more frequently he'd wondered. She was intelligent, funny, so kind, and beautiful. If a connection to him didn't mean the end of a person's privacy, he would have been begging her to date him, begging her to let him spoil her and take care of her... in more ways than one. He shook his head, trying to clear the mental image that had gone rushing straight to his brain and other critical organs at the mere passing idea of Maddy as his lover? Girlfriend? Wife? Who knows, but his baser side clearly wanted Maddy laid out beneath him, looking up into his eyes, writhing beneath him as he touched her...

He whistled to Bertie, tugging on his leash gently as he urged him back towards the warmth of the apartment. His stomach rumbled, reminding him that, despite Maddy's best efforts, he'd eaten very little the day before. As he wiped Bertie's paws and shrugged out of his jacket, Alex suddenly realized he had no idea where Maddy was. Was she still there? When had she left? The last thing he remembered was her soft voice reading his book to him, idly stroking his hair with one hand as she turned pages with the other. It had been dark outside, and she'd tried to coax him into eating some soup quite a while before he'd finally passed out. He glanced to where she would have left her shoes. Nothing. He had no idea what time it was, but it was still early. Frowning, he made his way back to his den and found his phone on the coffee table. He sank back into the sofa, exhausted even from just the short walk outside with Bertie. It was 7:30 a.m., and Maddy was definitely not in his house anymore. Picking it up, he saw that he had a text from her that had come in only a few minutes earlier.

THE HOT AMERICAN

How are you feeling today? Did you get enough sleep? When I left it felt like your fever had broken. Hopefully it hasn't come back.

Much better, thanks. When did you leave?

THE HOT AMERICAN

After you went to sleep.

Madeleine. What time did you leave?

THE HOT AMERICAN

It wasn't that long after midnight…

The way she was hedging told Alex it had been late, well into the night, and he found himself fighting off an itchy feeling that was equal parts anger, fear, and… some weird protective feeling that he was a little afraid to unpack too much.

Rather than continuing to badger her via SMS, Alex tapped the call button.

"Hey, how are you feeling?" Her voice was soft and dreamy, as if she hadn't been awake that long.

As if the first thing she did when she woke up was check on you? No, don't be such a self-centered idiot, Alex.

"I'm much better, but I need to know what time you left my house and how you got home."

"I told you, it was a little after midnight, and I got home just fine. I'm so glad you're—"

He cut her off before she could try to change the subject again. "Maddy," he said in an imperious voice he had never used with her, but that he knew that, when deployed, brooked no arguments.

He heard her sigh. "I fell asleep reading to you and woke up around one. You were passed out and your fever had broken, so I decided to let you sleep. I took the Tube."

"You took the *Tube*?" he practically yelled. A small part of him knew he was overreacting, but he couldn't take enough time to listen to that part. "At one in the morning! Maddy, that's absurd! God knows what could have happened to you!"

"It's not absurd. I was completely safe. I'm a big girl, Alex. I can take care of myself." He could tell she was placating him, but there was also a slight edge there, as if she had had just about enough of his bullshit. And yet, he forged onward.

"Maddy, I know you *can* take care of yourself, but do you ever actually do it? The more I get to know you, the more I'm starting to suspect that you spend so much time looking after other people that you rarely stop to consider the possibility of taking care of yourself!"

The silence on the other end told him he'd pretty near nailed it.

"Mads." He made a conscious effort to gentle his voice. "thank you so much for coming yesterday. Truly. It means so much to me that you'd just show up and listen to me babble and force red beverages down my throat for hours when you had plenty of other things you could have been doing. But the idea of you wandering around London in the middle of the night..." he trailed off, aware that he was overdoing it, but feeling a genuine, almost primal urge to protect this woman. "Just please promise me you won't do that again. I can get you a car anytime. I just want you to be safe."

"Alex, I'm fine. Nothing happened. I walked to the Tube. I was far from alone in taking the Tube even late at night, and I was texting one of my friends from college the whole time." She paused. "But I appreciate your concern."

He sighed. "You're not going to promise me, are you?"

"Unfortunately, as an American, I'm not one of your subjects, so I'm not actually required to obey you, Your Royal Highness." Her voice dripped with wry sarcasm. "Even if you had any real authority."

"Touché," he responded. "Well, again, thank you. Really. It's been years since anyone took care of me when I was sick. And I'm glad you got home safely."

"You're welcome, Alex," she said. "That's what friends are for."

His heart sank a little with her reminder of their purely platonic relationship. "What are you doing today?" he asked her, trying to remember what a normal conversation sounded like.

"The Stewarts are hosting a tea reception for American Fulbright scholars to the UK, so I'm working. How about you? Have you eaten anything yet today? Are you staying hydrated?"

"Food and hydration are next on the agenda."

"Good. Take it easy," she said. "You need to rest."

"I could say the same for you," he said pointedly. "If you left here at one, you didn't get home until two and you were texting me by seven."

"So you did learn deductive reasoning in that fancy education," she drawled.

"I was first in my class at Eton."

"And so modest too." She sighed and he heard rustling that sounded distinctly like bedding. He tried not to imagine her lying in bed, forced himself not to wonder what she wore to sleep in. "Okay, Alex, I have to go shower and get ready. Take it easy today."

"Yes, ma'am," he said. "Thanks again, Maddy."

"Anytime. Talk to you later."

As he hung up, Alex fought his very un-platonic urge to

imagine Maddy in the shower. The way her chocolatey locks would trail down her shoulders towards her breasts. The water sluicing down her naked body—

A sharp yip from Bertie pulled Alex from his X-rated fantasy. He adjusted his gray sweatpants self-consciously, and set about getting breakfast for both prince and pup.

Chapter 11

After Maddy spent the evening taking care of a fever-delirious Alex, she sensed a subtle shift in their relationship. He'd been incredibly vulnerable in front of her—albeit not entirely by choice—and she felt herself starting to wonder about letting her own guard down. She was scared, though. After several additional discreet and casual dinners and another afternoon at his place watching *10 Things I Hate About You,* she was reasonably confident that she knew Alex well enough to know how he'd respond, but she couldn't be sure. And she also knew that the closer she let him get, the closer she came to breaking her resolve. To getting too involved with yet another man whose career would push her back into public view. Anything more than a fling would be in direct contravention of the Maddy 2.0 plan.

A few weeks after Alex had the flu the Stewarts were in Paris on a diplomatic visit. As much as Maddy wouldn't have minded a weekend of *pains au chocolat* and, if she were being honest, respectfully ogling the French president, she was also glad to have a weekend fully off. Winfield House would be almost completely empty, and she had no responsibilities. No chance of being asked to escort the twins to dance class. No need to track down a specific skincare product for Mrs. Stewart. It was going to be glorious.

Maddy had turned in early Friday night after seeing the Stewarts off. After reheating some pasta she'd found in the embassy kitchen, Maddy had fallen asleep on the couch watching TV and then dragged herself up to bed. The next morning she treated herself to a real lie-in for the first time in weeks. When she finally rolled over, it was ten a.m. She couldn't remember the last time she'd felt so rested and relaxed. Picking up her phone, she saw she had a text from Alex.

MR. MARTINI

I saw on the news that the Stewarts are in Paris. Are you in town? Or did you go with them?

> Nope. I'm living my best goblin life at Winfield House alone.

MR. MARTINI

And what does a goblin life entail?

> Well, I'm still in bed and I have a full day of dissociating on my phone, watching trashy TV, and lounging planned. And obviously at least 3 beverages on hand at all times.

MR. MARTINI

Sounds amazing. Want company?

Maddy hesitated before responding. The real answer was of course she wanted to hang out with Alex. But she was also afraid that if they spent too much time together she'd let him get closer. That she'd have to explore the feelings that she kept resolutely shoving down each time they bubbled up. Decidedly un-casual feelings. That the closer he got, the harder it would be to keep her resolve to be independent, not beholden to another man with a powerful, public job. And she wasn't sure if she was ready for any of that.

MR. MARTINI

Of course, we don't have to hang out. I don't want to intrude on your solo-goblining.

Maddy bit her bottom lip and fidgeted with the chain around her neck subconsciously, the discs at the end clinking quietly between her breasts.

No! You should come over!

I mean, if you're allowed to do that? Are you allowed to just go to a friend's house? This friend's house very conveniently has pretty robust security…

MR. MARTINI

LOL. Yes, I'm allowed to go on playdates. Where's the best door to come in?

She gave him instructions on how to find the back door to the kitchen and they agreed on him coming over at 7:30 with a pizza. Which gave her eight hours to panic about hosting the second in line to the throne of England for a casual hang. A casual royal playdate.

By the time Alex arrived at 7:40 with a pizza and a bottle of Syrah that looked *far* too expensive to be enjoyed next to a pizza while wearing yoga pants, Maddy was slightly panicking. She'd spent the day alternating between sitting in an absolute stupor scrolling TikTok while not doing anything and frantic bursts of tidying in the hopes that her sitting room, at least, would not look like a slob lived there.

She led him downstairs, and he gaped. "Do you… live in the scullery? Am I walking into a Dickens book?"

She laughed. "Well, at one time it was that, but thankfully, nobody else is subject to my thoroughly mediocre cooking." She hung his jacket on the bottom of the banister and put the pizza on the coffee table before going to rummage through her postage stamp-sized kitchenette to look for a wine opener. "I usually eat on the couch…" she said, by way of apology.

"Perfect," he said, toeing off his leather sneakers and making himself comfortable.

She brought over two plates, two wine glasses, and the wine opener, and set about pouring wine and dishing out pizza. There was companionable silence as they tucked into the pepperoni pizza, Alex on the couch and leaning over the coffee table, Maddy sitting cross-legged on the floor opposite him.

"So, how was your goblin day?" Alex asked around his slice of pizza.

"Lovely," Maddy replied, pausing for a sip of wine. "What did you get up to today?" It was surreal to be sitting on the floor of her suite casually wiping pizza grease off her face with the second in line to the British throne, but she tried to sound normal.

"Well, my mum and dad are on an official visit in Scotland, and Ben and Hannah went out to their country house, so I mostly just bummed around. Read a few briefings for some events I'm working this week. Took Bertie for a jog through the park."

"You can jog?" she asked incredulously.

"I mean, I know we have a reputation for being inbred—" he started, slightly defensively.

"No, I meant, you're allowed to go out and move about

freely and exercise?" she said slowly, using two fingers to mime running, as if explaining to a very confused person.

"Oh!" he said, catching up to her. "Yes. Parts of Kensington Gardens are private for the family, so I can go there. I have a treadmill too, but it's nice to get outside, especially before winter really settles in."

"Ugh, the winter's going to be so cold, isn't it?" she groaned, shivering at the thought of enduring the long British winter.

"Well, it won't be *warm*," he hedged, clearly trying to protect her from the truth.

"I can take it. Just say it. It's going to be colder than a witch's tit, isn't it?"

"Those aren't the *exact* words I would have used to describe it, but yeah, pretty much. Sorry."

She sighed and topped off her wine glass. She looked up at the glass panes that made up the back wall and ceiling of her suite of rooms. "It'll be interesting to see how well insulated this place stays once the cold really sets in."

He glanced up and repressed a wince. "Well, based on my knowledge of British HVAC systems, it'll either be frigid or a sauna. There is no in-between."

She sighed again. "Yeah, I figured as much. I guess we'll find out." Maddy leaned back on one arm, relaxing into a cozy wine buzz. Gazing over at Alex it was hard not to stare. He was *so* attractive. It was honestly mind-boggling that he hadn't settled down with a nice aristocratic English person. After a brief pause, she looked at him and grinned. "Truth or dare?"

Alex narrowed his eyes slightly. "Truth."

"Okay," Maddy swallowed and then asked the question she would never have asked before two glasses of wine. "How are you still single? You could be banging every girl in Britain right now—and, hell, for all I know, maybe you are—but... I guess... how has someone not snatched you up and convinced you to put a ring on it yet?"

"I assure you," he said sardonically, "if I was banging *every* girl in Britain, at least one of the tabloids would have gotten a whiff of it." He took another sip of his wine and seemed to debate his options.

"Sorry, that was kind of a personal question—" she began.

"No, it's a fair question," he said, stopping her. "Usually when one gets to be thirty and has a public role in a family that relies on you marrying and producing offspring, one doesn't wait quite so long to start." He took a breath and another sip of wine, and went on. "Honestly, it always just seemed easier to keep things casual. The weight of expectation on anyone who gets involved with me is, frankly, absurd. The scrutiny, the lack of freedom. It asks too much for most people. And" —he paused for a second and then seemed to make a decision —"and I've been afraid of falling for someone and then having her realize that she can't do it, that it's too much for her. Which is a totally fair realization. But I guess it's been mostly self-protection.

"There was someone. Once. Just before I left for New Zealand. Imogen. She was a friend of a friend, and we met at a weekend in the country and... well, hooked up in what I thought was going to be just a simple 'just for the weekend' thing. But for some reason a weekend wasn't enough. So we started seeing each other. Casually. Mostly at people's country houses where there was no danger of the press seeing and starting to hound her. But then suddenly when we'd go on dates in London, the press started showing up. But only when we were together. And finally after a few weeks I realized she was calling them herself. She claimed she liked me, but she clearly also liked the publicity. So, yeah. That was my one kind of disastrous attempt at a more serious monogamous relationship." He let out a small sigh and shrugged. "I guess it wasn't —isn't—meant to be."

"Oh, Alex," she said, frowning. "That's horrible. Having someone use you like that must have just been awful. And really, *who* could possibly want that attention?" She also found herself angrier than she would have expected to be at the idea of someone taking advantage of Alex in that way.

"Okay, my turn." Alex leaned back as he picked up a third slice of pizza. "Truth or dare?"

Maddy took a deep breath. She'd vaguely realized that by starting this she'd have to play, too. She was not a daring person. "Truth."

"Same question."

Resignation settled heavy in her chest. Some part of her had known this was coming. And, if she really let herself be honest, *wanted* to tell him. Had wanted to tell him for days. This was it. This was the sign she'd been looking for. She took a large swig of wine and leveled her eyes on him. "Just promise that you'll let me finish the whole thing before you say anything."

"Mads, of course," he said, concern creasing his forehead as he leaned forward, forearms on his knees. "You can tell me anything. But also, you don't have to if you don't want to or aren't ready."

"No, I do," she said. "And really, this," she gestured between them, "will never be more than surface level if I don't tell you. Plus, it's going to come out sooner or later. I can't run from this forever." She took one more deep breath and began.

"So I was married," she started, and almost immediately, she saw Alex's eyes widen in surprise.

"You were—"

"You promised you'd let me finish," she said, chastising. "It's going to be hard enough for me to get this out without you interrupting me."

He nodded and sat back again.

"Our families were close growing up. His dad and my dad served in the first Desert Storm together with Ambassador Stewart. The three of them were good friends, and Evan's dad and my dad both re-upped their contracts. We wound up posted at the same place a few times and started spending a week on a lake in the Adirondacks every summer." She paused for a fortifying sip of wine and plunged forward. "Evan and I were always together during those weeks. We'd swim out to a dock a little ways out and climb out and lay there and talk for hours while we baked in the sun. It was kind of hard for me to make friends growing up—we moved so often, you know—but Evan was a constant. Once we were a little older we started texting and emailing all the time. He was one of the only people I knew well who truly got what it was like. His life was just like mine.

"And then came college. Evan, being the good Army son that he was, got a commission to West Point and half coincidentally, half on purpose, I wound up at Vassar. Poughkeepsie's only about an hour away from West Point, so we'd get together as often as he was allowed to leave campus. And gradually"—she closed her eyes briefly, then kept going—"we became more than friends. It was honestly partially puppy love and partially connection to a person who knew me better than anyone else, who understood me, who wanted me to be happy. And so, when he asked me to marry him at Christmas our senior year, I said yes. We were married at the Cadet Chapel at West Point the weekend after graduation.

"I knew it wouldn't be an easy life. We left for Fort Drum basically right after the wedding, and we lived in the middle of nowhere not far from the Canadian border for months. But I grew up in a military family. I'd watched my mom. She loved being an Army wife—getting to live in so many different parts of the country, hosting events, supporting the other wives and families, running a tight ship at home. My dad always jokes that he's a general on the battlefield, but she's the general at the Cartwright house. So I found a job on post, kept my chin up, tried to be supportive, and waited for things to get easier. I assumed once I got used to it, I'd flourish in that role the way my mom did. I assumed eventually our relationship would flourish too. Would..." She searched for the right phrase. "Would be *more*." She swallowed. "Would make the constant fear of deployment and having to move all the time worth it.

"Unfortunately, it just never really blossomed the way I hoped it would. On paper we had the perfect marriage. We got along, never fought, we had fun together, but there was no spark. And I gradually started to feel like I had less and less agency. And started getting resentful and itchy. I wanted to be able to choose where we lived together, to stay somewhere longer than a few years, to really put down roots. I had a job, but it wasn't something I was passionate about. I wanted to be able to develop a career without knowing that I'd have to pick up and move again as soon as we really got settled.

"His second deployment was to Afghanistan. It was eighteen months long. By then I was starting to realize that even though I loved him, I wasn't *in love* with him. We were good friends, but—" She swallowed. "He wasn't my soulmate. When he was gone I let myself start to dream about what it would be like to make my own decisions, get to choose where I lived based on what I wanted to do, maybe even go to graduate school. I played the good Army wife, talking to him on Face-Time as often as we could, supporting the other wives, volunteering, running events... but I also started looking up divorce attorneys.

"I realized one day when I was at a baby shower for one of the other wives in our cul-de-sac that even though all the other women's husbands were deployed too, they all seemed really happy. Like, fulfilled, excited, starting families... and I realized

I just... wasn't. I didn't want that. I wasn't ready to settle down. There was more I wanted to do before I started popping out his perfect West Point-bound babies." By this time, she'd risen from her seat on the rug by the coffee table and was pacing, not making eye contact with Alex, just trying to get the truth out as fast as possible.

"I'd finally decided I was going to tell him when he got back. That I wanted to end it. And that's when it happened. I was home alone on a Thursday afternoon, the day before I was supposed to meet with my divorce lawyer for the first time. Evan was six weeks from coming home. I was having a cup of coffee, watching TV, when there was a knock on the door. When I opened it and there were two soldiers there in uniform, I just knew. They told me his helicopter had been shot down. They were ambushed and his chopper took the heat, created a diversion, so that three others could get away. Evan and five other soldiers died."

"Oh, Maddy," Alex said softly.

"Would you believe," she said, finally looking at him, bitterness on her face, "that that isn't the worst of it?" He closed his mouth, his eyes full of unsolicited sympathy. "Because they had died so heroically, so publicly, the president invited the families to come to Dover to meet the bodies. There was press there, and a photographer happened to be standing right beside me." She fished her phone from the pocket of her leggings, unlocked it, and, after tapping a few times, handed it to him, with the photo on the screen. Masochistically, it was never far from the top of her search history, if she ever closed the tab. Maddy stood, silhouetted from the back and just to the side in a black-and-white photograph, wearing a black sheath dress and black hat. Her head was bowed, shoulders bent. The picture of a grieving wife. Flag-draped caskets were just visible out of focus in the background of the shot, being rolled off the military aircraft.

"That's you," he said, recognition and sorrow heavy in his voice.

She nodded. "That's why I just assumed you knew who I was. It was the picture seen 'round the world for weeks. I was the public paragon of a grieving young Army widow." She started pacing again, fingers subconsciously tracing the metal oblongs nestled against her sternum. "God, I hate that word, 'widow.' Talk about Dickensian." She gave a hollow laugh. "Everyone wanted to talk to me, comfort me, interview me, offer me sympathy. This amazing community of families whose servicemembers had also been killed in the line of duty reached out to try to support me." Another pause. "But none of them knew. Nobody knew. I wasn't this perfect grieving wife. I'd been ready to leave. I got this huge chunk of money from the Army, but the idea of using it for myself made me sick, so I just stuck it in an investment fund and tried to forget about it." She paused for a second, trying to collect herself. "I stuck with it for as long as I could." She sighed. "But after I'd been lying low, avoiding going out and being seen, just... moping around my parents' house for a year, my dad called Ambassador Stewart and asked him to find something for me. A few weeks later, he handed me a plane ticket and shipped me off to my new 'duty station' at Winfield House."

She was working up the nerve to actually face him, to confront the familiar and uncomfortable sympathy that would be in his eyes, the same way it appeared in everyone's eyes when they found out what had happened. The unwelcome pity that gnawed at her, reminding her of the lie she'd lived for so long. But then feet appeared on the carpet in front of her, strong arms encircled her, and Alex was holding her tightly, pulling her head to his shoulder.

"Who else have you told that all to?" he asked gently, smoothing a hand down her hair. "How long have you been holding that all in?"

"Nobody," she confessed, her voice slightly muffled against his chest. "Who could possibly hear how awful I was and understand? Even if I'd wanted to confide in anyone, I'd already become this patriotic icon," she said, disdain dripping from her voice, her body still tense in his arms. "I couldn't turn around and be the person who was going to divorce her war hero. I couldn't do that to my parents, I couldn't do that to Evan's family, and I couldn't do that to Evan and defile his legacy that way. So... yeah. It's been eighteen months," she said. "You're the first one I've told."

Her close friends from college had, she thought, had an inkling that all wasn't as it seemed between her and Evan and had gently tried to inquire. But she'd known that if she opened up at all, the entire truth would come flowing out. And she wouldn't let herself do that to Evan. So she'd held it in, swallowing the truest parts of her grief—the loss of not her husband, but of her best friend. The guilt over what she'd been planning to do. She'd dutifully kept it all to herself.

Alex placed a gentle kiss to the top of her head and then pushed her away a bit to hold her at arm's length. "Madeleine, you need to get something very clear." She hung her head, but he used a finger to lift her chin, forcing her to face him again. "Just because the situation wasn't what it seemed, just because you weren't willing to stay in an unfulfilling marriage does *not* say anything about who you are as a person." Maddy was slightly taken aback. She hadn't exactly expected him to run away in abject horror, but she also hadn't been sure how he'd react. In her darker moments the guilt still ate away at her. "If anything it makes you even braver than he was. Did it ever occur to you that he could have felt the same way? If you never talked about it, we'll never know. But that kind of feeling in a relationship isn't usually one-sided. And most importantly," he said, ducking his head a bit to look directly into her eyes, "just because you weren't in love with him like that doesn't mean you aren't allowed to mourn. It doesn't mean you're not allowed to be sad he's gone. You still lost someone really important to you." He pulled her close again, and she sagged a bit in his embrace, finally relaxing into the comfort he was offering. "Come here," he said, guiding her to the couch and snuggling her down next to him.

Maddy felt emotionally roto-rootered after revealing so much. Roto-rootered and slightly shellshocked after finally unburdening herself. The Army had sent grief counselors, but she'd struggled to open up to them. Even though they'd tried to reassure her that all of her feelings were valid and that they were a confidential resource, her total discomfort with the fact that there was a small, wriggling filament of relief, of freedom, infiltrating her brain alongside the grief and anger kept her from really being honest. Of actually doing the work to process. She'd sat through several insipid sessions, telling them what she knew they wanted to hear, were expecting to hear, numb and brittle, but convincing enough for them to believe that she wasn't going to hurt herself or go postal on the news. And after a few sessions they were convinced enough that they stopped making her go. And she'd been left to marinate in her own feelings of guilt, shame, and sadness. She'd told herself she was going to seek out a counselor when she got settled in London, but it had been several months and she still hadn't followed through on that commitment she'd made to herself.

Now, sitting next to Alex on the cozy and slightly droopy couch in her sitting room at Winfield House, she felt her entire body go almost limp. She hadn't realized how much tension she'd been holding in her body for so many months, but when it all left, it was almost as if she was the living embodiment of a "no bones day." Alex glanced at her and then, without saying anything, refilled her wine glass, and pressed it into her hand. He pulled her close, putting his arm around her shoulders and pressed another kiss to the top of her head, somehow both fierce and tender at the same time. "It's going to be okay, Maddy," he whispered, and then turned on the TV and turned his attention to an octet of bakers attempting to recreate a Twix bar on the television.

Several hours later, the pizza and wine were gone, as was most of a container of chocolate gelato they'd swiped from the Winfield freezer. Between the emotional exhaustion and several glasses of wine, Maddy was completely spent. As the baking show had segued into a historical drama about women behaving badly in the court of Henry VIII, Maddy had drifted off. When she woke up some time later, Alex was looking down at her, his eyes slightly crinkled with an emotion that, in her bleary state, she couldn't quite suss out.

"Sorry," he said, smiling apologetically. "I didn't mean to wake you."

"No, no," she said, rubbing her eyes and pushing herself to a sitting position. "If anyone should be sorry, it's me. I didn't mean to emotionally dump on you and then trap you on my couch until eleven pm."

He smiled at her again. Maddy felt like she was in a tractor beam. She knew she needed to look away, couldn't let herself get sucked in, and yet, somehow, his gaze was magnetic. "Allow me to reframe that," he said. "Thank you for being so vulnerable and then trusting me to help you decompress from what was a really emotional evening."

She blushed, looking down at her hands. "Thank you," she said quietly. "I... I didn't realize how much that was all eating at me until I got it all out."

"Anytime, Mads," he said, grabbing one of her hands and squeezing. "And now," he said, standing up, "I'm going to go home and get some rest, and you should too." She nodded and got to her feet. She stood awkwardly while he shrugged into his leather jacket, unsure of what to say, how to end this evening that had smashed through the remaining armor she wore around herself.

"Hey," he said, grasping her by both shoulders. "You deserve to feel happy. No matter what happened, you are worthy of knowing what real love can feel like. And don't let anyone tell you otherwise." He leaned down, kissed her forehead swiftly, and took the stairs back up towards the rest of the house two at a time. She knew she should walk him out, but the affectionate gesture and his kind words had been so startling that she just stood there staring after him until it was too late. After a few minutes she shook her head a little, quickly disposed of the trash from their dinner, and wearily climbed the stairs to bed.

Chapter 12

The next morning Maddy woke up with doubt gnawing at the pit of her stomach. Alex had been so nice the night before, so kind and understanding. But what if he was just trying to be nice? What if he was worried about being associated with her in case it came out in the press? Thinking to continue her panic spiral via doom scrolling, Maddy grabbed her phone from the nightstand and was surprised to see a text from Alex.

> **MR. MARTINI**
>
> How are you this morning? Last night was intense.
>
> I hope you haven't managed to convince yourself that I'm never going to talk to you again
>
> Because you'd obviously be wrong

How does he do that? Maddy thought to herself. *It's like he's a goddamn mind reader!*

Of course I didn't do that. Obviously not…

MR. MARTINI

Uh huh, ok, right.

I was wondering if you'd like to go on a
walk with me today?

Maddy's brow furrowed. How could they possibly go on a walk together without every tabloid photographer in London descending on them? She started to type a dubious reply when his next message came through.

MR. MARTINI

I know what you're thinking. No, not in
public. We'll be safe from the press, I
promise. What do you think?

Well, if you're sure we won't be seen, that
sounds good.

MR. MARTINI

I have a plan. I'll pick you up in an hour.
Dress warmly. It's going to be chilly today.

Thanks, DAD!

MR. MARTINI

Daddy kink is definitely not my thing, sorry,
Mads 😉

Maddy felt her cheeks flame. She truly hadn't meant to take the conversation in that direction, but despite her best intentions she found herself imagining what Alex's kinks were. And what it might be like to experience them. He'd been pretty adamant during their movie afternoon about his sexual partners being thoroughly satisfied, and even though she'd given him a hard time about it, she had to admit she believed him. And couldn't deny that she was curious.

She slipped into fleece-lined black leggings and a cream, cable-knit tunic sweater. Standing in front of the dresser at the foot of her bed, Maddy pulled her hair back into a high ponytail. As she replaced her brush on the dresser and glanced at her reflection in the small mirror, her eye was drawn to the chain that had hung around her neck twenty-four hours a day for the last eighteen months. Taking a deep breath, Maddy pulled it out from under her sweater. Evan's dog tags hung at the end. The officers who had come to notify her of his death had handed them to her on their visit, and she'd hung the chain around her neck instinctually, unthinkingly. At first she'd wanted to keep from losing them. She'd offered them to Evan's mother, but her former mother-in-law had insisted that Maddy should be the one to keep them. Had said that Evan would want her, his beloved wife, to have them. She'd gone on and on about how much Maddy had meant to her son, said things that would have been lovely and moving in any other context, but that only served to sicken Maddy. Nauseated by the guilt that ate away at her. And so she'd kept wearing them. Her own personal albatross. A constant reminder of the man who'd made the ultimate sacrifice for his country, even as she prepared to leave him.

Until the previous evening, she'd never told a soul the full story. The whole truth. And so she supposed she shouldn't be surprised that she suddenly felt lighter. That unburdening herself to Alex and having him not only accept her, but embrace her, validate her, might feel good. She still wasn't fully convinced that she deserved the wholesale absolution that Alex had offered her. But it had convinced her that she was allowed to at least consider moving on.

She reached behind her neck and unclasped the chain for the first time since she'd put it on. Holding the flat oblong metals in her hand Maddy was almost surprised by their small size and slight weight. She'd allowed them to become such a hefty burden over the months. She swallowed a lump in her throat and blinked back a few tears as she coiled the chain on top of the tags and slipped it into her top drawer. *I'm sorry, Evan. I hope you understand.* Taking a deep breath, she reached down to grab the boots she'd picked out and headed down to find coffee.

When Alex and his driver arrived forty-five minutes later, Maddy was more curious than anything else. "Good morning," Alex said, exiting the car to greet her with a European kiss on the cheek and a hug. Was that hug lingering? Or was it just in her head? "We're going to be in the car for about forty minutes," he said, "just a heads up in case you have any, er, needs you need to attend to before we go."

Maddy laughed, "I just went to the bathroom, Alex, but thanks."

"Alright, then, let's go." He opened the back door of a forest-green Range Rover with heavily tinted windows and closed it for her before going around to the other side and buckling himself in. "All set, thanks, Graham," he said to the driver, and they headed out into the quiet Sunday morning streets of London.

Maddy heard a noise from the trunk, and she turned around to see Bertie on a leash attached in the back. "Good morning to you too, my little friend!" she said, smiling at him, and reaching across to scratch his ears. The car was sumptuously appointed, enveloping her in the aromas of leather and coffee. Looking down, she noticed that in the arm rest between the two seats in the back, there were two to-go cups of coffee, as well as a small packet of what looked like pastries.

"Is this for me?" She asked, gesturing to the cup closest to her.

"I didn't know what your coffee order was," he said, smiling sheepishly. "So that one" —he gestured to the one closest to her— "is a flat white, and this one"—nodding at the other—"is a mocha."

"Yum," she said, smiling at him. "Which one do you want?"

"Lady's choice," he demurred.

"Well if you really don't mind..." She reached over to take the mocha. "I rarely actually order these for myself, but I do love them," she said, smiling.

"What do you usually order if you're depriving yourself of chocolate?" Alex asked with a teasing smile on his face.

"Either a latte or a flat white," she said with a shrug. "Feels healthier somehow," she added by way of explanation.

"You deserve a treat from time to time, though."

Maddy's cheeks flushed. She wasn't sure why him telling her that she deserved a treat made her insides go all gooey, but somehow it did. Redirecting the attention away from herself she asked, "What's your coffee order?"

"If I'm at home half the time I just raw-dog an espresso shot for efficiency's sake. If I'm ordering out, usually a latte or a flat white. But something told me a sweetheart like you might have a sweet tooth."

Maddy rolled her eyes. "That was *so* cheesy." But she felt her cheeks heating anyway. "Do I get to know where we're going now?"

"Windsor," he replied. "Of course there's the parts of it that are on display for the public, but there are also big sections of the ground that are private for family use. I like to go out there for a ramble when I can. Good for clearing the head."

"Sounds great," she said. "I know London has so many lovely parks, but I really haven't taken advantage of them much at all." She'd largely kept to herself since arriving in London, preferring the privacy of Winfield House to risking going to more public areas of town and risking being seen.

"Maddy, I had seen that picture, but I don't think it's as ubiquitous here as it is in America, and I definitely don't think Britons would recognize you out of context. Has anyone recognized you since you've been here?"

"*How* do you do that?" she demanded, shifting in her seat to face him. "It's like you're a mind reader or something!"

He shrugged. "I think we just understand each other. Don't forget, I've escaped to faraway places to avoid being hounded by the press too."

"I suppose you have," she said, sipping at her coffee.

They lapsed into companionable silence, drinking their coffees and snacking on the scones Alex had brought with him. "How much time do you spend in Windsor?" she asked finally.

"Eh, not too much," he said. "I was there more often when I was a kid. My parents knew that it was easier to shield us there, so we spent a lot of weekends there, and then, especially once I started at Eton, I was there all the time. But there's really not much to do there, and all of the work to do is in London, so I mostly stay in town now. My parents still go out for weekends, so sometimes I'll meet them for dinner, but I'm still trying to get settled in my new place in town."

"You didn't live there before you left for New Zealand?"

"No, it's new to me. My brother and I were sharing a different cottage on the grounds at Kensington for a few years before I left, but then he moved in with Hannah and that cottage got reassigned to some distant cousin, so they moved me into my own place when I finally came back." He paused to sip at his coffee. "I mean, it was mostly done and everything before I got there, but I'm still getting used to it. And there's Bertie to consider, of course, too. The last royal dog who spent much time at Windsor ate a priceless antique that had been a gift from Belgium, so people are a little nervous about having a puppy around."

Maddy laughed. "I guess that's a fair concern when you have that kind of stuff in your house."

"One of the many hardships of my life," he agreed drily.

Graham drove through a set of large stone and wrought-iron gates into the private part of Windsor's extensive grounds. Alex explained that most of the five thousand acres of Windsor's Great Park was open to the public for recreation, but that the family maintained a small portion of the smaller Home Park for their own private use. Graham stopped the car under a large oak tree that still clung to the last of its vibrant yellow leaves.

As Maddy stepped out into the chilly November morning, she was struck by the bright color of the lingering foliage against the slate gray sky. Although the top of the imposing Round Tower was visible over the rise behind them, the castle thronged with tourists felt quite distant. The only sounds around them were the creaking of trees in the light breeze and Bertie's snuffling as Alex let him out of the Range Rover on his leash.

"Shall we?"

"Sure," she said, falling in next to him with a shy smile.

They strolled in companionable silence for a while as meadows studded lightly with trees gradually became more densely wooded forest, pausing from time to time for Bertie to investigate a smell here, an exotic-looking mushroom there.

"So what was it like growing up here?" Maddy asked, her eyes sliding in his direction.

"Like I said, we mostly came here on weekends. When I was younger we'd drive out from the city when my parents could get away, and then when I was at Eton I'd come out to get away from school and have a decent meal." He walked a few steps further then paused while Bertie raised his leg towards a tree. "But it was nice. Even though it was still living in a literal museum, it felt like an escape. My parents were able to relax a bit more. It felt like there was less scrutiny."

"What's your family like?"

Alex paused, looking at her. "I mean, you know what they do for a living…"

Maddy rolled her eyes. "Okay, look. I've seen pictures of your parents, but I know nothing about them."

"You wound me!" he said, clutching at his chest melodramatically. Smiling at her, he continued walking, tugging at Bertie's leash slightly to pull him back towards the path and away from a squirrel in the distance. "Okay, fine. What do you want to know?"

Maddy sighed. "You're impossible. Start with the basics. Was your dad the king when you were born?"

Alex shook his head. "No. When I was little my parents had offices and an apartment at Clarence House, but we actually lived out here more or less full time when Ben and I were very small. At a cottage over there called Frogmore." He gestured behind them, beyond the castle. "My dad's mum passed away when he was a teenager, so I never knew her, but my grandfather was alive until I was seven and Ben was twelve."

"What was he like?" Maddy asked, prodding gently.

"I mean, he was very much of his generation. Not particularly warm, but I remember the way he smelled like the tobacco he smoked and the peppermints he always had on hand to try to cover up the tobacco smell. He taught me to play cribbage one summer at Balmoral and then would always try to make time for a game when we were together." There was a brief pause before he went on. "After he died, everything changed. And of course I was sad he was gone. But I think as I got older and looked back, I realized that I also resented his death because that's when we started being thrust into the spotlight more. My parents had started to take on more duties as he got older, but once they were officially king and queen, they were just as much the king and queen as they were our parents, if not more."

Maddy hummed sympathetically. She had at least some idea how it felt to have to share her parents with the general public, although to a significantly smaller extent than Alex had. She shifted slightly on the path to avoid a large rock, bringing her closer to him. Their hands brushed together just for a second, but Maddy almost recoiled in shock. Their momentary connection was so intense it almost physically burned. Her breath flew in, a sharp inhale, before she regained her composure and resumed her place on the right side of the path.

She glanced at him out of the corner of her eye, wondering whether he'd noticed. Other than a slight flush in his cheeks he seemed completely unaffected, so she forced herself to push past it. *Probably just the cold.*

Taking a deep breath, Maddy pushed herself back into the conversation. "That must have been hard," she said, hoping that the unsteadiness she felt in her voice wasn't audible. "Suddenly having to share so much more of your family with the nation."

He sighed. "It was. I think it was a bit easier for Ben. For one thing, he's like my parents. He's one hundred percent extrovert. His first real public appearance was coming to meet me at the hospital, and even at five years old, he loved it. The video is super grainy, but it comes through loud and clear. I've never been like that." He swallowed, pausing as Bertie stopped to scratch an itch. "And, of course, since he's the heir, he was getting special instruction as soon as he started primary school. He'd come home and go straight to lessons on how to greet guests from all walks of life, how to talk to people. Before Grandfather even died, my father had started taking Ben along with him on some of his public appearances and he just thrived." Alex's voice was wistful.

"You missed your brother," Maddy said. It wasn't a question.

"I mean, I was so young I'm not sure I knew what I was missing. But I guess maybe I did." They arrived at the end of the path, a small rise overlooking the river and down towards Eton and paused, taking in the view in silence. It should have been a companionable silence. Maddy hoped that Alex was experiencing it that way. But she was distracted by a strange sensation, a magnetic tugging that gave her an almost inescapable urge to take Alex's hand. To hold him. To comfort him for the childhood that he had, in many of the most important ways, lost. Even if his parents had done their best to raise him "normally," it had clearly impacted him deeply. She wondered if he realized how profoundly it had shaped who he was as an adult.

What happened next was like something out of a romantic comedy. By unspoken agreement, they both turned to walk back in the direction they'd come. Maddy stole a glance at Alex in her peripheral vision. She found herself wondering what he was thinking, lost in his recollections, and so she didn't notice the root protruding from the ground in front of them. She would have fallen on her face had Alex not reacted immediately, but as she started to trip, he grasped her wrist, pulling her back towards him, his other hand landing low on her hip as he steadied her. Their bodies were almost flush against each other, and Maddy, speechless, found herself looking into his eyes, mouth slightly open, intensely aware of the way their hips were gently pressed together. The magnetic pull that she'd been aware of at the overlook exploded into a near-frantic buzzing that he *had* to be able to hear.

"I'm so sorry!"

"Are you alright?"

They'd both spoken in the same instant, their gazes locked together, Alex's hand still anchoring her hip.

"Thanks," Maddy said, hoping that the flush she knew was creeping up her cheeks could conceivably be interpreted as wind burn. She went to step back, away from Alex's steadying grip, when she realized that Bertie, thoroughly enjoying the chaos she'd wrought, had somehow managed to completely tangle them in his leash, which was now wrapped around their lower legs.

She tried to look behind her, but almost lost her balance again, causing Alex to draw her closer with a firm hand in the center of her back. "Stay still," he said, softly, his mouth only inches from her ear. "I'll get us untangled."

Maddy was starting to wonder if she was coming down with something. That must be it. Nothing else could explain the way her breath was suddenly coming in shaky gasps and the burning heat in her cheeks, the unsteadiness in her legs, the preternatural awareness of her surroundings.

After an awkward moment of leash wrangling and corgi coaxing, Alex managed to free them and released her hips, leaving Maddy swaying slightly in a way she hoped wasn't visible. She found herself... disappointed? That she was no longer lashed to him with a leash? That couldn't be right. She was just hungry. That's why her brain was suddenly bereft of the sensation of being pressed against his body, knees to chest.

"Are you alright?" he asked, finally bringing Bertie to heel.

"Yes, of course, fine," she said quickly. "Let's keep going."

Their conversation remained firmly back in casual territory as they strolled back towards the meadow. As they neared the spot where Graham had dropped them off, Maddy noticed that a tartan blanket had been spread under a tree and a wicker basket was sitting on it. "Shall we have some lunch?" Alex asked.

"You arranged a romantic picnic? For our platonic walk?" Maddy asked.

"I mean, there's no distinction between romantic picnic and platonic picnic on the order form. It's not oysters or anything," Alex said defensively. "At least, I don't think it is..."

"Okay, but picnics, by definition, are romantic," Maddy countered.

"I beg to differ," Alex shot back. "If it's a summer picnic, there are usually bees. And bees are definitely not romantic."

"Well," said Maddy begrudgingly, settling herself on the blanket, "this looks lovely. Thank you. Getting out of the city like this was really what I needed."

"Good." Alex began to unpack the picnic hamper. He laid out sandwiches, a bag of chips, two small salads in containers, a wax paper package that looked like cookies, and two small bottles of sparkling water.

They ate leisurely, talking about everything and nothing: picnics of their childhood, the books they read over and over (him: *On the Road*, her: *The Song of the Lark*), which *Star Wars* movie was the best (him: *Empire Strikes Back* because "It's iconic!"; her: *Return of the Jedi* because "Ewoks. 'Nuff said."), their least favorite foods (him: pâté; her: yogurt), and everything in between. When they'd finished eating, Maddy sat up on her knees and started repacking their things back into the basket. After a moment she felt Alex's eyes on her. She looked up at him to find him gazing at her with a look in his eyes that she was afraid to analyze too much. "You don't have to do that," he said.

"I know, but you... ordered lunch and arranged all of this, the least I can do is tidy up afterwards," she said. Mentally, she wanted to keep tidying, but for some reason her body wasn't obeying her brain. She was frozen on her knees, her hands balanced on the side of the picnic hamper.

"Maddy." Alex's voice was raspy, barely louder than a whisper as he reached up and pushed an errant strand of hair behind her ear. She had to be imagining that his finger lingered against the side of her face for a moment, but she couldn't deny that the look in his eyes was something akin to desire. Desire that she knew she shouldn't return. Couldn't return. Not without losing her freedom. Nothing good would come out of getting more involved with him.

"Alex, we can't," she said, forcing her eyes away from his and finally recommitting herself to continuing to pack up the remnants of their picnic. She visualized the handwritten list she'd made of the plan for Maddy 2.0. He stopped her, taking one of her hands in his. She closed her eyes, hating how much she liked it.

"Remind me why not?" he said, sounding almost pained.

"Well, for one thing, I'm an American, and you're two horrible accidents away from being the king of England."

He huffed out a surprised laugh. "Okay, but we have very good security. The odds of that happening are astronomically low."

His thumb was rubbing the back of her hand in a way that made it hard to remember the rest of the talking points she rehearsed every night in bed to keep herself from thinking about other things... that she definitely should not be thinking about.

"Look, I know I'm not an easy person to be with," Alex began.

"Alex, it's nothing about you, it's just that... I've literally only been with one person in my entire life. And I lost myself in that relationship. His career, his service was the third person in our marriage, and I was priority number three." She sighed. "I just... I'm not sure I can do that again."

Alex squeezed her hand, shifting so that he was kneeling directly in front of her. "I know, darling," he said softly. Her cheeks flushed at the way he called her "darling." "We'll be completely discreet, nobody has to know. I promise the press won't get involved. I'm just so"—he searched for the right word—"enamored with you. Your strength, your sense of humor, your kindness." A pause. "How beautiful you are."

Don't look up, don't look up, don't look up.

She looked up.

When their eyes locked she knew she was done for. The way he looked at her made her feel things she couldn't put a name to and knew she didn't have a frame of reference for. "Please, Maddy," he whispered. "I think you owe it to yourself to have some fun. When was the last time you did something just for yourself?"

Her eyes slid closed as she swallowed the lump in her throat. There was truth in what he said. She owed it to herself. From what Alex had told her, casual hookups were his MO. He knew how to do discreet and casual. When she opened her eyes again he was still focused on her, his eyes a heady mix of arousal and tenderness, greed and awe. The word "Okay" had barely escaped her when their lips met. She wasn't sure who had moved first, but his lips were sliding across hers, and she was kissing him back. His kisses were soft but insistent. Maddy felt slightly unmoored by how adept he was compared with how out of practice she was. She forced herself back into the moment, refusing to let the specters in her past ruin what was, objectively, the best kiss of her life.

Her first kiss with Evan had been when they were teenagers. Fifteen, maybe sixteen years old—long enough ago and with so many experiences in between that she barely remembered. It was strange to be having that experience again after so many years. When for so many years she assumed she'd never have another first kiss.

She leaned closer to him, nudging the picnic basket out of the way with her knee as one of his hands slid up her neck to the back of her head, urging her closer, tilting her head toward him. Her hands slid up his chest, sliding under his charcoal gray peacoat and across his shoulders. He was wearing a cashmere sweater, and the softness against her hands paired with his lips, coaxing hers open, was exquisite.

Alex's fingers had slipped into her hair, massaging the base of her skull gently, easing tension she hadn't even been aware of. She edged closer to him on the blanket, needing more—more contact, more of his kisses, just *more*. He sat back, rearranging himself and somehow managed to ease her into his lap without breaking their kiss. He was sitting cross-legged now, her backside nestled in the bowl of his legs. One of his arms snaked around her waist, while the other rested on her thigh. "These pants," he almost growled, running a hand up the outside of her leg from her knee to her hip, "have been torturing me all day."

She giggled, breathless. "I'm...sorry?"

His forehead came to rest against hers, looking into her eyes. "I don't really think you are," he said with a mischievous smile, running a hand over the side of her head, smoothing back the hair that had come loose from her ponytail as they made out.

He dipped his head to nuzzle the tender place where her jaw and her neck met, making her squeal as his cold nose burrowed beneath her scarf, his lips teasing at her neck. She arched, giving him better access, his warm mouth chasing away the chill from the frosty air. He eased back, his fingers buried in her hopelessly mussed hair while his thumb stroked her cheek. Her eyes sparkled—desire, excitement, giddiness.

"I wish you could see yourself right now," he said, smiling

at her affectionately. "You're glowing. It's amazing." His eyes searched her face for a moment. "Are you okay? I know... I know this must be a big step for you."

"Alex," she breathed, "you have no idea how okay I am." She reached up for him, both of her hands busying themselves in his hair as she kissed him fiercely.

He shifted again, laying her across the blanket and draping his body over hers, one of his legs tangling between hers, plundering her mouth with his tongue. His hand had just started to roam when the sound of an engine pulled them out of their lusty haze. Alex levered himself up, his head falling back in defeat. "He just *had* to be on time, didn't he?" Maddy scrambled to sit up, hastily redoing her hair in an attempt to look slightly less like she'd just been making out with the prince of England. She quickly busied herself with closing up the picnic basket. She knew her face must be bright red and hoped that Alex's driver would think it was from the cold. Her brain immediately started spinning, spiraling as she thought about what he could have seen, what they had done, how risky it all was.

"Maddy, don't," Alex said.

"Don't what? Clean up?" Her voice was a little too bright. "We don't want to make your driver wait, Alex."

"No, don't start overthinking what just happened." His voice was patient, placating, but firm. "Worrying about what Graham saw. He has the world's most restrictive NDA, and he's been with the family for years. He's not going to say anything to anyone." She couldn't look at him. Her gaze was glued to her hands, fidgeting with the handle on the picnic basket.

"We should get moving," she said quietly. "It's not nice to keep people waiting, no matter how ironclad their NDA is."

Alex sighed in resignation and stood to help her fold up the red tartan picnic blanket, before ushering her back to the car, whistling to Bertie, who had been dozing under a tree nearby. Graham hopped out of the front and opened the rear doors for them as they approached. Maddy thanked him quietly and slipped into her seat.

The drive back to London began in silence. After a moment, Alex pushed up the armrest that had held their coffee on the way out and reached over to cover her hand with his, squeezing gently. "Do we get to talk about this, or are we going to pretend that didn't happen?" Her eyes shot quickly to Graham in the seat in front of her. "Graham, are you paying attention to what we're saying?" Alex asked, raising his voice.

"No, sir," he responded, his eyes never leaving the road ahead of him. "I'm trying to figure out how to get myself out of the corner I wrote myself into. In addition to driving you safely, sir." The last sentence was tacked on hastily.

Alex turned back to Maddy. "Graham writes cozy mysteries under a pen name when he's not keeping me alive," he said, by way of explanation. "And apparently some of the time while he is keeping me alive, it would seem," he added wryly. "But, you see, he doesn't care what we're talking about unless it's going to help him figure out how not to give away who the murderer is too soon." He paused. "It's the vicar," he added in a stage whisper. Maddy let out a puff of mirthless laughter.

"Okay," she said quietly. "If you want to talk, talk. You're the prince of England. How does this work? What do we do now? You say we can be discreet, but how long do you really think we can hide this from the press?"

Alex turned so that he was facing her on the bench seat, still holding her hand. "It works like this," he said, intertwining their fingers. "We go to quiet dinners in private places where photographers don't go. I take you on walks and picnics on my family's properties where the public isn't allowed. I whisk you away to private islands with only your tiniest bikinis in a carryon and feed you exotic fruit for days."

"Alex, be serious."

"I am being serious, Mads." Nobody called her Mads. She kind of hated how much she loved it. "I know the only relationship you've ever had went from puppy love to marriage, but they don't all have to go like that. We can keep it casual—watch movies together, lay low, get to know each other, just hang out. Who knows what I'm going to find to do with myself after the wedding? Maybe I'll bugger off back to New Zealand and you'll go back to the States, and it will all be a lovely memory. But at least for now, we can enjoy each other's company. Please, Maddy. At least consider it."

She closed her eyes, trying to think. But every time she closed her eyes, all she could see was the way he looked as he lay her down on the picnic blanket. Memories of the way his warm breath felt against her cold skin, the way his fingers combed through her hair, the way his voice had gotten deeper when he'd told her that her pants had been driving her crazy. "Alex," she exhaled, finally forcing her eyes open to look at him. "This feels like a spectacularly bad idea."

"I can protect you," he said, with a self-assuredness that Maddy was certain she'd never experienced in her life. "Please," he said, looking into her eyes earnestly. "Let me take care of you. Casually." The last word was added somewhat weakly, but it made her chuckle faintly, all the same.

"Okay, *but*," she added as she saw victory start to unfurl across his face, "I mean it when I say this has to be casual. Low-key, nothing public. This is not a relationship. This is a casual hookup. Between friends. We're just hanging out, and if there happens to be more kissing, I won't stop you."

"And what if there happens to be more than kissing?" He leaned closer, murmuring the words in a low, sultry voice that caused goosebumps to erupt all over her body.

"I...we..." The way he could disarm her with one sentence was alarming and spelled disaster for their whole "keep it casual" plan. "We'll cross that bridge when we come to it," she managed to get out, knowing that she was once again closer in color to a tomato than anything else.

"Excellent," he said, smugly resituating himself in his own seat. "I look forward to that very much." Maddy wasn't going to give him the satisfaction of saying it out loud, but holy mackerel, so did she. From the way he kissed, she had an idea that the ways he might "take care of her" were likely to be pleasurable in a way she'd never experienced.

Chapter 13

The next evening, Maddy was posted up at the counter in Nadia's small pastry kitchen half watching her assemble tartlets for the Stewarts' expat Thanksgiving dinner and half working on graduate school applications. It had started as another one of their baking lessons (Maddy 2.0 item 4), but after she'd almost cost them an entire batch of cranberry filling by getting distracted while she was supposed to be stirring the pot of compote on the stove. Nadia had relieved her of her duties, so she'd brought her laptop up to work on Maddy 2.0 item 2: apply to master's programs.

She'd always thought she'd like to get a master's or even a PhD. The transient life of a military spouse, however, had convinced Maddy that trying to make progress on a degree would have been too difficult. The added complication of finding duty stations that were near the right institution had always kept her from applying. She knew if she'd said something to Evan about it, he would have been thrilled for her. Would have done what he could to plan his postings so she could be near a good program. And she knew of other military couples where one person had lived away from a duty station in order to pursue their own careers. But she had grown up with the paragon of Army spouses. Virginia Cartwright would *never* have left the general to go to graduate school. And so Maddy had dutifully pushed ideas of advancing her own career, of getting a graduate degree, to the back of her mind. Instead, she focused on supporting Evan while working a job that gave her something to do during the day, and had even given her some skills that had proven useful since coming to London, but that hadn't made her tick. It had been a job, not a career.

But in the last several months of work at the embassy, she'd realized that she *did* want the degree. She was doing good, meaningful work for Ambassador Stewart, but she also knew that with more education she'd be even better equipped and have a better shot of getting more serious jobs. And even though she knew a lot of master's degrees were scams, she also had always loved learning. She'd devoured the readings for her American Studies classes at Vassar, had enjoyed the long weekend days nestled in the golden sunlight below the stained-glass windows of Thompson Library studying for exams and writing papers. Maddy had never really allowed herself to dream about what she'd do if she could decide what *she* wanted to do, where *she* wanted to live. At first she wasn't really sure what she even wanted to go to graduate school for. But she figured that even though her sharp pivot into diplomatic work had been purely circumstantial at first, in actuality, it could be an interesting and viable career. And so she'd decided to just try a few applications for programs in foreign service and government. If it was meant to be, it would happen, and if not, she probably had at least fourteen months before the new president was elected and got their ducks in line enough to appoint a new ambassador. That was plenty of time to devise a plan for Maddy 3.0 if it came down to it.

"How's the personal statement coming?" Nadia asked, her softly accented voice cutting through Maddy's wandering thoughts.

She sighed. "It's coming. I think I'm almost there. Pretty sure it helps to say, 'Well, since I've been working in an American embassy for the last four months, I've learned a thing or two about what a master's in the field could do for me.'"

Nadia laughed. "I'm sure it doesn't hurt. Is the ambassador writing a letter of recommendation for you?"

"No. I thought about asking, but since he's such a close friend of the family, I don't want it to sound like nepotism."

"Good point." Nadia said as she passed over a spatula covered in cranberry filling for Maddy to lick.

"Mmmm, Nadia, these are going to be amazing," Maddy moaned around the spatula.

"Have I ever made you anything that wasn't amazing?" her friend replied, hands on her hips in mock accusation.

"Of course not! I'm just appreciative as always."

Just then, Maddy's phone vibrated on the counter next to her laptop. She picked it up and immediately felt her cheeks flush as she read the message.

MR. MARTINI

How are you? I can't stop thinking
about you.

Before she had a chance to respond, another came through.

MR. MARTINI

And what I wanted to do with you before
we were so rudely interrupted yesterday.

Maddy suddenly felt as if the room had grown fifteen degrees warmer.

"Ooooh, who is texting you to put *that* look on your face?!" Nadia said, keen interest in her voice.

"Nobody!" she squeaked out in a way that immediately betrayed her answer for the lie that it was.

"Uh-huh, sure, and does this nobody have a name? Ohmigosh, is it the guy from the party? Mr. Martini?"

Maddy wracked her brain for how to answer. She trusted Nadia. And as she'd developed a closer relationship with Alex, she'd realized how sorely she'd been missing true friendship. How nice it was to have someone to confide in. She thought, particularly now that she was moving beyond friend territory with Alex, she should try to let Nadia in more.

And yet.

She and Alex had agreed to keep it very casual. On the DL. It was barely twenty-four hours since their first kiss. But Nadia didn't know that Mr. Martini was Prince Alexander. So maybe she could answer semi-truthfully. "Maybe," she said slowly, drawing out the vowels, as her cheeks, somehow, managed to flush more.

"Girl, spill!" Nadia demanded, sinking onto the stool next to Maddy, propping her chin on one arm, and looking at her eagerly.

Maddy scrunched her face up and tried not to squeal. She'd forgotten what it felt like to have a crush. To get to share it with a friend. Had she *ever* felt this way about Evan? Their relationship had morphed so gradually from friends to more that there hadn't ever really been a "crush" phase. Just a slow deepening and shift.

"Well, it turns out his name is Alex." His first name was common enough that she felt comfortable using it without worrying Nadia would make the connection. "He texted me after he sent the flowers asking about my dry cleaning bill...

and... well, I guess we just started texting after that?" Just as she'd never really done the whole "crush" scenario, she'd never really done the whole "spilling to a friend" scenario and suddenly wasn't sure what to say. Luckily, Nadia took over.

"And? Is he cute? Can I see a photo?"

"I don't have any photos of him." At least none that she'd taken. "But yes," she said, trying to stifle a grin and utterly failing, "he's very cute."

"How many dates have you been on? Is he a good kisser?"

"Not many—we're keeping it casual." That was true, too. "Maybe like three? We've been to dinner a few times, and he took me on a really lovely walk and a picnic yesterday. And yes. He's a *very* good kisser." Remembering the way he had held her while driving her crazy with his mouth yesterday caused heat to pool low in her stomach.

Her phone vibrated again.

MR. MARTINI

When can I see you again?

"Maddy, you have a man begging to see you again? You little minx! Walking around here all innocent in your pantsuits. Are you secretly a freak?"

"No!" Maddy giggled. "But, yeah. I won't lie, it's kind of nice to have a guy who is not shy about telling you how into you he is."

Nadia pushed herself back to standing. "'Kind of nice'? Maddy, that's the dream! Does he have any friends?"

"I can ask," Maddy said with a smile, and turned back to her phone.

When do you want to see me again?

His response was immediate.

MR. MARTINI

Now. Preferably in private. Ideally naked.

Tell me how you really feel, Alex 😊

MR. MARTINI

Can you come over for dinner on
Thursday?

Sorry, Thursday's Thanksgiving.

MR. MARTINI

I hate to break it to you, Mads, but
Thanksgiving isn't a holiday here.

I know that, you dork, but I work for the
American embassy. *We* are still
celebrating Thanksgiving.

MR. MARTINI

Did you just call a member of the British
Royal Family a dork?

It would appear that I did.

What are you going to do about it?

MR. MARTINI

You'll find out 😈

Okay, well if Thursday is out, what about
something later on Friday? I have to make
an appearance at a cocktail reception, but it
shouldn't be late.

That works for me. But won't they feed you
there?

MR. MARTINI

I'm not really supposed to eat at those
things. It gets in the way of the
gladhanding.

Maddy looked up at Nadia. "Nadia, do you think there will be leftovers after Thursday night?"

"Do I think there will be leftovers?" Nadia laughed. "Maddy, have you *seen* the turkeys—yes, plural, turkeys—that Pierre bought? We have like seventy-five pounds of potatoes. And this is only my first batch of forty-eight tartlets. Yes, I think it's safe to say we'll be drowning in leftovers for days."

"So you think it's safe to assume I can bring some to Alex Friday night?"

"Oh, absolutely. Any guy who makes you smile like that gets his choice of leftovers."

Maddy smiled, "Have I told you you're the best lately, Nadia?"

"Yes, but I never get sick of hearing it!"

Ok, Nadia says there will be tons of leftovers. Why don't I bring over a Thanksgiving feast for two?

MR. MARTINI

Is this the same Nadia who made those brownies from the meeting?

She's the only Nadia I know.

MR. MARTINI

I'm still thinking about those brownies.

I did happen to notice you enjoying them that day. You ate in *that* meeting!

MR. MARTINI

Yes, and I wasn't really supposed to, but those sweets looked so good I couldn't help myself!

They *are* really good. I think she's making more for Thursday, so I'll be sure to bring some. But the cranberry tartlets she's making right now are to die for. We'll be well provisioned, either way.

What time should I come over?

MR. MARTINI

7ish? I should be back by then?

If I get there early do I get a better chance of seeing you in a tux? 😊

MR. MARTINI

She likes a tuxedo, does she?

puss in boots sad eyes.gif

MR. MARTINI

Well, unfortunately it's not that kind of reception, but I am definitely filing that information away for later.

How was your day? What are you doing?

Day was fine. Spent an unreasonable amount of time cutting out feathers for a stupid turkey craft for the dinner Thursday night. This is what they pay me the big bucks for.

And now I'm sitting on my ass watching Nadia make mini pies.

MR. MARTINI

Mm, but it's a very nice ass.

She felt her cheeks heating again and was glad that Nadia had chosen that moment to turn around and put the tray of tiny pies in the oven.

"Don't think I didn't see that blush!" her disembodied

voice said, floating over from where she was bent over the oven. "You've got it *bad*, Maddy."

She sighed. Much as she didn't want it to be the truth, she was afraid Nadia was right.

* * *

Alex was having a nearly impossible time remaining focused on the cocktail reception for some environmental activism fund that he was attending. He cared about the environment. Truly, he did. But he cared even more about finding out how much time remained before he could reasonably leave to go home and see Maddy.

They'd had several additional flirty text exchanges through the rest of the week, but she'd been busy getting ready for their big Thanksgiving celebration and she'd also seemed hesitant enough about getting involved with him that he hadn't wanted to push too hard. So he'd resisted calling her about four times over the course of the week and just waited impatiently for their Friday night leftovers date.

Every minute of greeting and shaking hands and nodding with a studied look of interest on his face seemed to take roughly six months. Royals absolutely did not check their phones or watches during events to see how much time had elapsed, so when Eric appeared at his elbow at 6:30, Alex almost threw up his hands in celebration. Almost. Thankfully, he managed to control himself, and simply shook hands with the foundation's chairwoman one more time before striding out a side door and into the waiting Range Rover that would take him back to Kensington.

When he rushed into his apartment it was 6:52. Traffic had been worse than he'd hoped and Maddy had so far been very punctual, so he had very little time to prepare. He'd practically tossed Bertie bodily out the back door to pee and then hauled him back in immediately, like a fisherman reeling in a recalcitrant fish. The dog gave him a decidedly disgruntled look, but Alex didn't care. He checked his phone: 6:55. He sprinted to his bedroom, shedding the blazer he'd worn to the event and tossing it and his tie over the chair in his walk-in closet before closing the door hastily behind him to hide his mess. Thankfully, the housekeeper had been through that day so his room had been tidied. He didn't want to get presumptuous, but he also didn't want to be unprepared for the evening to end in his bed.

Satisfied that his space didn't look a shambles, he strode back towards the lower floor, unbuttoning his collar and rolling back his sleeves as he went. Much as he found himself uninterested in other women lately, his previous exploits had taught him one thing if they had taught him nothing else: women tended to go feral for forearms. And forearms he could certainly provide.

He was standing in front of the wine rack in his kitchen, contemplating his options, when he heard Maddy's knock at the door followed immediately by Bertie's bark—which he was sure was intended to be welcoming and not menacing—and the skitter of claws against the wood floor in his entry way. Alex tried to moderate his pace as he hurried toward the front door, but the absurd desperation he was feeling to see her won out. He leaned down to grab Bertie by the collar as he opened the door to see her standing there, her purse over one shoulder, a large paper sack of to-go containers in her arms, and he felt his face break into what he feared might be a slightly absurd grin. "Hi," he said, opening the door further and dragging Bertie back to let her in.

She smiled up at him as she stepped through the door. "Hi." She seemed almost shy. It was very endearing. Maybe she'd been anticipating seeing him the same way he'd been looking forward to seeing her? And he didn't miss the way her pupils flared when her eyes darted down to his rolled-up sleeves. The forearms did it every time.

She looked down at Bertie, who was pogoing up and down where Alex still held him by the collar. Placing the sack of food on the floor behind her, she crouched to greet the small dog, scratching his ears affectionately and making the cutest little scrunchy faces at him.

"I can take that," Alex said, reaching past her for the sack before Bertie decided that in addition to monopolizing his woman he was also going to make a pass at his dinner.

"Thanks," she said, rising and unzipping her long blue coat, shrugging out of it to reveal another pair of those yoga pants she wore that filled him with unbridled lust. She had on a soft-looking red shirt under a long gray cardigan. He loved that she was comfortable showing up at his house with leftovers in casual clothes. Most of the women he'd dated before were constantly dressed to the nines, but not Maddy. When she was off work, she tended towards cozy, soft materials that just made him want to cuddle her even more.

She shoved a cream-colored knit hat into the sleeve of her coat before hanging it on a hook inside the door and stepping out of brown booties. "How was the reception?" she asked, following him back to the kitchen.

"Honestly, I couldn't tell you," he said, setting the bag of food on the kitchen island and pulling her to stand between his legs, his hands clasped low behind her back. "I couldn't get my mind off this gorgeous American girl I knew I got to see afterwards." Her cheeks flushed a beautiful pink color, and he leaned down to steal a kiss. "Hi," he said, smiling down at her.

"Hi," she said back, grinning up at him.

"I missed you this week," he admitted, pulling back a bit, but not letting her go.

"Me too," she replied, her hands coasting up the front of

his shirt to rest on his chest. "Last night I was kind of wishing I could have brought you to Thanksgiving dinner."

"But you brought me the next best thing!" he said, turning to start unpacking the large bag of black to-go containers she'd brought with her. If he kept kissing her, he wasn't going to stop and they were never going to eat anything. At least, not any food.

"According to some people, this *is* the best thing," she said, moving to his side to start opening containers. "A lot of people think Thanksgiving leftovers are better than the real thing."

"Okay, then," Alex said eagerly, pulling the last container from the bag. "Teach me. What do I do?"

"Well, Alex," Maddy began in a jokingly pedantic voice, "these are leftovers. You put them on a plate and then reheat them in the microwave..."

He grabbed her sides, tickling her gently and pressing a mischievous kiss to the side of her neck from behind. She giggled and squirmed in his arms, but didn't pull away. His heart soared. "I meant, what do we have here, and what's the order of operations?"

She turned in his arms to plant a sweet kiss on his cheek and then turned back and started pointing. "Turkey, stuffing, mashed potatoes. All of those should get gravy on them. Brussels. I'm going no gravy there, but won't judge you if you choose otherwise. If we're feeling fancy, Nadia said we can wrap the rolls in foil and put them in the oven while everything else microwaves, but I won't tell her if we just decide to throw them in the microwave for the last 10 seconds with everything else. Then cranberry goes on after everything else is heated up, although I have to tell you, this bougie whole berry stuff is an abomination. The real deal has ridges to show you it's straight out of a can." He stepped away to grab two plates and passed her one, watching as she started dishing out her plate, paying attention to which things she took more of (mashed potatoes), which less (everything else). "And then obviously we'll come back for dessert later."

"Obviously."

"Just don't forget to save room! There are two kinds of tartlets, plus brownies and gingerbread."

"Definitely will be saving room. If this woman's pies are anything like as good as her brownies, part of me wants to skip the dinner part and go straight to dessert."

Maddy laughed. He loved that sound. "No, Pierre is every bit as good with savory foods as Nadia is with the baking. You don't want to miss any of it."

She turned toward the microwave and carried both of their plates there, stopping along the way to grab two paper towels from the roll next to the kitchen window. He found himself just standing there, smiling like a loon, watching her. She was such a caretaker that she couldn't even stop herself from microwaving his leftovers. She even had a method that involved alternating the plates so that both of their meals would be warm at the same time. He sobered as he realized that, yes, of course, the domesticity of cooking—or, reheating, rather—for two came naturally to her. She'd been someone's wife. He certainly didn't want to erase that part of her, but he didn't love dwelling on it, either.

Pushing himself off the counter, he went back to the wine rack. "Red or white?" he asked over his shoulder.

To his surprise, Maddy's arms came around him from behind, peering past his bicep to the extensive collection. "I mean, I'm not particular, but I'm generally more of a red drinker."

"Red it is," he said, leaning forward, her arms still around him, to select a red blend that went well with everything. The microwave beeped, and she slipped away again to retrieve their food as he set the bottle and two glasses down on the small table for two in his kitchen.

"I thought we'd eat in here if it's alright with you?"

"Of course," she answered, bringing their plates over. He marveled at how comfortable she was, finding her way around his kitchen. People tended to tiptoe around him, so to find someone who just made herself right at home was refreshing. He forced the feelings he was having back and tried to stay in the moment. They'd agreed to keep it casual. Thinking of how comfortable their domestic situation would be was the opposite of casual.

"So are these all the foods you had growing up for Thanksgiving?" he asked, forcing himself back into the moment.

"Pretty much," she said. "The weird thing about Thanksgiving is that it's so reliant on the food and everyone does it a little different, so you never quite know. Also, since I grew up doing a lot of big community Thanksgiving dinners with my dad's soldiers, it wasn't like my mom was always making the same home-cooked meal, so I'm maybe a little less particular than the average American." She took another bite. "But this cranberry really is bullshit. Don't tell me he can't import the good stuff. He's the freaking ambassador. They can slip two cans in with the diplomatic post," she grumbled, examining the small pile of whole berry cranberry sauce she'd begrudgingly put on her plate with a face of pure derision.

It was basically the only thing he'd ever seen make her grumpy, besides his inability to take care of himself when he was sick, and now that he wasn't the victim, he found her disgust thoroughly adorable.

"So, what do you think of your first Thanksgiving?" she asked, smiling over at him. "I should have taken a picture or something."

"Delicious," he proclaimed. "Part of me wants more, but I know there's so many treats to come..."

She sighed contentedly, sitting back in her chair. "I think I'm going to need a break before I can tackle dessert."

"Okay, well, what if we take it and the rest of this wine upstairs with us and we can hang out for a bit and then when we're ready we can go for round two."

"Perfect," she said, standing and moving to clear their plates.

"Oh my god, Maddy, you're not allowed to bring the food, heat the food, *and* do the dishes. Take this upstairs," he said, handing her the bottle of wine and her glass, "make yourself comfortable, and I'll be right behind you."

"Okay," she said. "But I really don't mind—"

"Go!" he said, swatting at her playfully with a dishtowel.

"Going!" she called over her shoulder.

Chapter 14

After hastily closing up the remaining dinner food and putting their dishes in the sink, Alex grabbed the container of pastries and headed upstairs. He found Maddy curled up in the corner of his couch, sipping her wine and scratching Bertie's ears contentedly.

He flipped a switch next to the door, and a gas fire sprang to life in the fireplace across from the sofa. "Oh, lovely!" Maddy said, smiling brightly. "I always loved it when our houses had fireplaces growing up."

"I wish it was real wood, but once a building gets to be this old, they're pretty reluctant to let us introduce any more significant fire hazards than is truly necessary." He shooed Bertie off the couch so he could sit down next to her. He reached for her feet, pulling them across his lap, and starting to knead one gently.

"Mmmm," Maddy sighed, "that feels so good." He suppressed the decidedly adult images that raced to the front of his brain as he thought about other ways he could make her say that and tried to focus on her feet. Toes, ball, arch, ankle. And then the other one. Toes, ball, arch, ankle. They were quiet for a few minutes. "A girl could get used to this," she said, her voice relaxed, her eyes gazing at the blazing fire.

He fought the urge to think about what else they could get used to: romantic nights in, putting away grocery orders together, walking Bertie around Kensington Gardens. But no. They'd said casual. He couldn't take this further than she wanted to, or he'd wind up with his heart stomped over.

Needing to distract himself from the things he couldn't have with Maddy, he forced himself back into the present and, taking her wine glass from her hand and placing it safely on the coffee table, cradled her jaw in his hand and kissed her. She tasted like wine and cranberries, and he'd never tasted anything better.

Kissing Maddy was almost surreal, unlike anything Alex had ever experienced. And that was, frankly, saying something. He hadn't ever been a real relationship guy, but at some point as a teenager he'd realized that "proficiency in bed" was a viable skill to make a priority for him. His first sexual encounter had been with the daughter of a baronet four years his senior who had—kindly, gently, but in no certain terms— told him afterwards that his technique was shoddy, to say the least. Ever the people-pleaser, Alex had immediately set about rectifying the situation. He had already known that asking someone to commit to the life that would be expected of the wife to the Spare was likely asking too much. But if he didn't want to live a life of celibacy, which he was already certain he did not, the least he could do was offer his partners a pleasur- able experience. So while Ben had been busy learning how to greet the king of Bahrain and parse the government memos that would one day show up on his desk each day, Alex had set about spending his spare time at Eton and on long summer weekends at various country homes learning exactly how to please a partner. He never spent more than a few nights with each one, and he made very sure that they knew what they were getting into, but also made sure that his partners left satisfied.

Over the years he'd developed a quiet reputation among the upper crust of British society. And then when he went to New Zealand he'd had even more opportunities to hone his craft. It made him feel accomplished, powerful, and like he was finally the best at something. And it turned out, having something that was "his thing," even if that "thing" was being the orgasm whisperer, was highly motivating for Alex.

As he worked his way down to the spot where Maddy's jaw and neck met, he nuzzled against her, alternately licking and nibbling gently. Her hips were writhing beneath him on his couch, driving his own arousal even higher. Her hands raked through his hair, her head thrown back. Her cheeks were deliciously flushed, her lips slightly parted and bee-stung from their kisses. The sensations of kissing her, and the sweet needy noises she was making, combined with the incredible softness of her clothes and her skin, were almost overwhelming. He had one hand buried in her hair and the other started to drift from where he'd been running it aimlessly up and down her back towards the curve of her breast.

He could see that she was wearing some kind of lacy bra under the tank, but it was thin and her nipples were clearly visible beneath. She moaned quietly as he grazed her nipple. "Is this alright?" he asked, desperately needing to hear her say yes.

"Yes," she exhaled, her breaths growing ragged. "Oh my god, yes." She pulled his head back to renew their kiss while he busied himself teasing her. He'd never wanted anyone like this and he was struggling to restrain himself. All he wanted was to rip her clothes off and worship her body, slowly and very thoroughly. But he was also acutely aware of wanting to be sure he was giving Maddy what she needed. She protected this part of herself so much that it was sometimes hard to tell what it actually was that she needed. Although, the way her pelvis was moving against his thigh made him fairly confident that she was a fully willing participant.

He pulled back, looking down at her. Her eyes were glassy with desire as she blinked up with him. He moved his hand away from her hard nipples to rest just below her clavicle. "God, you are stunning," he breathed. She flushed and pushed an errant lock of hair behind her ear, breaking their eye contact. "Your reaction makes me think that you haven't been told that enough." A blush creeped over her cheeks, and she looked away but didn't say anything. "Hey," he said gently, "eyes up here." When she complied immediately he wasn't sure whether his heart or his cock swelled more. "Maddy, I don't know our future. And even if I wanted to, I can't change your past. But you deserve to believe how beautiful you are. You deserve to feel sexy and cared for and to experience pleasure. Will you let me try to do that for you?"

She hesitated for a second, but then nodded again. "I need to hear you say it," he said gently.

"Yes," she exhaled. He reclaimed her lips, trying to channel words that were too hard for him to say—and also, he suspected, hard for her to hear—into his actions. Her hands were raking up and down his back, making his entire body break out in goosebumps with the feel of her fingernails through his shirt. He needed more and he hoped she did, too.

He pulled back and ran a finger tantalizingly around the curve of the neckline of her tank top. "Can I take this off?" he asked in a low voice.

"Yes," she practically groaned. "Please." He helped her sit up and peeled the cardigan off her arms, applying his lips to her neck and then, as they were exposed, her shoulders, before relieving her of her shirt. She lay below him, panting as he took in the sight of her in those skintight yoga pants that he couldn't think about if he wasn't in private, and a lacy pale pink bra. His system was going to overload if he didn't get her naked in his bed soon.

"I'm not sure those are legal in the UK," he said raggedly, his eyes greedily drinking in the sight of her.

"My boobs or bralettes?"

"Yes," he said. She giggled as he resumed his place on top of her, their legs tangling together again as he palmed her breast through the item she'd called a "bralette." He wasn't exactly sure what made it different from a bra, but at that moment he couldn't care less. She arched into his hand as he leaned down and started placing kisses around the lacy edge of the band of fabric that was the only thing keeping him from tasting her nipples. Pulling back to look at her, he found desire mirroring his own in her brown eyes. "What if we...?" he said, looking towards the door to the hallway and his bedroom, hoping his intention was clear.

"Yes," she replied immediately.

He stood, taking her by the hand and, making sure to quickly flip the switch to turn off the fire, led her swiftly from the room and down the hall.

* * *

They tumbled back onto his bed in a tangle of limbs. Maddy was frantically, yet futilely, working at the buttons on his shirt as he kissed and licked his way down her neck, stopping to lavish attention just above the curve of her collarbone.

"Alex," she gasped, still fighting the uphill battle against his shirt buttons as he thwarted her with his mouth at every turn.

"Yes, darling?" he asked, seductively, not looking up from the task at hand.

"If you give me a hickey, I will not hesitate to cause an international incident," she managed to get out, before a moan overtook her as he began inching the fabric of the bralette down over her breasts at a glacial pace, his lips following closely behind the thin material.

"Duly noted," he said, finally sitting up and taking mercy on her, unbuttoning a few more buttons before pulling the partially unbuttoned shirt over his head.

Maddy's eyes were almost cartoonish as she eagerly took in the planes of his chest. He was fit, but not obnoxiously so, with enough definition in his biceps and abs to show that he worked out, but not so much that it screamed "gym rat."

Leaning back on his haunches, he ran his index finger slowly under the waistband of her yoga pants. "May I?" he asked, his eyes glowing with arousal, but also seriously asking for her consent. She'd never felt so cared for—or so turned on—in her life. That was a weird feeling, and not entirely a good one, but she forced that thought back into the furthest recesses of her brain and refocused on the incredibly attractive half-naked prince who was asking permission to undress her.

"Y-yes," she rasped out. "Please."

There was heat in his gray eyes as he smiled up at her wolfishly and started to ease her pants and her underwear off. When he'd finally freed her ankles—really, there was no sexy way to remove yoga pants—he nestled himself between her legs and smiled up at her. He gently pushed her thighs apart with his hands and let out an almost pained exhale.

"Christ, you're so gorgeous," he said, pushing up on one elbow as he used the first two fingers of his other hand to gently trace the outlines of the curve of her sex. "So smooth," he rasped, stroking her tantalizingly with his index finger.

Maddy writhed and tried not to whine, desperate for his fingers to find where she was wet for him, the bud that was screaming for his touch. He was clearly a prince with a plan— to drive her completely mad. His unhurried strokes explored the sensitive crease between her thigh and her pelvis before taking another lap around her sex and up to the other hip. "So smooth," he repeated, almost reverently.

"Don't get too used to it," she said self-consciously. "It's pricey and painful." Having had some inkling that he might be seeing her naked that weekend, Maddy had found a sugaring salon in Chelsea and paid a small fortune to have most of her pubic hair removed earlier that week. Although it had hurt like crazy at the time, she had to admit that she'd felt uncharacteristically sexy for the last several days, reveling in the unfamiliar sensation of being very aware of the friction of her panties against her newly smooth skin, luxuriating in the sexy secret of what she'd done.

Alex pushed up on both elbows, looking her squarely in the face. "I need to make one thing very clear," he said, resting his palms firmly on the tops of her thighs. "You are sexy as fuck, no matter what. If this," he said, two of his fingers returning to stroke where she was smooth and so hot for him, finally easing one finger into her hot, tight pussy and drawing her wetness up to circle her clit, "makes you feel sexy, then by all means. I love it. If you want to grow it all out, fine by me. Or maybe you'll let me take care of it myself," he said with a seductive quirk of his eyebrows. She moaned, so turned on she wasn't able to form coherent sentences. "But I mean it when I say that you are stunning, no matter what." He slid a second finger in, pumping languidly. Slowly, he lowered his head. "May I?"

He looked up at her, awaiting her response, and Maddy swore she'd never seen anything sexier. "Oh my god, yes, Alex," she hissed.

Withdrawing his fingers, he used his thumbs to spread her open, his shoulders coaxing her thighs even further. "Fuck, Maddy, you're so wet for me," he said, seconds before his tongue made contact with her opening, teasing her entrance before gliding north. She writhed beneath him, one hand gripping his hair, the other holding on to the sheet for dear life as he licked her everywhere except the one place she needed it most.

"Alex," she was practically begging and too turned on to even care. "Please."

When his lips finally closed around her clit she nearly screamed. "Ohmigod, Alex, I'm close. Jesus Christ, I'm close."

He backed off almost immediately before looking up at her sternly. "Don't you dare. I'm not nearly done with you yet."

"Alex." She was almost whining, dripping for him, begging for release.

He shifted, moving up to bring his lips to hers again in a searing kiss. She'd never been particularly keen on kissing after oral, but somehow with Alex, it was unimaginably hot. The way his damp, slightly stubbly skin ravaged her, how he alternated pumping two fingers into her and circling them around her clit while he kissed her. She arched her back, desperate for more, and he finally relented, resettling himself between her legs, his lips and tongue driving her absolutely wild with need while his fingers continued urging her towards her climax.

Maddy's brain was on the verge of short-circuiting. The sensations were overwhelming. It had been so long since she'd been with anyone, and even longer since she'd been with anyone new. The novelty combined with the excitement and, frankly, the anxiety about her ability to perform after so long kept threatening to distract her from the exquisite pleasure Alex's mouth was bringing her.

Just then, Alex simultaneously found that particular spot inside her with his fingers and sealed his lips around her clit, ravishing both at the same time and pulling her squarely back into the present. Her hips bucked wildly, stars clouding her vision. Alex's strong hand anchored her hips firmly to the mattress as his lips and fingers coaxed the last drops of pleasure from her.

When she came back down, he was still idly pumping two fingers in and out of her, lavishing light kisses and licks on her overheated skin. He wiped his chin with the back of his hand with a deeply satisfied grin and crawled up to cradle her in his arms.

"That was outrageous," Maddy panted, barely conscious. "I'm not sure that's legal in the States." She sighed contentedly and then reached for the prominent tent in his pants. Her fingers had barely grazed the outline of his erect, fabric-imprisoned cock, when he grasped her hand and pulled it first to his lips, then to nestle between their chests.

"Just relax," he said, stroking his hand gently up and down her back.

"But you didn't—" she began.

"And you *just* did," he interrupted gently. "Let me hold you for a moment. Take care of you. Then maybe I'll let you show me what you can do."

She sighed and snuggled a bit closer to his naked chest, allowing herself to fully relax after her intense release. After a moment she realized a tear was rolling down her cheek. First just one, then a second followed, and soon her face was flooded with silent tears.

"Hey," he said, pulling back to look at her. "What's wrong?"

She shook her head, suddenly crying so hard she couldn't speak.

"Did I push this? Did we go too fast?" he asked, starting to look almost panicked. She shook her head vehemently as small sobs wracked her body, her breath catching and coming in gasps.

Looking slightly relieved but still concerned, Alex pulled her more tightly to his chest, wrapping his arms around her snugly, like a weighted blanket. He started running his hands through her sex-mussed hair and down her back, murmuring comforting nothings into her ear, shushing and soothing. After several long minutes her sobs started to abate, slowing to hiccups, and then ragged sniffles.

She squirmed, and he eased his grasp on her so she could roll onto her back, scrubbing at her swollen, tear-streaked face with her fists. "Wow. That was supremely unsexy."

"Hey." He placed his hand on the side of her face, turning her gently to look at him, and offering her a tissue from the box on the nightstand. "It's okay. That was a really powerful release. And sometimes powerful releases of one kind can lead to powerful releases of other kinds as well." He used the side of his thumb to wipe away an errant tear that was drifting towards her neck. "But I would very much like to confirm that it wasn't anything to do with anything I did," he added.

Maddy inhaled deeply, wiped at her eyes one more time, and then looked at him again, pushing herself up onto one elbow. "Alex, no. You were... you were perfect. That was... just, wow. Truly." She paused for a moment, gathering her thoughts. "Did I tell you I never cried?" she asked. "After Evan died?"

He let out a lungful of air. "Oh, Maddy."

She nodded. "I was just so... numb, at first. And then so eaten away with guilt. Like... I don't know, but like I didn't deserve to be sad when I was ready to leave him?" He looked like he was about to interrupt her, but she lifted her hand to stop him. "I know. I'm working on those feelings." She'd finally forced herself to start combing through the therapists that took her insurance and had an appointment lined up with one for the following week. "But grief isn't rational, right?" He nodded and waited for her to go on. She swallowed and then continued. "And then of course, that's the first time I've been with anyone since Evan. And Evan had been deployed for over a year before he died." She swallowed again, but kept going. "And, well... I'd never been with anyone else. I had virtually nothing to compare it against until ten minutes ago. And you fucking blew my mind. Literally." She let out a watery laugh before sobering again. "And I think all of that combined with the fact that it kind of confirmed that our sex life wasn't that great and the fact that you were so wonderful and caring and—holy shit how do you make consent so sexy?" She paused again. "I just, I think you broke the dam a little bit."

Alex sat up enough to draw her into his arms again. He kissed the top of her head. "Thank you. Thank you for trusting me with that." Her body shuddered with an emotional aftershock, and he shifted them back, tucking her under his arm and pulling the duvet up to cocoon them.

A few minutes passed in silence before Maddy said, "Sorry I kind of killed the mood. This feels like a very one-sided evening."

He turned his head to look down at her. "You're really not good at letting other people take care of you, are you?"

She bristled a little. "I mean, that's just not how it works," she said, somehow simultaneously defensive and dismissive. "I'm the one who takes care of other people. That's just what I do."

"And how do you feel when you take care of people?"

"Good," she answered promptly. "Needed, helpful."

"And has it ever occurred to you that other people might enjoy that feeling too?"

"I mean..." she trailed off.

"Exactly," he said, slipping out from beneath the covers and tucking them more firmly around her. "So what's going to happen is that you're going to stay here, I'm going to go make you a cup of tea, and then you're going to drink it while I cuddle you and we watch absurd videos on TikTok."

She looked up at him, her eyes going a bit watery again and gave a small nod.

"Alex?" He turned back from where he was headed toward the door. "Thank you."

The only response she got was the hundred-watt smile that he flashed her as he left the room and she snuggled down into the duvet.

He returned several minutes later, as promised, with not only a cup of tea, but also the box of desserts Nadia had packed and proceeded to feed her bites of pastries while they watched inane videos on his iPad. A few times she tried to turn the topic back to his unmet sexual needs, but Alex always shot her down, insisting they had plenty of time for fooling around later and that all he wanted to do was hold her and enjoy spending time together. And so, even though Maddy hated feeling like she hadn't reciprocated, she allowed him to take care of her and even, if she looked deep, found herself enjoying it. His sheets were unbelievably soft, the pillows were plush and plentiful, and the way he cuddled her close to him, the iPad leaning against their bent knees in front of them, made her feel precious in a way she wasn't sure she'd ever felt before. It was a gentle domesticity that would be easy to get used to. Too easy to get too used to, even.

At some point she realized Alex was gently shaking her awake, pressing kisses along her temple. "Sorry," she said, blearily, "I fell asleep on you again."

"Don't apologize," he said, smiling at her tenderly. "I liked it. But it's late. We should get ready for bed."

She glanced at the clock on the iPad and realized it was almost midnight.

"Oh my gosh, I can't believe it's so late!" she cried, tangling herself in the bedsheets in her hurry to get up.

"You can stay if you want," he said, smiling in a way that almost looked shy.

She closed her eyes, thinking for a moment of how nice it would be to go back to sleep in his arms. And his amazingly comfortable bed. "Alex, I'd love to," she said wistfully, "but I should really go sleep at Winfield."

"Okay," he said, pulling back the covers and swinging his legs over the side of the bed.

"Really, I want to," she said, trying to make him understand. "But we agreed to keep this casual. And low-key. And spending the night definitely doesn't count as casual. And me trying to explain sneaking into Winfield house tomorrow morning probably doesn't constitute low-key."

"I know, you're right." He sighed. "It just feels so good to have you in my bed."

"And it feels so good to *be* in your bed," she said, circling the bed to where he still sat on the side, shirtless and in a sinfully good-looking pair of gray sweatpants that he'd slipped into when he went to get dessert. She ran her fingers through his hair and he leaned into her touch. "But this is just the beginning," she promised. "Don't think you're going to be able to keep me away from that bedding. Or"—she leaned down and licked the shell of his ear seductively—"your mouth."

He groaned. "Don't you dare tempt me, Madeleine Cartwright, or I will have you back in that bed and screaming in ten seconds flat."

She giggled and fled the room, making her way back towards the entryway. She'd gotten dressed when she got up to use the bathroom during their TikTok scrolling session, so all that remained was to slip on her booties and shrug into her coat. Alex came padding down behind her, Bertie at his heels. He'd put on an old hooded sweatshirt and reached for Bertie's leash as she finished zipping her coat and threw her purse over one shoulder.

"Dinner one night this week?" he asked, tweaking the

pom-pom on the top of her hat fondly. "There's a French place I think you'll love that I've been dying to take you to."

"Sure," she said. "Text me."

"Graham will just be a sec," he said, slipping his feet into a hideous pair of athletic slide sandals.

"What?" she asked, turning to him in confusion.

"To drive you home."

"Alex—"

"No, Maddy," he interrupted her. "Look, I know what we're doing isn't serious, but I am serious about you getting home safely, and I hate the idea of you traipsing across London at this time of night."

"The Tube is perfectly safe!" she insisted.

"Please, Mads," he said. "Just humor me on this one, okay? I don't want to be worrying about you."

The stubborn determination that had settled across her face softened. "Okay," she said. "But only because it's late, and frankly it looks cold out there." The idea of walking to the Tube stop was definitely not appealing.

Alex opened his front door just as Graham pulled up in a dark Range Rover. Alex and Bertie walked Maddy down the walkway, and he opened the back door for her. She stopped and looked up at him. "Thank you," she said softly, her voice slightly husky with emotion. "Tonight was..." She paused, looking for the right word, and then started over. "I really needed that. All of it." With a quick look behind them to make sure nobody was around to see, she reached up on tiptoe and pressed a kiss to his lips. Worried if she didn't stop they'd wind up back in bed, she ended it quickly and then slid into the back seat without another word. She blew him one more quick kiss as he shut the door behind her and Graham steered them away from the curb and into the night.

Chapter 15

As November turned to December, the halls at Winfield House were thoroughly decked. The Stewarts hosted a grand tea where a selection of American expatriates in London were invited to come help decorate the lavish tree that had appeared in the grand salon, and a children's Christmas party where children and their families came, ate, drank, and received a small gift from the ambassador and Mrs. Stewart. Maddy was simultaneously loving all the merriment and also starting to get exhausted. Her weekends had been completely scheduled with festive events, and she hadn't had a full day off in several weeks. Between the embassy's busy slate of events and the royal ramp up to the holidays, finding even stolen moments to see Alex was getting harder and harder. They'd had late-night carryout followed by making out at Kensington a few times, but real dates had been hard to schedule.

One Tuesday afternoon a few weeks before Christmas, Maddy's phone vibrated on the long oak table in the formal dining room that was currently serving as the embassy's conference room.

MR. MARTINI

What are you up to, gorgeous?

I have a problem I really need your help with…

[img4589.jpg] Image could not be delivered because the content has been blocked.

Yowza! What was in that picture that made the work firewalls block it?

Sorry, I'm in work meetings all afternoon ☹

MR. MARTINI

You'll just have to come over and find out…

Call out sick!

Hah, I wish, but I have to work, Alex. Sorry.

MR. MARTINI

Tell them someone is having a medical emergency and that you have to come for him. Immediately. 😏

Maddy rolled her eyes and flipped the phone over on the conference table after putting it on "Do Not Disturb" mode. She hoped her cheeks weren't as flushed as she was afraid they might be. She tried valiantly not to think about what other scandalous texts Alex might be sending her as she refocused on the meeting she was sitting in where they were discussing a cocktail reception the Stewarts would be hosting for visiting senators just after the new year.

Alex's texts were flattering, of course. Her relationship with Evan had morphed so gradually from childhood friendship to more that there had never really been a period where they were so desperate to be together that they were sending each other salacious texts. And regardless of how their relationship had progressed, there was no planet on which Evan would have abandoned his duties for any reason, up to and including sex. But even though Maddy was flattered, she found herself fighting down irritation. In so many ways Alex was considerate, thoughtful, and attentive. But occasionally there would be times when his complete ignorance of normal life things like jobs and finances was glaringly obvious. And kind of annoying.

By the time her meeting ended at four, she'd missed another few texts from him. Although the first few had been in the same NSFW vein as the ones she'd seen, he'd taken a quick left turn into contrition when he'd realized she was serious about not responding and had even tried calling her. Twice. Maddy sighed. It had already been a long day, and she didn't really feel like calling Alex back, but felt bad leaving him on read.

After changing out of her work clothes into leggings and a worn long-sleeved shirt, she tapped the button to call him, putting the phone on speaker as she started pulling ingredients out of cupboards and boiling water for pasta.

"Hi there," he said, answering on the first ring. His voice was warm, but he also sounded a bit guarded. As if he knew that he was probably in trouble.

"Hi," she said, rinsing a head of broccoli to throw in with the pasta.

"How was your day?" he asked, sounding a bit cautious.

"Long," she said. "Busy. How about you?"

"Fine. Boring."

"Yeah, I got that."

"I think I may have gone a bit too far today..."

"You think, Alex?" Maddy tried to temper the irritation in her voice, but struggled. She was tired. She'd had a long day of being the problem-solver at work, and her energy for explaining things to people was running very low.

"So I did?"

"Alex." She halved the head of broccoli slightly more aggressively than was strictly necessary. "I am flattered that you were thinking of me today. But I have to do my job." She struggled not to talk to him like he was five. But in this particular area, it kind of felt like he was. "If I don't work, I don't have money. If I don't work, I don't have a visa. If I don't work, the ambassador calls my parents. I know you've never had to rely on a job to make money, but it's like you don't even realize that other people do."

"I mean, I could get you a new visa," he said flippantly.

"*Alex.*" Her frustration bubbled over. "If you want to continue to spend time together, you have to at least pretend to figure out what real life is like for mere commoners like me. I can't just rely on you for everything. I'm supposed to be figuring out how to live as an independent adult. When I go back to the States, I can't have just spent the year living as your kept woman. Not to mention, this is supposed to be casual. Offering to get someone a new visa isn't casual."

There was silence on the other end of the phone, and for a moment Maddy wondered if she'd gone too far.

"You're right," he finally said. "I'm sorry." She could hear the real regret in his voice, could tell he was finally starting to get it.

"Alex." She made a real effort to gentle her tone. "Spending time with you is so much fun, and I really appreciate how generous and caring you are. It's just hard sometimes that you can see the way your privilege shows up on a Commonwealth-wide macro level, but that you can't see it on this level."

She heard him sigh through the phone. "You're right. You are. I'm so sorry. I know doing things for yourself is important to you. I really like taking care of you, but I also need to respect that you want to take care of yourself. I'm going to get better about this."

"I appreciate that."

A few weeks later Maddy was summoned to Ambassador Stewart's office just before five p.m. When she arrived, the ambassador was seated behind his large desk, poring over a report, a cut-crystal glass of whiskey at his side.

"Ah, Maddy, thanks for coming," he said, standing when she entered.

"Of course," she said, somewhat uncertainly. Despite Ambassador Stewart being one of her father's closest friends, she still didn't see him that often, and certainly not alone. She could only think of one or two times when he'd asked to see her in the nearly six months she'd worked at the embassy.

"How are you doing?" he asked kindly, retaking his seat. "The embassy staff is very pleased with your work, and Delia says you seem happy."

Maddy relaxed slightly. She hadn't actually thought she'd been about to lose her job, but she also couldn't have ruled it out based on the zero information that came with her summons to see the ambassador. "I'm fine," she said, trying to figure out what other kind of information he might be looking for. "I enjoy my work, and of course living in London is a dream come true."

"Good, good," he said, smiling broadly. "I'm so glad it worked out for you to come."

"Thank you, me too."

There was a pause that felt awkward to Maddy. "Maddy, I talked with your father last night."

Ah, there it was. She should have guessed this was what he wanted to talk with her about. She sighed. "Let me guess," she said, before he had a chance to go on. "He wants you to convince me to go home for Christmas."

"Well." The ambassador looked a bit sheepish. "Yes, that's exactly what we discussed."

"I'm sorry," she said, looking at the ceiling in exasperation. "He shouldn't have put you in that position."

"Maddy, it's a fair request. You're their only child. The idea of you spending Christmas rattling around this place by yourself while they're back in Kansas, just the two of them... your mama can't bear it."

She sighed, "I know they want me to come home, but—"

The ambassador interrupted her gently, "Why don't you want to, Maddygirl?" he said, using the nickname she hadn't heard since she was a child. "If it's the money—" He knew she hadn't wanted to touch the death benefits she'd received from the Army when Evan died.

"It's not the money. I just..." Her voice trailed off. "I just feel like I need something different this year. Doing the same old routine was so hard last year—it just reminded me of who wasn't there. I don't think I can do that again." She couldn't quite bring herself to say Evan's name out loud. "It's been so nice to get away from all the sympathy and the stares and... I just think staying here is the right thing for me."

He sighed and looked across at her. "I understand," he said quietly. "The Christmas after I lost my first soldier, the idea of just celebrating as normal felt terrible. Pointless, even." He seemed lost in his own recollections for a moment. "I think your dad gets it too. He just hates to see your mama so broken up about it."

She bowed her head. "I know. I feel bad. I don't want to hurt her, I just... I really think this is what I need to do."

"Ok, sweetie. If you're sure."

She nodded. "I'm sure."

"Well if you change your mind, you just let me know and

we'll get you there before you can say 'Self-Licking Ice Cream Cone.'"

She giggled at the Army slang. "Thank you, sir."

"You betcha, Maddy."

She stood and walked out of his office, slipping her phone from the pocket of her navy-blue suit pants as she headed back towards her office. The workday was over, but she was going to bring her laptop down to her rooms to confirm details for the last big Christmas event that the Stewarts would be hosting before their own flight back to their home in Birmingham, Alabama, on the twenty-second.

Glancing down she saw that she had a text from Alex, confirming their dinner plans for that night. She was meeting him at a French bistro in Mayfair for dinner at 6:15. Looking at the time, she realized she didn't really have time to do her work. In fact, at almost 5:30, she was starting to run short on time. Abandoning her idea to get her laptop, she hurried back to her room to run a brush through her hair and reapply her lipstick before shrugging into her long winter coat and slipping out the kitchen door to head for the tube.

Maddy's nose and cheeks were delightfully flushed from the cold when she rushed into their private room at Aubaine. She'd already given her coat to the staff out front, so Alex was free to drink in the sight of her in her navy-blue pantsuit with a cream-colored blouse and black heels. He stood and went to her, leaning down to give her a lingering kiss, using his hands to try to warm her cheeks. She pressed her nose into the side of his throat, and he jumped back, laughing, at the icy sensation over his already heated skin. "I love seeing you in your work clothes," he murmured, leading her to their table and pulling her chair out for her. As she sat, he pushed her hair to one side, exposing her neck, so he could whisper right in her ear, "It's so sexy imagining you bossing the entire embassy around."

Her cheeks flushed, this time from his words and the sensation of his breath on the shell of her ear, not from the cold. "I don't think anyone would refer to my job as 'bossing around the entire embassy,'" she said dryly, "but if that's what gets you off, I'd never deprive you of that mental image."

Alex felt himself rapidly growing hard imagining fucking her in just her black heels. Or finding an office to defile. He turned toward the table, eager to sit before he embarrassed himself. Their server came in as Alex took his seat again, carrying the bottle of Côtes du Rhône he'd ordered. Alex waved off the formality of being offered a taste and just asked the server to pour them each a glass. Another member of the waitstaff came in carrying the butternut squash and burrata appetizer he'd also ordered, and he smiled as he saw Maddy's eyes light up. "Mmm, my favorite. I'm so hungry!"

"Did you skip lunch again?"

"No!" she cried defensively. "I had half a sandwich between meetings and a few peanut butter crackers around four!"

"Mads, that's not enough to keep you going all afternoon."

"Okay, *Dad*," she said, rolling her eyes and turning her attention to the dinner menu. "Mmm, the burger sounds divine," she said. "Oooh, and they have truffle parmesan fries!"

Alex ordered a steak and something called "pomme puree" that he sincerely hoped was going to turn out to be normal mashed potatoes and not some avant-garde interpretation, and the server left them in peace.

"So, how was your day?" she asked, taking a sip of her wine. He had trouble understanding the question, completely entranced by the way she savored the red wine, a tempting drop lingering on her lip. His brain almost short-circuited as her tongue darted out to clear the errant wine.

"Sorry, what was the question?" he asked, somewhat dazed.

She gave him a Look. "You inveterate horn dog," she chastised. "I asked how your day was."

"Oh! Fine," he said, trying to refocus on the woman in front of him and not the things he wanted to do to her later. "I had a few meetings about the new environmental initiative they want me to support in the new year, and then I went to Westminster Abbey with Ben to talk about..." he trailed off, thinking for a moment. "I honestly don't have any idea what that meeting was about or why my presence was required, but when you're the best man and the groom says he needs you to come meet with the archbishop, you don't say no."

Maddy laughed. "No, I suppose you don't."

"So when's your flight?" he asked. "How long will you be gone?"

"What flight?" she asked. He could see the moment she realized what he'd meant and noticed a shift in her demeanor. As if she were steeling herself for an argument. "Oh. I'm not going back for Christmas."

"You're not?" he asked, stunned. "But what are you going to do?"

"No," she said. "I need a change of scenery. I'm going to stay here. Check out the Christmas lights in Regent Street. Maybe go to the Leadenhall Market."

"Maddy, I can take you to do those things and be done in like three hours. What are you going to do for the rest of Christmas?"

"Relax? Watch *The Sound of Music* on TV? Read some cozy romances? I haven't had a real day off in weeks. I'm honestly looking forward to having nothing to do."

Alex frowned. He hated the idea of her rattling around the

huge ambassadorial residence by herself at Christmas. Especially her second Christmas alone. He sighed. "I wish you could come to Sandringham with me."

She barked out a laugh. "Oh yes, because that's the epitome of casual. 'Hello, yes, did I mention I have a secret girlfriend? Well, she's not really my girlfriend, but she's not *not* my girlfriend. Anyway, here she is! Oh, and she's American! Merry Christmas!'"

He sighed. "I know, I know. I just hate the idea of you being alone on Christmas."

She gave him a small smile. "You and everyone else in my life. The ambassador hauled me into his office today to try to convince me to go home. Because my father asked him to. Nadia even invited me to go home to Oxford with her. It's all very kind and well-intentioned, but it's not what I need." He could see the conviction in her face and knew she wasn't going to change her mind.

Sighing, he tried to resign himself to the idea and move on. "Alright. What would you be doing if you did go home?" he asked.

"Church on Christmas Eve. Quick presents on Christmas morning and then off to volunteer somewhere on post. My father serves food at a Christmas luncheon for servicemembers, and then my parents host dinner for the other officers somewhere. It's all I've ever known, but sometimes I wished Christmas could just be our family. That instead of having to smile for picture after picture with people I didn't know that we could just have a relaxing day at home celebrating just the three of us."

"I see," Alex said. *Just another time when everyone else came before her.*

"What about you?" Maddy asked. "What does your family do for Christmas?"

Alex smiled. "Well, we go out to Sandringham. My parents

host a fancy dinner one night, and we have to parade past a bunch of people to go to church on Christmas morning, but other than that, I think it's closer to normal than you'd expect. We open presents at teatime on Christmas Eve. There's usually a handful of completely absurd joke gifts." He gave a cheeky smile. "I got Hannah *The Corpse Bride* on DVD this year."

Maddy giggled, "Will she think that's funny?"

"I think so? I hope so. I got her a nice necklace too."

"That's bold," Maddy said. "I hope you know her taste in jewelry."

"I mean, I didn't pick it out," he said. "I had help."

"Okay, so please, yes, go back to telling me how normal your Christmas is with people who help you do your shopping."

"I said *close* to normal!"

"Mm-hmm." She smirked into her glass of wine.

Just then their server returned with the food and the conversation turned. They enjoyed the rest of the evening, talking, sharing stories about holidays of the past. After dessert was served, Alex found himself with a slightly wine-tipsy Maddy in his lap kissing him, which he enjoyed thoroughly, only managing to hold himself back when he realized that a public indecency charge would definitely blow their cover. But in the back of his mind, he couldn't stop imagining her alone at Winfield, curled up on her old couch, alone on Christmas. He hated it.

Chapter 16

Christmas morning Alex was up early. They didn't have to arrive at church until eleven, but the old plumbing meant that hot water tended to run out at Sandringham early when the whole family was in residence and he didn't want to miss his chance. As he headed down to breakfast after his shower, he found himself thinking of Maddy. Wondering what she was doing. Imagining her waking up alone in her drafty space.

When he arrived in the dining room his brother was its only other occupant. "Morning, Ben," he said, helping himself to a cup of coffee from the antique silver urn on the sideboard.

"Happy Christmas, mate," Benjamin said, looking up from a plate loaded down with eggs, toast, and bacon and setting aside the newspaper he'd been looking over.

"Happy Christmas," Alex said, setting his own breakfast down and leaning over to give his brother a half hug. "Is Hannah still asleep?"

Ben barked out a laugh. "She's been getting ready for the Merry March for hours," he said, referring to the family's traditional walk from Sandringham to the local church. Their route was always lined with fans and well-wishers, which meant that the family had to be perfectly cheery and "on" for the entire walk, no matter what. "I brought her a cup of coffee and some toast and then beat a hasty retreat. She's up there with Mum and Colette and Elise, and the hairspray fumes are deadly. Seems like a bloody nightmare." He shuddered and turned his attention back to his food.

Alex grunted his agreement and tried not to imagine what it would be like to have Maddy upstairs with his mother, aunt, and cousin, all getting ready to walk to church together. How well she'd do greeting all the people who came out to see them. How pretty she'd look in a coat dress, her cheeks flushed from the cold, walking next to him from the house to the church. And then he wondered what she was doing now. He glanced at his watch. It was just gone eight, so she might still be asleep. His mind wandered, imagining surprising her in bed. Creeping up the ridiculous stairs to her lofted bedroom, climbing under the covers with her, and kissing her awake...

"Alex?" His brother's voice cut into his daydream.

"Sorry, what?" he asked, shaking himself back to the present and turning to face Ben.

"Where'd you go?" his brother asked, an inquiring look on his face.

"Sorry, not enough coffee yet," Alex said, trying not to look guilty. His brother was five years older and had always been able to tell when Alex wasn't being straight with him, and Alex knew he wasn't being terribly convincing, so he tried to take control of the conversation. "What were you saying?" He forced himself to concentrate on his brother, keeping his mind firmly in the present.

"I was asking how long you were planning to stay at Sandringham. Hannah and I will be here until lunchtime tomorrow, and then we're heading out to spend a few days with her family in the Cotswolds."

"Oh, very good," Alex said. He'd been planning on staying several more days, but suddenly found himself saying, "Do you think anyone would be terribly put off if I left after tea today?"

"Today?" Ben asked, recoiling, surprise written across his face. "Where would you possibly go? And why?"

"Oh, no reason," Alex said, unconvincingly. "Just wondering about getting back to the city. Bertie does better in his own space," he added, hoping that it didn't sound as if he'd just made the last bit up on the spot. Which he definitely hadn't.

"Mm-hmm," Benjamin said, eyeing him suspiciously. "Who is she?"

"She's... wait, what?" Alex tried not to let the panic show on his face.

His brother looked over his shoulder to make sure they were well and truly alone before saying quietly, "Who are you fucking right now that you're so eager to get back to London for?" He hadn't said it unkindly. If anything, he seemed maybe a little eager for gossip in the way that people who have been in long-term committed relationships often do. And really, Alex rationalized to himself, trying not to unleash fury on his brother, it wasn't an unfair assumption. Alex's previous "relationships," if one could even call them that, had, with one notable exception, all been short, transactional, no strings attached.

But despite the rational knowledge that it wasn't a totally off base logical leap to make, Alex found himself offended that his brother would think he'd actually ditch his family on Christmas for a random hookup. "It's not someone I'm fucking!" he hissed fiercely, keeping his voice low to avoid being overheard by the servants or anyone else. The rest of the family would be trailing in for breakfast any minute.

"Oh ho! So it's more than that!" Ben crowed.

"More than what?" their father asked, coming around the corner and into the breakfast room, looking at them with fond curiosity.

"Erm…" Alex frantically searched for something that made sense to say.

"More than just the rubber chicken he gave me yesterday. I knew there had to be a better present than that," Ben filled in smoothly. "I'm just trying to get it out of him."

Their father chuckled affably as he set about filling his breakfast plate. "You boys and your practical jokes."

"How's it going up there?" Alex asked, thinking of anything possible to change the subject.

"Cousin Charlotte has entered the fray," his father said with a meaningful look. Cousin Charlotte was Alex's grandmother's cousin who was about eighty-five years old and nuttier than a Christmas cake. "When I came down, your mother was trying to convince her that lighting her cigarette in a room with that much aerosol in it was likely to burn down one of the most important buildings on the National Registry of Historic Buildings." He set his plate down and went back for a cup of coffee muttering, "Bloody nightmare."

Maddy answered on the second ring. "Hey, Merry Christmas."

"Happy Christmas," he said. "What are you doing?"

He heard the sound of a utensil scraping against a dish. "Eating mashed potatoes and watching TV." What she was actually doing was watching coverage of the king's Christmas day speech, His Majesty's pre-recorded annual message in a small video inset over footage of Alex and his family walking to church earlier that day. But it felt weird to say that. "What about you?"

"Why don't you come open the door and see?" he said, grinning ear to ear even though she couldn't see him.

"Wait, *what?*" she shrieked. He heard the clatter of a utensil against a dish. "What do you mean, open the door?"

"Mads, come open the door," he said, patiently, waiting for the other shoe to drop.

"You can't... you didn't...you're supposed to..." He heard shuffling as she sputtered in disbelief. He stood outside the side door to Winfield rocking back and forth on his heels, trying not to think too hard about how excited he was to see her after only a few days apart.

When she finally opened the door, phone still to her ear, her eyes were wide in utter shock. She was wearing red tartan flannel pajama pants and a well-loved oversized Vassar crewneck sweatshirt. Her hair was piled on top of her head in a droopy bun. Alex drank in her appearance as if she was wearing head-to-toe La Perla. "Alex," she gasped in what appeared to be half shock and half horror, "what in god's name are you doing here? You're supposed to be at Sandringham with your family!" She was so stunned, she was still holding the phone to her ear, even though he'd long since hung up.

Alex moved closer and gently took her phone from her hands and, after giving a quick look around, leaned forward, took her face in his hands, and kissed her gently. "But I'm not at Sandringham. I'm here."

The kiss seemed to pull Maddy out of her state of shock, and she quickly pulled him into the Winfield kitchen.

"Alex, what are you doing here?" she asked again.

"I'd sort of hoped you might be happy to see me?" he said, suddenly starting to wonder if maybe he'd made a mistake.

"No, I mean, of course I'm happy to see you!" she said. "I'm just confused. You're supposed to be with your family. It's Christmas! You spend Christmas with your family!"

"Well, at the risk of pointing out the obvious, you're not," he began, "and really, we do most of it on Christmas Eve. We did presents and the big dinner last night, church this morning, and then boatloads of more food at teatime, and now they're all sitting around in a food coma. Ben and Hannah are leaving to go to her family tomorrow, so it's not like I'm really going to miss much. Plus, my cousin Charlotte and Bertie don't really get on..." He shuddered a bit, thinking about the hideously expensive shoe Bertie had somehow managed to steal and mangle. "And when I thought about what I wanted to do with my time, I realized I really just wanted to spend it with you."

"So, you... left your family. The king and queen of England. To spend time with me?" Maddy still seemed to be in shock. "Weren't they upset?"

"Really, once you've watched my father make a Christmas speech once, you get the gist. And I've seen like twenty of them. Honestly, I'm the quietest one in my family by a pretty significant margin. If it weren't for Bertie being such a menace all the time and the fact that I announced our departure, I'm not sure how long it would have taken anyone to notice I was gone."

"I'm sure that's not true."

"No, really," he said, "my family is great. Truly. We all love each other. But when being the ruler of a country is your birthright and you also happen to be extremely extroverted and you're surrounded by a whole bunch of other weirdos who are just like you, it's easy to be benevolently self-centered. I'm the only introvert in the whole bunch. I love them, but when the whole family gets together, it honestly gets exhausting. It's so much nicer to be here, where it's quiet." He paused, fighting past the vulnerability that threatened to choke him. "Where you are."

Her face softened a bit. "Oh, Alex." She smiled up at him and then reached up to kiss him. "Thank you. I..." Her voice trailed off a bit and he saw her swallow before she continued.

"I still know that staying here was the right thing to do. But I won't lie and say I wasn't having the slightest bit of a pity party for myself." She kissed him again. "It's so good to see you."

The relief of knowing his instincts to come to her combined with the sweet smile on her face just about made Alex's heart explode. "Come here, you," he almost growled, locking his arms beneath her ass and lifting her. She wrapped her legs around his waist and he almost lost his balance before coming to lean against one of the stainless steel countertops in the Winfield kitchen. They were both laughing, and he savored the moment. Their shared mirth. The sound of her completely free laughter. It was intoxicating. He wanted to bottle that sound and then figure out all the ways to make her do it over and over again.

Another thought suddenly intruded into his thoughts. "There's no one else here, is there?" he asked.

"Nope, just you and I."

"Really? They actually left you entirely alone in this huge place?" He couldn't decide if he was relieved to hear that there was no chance that they'd be interrupted or aghast to realize that she had truly been here all by herself for god knows how long.

"I mean, I'm a grown-up, Alex. They're not worried I'm going to burn down the embassy or something."

"No, I just meant... I worry about you being here all alone."

She smiled at him. "Really yesterday and today are the only days I've actually been alone. It's been a skeleton crew for sure, and the chefs haven't been here since the Stewarts left a few days ago, but at least a few folks have been coming in to work at least part time every day until Christmas Eve. And there are security guards who make rounds outside periodically."

He relaxed slightly. "Good." He looked past her towards the door that led to her rooms. "Shall we take this somewhere more comfortable?"

"Oh! Yes, of course, sorry!" Maddy said, adorably flustered. "I should have invited you past the kitchen ages ago." She turned towards the stairs, then stopped. "Are you hungry? The cooks did leave some—"

"Maddy, I ate enough to last me three days like two hours ago. There's only one thing I'm hungry for right now and it's. not. food." He punctuated the last three words with kisses as he herded her gently towards the stairs. She smiled up at him with a sassy glint in her eyes.

"Well, I wouldn't want you to go hungry." She took his hand and led him through the door and down the stairs to her sitting room. When they got to the bottom, she turned and pinned him to the wall, leaning against him on tiptoe, kissing him as if she was dying of thirst and the only way to quench it was his mouth. Not that he was complaining. Without breaking their kiss, she unzipped his leather jacket and pushed it from his shoulders onto the floor.

She ran her hands down his chest before pulling back, a puzzled look on her face, to look at what she was feeling beneath her hands. He groaned, realizing that in his urgency to leave Sandringham and get to her, he hadn't changed his clothes. When he managed to force himself to open his eyes, she was giving him a quizzical look. "Sooo, after church on Christmas we have this tradition of an ugly sweater lunch..."

Maddy burst out laughing. And, to be fair, Alex couldn't blame her. He'd outdone himself that year, finding a chartreuse crewneck sweater festooned with green and gold tinsel, miniature globe ornaments, and a huge applique rendering of the abominable snowman, complete with large googly eyes. Realizing that he looked utterly ridiculous, Alex pushed off from the wall, held his arms out, and did a little spin. "That's it, drink it in," he said, smiling at her, enjoying her reaction, even if it was at his expense.

"That is truly hideous," she said, finally stopping laughing for long enough to gasp for air. "And I think I only have one choice," she said, mock regret filling her voice. "I'm going to have to take it off of you."

He heaved a fake sigh. "Well, I suppose, if you must, you must."

She approached him and gingerly removed the offensive garment, being careful not to scratch him with any of the many absurd ornaments that dangled from it. When she'd safely gotten it over his head and tossed it on top of his abandoned jacket, her eyes went dark with desire and immediately went after the tight white undershirt he had on underneath. "I mean, while I'm at it, I might as well," she said, pulling at it until they managed to work together to get it off.

He tried not to preen as he enjoyed the way she was ogling his chest. Lots of women had looked at him that way, their eyes full of desire, over the years. But nothing compared to the way it made him feel when Maddy looked at him like that. As if she was unwrapping the best present she'd ever received and it was something delicious to eat. She ran her hands up his bare chest, the combination of the slight chill in the air and her fingernails causing his nipples to jump to attention. Her warm breath felt incredible as she drew nearer, pressing almost timid kisses up his sternum toward his throat. She started pushing him gently toward the couch and, when his calves found it, he sat, pulling her down to straddle his thighs.

Their mouths met in a searing kiss and he moaned as she ground her hips against the rapidly growing bulge in his jeans. He ran his hands under her sweatshirt and almost lost control when he realized she was completely naked underneath. He reached one hand around her lower back to anchor her to his lap while the other slid up to cup her breast, his thumb brushing over her nipple. They kept going until Alex wasn't sure he could take it anymore. "Upstairs," he finally said, his voice dark, sultry, demanding. "I want you naked in that bed before I get there." Her cheeks flushed with arousal as she almost tripped over her own feet in an effort to do his bidding.

* * *

When Maddy reached her lofted bedroom, she frantically tore off her clothes, dumping them on the far side of the bed in an attempt to make things look neat. She clicked on the bedside lamp, pulled back the covers, and slid under, her skin hot and tingly against the cool sheets. She'd been blindsided by the force of her emotional response to their first time being intimate. She supposed she shouldn't have been. It wasn't a small thing to be intimate for the first time since the death of your husband. Especially when that husband was the only person you'd ever been with. And yet she still hadn't expected it. Even though it had been somewhat embarrassing to totally lose it in that context, the emotional release had also been cathartic. She certainly hadn't gotten over what had happened to Evan, would probably never really get over it. But allowing herself to really engage with the gnarled mess of conflicting emotions she had about their relationship, even the ugly ones—especially the ugly ones—and having Alex validate them. Having him hold her and comfort her. That had been healing. It felt productive when she looked back. She'd held so much in for so long, that she supposed there needed to be some ugly catharsis before real progress could be made. She made a mental note to add that to the list of things to discuss with her new therapist in the New Year. She obviously still had work to do, but now, as she laid there, her body nearly vibrating with need for Alex, she knew that she was on the right track.

She was practically humming with arousal and didn't

think it was possible for her to be more turned on, but somehow her desire grew more intense as she heard him climbing the stairs, his steps heavy and intentional.

When Alex ducked behind the curtain that separated her bedroom from the steps, his eyes were dark with want. He stalked to the bed like a predator contemplating his prey and, without a word, whipped back the covers to reveal her naked body.

Alex put one knee on the side of the bed, his dark gaze drinking her in. Maddy felt like she was going to combust. She tried to be still, tried not to fidget, fought against the urge to cover herself.

Leaning over her, he grazed a hand from the curve of her hip up to tease her breast briefly before cupping the back of her neck and taking her mouth with a groan. She moaned into his mouth, running one hand up the close-cropped hair along the back of his head, enjoying the slightly prickly sensation against her overheated skin. Her other hand snaked down his spine before grabbing his ass and squeezing.

Alex kissed his way sloppily down her neck before turning his attention to her breasts, laving one nipple with his tongue while he plucked at the other with his fingers. "Alex," she breathed, her head falling back on the pillow, running her hands through his hair as she writhed beneath him. He took his time in a way that Maddy had never experienced. Every time she thought she couldn't get more turned on, he did something new— tugging on her earlobe with his teeth, pinching her nipple just hard enough to hurt in a way she never could have imagined would be pleasurable, running his tongue up the underside of her breast along a pathway that seemed to have a direct line to her pussy.

When she couldn't take it anymore, one of her hands snaked past him, seeking to take the edge off, but he grabbed it and pinned it above the pillow next to the headboard. She soon found her other hand there too, both wrists clasped in one of his hands in a way that wasn't painful but made his intention clear. "Is this okay?" he asked, taking a break from the exquisite torture he was carrying out on her breasts to look up at her, searchingly.

"Oh god, yes," she gasped, her hips writhing, seeking friction. He smiled, devilishly, shifting her wrists to his other hand. She felt his fingers running sensuously down her side, before two fingers pushed into her dripping pussy, just for a moment, before spreading her open, massaging, rubbing rhythmically up and down on either side of her clit. "Alex," she groaned, her eyes rolling back in her head. "Just like that... Fuck, yes."

He smiled seductively and pressed her hands against the underside of the headboard. "Grab this and don't let go." She did what he asked and was rewarded with a husky "Good girl," which was somehow so sexy that she thought his words alone might push her over the edge.

Alex made his way back down her body, stopping to press kisses along the way—the side of her neck, her sternum, one hip, the crease at the top of her thigh—before settling between her legs. "God, Maddy, you're soaked. You're so ready for me, aren't you?"

"Yes, fuck, Alex, please!"

"Yes, that's it. I love hearing you scream my name," he said, looking up at her with hooded eyes, his pupils blown wide with desire.

And then—*finally!* —his lips were there. At first, just featherlight kisses up and down her sex, but then his tongue was dipping into her, spreading her wetness up and around, his hands pushing her legs even wider, thumbs massaging her inner thighs.

"Alex, I'm close, I'm so close," she panted.

"Good. Come for me, Maddy."

"No," she choked out. His head stilled immediately, and his eyes flew to hers. "I want to come on your cock this time."

He pushed up onto one elbow. "You're sure?"

"Absolutely." She knew this was a big step, and this time, she was ready. She didn't think she was going to cry again, but she was prepared, and more importantly, she knew that she was safe with Alex. That he was a safe place for her emotions to let loose. It was one of those moments where, without being able to pinpoint the reason, she was confident, self-assured even. She looked straight in his eyes to show him how ready she was. "There are condoms in the bottom drawer," she said, indicating the nightstand. "And"—she wavered momentarily before fighting past the awkwardness—"I have my test results downstairs if you want to see them."

"I trust you. I have mine on my phone, too," he said, "but Maddy, I need you to know that we don't have to do this. I can wait until you're ready. There are plenty of other—"

"I appreciate that so much," she interrupted, leveling him with a serious look. "Truly, I do. But if you don't suit up and put it in, I'm going to have to take matters into my own hands."

Alex snorted, shaking his head. "The mouth on this one," he said, almost to himself, as he pushed himself to standing and unfastened his pants. When he looked at her again, his eyes were full of lust and something that almost looked like awe. His gaze never left hers, even as he tore open the packet and slid the latex up his impressively erect cock.

He eased back onto the bed, lying next to her, one finger teasing at her entrance, holding her on the edge of pleasure. He looked at her, his pupils flared with desire. "Get your favorite toy."

"My... I don't... How did you... We don't have to..." she sputtered.

"Maddy," he said, looking at her knowingly. "You're a

twenty-first-century woman who's been without a partner for quite a while. I'd be shocked if you didn't have one, and I want to make this good for you. *So* good. Why would I set myself up for anything less than smashing success when I know there's a battery-powered accomplice somewhere in this room that could make it that much better for you?" He added, "When it's better for you, it's better for me. If it's too awkward, you can tell me and we'll ditch it." She finally nodded and was rewarded with an approving "That's my girl," as she pushed back towards the head of the bed, opening the top drawer of her nightstand and withdrawing an oblong purple silicon toy.

"Show me how you use it," he said, his eyes never leaving her.

"Alex," she started, blushing.

"Please, darling. I want to see what you do when you're here alone."

She was so turned on that she quickly overcame her shyness, pushing a button and filling the small space with the sound of vibration. She eased the toy down her pelvis, running the side of it next to her clit, alternating between sides, getting closer and closer. Through half-closed eyes she could see him watching her intently, his hand running up and down his sheathed cock gently. After a moment, he put his hand over hers and said, "May I?" his voice deep and raspy.

She nodded. "Alex, I need you."

"Shhh, I know, darling, I know," he said, taking the toy from her and kneeling between her legs. He ran it around her mound, looking at her, something akin to reverence on his face, as he eased a finger into her, and then another.

"Maddy, fuck," he bit out, "you're so wet, so tight."

"Alex, I swear to god, if you don't stop torturing me and put it in—" He huffed out a laugh and withdrew his fingers, never breaking eye contact as he sucked them clean. He set the toy on the mattress next to her hip. The sound of the vibrations against the firm surface of her bed felt deafening. But in the next moment, she couldn't think straight as he positioned himself at her opening and started to gently ease into her. Reaching for the toy again, he returned to his slow torment, moving close enough to her clit to drive her wild with pleasure, but not close enough to send her over the edge. And then he kept doing it, again and again.

Maddy felt her eyes rolling back in her head. The exquisite stretch as he entered her coupled with the skillful way he kept her just on the brink of pleasure with her vibrator was masterful. It was her first time using a toy with a partner and she was stunned by how different it felt, ceding that control to someone else. Nothing about the toy itself had changed, but when Alex controlled the way it was deployed, it was an entirely new experience.

"Maddy, god, you feel so good." He was finally fully in, his eyes closed momentarily, clearly trying to maintain control. His eyes found hers. "Are you okay?"

"Alex," she begged. "Please, I need more."

And with that, he finally started moving. Slowly, at first, and then faster, at her urging, her fingernails gripping at his ass. She was completely overwhelmed by sensations. The steady vibration of the toy, the unfamiliar fullness, the intense intimacy of their steady eye contact. After the emotions of their first time together and the way she'd struggled to get out of her head, Maddy had been slightly concerned that when they were together again the same thing might happen. Alex shifted slightly on his knees, using his free arm to bring her hips closer and simultaneously finding a new, deeper place inside her.

"Yes... ohhh... Alex!" she panted, chasing her orgasm.

After a few moments he passed her the toy so that he could lean forward, bracing himself with one hand on the mattress next to her head and the other on the headboard behind her. The new angle and his closeness only served to heighten both the emotional closeness and the physical sensations. She held the vibrator to her clit, grinding into him. "Not yet, Mads," he said, even as she could tell by the way his eyes were losing focus that he was close too. "Don't end this too quickly."

She eased her hand back slightly, unquestioningly. She didn't want it to end either. He slowed his strokes slightly and smiled down at her. "Christ, you feel amazing, so hot and wet for me," he rasped, leaning down to kiss her.

"Alex," she moaned, as he moved to pull one of her legs up over his hip. "I can't hold on much longer."

"Maddy," he bit out, his grasp on control clearly fraying by the moment. His hips were pumping furiously, the gentleness gone, and instinct taking over.

"Fuck, yes, Alex!" she called as she went flying over the precipice, her body clamping down on him, riding her orgasm as it went on and on. She felt him let go as well, still pumping into her, chanting almost unintelligibly as she rode out what had to be the longest orgasm she'd ever had.

When it finally ended, he collapsed on her, pulling the vibrator from between them and tossing it to the other side of the mattress after turning it off.

They lay there, panting, for a moment, before he gingerly eased out of her and rolled to the side. "Oh my god," he gasped. "I think I'm dead. You killed me."

She chuckled, catching her breath. "I should probably get dressed then if Interpol is about to show up."

He grabbed her and cuddled her against him, reaching down to pull the sheet up to cover them. "Don't you dare, you absolute vixen." He kissed the top of her head. "That was unreal."

"It was," she said, slowly running her finger up and down

his chest. "I..." She trailed off. "It was," she said again, her voice slightly thick but steady. He just held her closer, tighter.

"You are remarkable," he said, squeezing her closer and kissing her again. "So brave," he said, trailing his fingers up and down her arm, "and fierce... beautiful... sexy... perfect."

She pushed up on one elbow to look him in the face, her eyes shining with tears, but a smile spreading across her face. "Thank you." She took a breath.

He pulled her down to kiss her and then tucked her head against his chest, under his chin again. "Happy Christmas, Maddy."

Chapter 17

After a few minutes of post-coital cuddling, Alex slipped out of bed, tied off the condom, and wrapped it in a tissue before putting it in her bedroom trash and starting to collect his clothes. He turned back to where she was still splayed across the bed, her hair fanned across the pillow, her cheeks still flushed from their exertions. "I was thinking," he started slowly, "maybe you might like to come spend a few days at my place? We can hunker down with movies and take Bertie on walks and, y'know... just hang out?" He was starting to sound desperate and a little pathetic. "I mean, if you want."

She blushed and smiled up at him, "Of course I want to. That sounds great. Nobody will really be back here to wonder where I've gotten off to until after New Year's either."

He was irrationally excited to hear her agree to the plan he'd been rehearsing in his head the entire two-hour drive back from Sandringham. "Excellent. Want to pack a few things? I plan on keeping you mostly naked, but if we want to go on a walk or something, I suppose pants might be in order."

She giggled and stretched. "Yes, I don't think I want to find out what frostbitten lady bits feel like." Pushing herself to sit, she suddenly became concerned. "Wait, where *is* Bertie?"

"In the car," Alex replied.

"In the *car*?" she shrieked.

"He's fine," Alex reassured her. "I gave him a bone big enough to keep him happy for at least two rounds."

She laughed and started opening drawers to pull out clothes. "Well if he can wait another ten minutes, I could really use a shower…" she said ruefully. "I kind of can't believe I let you get that close to me like this."

Alex came up behind her and wrapped his arms around her torso, clad only in a bra, kissing along her neck. "I was too busy thinking about all the ways I wanted to defile you to even notice." He paused. "And if you can stand it for just a few more minutes, you could shower at my place?" He couldn't understand why asking her things like this made him feel nervous and vulnerable. That was totally not his way with women—he was assertive, a little dominant even, and always had a clear plan. But for some reason with Maddy he found that, outside of the act itself, he felt less sure. He tried not to think about the fact that it might be because he cared a hell of a lot more for Maddy than he had for any other woman he'd ever been with and forced himself back into the moment. Those thoughts were decidedly *non*-casual. He leaned down, getting his mouth right up next to her ear, even though they were completely alone. "I've seen your shower. It's tiny. If we go to my place maybe I can help you wash your back," he said in a husky voice.

He swore he could feel her heart racing in her chest as he heard the slight intake of air, and her breathy "I think I can wait a few more minutes."

"Excellent," he said, reluctantly dragging himself away

from her before he gave up and threw her back into bed. It was true that Bertie would wait up to a certain point, but if they actually went in for round two he'd have real reason to worry about the interior of his car. "Grab what you need for a few days, and I'll meet you down there," he said, indicating the absurd conversion of a sitting room the embassy had put her in—really, they couldn't find an actual suite of legitimate rooms for her?

"Oh, and one more thing," he added, looking over his shoulder as he headed for the stairs. "Bring the toy." He watched her cheeks flush and her pupils dilate as he winked at her and started back towards where they'd left his shirt.

Her cheeks flushed, but she looked up at him with evident desire in her eyes. "Okay, just give me a few minutes."

He wandered around her sitting room. It was the first time he'd been alone in her space for any real length of time and he suddenly was noticing that there were essentially no personal touches. No photos, no tchotchkes, nothing that reflected the warm, thoughtful, caring person who lived there. Before he could let his brain go too far down that path, he heard her clattering back down the stairs, a canvas duffel bag thrown over her shoulder, the sleeve of a sweater sticking out. She'd changed into an oversized striped turtleneck sweater and another pair of those irresistible black leggings that made her ass look fantastic and turned Alex's brain into a horny cauldron of goo. She darted into the bathroom to grab a few more things and emerged seconds later, zipping the duffel as she grabbed her coat from the rack at the foot of the staircase into the main house. Alex took the bag from her so she could slip into the knee-length sky-blue coat and pull a white knit hat topped with a fur pom-pom on it over her hair, which he noticed she'd wrangled into a slightly less messy bun when she changed. Pointedly ignoring her attempts to take the bag back from him, he ushered her up the steps and out to where he'd left his car by the kitchen entrance to Winfield House.

When they walked out, Maddy seemed surprised to see his black Audi e-tron GT, with Bertie peering out the back window. "Where's Graham?" she asked, the surprise evident in her voice.

"Home, with his family," he said, as if that should have been obvious. "The man's not a serf. He's allowed to take holidays off." He opened the passenger door for her and waited as she settled herself in the cognac leather seats before closing the door and jogging around to the driver's side. He leaned in to toss her bag into the backseat next to where Bertie's leash tethered him, before settling himself in the driver's seat. "I use a driver when I'm going to official events or when I want to be able to do other things on the way." He smirked thinking of their trip to Windsor. "But I *am* allowed to drive myself."

"Wow, this thing is silent," Maddy marveled as she took in the luxurious surroundings.

"Fully electric," he said by way of explanation as he pulled out into the mostly empty streets of Marylebone. "It's the way of the future."

She smiled over at him. "I still just can't believe you're here! Are you sure your family isn't upset?"

"Mads, I want to be here with you." He was afraid to admit how much. "And really, one less person taxing the aging infrastructure of that place is a blessing to everyone else." He reached over and took her hand, bringing it to his lips before settling it on his thigh as he navigated the route back to Kensington. The ride, which sometimes took as much as half an hour in London traffic, barely took half that, and before long they were pulling into the security gate. Alex waved at the guard on duty and noticed that Maddy ducked her head to avoid her face being seen as they drove past.

He begrudgingly allowed Maddy to carry her bag as he

managed his own small suitcase and the exuberant corgi on his leash. He unlocked the door and pushed it open to let Maddy go ahead of him. As she slipped out of her sneakers, he placed his suitcase just inside the door. "I need to let this maniac go do his business," he said as Bertie hopped and danced on the end of the lead. "Why don't you"—he leaned closer to place a kiss on the side of her face—"make yourself comfortable"—another kiss, this one on the tender underside of her jaw—"maybe hop in the shower"—a nip at her earlobe—"and I'll be in in just a moment."

He felt rather than saw her shiver and she said, "Okay. But don't be long."

He finally kissed her lips and then had to drag himself away before Bertie dislocated his arm. "Two minutes. Tops," he promised as he pulled the door closed behind him and followed Bertie towards his favorite tree.

"Ok, mate," he said to the dog, "we need to do this and get it done. And then you're going to be a good dog and go to sleep. In the study. In your bed. Not in mine. Got it?" He hoped his voice didn't sound quite as desperate out loud as he thought it did. *You're talking to a dog*, he chided himself. He had to have been imagining it, but he swore when he looked down, Bertie was giving him a look that said the exact same thing.

He bounced up and down on the balls of his feet as he waited for Bertie to do his business, imagining Maddy in his house, undressing in his bathroom, standing there naked as she waited for the water to heat up. He pictured the way her chocolate-brown hair would cascade down her naked back as she released it from the tie—how was a woman's naked back so damned sexy? —the perfect curve of her ass—and *fuck*, the things he wanted to do to that ass—as she stepped into the shower, and the way her smooth skin would feel with the water streaming down.

Despite the frigid temperatures he found his cock starting to stiffen as his mind wandered, and he turned his attention back to Bertie impatiently. "Are you done yet? Come on, mate!" The dog yipped back, as if in agreement, and they walked briskly back to Alex's apartments, where he rushed through the process of settling his canine companion as quickly as possible before racing to his bedroom and shutting the door firmly behind him.

He heard the shower running and could see steam starting to fill the en suite through the partially open door. He ripped his clothes off in a manner that he hoped was closer to Superman in a telephone booth than flailing muppet, but frankly it didn't matter that much. All that mattered was that clothes were the only things standing between him and Maddy's luscious, wet body in his shower.

He slowly opened the door, stopping for a moment to admire the sight before him. It was much as he'd imagined it: Maddy, her back to him, standing under the showerhead of his large shower. He wasn't entirely sure she'd heard him come in, so he wracked his brain for some even remotely sexy way to let her know he was there without startling her. He finally landed on striding over to the shower and knocking lightly on the glass door before opening it. She turned to him, her eyelashes catching water droplets as she took in the full view of his naked form. "Hi," he said, stepping in and joining her under the generous streams of water pouring from the twin shower heads.

"Fancy meeting you here," she said, giving him a sassy smile.

He slid his hands down her sides, coming to rest on the curves of her hips, relishing the slick feeling of her smooth skin. Her hands slid up his chest, coming to rest briefly on his shoulders, before moving to the back of his neck to pull him down to kiss her. He sank into their kiss, drawing her closer and wrapping one of his hands around the base of her skull, lacing his fingers into her wet hair. Even though it had been barely an hour since he'd been inside her, his cock was starting to harden again.

Apparently Maddy was having similar thoughts, as one of her hands snaked down between them to take him in her hand, stroking gently but firmly as she moaned into his mouth. One hand still cradling her head, he used his free hand to cup one of her breasts, teasing her nipple into a stiff peak with his thumb. After several minutes she broke their kiss, glancing around the shower briefly before adjusting one of the showerheads to point toward the tiled bench and pushing him in that direction.

If possible, his cock got even harder as her intentions became clear. As he sat on the bench, she followed him, straddling his thighs and undulating her hips against his erection. If they hadn't just had sex he would be coming all over her right now, because *Christ* was she sexy. Based on her slightly submissive nature the previous times they'd been intimate, he was surprised and incredibly turned on by the way she was taking charge, and he leaned back, holding her lightly by her hips, and let her have her way with him.

Minutes passed, filled with unhurried kisses before she slid away from him, dropping to her knees on the tiled floor. She adjusted her grip on his length and looked up at him, a sexy question in her eyes. "May I?" she asked over the steady rainfall of the shower.

"Fuck, yes, Mads," he groaned out, his head hitting the tiled wall behind him as she immediately extended her tongue to lick him root to tip, swirling around the head of his cock before starting over on the other side. He hissed as she gently cupped his balls, fondling him as she set to working over his rock-hard length. The way her mouth felt around him was unreal. If he was objective about it, she wasn't doing anything he hadn't experienced before. But the fact that it was Maddy and that he could sort of tell by the way her grip was slightly too tight that she hadn't done this for anyone in quite a while somehow made it ten times sexier. One of his hands slid into her hair, just behind her ear as used the other to brace himself on the bench, slightly worried that if he got too enthusiastic he could slip right off. His hips were bucking slightly as he moved closer to losing control and he tried valiantly to hold himself back, not to push too far or cause her to slip. But she just kept going, bobbing up and down on his cock, making sexy little sounds that he could just barely hear over the sounds of the rushing water and his own barely coherent moans mixed with praise.

"Fuck, you're so good, Maddy. So fucking good." She hummed around him and he almost lost control, the sounds, the sensations, all of it was overwhelming. "Oh god," he bit out. "Mads, I'm close. I'm so close." She looked up at him, her brown eyes smoldering as she smiled around him and redoubled her efforts. She reached beyond his balls to put exquisite pressure just behind them and moaned as he came in her mouth, swallowing until she'd taken everything he gave her. He twitched when her tongue traced the sensitive seam on the underside of his cock as she slowly released him from her mouth and sat back, wiping her mouth with the back of her hand and looking up at him.

"Jesus Christ, woman," he said, running a hand down his face as she got to her feet, smiling at him with shy satisfaction.

"Was that okay for you?" she asked, a hint of self-consciousness overtaking the woman who had just blown him out of the water... literally.

"Okay?" he asked, incredulously. "That was... a far cry better than okay, you absolute sex monster. Here I was figuring we'd conserve water by sharing a nice innocent shower before going to bed and getting our rest, and there you go absolutely blowing my mind." Finally feeling like his legs might hold him, he stood and joined her under the main showerhead, adjusting the second one on his way so that they were getting the warmth from both. He leaned down and kissed her gently. "That was incredibly sexy," he said, touching his lips to the sensitive spot behind her ear. "Thank you."

"My pleasure," she said, blushing slightly.

He reached past her to pump some shampoo into his hand and, drawing her slightly out of the stream of warm water, began massaging it into her hair. She sighed contentedly as he worked the lather down to her scalp, paying special attention to the base of her head where he'd learned she held most of her tension. She closed her eyes and let her head fall back as he kept working, probably longer than one really needed to wash someone's hair, but she was so clearly enjoying his ministrations that he couldn't bring himself to stop. After a few more moments he gently edged her back towards the spray and started to rinse the lather from her hair, realizing that he thoroughly enjoyed knowing that she'd smell like his shampoo until the next time she washed her hair.

Maddy reached past him and grabbed a washcloth from the shelf and, after applying soap to it, started to gently wash his chest, making sudsy circles across his pecs and then down his flanks. She was almost tender in her attentions, and as his head fell back, enjoying the soothing sensations, tried not to imagine this becoming his new normal. He felt his dick quiver as she drew the washcloth up between his asscheeks, and continued her soapy and thorough exploration of his body.

When she finished he felt her lean her wet forehead against his upper back, putting her arms loosely around his waist. He turned in her embrace to kiss her before taking the washcloth from her and returning the favor. He wanted to memorize every inch of her body, from the modest swell of her breasts topped with rosy pebbled nipples to the curve of her hips to the tiny mole at the corner of the crease between her butt and her thighs. When he finished he stood behind her, his front to her back, kissing her neck languidly. She moaned sweetly for him, and he nudged her slightly forward, angling her so that when he used his right hand to splay the lips of her sex, the stream of water fell directly on her clit. He watched for her reaction, noticing that even as her eyes flew open in surprise, her lips parted in obvious arousal. "Yeah?" he rumbled in her ear, as he used his free hand to anchor her left hip to him.

"Uh-huh," she whimpered, her breaths coming in short pants already. "Oh my god, *Alex*!" Her hands were raking up and down his thighs, desire carrying her higher and higher.

"I've got you," he said, "Just relax. Let me take care of you."

Her head fell back onto his shoulder, her hips writhing. He moved his right hand to reach up and pull down the removable showerhead, bringing his left hand around to hold her open as he aimed the stream of water at her pussy, making gentle circles, careful to keep it far enough away that the pressure wasn't too intense. She keened, still clawing at his legs as he sensed her impending climax. "That's it, that's my good girl. Here, hold yourself open for me." When she did what he asked, he reached down to thrust two fingers into her, continuing his assault by showerhead. "You are so fucking hot," he growled into her ear. "So wet and needy for me." He felt her core beginning to tighten around his fingers, still plunging rhythmically into her center. "You're going to come so hard for me, aren't you, Mads? Come on, give it to me." When she came it was fast and hard, her cries echoing throughout the tiled room. He moved the showerhead away, not wanting to overstimulate her, but continuing to pump his fingers slowly in and out as she came down from her second orgasm of the evening.

She slumped against him, out of breath, and he reached

past her to turn off the water, before sliding one arm out the glass door to grab two towels from the ledge just outside. After wrapping one around his waist, he cocooned her in the other, kissing her gently and murmuring sexy nothings in her ear as he swiftly bundled them out of the shower and towards his waiting bed.

Chapter 18

The next several days passed much as Alex had planned them—cozy snuggle sessions watching movies in front of the fire in Alex's sitting room, brisk walks through Kensington's private gardens with Bertie, and a healthy dose of time spent naked, giving and receiving orgasms on almost every surface of Alex's apartment.

By the morning of December thirty-first, Maddy was starting to feel uneasy about the whole situation, though. It wasn't that she wasn't comfortable around Alex or spending time at his place. Quite the opposite, actually. She had settled into their casual inter-holiday domestic bubble with startling ease. Even after living with Evan for four years, she wasn't sure they had ever co-existed as seamlessly as she and Alex did after just a few days. Alex wasn't exactly what she'd describe as "useful" in the kitchen, but rather than being underfoot as she whipped up easy meals to sustain them between bouts of sex, they had perfected an easy dance of sorts with her taking the lead and him accomplishing the easy tasks she assigned him in perfect sync. To be fair, Alex's kitchen at Kensington was about twice the size of the largest kitchen she and Evan had ever shared. They even worked out well together in his small home gym—him taking enthusiastic Peloton rides and her jogging on the treadmill while giving him a hard time about his faddish exercise routine during her walking recoveries. And him spotting her while she lifted weights had only turned into sex once...or was it twice?

All in all, it had been a blissful week. So as she woke and stretched on the morning that would be her last time waking up at Kensington before returning to Winfield House, she was confused as to why she was feeling antsy, her stomach twisted up in knots. Quietly slipping out of the bed so as not to wake Alex, who was adorable in sleep, one arm thrown over his head, the other reaching across where he'd been holding her, Maddy crept into the bathroom and turned on the shower, hoping the hot water would wash away her feeling of unease.

As she shampooed her hair, she tried to pick apart her feelings. The week had been lovely. Alex was caring and attentive, an adorable dog dad to Bertie, and practically insatiable in bed. She was more relaxed than she'd been in... well... since long before her world had turned upside down. Spending time with Alex was easy, uncomplicated. She could imagine doing this for a lot longer than five days.

And there it was.

This was supposed to be casual. It wasn't supposed to be a real relationship. She'd submitted her graduate school applications just before the holiday rush began. She'd start hearing back in just a few months. Alex hadn't said anything about his plans after the wedding, but, as far she could tell, he still didn't really have a plan for how he would find his place in the royal family post-wedding, particularly since as soon as Ben and Hannah started having children, Alex would be pushed further and further down the line of succession. For all she knew he could be planning to go back to New Zealand as soon as the wedding festivities ended.

So in terms of talking about plans, the future, their feelings they'd certainly been keeping things casual. But playing house wasn't casual behavior, even if it was a totally unrealistic end-of-the-year liminal space where time didn't matter and the real world and responsibilities didn't exist. And she found herself enjoying this stint of cohabitation more than she should have. It was easy. Too easy.

Evan and Maddy had cohabitated perfectly naturally – after a lifetime of friendship, it was easy. They'd gone to work, had dinner together, sat on the couch after dinner while she read a book and he played video games or watched football. On weekends they'd each take care of their respective chores, go to gatherings with their friends where the men would circle around the grill or the TV, depending on the season, while the women chatted in the kitchen, picking at cheese and crackers and drinking wine or hard seltzers. They'd enjoyed each other's company and wanted the best for each other, but their relationship hadn't been one of passionate love. It had been easy friendship and companionship. They'd gotten along just fine, but their lives existed in parallel, not in sync.

And with Alex, everything synced almost immediately. Even when they were curled up on his couch each on their phones or reading, Maddy felt deeply connected to Alex after just a few weeks. Things had clicked into place and seemed so effortlessly *right*. And suddenly Maddy was scared that that was wrong. This was getting too serious, too quickly. If they kept it up like this, they were sure to be discovered by the press. And one of them was going to get hurt when she left. Because eventually she'd have to. Coming to London wasn't a long-term plan. It never had been. It was an "escape the prying eyes of the American media" plan, get a change of scenery plan, a "take time to figure out who Maddy 2.0 is" plan. Even if she didn't get into grad school and decided to stay in England, the very nature of diplomatic work meant that the ambassador's job was only slightly less term-limited than the president's. Sure, it would probably take whoever the new president was some time to figure out who he wanted to represent him at the Court of St. James, but this position was far too visible and important. Even if it was another Democrat, there was almost no chance that Andrew Stewart would be able to stay on past the end of the administration. And since Maddy's job had been obtained with far less than the normal amounts of rigor and due diligence, there was pretty much no chance she'd be able to keep hers either.

As grateful as she was for the opportunity to get away, she also knew that London wasn't her forever home. And she knew that no matter what kinds of feelings he might have for her, there was no way that Alex could make a forever home anywhere else.

No, whatever their relationship was, they had to do a better job of keeping it casual. Even as she came to that conclusion with confidence, Maddy's heart sank. The idea of going back to her drafty Frankensteined rooms at Winfield House, to being half embassy staff and half Delia Stewart's gofer filled her with dread. The idea of waking up without Alex's long arms wrapped around her in a protective cocoon made her miserable. And that was exactly why she had to do it. She had to go back to her regular life. She had to remind herself why she was in London in the first place. And she needed to get some distance. If she didn't it would spell heartbreak for both of them.

She turned off the water and wrapped herself in a towel before heading back into Alex's bedroom. He stirred as she entered. "Good morning," he murmured sleepily.

"Morning," she replied quietly, locating the leggings he'd peeled off of her the night before bending her over the side of the bed and fucking her so hard she thought she was going to pass out from pleasure. She pulled a Breton-striped sweater over her head, trying to avoid looking at him.

"Why don't you come back to bed?" he said, his voice husky with sleep and desire.

"I need to pull my stuff together," she said, still not making eye contact. "I have to get back to Winfield today before people start to notice I'm not there. If the Stewarts get back and find out I've been away for so long, they'll definitely ask questions."

"I thought their flight didn't get in until tonight?" Alex asked, sitting up in bed and rubbing the sleep from his eyes, looking over at her with a frown.

"They don't, but my stuff is everywhere. It's going to take me a while to corral everything." Maddy turned her attention to her assorted belongings, which had somehow managed to end up strewn not only all across Alex's bedroom, but also all over the apartment.

As she walked toward the window seat to collect a sweater and a book she'd been reading, she heard Alex padding across the sumptuous carpet towards her. She stilled as his arms slid around her from behind. "Why are you freaking out?" he asked quietly, pressing a soft kiss to the side of her head.

"I'm not freaking out, who said I was freaking out?" Maddy said, the words coming out too quickly, her voice clearly belying every word she uttered.

"You haven't looked at me once since you got out of the shower and you're packing a bag before you've even had coffee." Alex said, stating the obvious in a remarkably calm voice. "Tell me what's going through that brilliant brain of yours."

Maddy sighed. As much as she might want to, she couldn't just race out of Kensington without talking to him. She wasn't an impetuous, immature teenager, and he wasn't stupid. "We said this was going to be casual," she said, turning to sit on the padded window seat and finally looking up at him. "Casual isn't shacking up for five days playing house. What were we thinking?"

He dropped down next to her. "I was thinking," he began, "that it would be much easier to keep you high on a steady dose of orgasms if we were here." He pressed another kiss to the spot where her shoulder and her neck met. "But you're right. This doesn't exactly scream casual relationship, does it?"

"It doesn't. The fact that the entire city is tucked away watching Christmas specials and getting tipsy on fruit cake has meant that we've been safe here, but in two days the world will reawaken and we're going to have to go back to pretending that this isn't a thing."

"Are you sure?" he wheedled like a little boy.

"Alex."

"Yeah, okay, I know," he said, hanging his head. "You're right. We agreed that this was casual." He sighed heavily. "But I can still take you on secret dates, right? I was hoping next month maybe I could sneak you up to Scotland for a long weekend?"

Her resolve softened a little bit, seeing the eagerness in his eyes, remembering the seriousness with which he took his mission to take care of her—in every sense of the word. "Of course," she said. "But the sleepovers can't keep happening. That's a recipe for being caught."

"Right, okay," he agreed.

"And Alex..." Her voice trailed off. "Are you sure this is a good idea? I obviously love spending time with you. This week has been a dream." She swallowed, melancholy washing over her in waves. "But you have to know that this can't really go anywhere. What are you going to do once the wedding is over? Are you even staying?"

"I... don't know." Alex's voice was heavy. "Part of me would love to run away back to Christchurch. Life there was easy. Or, at least, easier. But I hated being so far from my family. If I know Ben and Hannah they're going to start popping out kids about forty-two weeks after the wedding. I don't want to miss that. I don't want to be the odd uncle who lives half a world away and only shows up on a computer screen. My parents aren't getting any younger. They could use help spreading out the royal duties. But it's as if they still see me as this little boy who couldn't even recite his one line in the coronation, who needs to be shielded."

There was a long pause. "Maybe if I had a cause, had an obvious role to step up into, it would be different. But until I can find that, I feel like I'll just be stuck on the sidelines. So that's a long way of saying that I have no idea what I'm going to do after the wedding, Mads. And you're absolutely right that what we've been doing the last few glorious days isn't going to fly in the New Year. But right now as I see it I've got two jobs: one is being Ben's best man, and the other is taking care of you however you'll let me, even if I have to fight you for it. We can keep it casual, we can be discreet. I just..." He searched for the right words. "I want you to know what it feels like when someone puts you first." He swallowed. "I've been at sea since I've been back, drifting, purposeless... and since we met, I feel like I have a purpose again. To be yours. You were so unhappy for so long. You put everyone else first all the time. You still do. I want to be the one who shows you what it feels like to be someone's number one priority. Please, can we keep trying this?"

Maddy's heart had been steadily melting and breaking as he spoke. He'd told her about his childhood early on when they'd started spending time together, of course, and he'd made the occasional passing comment that showed her how unmoored he felt. Even though he was excited about the reparations project he and Eric were working on, he was careful to specify that it was Eric's project. He was just there to support it. She hadn't fully realized how directionless he was. When he talked like this, he got a lost look in his eyes that made Maddy want to pull him into her arms and never let go.

"Of course we can keep trying," she said, putting her arms around him and resting her chin on his shoulder. "We just have to be careful. We can't get caught." *And we can't get too attached*. But she feared it might already be too late for her.

Chapter 19

After their talk on the morning of New Year's Eve, Maddy and Alex had fallen back into something closer to the rhythm they'd had before the holidays. They slipped in and out of a handful of discreet restaurants, took the occasional trip to Windsor to go on long rambling walks with Bertie, and found ways to be together whenever they could. Sometimes Maddy wondered if Alex wanted more, but she tried to push her suspicions aside, reminding herself that their relationship had a "best by" date and taking things any deeper would be bad for both of them.

One Thursday night in early February, Alex rushed into their private dining room in a storied Mayfair restaurant fifteen minutes late. Maddy wasn't complaining—the small space boasted luminous green floors and stunning works of art by famous painters on the mirror-paneled rooms. She'd been quite occupied examining the priceless paintings and the glitzy surroundings.

"Sorry, darling," he said, slightly out of breath as he loosened his tie and leaned down to kiss her. Maddy slid her hands up his shoulders to the nape of his neck, looking to prolong the kiss, which had started as a quick peck on the lips. He tasted like minty ChapStick, the sensation heightened by the chill lingering on his face from the wintry evening air outside.

"No apologies necessary," she said, as he took the seat next to her and reached across to where his menu had been laid at the chair directly across from her. "Long day?"

He sighed heavily, flipping to the cocktail list. "Just when I thought we were finally starting to make progress on this reparations project, the prime minister caught wind of it and suddenly wanted to stick her fingers where they don't belong. But of course we have to play nice, so we had to take three steps back to include her and two of her staffers. I don't know how Eric stays so calm and patient about this crap. I was ready to flip the table after two hours." He finally paused for breath, raking his hand through his already disheveled hair in frustration. Maddy had learned, after several months of after-work dinners with Alex, that the state of his hair was a direct correlation to how his day had gone. Slightly mussed meant things had gone well. The more it was standing up, the harder things had been. If it was still perfectly combed, it either meant he hadn't worked at all that day, or it had been so bad that he'd had to go home for a shower to cool off before meeting her.

"That sounds maddening," Maddy said placatingly. After their server had taken their order, she returned to the topic at hand. "Are you open to feedback on this whole reparations project?" she asked, gently.

"Of course," he said immediately, looking her square in the eye. "I always want to hear what you have to say."

Maddy took a breath, choosing her words carefully. "I wonder if Eric has an easier time keeping his cool because he knew this was going to be an uphill battle? I know he's grateful for the effort you're taking to try to make this happen, but I wonder if some part of him has set a very low bar?"

Alex drew back slightly. "You think he thinks I'm not

going to follow through?" The defensiveness she'd been afraid of lurked just behind his eyes.

"Of course not. I know he trusts you. But as someone whose lived experience has told him that his needs aren't a priority for his entire life and many centuries before that, I wonder if he was going into this with a slightly larger dose of realism than you have?" When he didn't respond, Maddy went on. "What you're doing is really admirable, Alex. Truly. This has the potential to change the course of history. But it's also literally *changing* the course of history. This is a gigantic departure from centuries of practice, philosophy, and mindset. Your optimism about it is so necessary, but so is Eric's realism. This is a huge project and not an easy one, and I think Eric might have had a clearer picture of that than you did."

Alex sighed and took a long pull of the apple highball their server had silently deposited at his elbow while Maddy was talking. "Christ, I'm an idiot sometimes," he finally said in a low voice.

"Not an idiot," Maddy corrected. "This is just new to you. There's a learning curve. You may just need to adjust your expectations. This isn't something that's going to happen overnight."

"I know you're right." Sighing again, he looked up at her. "Do I owe Eric an apology?"

Maddy stopped to think. "I don't know that you've done anything that requires an apology..."

"Besides coming from a family that has profited massively off colonialism and white supremacy for centuries?"

"Well, I mean, there's that. But in this case, since you haven't actively intentionally subjugated anyone, I suspect what is more meaningful is your actions. You're the one person in all these centuries who has really stopped to say, 'How can I bring about meaningful change here?' and that's not nothing." She took a pensive sip from her martini—which had become one of her favorite cocktails almost overnight. "I was going to say, it might be worth having another conversation about it with him. Admit to him that you've been operating under unreasonable expectations about how this project is going to go. Ask him to share how he sees it going so that you can both be on the same page and you'll be able to moderate your expectations."

Alex reached over to cover her hand with his. "You're so wise," he said, smiling at her fondly.

"I don't know about that," she said, brushing off his compliment. "I just spent the first twenty-seven years of my life as a cog in a massive bureaucracy. I know a thing or two about procedural red tape."

The conversation moved on to lighter topics as their server brought in a decadent array of courses. They were lingering over coffee and petit fours when there was a short knock on the door to their dining room and then, without waiting for an answer, Graham entered, quickly shutting the door behind him. Maddy could tell from the look on his face that something was wrong.

Clearly Alex could too. "What is it?" he asked, his face registering slight alarm.

"Sir, it would appear the press have discovered you're here. There's a growing crowd of paparazzi out front. It's starting to create something of a scene..."

Maddy was pretty sure Graham kept talking and she was aware of Alex saying something in response, but she couldn't process any of their conversation. A dull buzzing had started in her ears. Her legs had gone all tingly and she couldn't feel her hands. Her eyes focused on the half-eaten cake bite on her plate, but she wasn't really seeing it. Horrendous scenes from almost two years earlier were playing in her mind's eye. She heard the loud clicks of the cameras, the strange voices shouting her name. Felt the jostling of her body as photographers tried to get to her, indistinguishable from the touch of those trying to hurry her away to privacy.

Suddenly she was jolted back to the present. Alex had turned her chair to face him and taken both of her hands in his own. "Mads," he was saying, insistently. "Maddy, darling, it's okay." She could tell by the tone in his voice that it wasn't the first time he'd said it.

She blinked and tried to recenter herself in the present moment, but it was a struggle and she was only half hearing what he was saying. "...Really, it's all right. I'll saunter right out the front door, and Graham will take you home. Nobody will see. Truly, darling. It's not that bad."

She was vaguely aware of Graham standing over Alex's shoulder, a look on his face that seemed almost... disapproving? Although that couldn't be right. Graham was more loyal to Alex than Bertie was. As quickly as she'd registered it, Graham was turning away to answer his phone. A moment later he turned back to them. "Your Royal Highness, the other car is out front. You go out that way, and I'll get Miss Maddy back to my vehicle."

Maddy stood numbly and let Alex help her into her coat. He held her face in his hands gently and said something reassuring before kissing her quickly and slipping out into the main part of the restaurant.

"This way, Miss Maddy," Graham said gently, leading her out the same door Alex had left, but turning in the opposite direction, toward the back of the restaurant. She followed him through the kitchen, ignoring the curious looks of the staff. After having her wait at a back door for a moment, he returned and ushered her directly into the backseat of his waiting Range Rover.

As Maddy sank into the black leather interiors, engulfed by the warmth from the blasting heat and the sumptuous interiors, she felt her awareness returning, measure by terrifying measure. Realizing how close they'd been to getting caught, how narrowly she'd escaped finding herself in the exact media circus she'd been subjected to after Evan's death. Graham slowly pulled away from the curb and out of the alley behind the restaurant. As they swept past the front of the restaurant, she caught a glimpse of Alex posing gamely for a small handful of photographers on the front steps of the restaurant, allowing her and Graham to pass unnoticed.

The initial numbness had started to wear off, and Maddy realized that she was trembling violently and tears were running down her cheeks. In her periphery she was abstractly aware of the fact that Graham was sneaking frequent, concerned looks at her in the rearview mirror, but either out of respect or his years of training, he didn't say anything, just drove her silently back to the side entrance of Winfield House and escorted her to the door.

* * *

An hour later, Alex was sprawled on his sofa, a tumbler of whiskey on the rocks in one hand, his other hand idly scratching Bertie's ears. He'd changed from his suit into his favorite gray sweatpants and a worn black long-sleeved T-shirt. There was a football game he'd recorded on the TV, but he wasn't really paying attention. He gazed into the fire in the fireplace, reflecting on Maddy's insights into his expectations of the reparations project with Eric. He was turning over something she'd said when his phone buzzed on the couch next to him.

Alex sent a quick response before loping downstairs to let his driver in. Bertie made a nuisance of himself, showing off and prancing around on his back legs, trying to get the attention of one of his favorite people, while Alex tried to convince Graham to take his jacket off and relax.

"This won't take a moment, sir," he demurred quietly but firmly.

"Okay, well, at least come upstairs and stop loitering in the entry like an encyclopedia salesman."

"Very good, sir," Graham replied, following Alex begrudgingly up to the sitting room.

"I wanted to apologize, sir," he said when they were both finally seated back in the sitting room. "I'm not sure how the paparazzi found out where you and Miss Maddy were dining, but I promise we'll be more thorough in the future."

"These things happen, Graham. I think we handled it well. Maddy got out of there without being seen. No harm, no foul, as they say, eh?"

"Well, that's the thing, sir," Graham said. Alex registered that Graham was fidgeting with his hands, the man's clear tell that something was bothering him. He should have noticed it sooner.

"What is it?" he asked, a bit more sharply than he'd intended.

"Well, it's Miss Maddy, sir," he began slowly.

"She was pretty rattled," Alex acknowledged.

Graham leveled him with A Look. "She was having a panic attack, if I may be blunt about it."

Alex's eyes narrowed. "I mean, I know she was uncomfortable—"

"Respectfully, sir, you didn't see her once she got into the car," Graham interjected.

"Go on," Alex urged, leaning forward in his seat, suddenly wondering what he'd missed.

"She was a fair sight more than rattled, " Graham told him directly. "The poor girl started shaking like a leaf and crying as soon as she got into the car."

Graham's words hit Alex like a physical blow. "Wait, really?"

His driver nodded somberly.

"Did she say anything?"

"She didn't, and I didn't want to pry," Graham said. "But she was more upset than I've ever seen her."

Alex slumped back into the couch, running a hand down his face. "I'm an idiot," he sighed. Graham didn't say anything. "I should have realized she wasn't going to be okay."

"If I may, sir?" When Alex nodded, Graham continued, "It may be that this is bringing up painful memories for her?"

"You know about that?" Alex asked, surprised.

"It's my responsibility to know about the people with whom you're spending time, sir."

"I guess that's true," Alex responded. "But I'm sure you're right. I suppose I didn't realize the degree to which that would still impact her." Graham stood as if to leave, and Alex suddenly felt extremely vulnerable. "Graham?"

"Sir?"

"What should I do? Should I go to her?"

Graham thought for a moment before responding. "Maybe just check on her, sir? She's had a long night, and it's getting late."

Alex sighed. "And once again, you're right." He stood too. "Thank you, Graham. I needed to hear that. I appreciate it."

He walked the older man back to the front door and locked it behind them before returning to his place on the sofa. He picked up his phone, intending to call Maddy, but something made him stop. He set it down again, staring pensively into the fire. He found himself sifting through thoughts that swirled in his mind. How much he wanted Maddy. How badly they were failing at keeping things casual. How desperately he wanted their relationship to be something more, if he really got honest with himself. But also how hard his life would be for her. How fervently he wanted to prove to his family that he could be useful. He found himself wondering if there was any way to reconcile the seemingly contradictory ideas that were floating past his mind's eye.

He was pulled from his thoughts by the vibration of his phone, still in his hand.

THE HOT AMERICAN

I'm so sorry about tonight. I totally freaked out and that was absolutely not what you needed. I think maybe I haven't been entirely honest with myself about how much of that has stuck with me from before…

Regret and something bordering on outrage shot through Alex as he read her message. Without allowing himself to think further, he tapped her picture at the top of his contacts list to call her.

"Hey," she answered. She sounded tired.

"You have absolutely nothing to apologize for," he said fiercely, by way of greeting. "None of that was your doing. If anyone should be apologizing, it's me. Graham came by after he dropped you off to tell me how upset you were. I should have realized it, should have made sure you were okay before leaving you there. Maddy, I'm so sorry."

"Alex, no, it's not your fault. This is something I need to work on." He heard a small sigh before she continued. "I don't think I knew how *not* okay with it I was until tonight."

"Right, but I should have realized how not okay you were."

"You're not a mind reader, Alex."

"I'm not, but I am your—" He paused, realizing that they really hadn't discussed labels for their situation, much as he'd love nothing more than to be able to call himself her boyfriend. Starting over, he said, "I've spent enough time with you that I should have been more aware that you were panicking. Should have noticed that you were more than just a little shaken up."

"Alex, it's okay. You were in damage control mode. I'm the one who just completely froze."

"Darling, you froze for completely understandable reasons," he said, his tone gentling. "I just wish I'd stopped being in solutions mode for two seconds to realize that so I could have helped."

"I'm fine," she said quietly. "Graham probably thinks I'm a nutcase, but I took a hot shower and made myself a cup of tea when I got home and that helped."

"If Graham thinks anyone is a nutcase, it's me," Alex retorted. "The way he had to explain how not okay you were to me like I was five..." He heard a small chuckle from Maddy's end of the phone and some of the anxiety that he hadn't fully processed unwound itself from around his chest. "Are you sure you're okay?" he asked. "Do you want me to come over?"

"I'm fine." He heard a stifled yawn. "Now that the adrenaline is wearing off, I'm mostly just exhausted. I really just wanted to apologize for totally losing it tonight."

"Don't you dare try to apologize again, okay? Your feelings, your responses are valid. We'll just be more careful in the future, yeah?"

She murmured her assent, and after saying goodnight, they rang off.

An hour later, Alex found himself still staring into the flames in the fireplace again, wondering how far "more careful" could really take them.

Chapter 20

MR. MARTINI

U up?

You did not seriously just say that to me.

MR. MARTINI

What do you mean? I just didn't want to be
blowing up your phone if you were asleep.

Maddy sighed, realizing that this was likely another of the strange but significant lacunae in Alex's pop culture knowledge that she'd have to explain to him at some point not over text.

Never mind. I'm up.

MR. MARTINI

I miss you

Oh yeah? What do you miss about me? 😉

MR. MARTINI

That sassy mouth, for one thing

The noises you make when I'm driving you
over the edge

Your incredible tits

> Well now that I've been thoroughly
> objectified...

MR. MARTINI

Mads! Of course I miss everything
about you.

> I know, I was only kidding
>
> I miss you too
>
> How has your week been?

MR. MARTINI

Unbelievably busy. I think the press office is
worried that people think I'm only here for
the wedding, so they've been sending Ben
and me out on joint appearances to build
up this image that we're inseparable

> I mean, you like your brother... that doesn't
> sound so bad?

MR. MARTINI

I mean, it's not terrible. But have you ever
been required to spend copious amounts of
time with someone who was so much more
high-profile than you that you basically
blended into the background?

> ...literally every day of my childhood
> growing up as the child of a heavily
> decorated high-ranking member of the
> United States Army

MR. MARTINI

Oh. Right.

> But yes, I know it kind of sucks. Sorry, A.

MR. MARTINI

It's fine. It's the job. I just hate that it means
I haven't seen you in days.

Me, too. What's on the docket for today?

MR. MARTINI

We're on the train on our way out to Wales.
Ben will get dubbed Prince of Wales
basically the second he gets married, so we
have to be sure it doesn't look like he only
set foot in Wales once he got the title.

...by setting foot there for the first time a
month before he gets the title?

MR. MARTINI

Precisely

"Who are you messaging with that goofy grin on your face?"
Ben's voice cut into Alex's mind, pulling his focus away from
his phone.

"No one," he answered quickly, pocketing the device
before his brother could see. Even in their thirties, they'd been
known to play keep-away, and he definitely didn't want Benji
seeing all of the things he'd said to Maddy lately. He'd been so
busy their relationship had been almost exclusively via text
and, despite both of their concerns about security leaks, they'd
gotten a bit racy several times.

"Bullshit." Ben said. "Is it the same girl from Christmas?
The one you ditched the family for?"

"I did not ditch the family!"

"Mate, you left like five seconds after they cleared the
dessert plates from Christmas tea."

"If we'd stayed much longer, cousin Charlotte would have
made a corgi-skin coat."

"True." Ben snickered. "But we both know that's not the only reason you went flying out of there at the earliest opportunity."

Alex sighed. He and his brother didn't always see eye-to-eye on things, but he knew he could trust Ben. He didn't always give the soundest advice on everything, but, he forced himself to acknowledge, it might be good to have someone he could confide in besides Maddy.

"Okay, but you have to *promise* not to tell anyone—especially not Mum and Dad."

Ben's face somehow turned simultaneously immediately serious and completely giddy with glee. "Of course not, bro. Tell me!"

"Her name is Madeleine. Maddy. She's American." Alex saw his brother's jaw drop slightly, but ignored him. "I met her doing that gala concert in November. She works at the embassy." The story came out in fits and starts—starting with their first few hangs as "friends," which was never what he wanted at all, to taking her to Windsor and kissing her for the first time, to their blissful five days over the holidays. He left out Maddy's personal backstory. That wasn't his tale to tell. But he gradually revealed the full story of him and Maddy until he was confessing, "So yeah. I guess we just try to see each other as much as we can and keep it really casual."

Ben let out a low whistle. "Mate, you've gotten yourself in a heap of trouble there, haven't you?"

"What do you mean?" Alex asked defensively.

"You can't marry an American!"

"Who said anything about marriage? We're just fooling around!" He hated himself, even as the words came out. No matter how secret their relationship had to be, no matter how casual they insisted they were keeping it, what they had had never been anything as tawdry as "fooling around," and he damn well knew it.

Apparently Ben did too. "That's absolutely nonsensical. I can tell just by the way you're talking about her that you're totally gone for her. I've never heard you talk about anyone that way before."

Alex hung his head. "I mean," he began, trying to formulate a response when he knew his brother was right. "Yes. I know we can't get married. And I don't think she wants to. She's... she's had a hard time. She's not ready for anything serious. I just... I just want her to feel special. And cared for."

Ben's face softened. "I mean, that's admirable as fuck, mate, but what are you going to do when her ambassador gets recalled?"

Alex sighed again. "No idea. That's why we're keeping it casual. She's terrified of being exposed by the press, she's not ready for anything serious, and by the end of the year her boss will probably be out of a job and they'll all be packing it in and flying back to the States."

Ben clapped him on the back sympathetically. "That's shit, man. I'm sorry."

Alex shrugged. "I mean, who knows where this will go. But we're having fun for as long as we can."

He didn't miss the sad look on his brother's face when he said, "As long as you think you know what you're doing..." He sounded very doubtful on that front, and frankly Alex didn't entirely blame him. He was starting to feel like he didn't really know what he and Maddy were doing either. But he knew that he was starting to feel like he couldn't live without her. "You should bring her around to dinner or drinks or something sometime," Ben went on, pulling Alex out of his thought spiral. "I want to meet the girl who has you looking so lovesick you're about to puke."

"I am *not* lovesick!" Alex exclaimed.

"Yeah, sure, okay," Ben replied with a grin. "But really. I'd like to meet her."

Alex smiled. "I think you'd like her."

"If she makes you that happy, I'm sure I will."

Their conversation was interrupted then by the announcement that they were pulling into their station. Alex slipped his iPad back into the shoulder bag he carried on these daylong events and stood to shrug into his overcoat. As the train slid into Cardiff Central Station, he took a few deep breaths, slapped on his publicity smile, and followed his brother out into the throngs. A camera flash went off right in front of them as they both waved to the gathered crowd, and he suddenly realized two things: one, he couldn't ask Maddy to go back to this if every flash was going to send her straight back to the panic and grief that had consumed her after Evan's death; and two, Ben was right. He was totally lovesick.

Chapter 21

March turned to April, and spring started to come to London in tiny fits and starts. The slush had mostly melted away from the gutters and tiny pops of bright green were starting to appear on the barren branches of the trees in Regent's Park. Maddy had returned to her habits of the preceding fall, trying to get back to being able to run the full four and a half kilometers around the outer circle of the park. She didn't get out every day, but she found it so useful for clearing her head when she was able to move her body, so she tried to make it a priority at least two or three times a week.

On one of these days, Maddy found her thoughts drifting to her relationship with Alex. After the near-miss in February, they'd made more serious attempts at keeping things casual, aided by his rapidly filling schedule of pre-wedding events. His parents had reluctantly handed over a few smaller patronages to him, mostly ones that didn't require public events, she'd noticed, but still, between those and Maddy's work at the embassy, they were only able to see each other once or twice a week most weeks. As Maddy's legs carried her past the gleaming dome of London's Central Mosque and towards the lake, she knew the time was coming when she'd have to make a choice.

The email telling her she'd been accepted to Georgetown had come the day before. The surge of immense pride she felt seeing the words "It is our pleasure to inform you of your admission…" was pretty much unparalleled. She'd experienced a number of proud moments in her past, but, upon reflection, a lot of them were being proud of someone else: seeing her father and Evan receive military promotions, seeing Alex and Mrs. Stewart carry off the gala concert, hearing Alex tell her about the progress he and Eric were making on the reparations project. Rarely had that pride been directed inwardly. Yet the pride was almost immediately followed by a surge of heartbreak, knowing that she'd have to decide between forging her own path and continuing to feel the warmth of Alex's affection.

She hadn't actually told Alex that she'd applied for master's programs. The applications had been due right around the time of their first dinner date, so it hadn't come up in conversation then. And then the moment had just never seemed right. Maddy knew that Alex would be thrilled for her. He'd made it clear that her happiness and fulfillment was a priority for him, and as someone who obviously felt that he lacked agency in the trajectory of his own life, she was confident that he'd support anything she did to take her own life path by the horns. And yet she still hadn't been able to bring herself to tell him. Alex seemed so singularly focused on her own happiness and satisfaction. He constantly reminded her that he wanted her to know what it felt like to be someone's priority. It felt amazing. But she also suspected that he'd push her toward her own accomplishments and happiness at the expense of his own. Because as much as he wanted her to feel like someone's priority, she also suspected that his desire to make her feel valued and important came from a deep need to feel the same way. It was just one more thing that had the potential to torpedo their relationship, and she didn't relish the idea of facing that reality any sooner than she needed to.

But the fact of the matter was that soon she'd have to decide whether she was leaving London over the summer or sticking it out a bit longer to see what happened after the election. To potentially give her relationship with Alex, such as it was, more time. The stark lines of the Marylebone Green playground's concrete structures came into view as she turned her thoughts over in her head, the shrieks of children flying down the slide and the feeling of her sneakers pounding along the path accompanying her attempts to sort out her feelings. When it came down to it, the pros of staying were:

- Alex
- Staying out of the public eye
- Alex
- Not having to move
- Nadia's friendship
- Nadia's brownies
- Alex.

The pros of going were:

- Getting to choose her own path for essentially the first time
- Forwarding her career with an advanced degree
- Her love of learning
- Not having to constantly figure out the time difference from London to her parents' home in Kansas.

She had to admit that, on paper at least, the pros of going far outweighed most of the pros of staying. But the fact of Alex threatened to tip the scales. Even as they tried to keep things casual, Alex made her feel seen, important, treasured in a way she'd never felt before. When he asked about her day, her work, even what she was reading, the way he listened intently was unlike anything she'd ever experienced.

And the way he worshiped her body was entirely new, as well. She tried to push back the thoughts of how exactly he'd become so proficient in bed and instead focused on the many scintillating and creative ways he found to send her into orgasmic bliss. After their first time having sex on Christmas night, new toys not infrequently found their way into the drawer of his nightstand. Once he discovered exactly what she liked, it was as if he made an academic study of bringing her pleasure.

On one very memorable occasion he'd even had a small, discreetly wrapped package delivered to her at Winfield House containing a pair of lacy black panties that, as she discovered on their date that night, could be controlled by a remote that he hid in his pocket. After their entrees had arrived, he'd told their waitstaff not to come to take their dessert order until he called for them, and had spent a deliciously torturous thirty minutes teasing her while she tried to eat a piece of salmon.

But was the promise of their high-flying physical relationship and the burgeoning emotional intimacy enough to keep her from pursuing her own dreams? Maddy wasn't sure. As much as she wanted to think that if she stayed somehow they'd be able to work something out, a big part of her knew it was impossible. No matter how many lovely things Alex said about his gregarious but caring family, she knew there was no way they could ever accept a thoroughly average American as his serious partner. He needed someone who could stand up with him in the most important, weightiest occasions of state.

Someone who had been brought up amongst England's upper crust and inherently understood the ways of high society and the appropriate form of address for each tier of nobility. An American army brat was never going to be accepted by the upper echelons of British society, and she knew it. Alex already had to fight every day to prove his worthiness to represent the family on the international stage. He didn't need to have to fight to prove the legitimacy of his relationship on top of everything else.

And besides, she knew all too well that it was only a matter of time before the press found out about them. The British tabloid media was notoriously cruel, and the fact that they hadn't been discovered yet truly surprised her. And the last time she'd subverted her own dreams and desires for a man, it had ended in heartbreak and a raft of unwanted press attention, and no matter how she spun it, she couldn't imagine a scenario in which this flash-in-the-pan romance didn't end the same way.

The London Zoo came into view as she continued to ruminate. All signs pointed to accepting Georgetown's offer and pursuing her own dreams for once in her life. And yet. When she closed her eyes and saw Alex's gray ones boring into her soul, the way he smiled at her, lifted her up, made her feel seen and cared for, it threatened to stop her in her tracks. She rarely let herself really examine her deepest feelings on the matter because the truth scared the crap out of her. But when she did, she found herself realizing that she wasn't sure how she was going to live without him. That the collection of stolen moments together, of backroom kisses, of late-night cuddle sessions that turned into languorous sex at his apartment—they were knitting her soul back together. Alex's attentions made her feel strong and motivated in a way she couldn't remember feeling before. And something told her not to discount that, even as it flew in the face of all the rational thoughts she had on the subject.

She really wished she could talk to Alex about it, but she knew inherently that he'd push her towards her own dreams, even at the expense of his own happiness. As much as she didn't want to hurt him, if someone was going to do it, it needed to be her. She couldn't let him lay down on his own sword, which she knew he wouldn't hesitate to do if he thought it was best for her. They hadn't talked about it, but she was starting to suspect that Alex might also be developing the feelings they'd promised to avoid. Much as she hated to admit it, she was concerned that they might be failing at keeping things casual.

Passing the running track where the real runners practiced, Maddy gasped for breath as Winfield House came into view. Despite forty-five minutes of movement and mulling, she still didn't feel any closer to a decision than she had been when she set out. So as she approached the back door of Winfield House, she shoved her thoughts back down deep into her brain and refocused on the day's work at the embassy.

Chapter 22

"Sorry I'm late," Alex gasped, striding into the private greenhouse at One Marylebone restaurant ten minutes late. Maddy was sitting at the table and put down her phone to stand as he rushed in.

"That's okay," she said, pushing onto tiptoe to kiss him sweetly. Alex resisted the urge to draw out the kiss, knowing that once he started he wouldn't be able to give her up. "How was your day?" she asked as she retook her seat and slipped her phone into her purse.

"Busy," he said, running a hand through his hair distractedly and pulling a menu toward him. "I swear they have five wedding planners, and yet somehow my parents want all of us to be involved in every aspect of this wedding. Aside from the dress, poor Hannah probably hasn't had a single unilateral choice about her own wedding."

Maddy smiled ruefully. "I mean, presumably she knew what she was getting into. She's a Cromwell, for Christ's sake. I imagine even before she and your brother started dating she knew how things like this went in your set. And it's not like they started dating last year or anything."

"True," Alex agreed. "But still. When I managed to disentangle myself from the wedding war room, they were going back and forth on what kind of flowers should go on the cake and whether they should mirror the wedding flowers or should they be another opportunity to bring in additional symbolism or some nonsense like that."

Maddy looked at him placatingly. "Well, you're here now."

"I am here now," he said, taking a deep breath and trying to recenter himself on the beautiful woman sitting across from him and shed the contagious frenetic energy he'd absorbed from the chaos he'd left at Buckingham Palace.

"How was your day?" he asked, taking a sip from the glass of water that was already sitting in front of him.

"Oh, fine," she said. "Nothing too exciting. I went with Mrs. Stewart and the girls for the final fitting for their dresses for the wedding." In addition to being the American ambassador, Andrew Stewart's relationship with King Alfred went back to his days in the service when they'd both been involved in the NATO efforts to defuse tensions in the Balkans, which had garnered their family seats at the royal wedding. Alex thought she looked slightly wistful as she said, "Amelia is so excited she could barely stand still, and Audrey is so bored by the idea that she could barely be bothered to stand up."

Alex laughed. He'd only met the Stewart twins a few times in passing, but Maddy's description of the fitting tracked with what he knew of their divergent personalities. "So about that," he began slowly, but was interrupted by the server coming to take their dinner order.

"Sorry, what were you saying?" Maddy asked, taking a sip from the gin cocktail she'd ordered and looking over at him.

"Right," he said, trying to decide where to begin. "So, I know we agreed that this was strictly casual and out of the public eye... but have you told anyone about us?"

She seemed a little puzzled by the question, but answered

readily enough. "Nadia knows I'm seeing someone. I told her about martini-gate and that I'd started dating the guy who dropped a whole drink on me, and that his name is Alex. But that's all. Why do you ask?"

"Well," he said, "my brother kind of figured out something was up, so I had to tell him." He was slightly worried she might be upset.

"Oh, that's fine," she said mildly. "Of all people, I'm sure he understands why we're not going public with it."

"He wants me to bring you to their wedding reception."

Maddy coughed, choking slightly on a sip of gimlet that had gone down the wrong pipe.

"I'm fine," she wheezed, gulping from her water glass. "I'm just. He what?"

"So there will be an official early afternoon reception at Buckingham Palace for like half of the gazillion people who will be at the ceremony," Alex explained. "And then in the evening my parents are hosting a more intimate dinner party for like two hundred and fifty of their closest personal friends. And then after that there will be an actual party for just people Ben and Hannah actually know and like. Cocktails, dancing, no press, no parents. Ben was hoping I'd bring you to that."

"But he doesn't know me?" she said, baffled.

"No, but he wants to meet you."

"At his own wedding?" Maddy asked, still confused.

"I guess?" When he thought about it, it was kind of a strange context in which to meet one's brother's secret girlfriend. "I suppose he also figured I might enjoy having someone to dance with." He smiled at her, suddenly worried that maybe she didn't want to come. Maybe this was too much too fast. "But of course you don't have to if you don't want to come."

"I... I just..." Maddy seemed to be searching for a way to put words in the right order. "Of course I *want* to come," she said, smiling at him. "Obviously I want to come. It's just— I... it feels risky. And decidedly not casual."

"I mean, is it entirely without risk? No. But for one thing, by the time this is going on, it will be the end of the day. People will have done all the people watching they want to do. We'll slip you in when the dancing starts. And no offense, darling, but most of these people are a) too self-absorbed to notice anyone else, and b) going to be more concerned with seeing how close they can get to Adele and Ed Sheeran and my brother than with me casually whisking you around the dance floor."

Maddy barked out a laugh. "Fair point." She paused again. "I also have no idea what the dress code is for something like this, but I feel confident I don't have anything nice enough to wear."

For this protestation, Alex had at least been prepared. "If I told you you didn't have to worry about it, would you agree to come with me?"

Maddy paused again, just momentarily, and then seemed to decide. "Yes," she said. "But why wouldn't I have to worry about that?"

Alex pulled a small white card from his interior jacket pocket. "This is the name of Hannah's personal shopper at Harrod's. Just text her and set up a time to go in. She's expecting to hear from you."

Maddy's eyebrows shot up as she accepted the card. "Wow," she said, looking at the letter-pressed black writing. "Okay," she said, still sounding a bit uncertain. "If you really want me there."

His heart warmed. "Darling, there's nobody I'd rather dance with."

. . .

Two days later, Maddy was walking somewhat trepidatiously into the iconic main entrance of Harrod's and, after locating the elevator, took it to the fifth floor as Hannah's private shopper, Liz, had directed via text. Alex had assured her that Liz would know exactly what she needed, although Maddy was a little afraid the limit on her credit card wasn't high enough for that. She reminded herself that this was literally a once-in-a-lifetime opportunity and she'd figure the money out later, and took a deep breath before approaching the entrance to the penthouse.

Maddy tried to exude confidence she did not feel as an attendant led her into the sumptuously appointed white and black suite of rooms. A tall woman with a bouncy blonde ponytail who looked to be in her late thirties or early forties walked towards Maddy, her hand extended warmly. "You must be Maddy. I'm Liz." She air-kissed Maddy on both cheeks as Maddy's khaki trench coat was taken by the attendant, who, after Maddy declined the champagne they offered, left them.

"Come right through here," Liz said, leading her toward a smaller room to the right. "Now, I wasn't sure exactly what you'd like, so I pulled a bunch of different things and we'll just start trying them on and see what suits you."

Maddy's eyes went wide as she walked into the fitting room. The furniture was all rose tufted velvet with gold accents. Soft uplighting seemed to exude from behind the walls, and a rack of dresses in almost every color waited at one end of the room.

"Why don't you slip into this and then we can talk a bit," Liz said, handing Maddy a cream satin robe.

"Okay," Maddy said slowly, trying to not let her complete and total overwhelm show.

"It's okay, love," Liz said conspiratorially, "this will be fun. Just let me take care of everything."

Maddy took a steadying breath, nodded, tried to smile at

the enthusiastic woman, and watched her leave the room. Stepping out of her nude heels, Maddy forced back the feeling that she'd made a terrible mistake by agreeing to attend the reception with Alex. She was an army brat from everywhere and nowhere. Sure, she'd attended her fair share of Army balls with Evan, but never anything like this, and from the looks of the dresses Liz had pulled for her, her wardrobe was even farther from appropriate than she'd thought. Trying not to think about how much the dazzling rack of gowns cost and how far from casual attending the royal wedding after-after-party fell, Maddy slipped out of her tan pantsuit, thanking her lucky stars that she'd remembered to wear shapewear, and was just tying the robe around her waist when Liz came back.

"Look who I found!" Liz crowed, moving into the room.

Maddy's jaw just about hit her chest as Hannah Cromwell followed Liz into Maddy's dressing room. Maddy hardly had time to react before the statuesque woman with incredibly shiny dark hair who would one day be the queen of England was... hugging her? "It's so nice to meet you, Maddy!" she gushed.

"I... you too..." Maddy said, knowing the shock was written on her face and too stunned to even try to hide it.

Hannah beamed at her as she pulled away. "Sorry to just burst in like this, but Alex said you'd be here—"

Finally recovering both her voice and her wits, Maddy burst out, "He didn't put you up to coming here, did he? I know you're so busy."

"Of course not, silly. I've been dying to meet you, and so when he said you'd be here, I decided to capitalize on that opportunity!"

There was a quiet knock on the door, and the attendant who'd brought Maddy in returned with the bottle of champagne that Maddy had declined but Hannah had clearly accepted, along with two coupes. Hannah pressed one into her hand before clinking the rims together. "Cheers, darling!"

"Cheers..." Maddy said, still trying to get her wits about her. She was in a private shopping area of Harrods. With the future queen of England. Getting ready to try on dresses that probably cost more than three months' rent on the last house she and Evan had lived in in Fort Bliss, Texas.

"It's a lot, isn't it?" Hannah said kindly, putting an arm around her and guiding her over to the rack of gowns. "I mean, I grew up on the periphery of all this, and even for me it took some getting used to."

Maddy tried to force herself to relax. "Yeah." She exhaled shakily. "I just..." She trailed a hand down the row of pinks and blues, blacks and golds, satins, silks, and sequins.

"Suck that down and grab the one that speaks to you most," Hannah said decisively. "We'll start there."

"Good idea," Maddy said, appreciating the other woman's direction. She swallowed the second half of her coupe of champagne and, after taking just a moment to glance at what Liz had pulled for her, selected a black McQueen gown.

Liz took it and hung it on the backside of a privacy screen, unzipping the gown on its hanger before pushing Maddy behind it to change. She slid into the black crepe, luxuriating in the feel of the fabric. Apparently this was the difference between designer and regular clothing. The materials felt amazing.

"Alright, let's see you!" Liz's voice called from the other side of the screen, and Maddy stepped out. As she emerged, Liz bustled behind her, zipping up the back of the dress and smoothing it over her hips.

Maddy walked toward the mirror. The black column dress made her feel a million feet tall with its simplicity and long lines, adorned only with large metallic floral appliques at each shoulder. She couldn't suppress a smile at her reflection, and she saw Liz and Hannah look at each other knowingly behind her.

Hannah came to stand next to her. "So you look absolutely fantastic in this… and this is also exactly the kind of dress that Alex sent me here to talk you out of."

"So he *did* put you up to this!" Maddy said, turning to her accusingly.

"He just mentioned you would be here and could use a friend." She moved on quickly. "Okay, now that you've got a bit of confidence, let's find something that will really make his jaw drop."

Liz and Hannah coaxed Maddy in and out of half a dozen other gowns—strapless, long-sleeved, plunging necks, plunging backs, delicate embroidered flowers, sequins, she tried it all. They'd tried valiantly to talk her into a head-to-toe sparkling gold number, but she'd insisted that it made her feel like an Oscar and they finally relented. Maddy was just starting to worry that maybe she just wasn't fancy enough to wear dresses like this when they found it.

As she walked out from behind the screen in the dark green Jenny Packham gown, she could tell by the looks on Liz and Hannah's faces that it was the dress. It had short sleeves and a plunging V-neck that might have felt too risqué except for the delicate green illusion netting that held everything in place. The fabric gathered just below her rib cage and then cascaded to the floor in a waterfall of sequins. Despite the total glitz of it, it still managed to feel slightly understated and, as Liz zipped her up and Maddy stepped to the mirror, she knew they were right. This had to be it.

"It's perfect," Hannah breathed. "Alex is going to go absolutely bananas. I'll be lucky if he doesn't just whisk you away before I even get to see you in it!"

Liz nodded. "Yes, this is definitely it. Not too long to dance in, not too fussy, and it fits you like a glove."

Maddy flushed and knew they were right. She started to reach for the tag that she could feel dangling by her ribs, but Hannah swatted her hand away. "Don't even think about the price, darling, this is the one."

"Yes, but—" Maddy started.

"Liz, put this one on my bill." Hannah said, steamrolling over Maddy's protestations.

"Hannah, that's very—"

"Maddy," she said, turning Maddy to face her and placing her hands gently on her shoulders. "For one thing, this is a drop in the bucket for my future in-laws. Nobody will think twice about it. For another thing, Alex has been different these last few months. More confident, happier, less brooding. And I can't say for certain, but I'm pretty sure you've got something to do with that. So at least let me do this to thank you."

"Hannah," Maddy stammered, "I don't know what to say."

"Really, darling, I should be thanking *you*! Even when Sarah is around, the testosterone in that family is overpowering. At least now the score will be a bit more even."

"Oh, we're not— I mean—" Maddy stammered, trying to tell her that she and Alex were casual, that she doubted she'd ever meet his parents.

"Okay, I have to run to my next meeting. Lovely to finally meet you, darling, and I'll see you in a few weeks, yeah? Oh, and Liz? Don't forget shoes and a bag!"

"Oh, but I have—" Maddy tried to get out.

"Shoes and a bag, Liz!" Hannah called, waving over her shoulder as she disappeared in a cloud of expensive-smelling perfume and bouncy hair.

Maddy stood, still wearing the green dress, shell-shocked.

"She's a force, isn't she?" Liz said, coming to stand beside her.

"Uh-huh," Maddy managed, still trying to wrap her brain around everything that had just happened.

"Now let me just find you shoes and a bag, and we'll get you all set up," Liz said, patting her shoulder as she bustled out in search of accessories.

Text Thread "The Heirs and the Spare"

HANNAH

OMG Alex, she's a gem!

BEN

Wait, you MET her? How?!

HANNAH

Yes! I helped pick out her dress for the after party. Alex, you're going to DIE 💀

BEN

Well! What's she like?

HANNAH

I mean, to be fair, I think she was a little surprised, but I can tell she's got a feisty side. And she's a stunner, that's for sure.

BEN

I bet she does have a feisty side... 😈

What did she pick?

HANNAH

You'll just have to wait and seeeee 😇

HANNAH!

HANNAH

I promised not to ruin the surprise. But trust me: she's not going to blend in and you're going to be very happy.

Chapter 23

The morning of the royal wedding dawned bright and sunny, and Maddy spent it the way most of Britain did: on the couch in her pajamas, glued to the TV. Unlike most of the rest of Britain, Maddy was perhaps a bit more invested in the way the groom's brother looked in his impeccably tailored morning suit, but who could blame her? The entire event was, as expected, stunning. From the literal trees planted in Westminster Abbey to the new choral pieces commissioned for the day to Hannah's stunning bespoke Sassi Holford dress, to the way Prince Benjamin was visibly fighting back tears as she glided down the aisle on her father's arm, it was magical.

Yet Maddy pretty much only had eyes for Alex the whole time. She thrilled as he looked over his shoulder to get the first glimpse of his sister-in-law-to-be and then whispered something to Ben, making his brother blush. The way he and Hannah's sister had to shepherd the tiny attendants out of the Abbey. She found herself imagining what another wedding could look like, in spite of herself.

The king and queen had, as expected, declared bank holidays both Friday, the day of the wedding, and the following Monday, so between the end of the televised wedding content around one p.m. and when Graham was picking her up for the after party around 8:30, Maddy was kind of at sixes and sevens. The Stewarts had received invitations to the more formal luncheon reception following the wedding, so they weren't home. None of the other embassy staff were working. And, even if she took the longest she'd ever taken to get ready, Maddy didn't need to start showering and getting ready until at least 5:30.

She decided to try to work out some of her restless energy, but her standard longer run around the park only took an hour, so even after she got back, took a long shower, and started poring over some of the early wedding photos starting to appear on social media, she still had plenty of time.

Finally it was time to put on The Dress. She realized when she thought of it, she'd been capitalizing The Dress. Liz had found her some black peep-toe heels and a black clutch, which Maddy not only liked but could see herself using again, which was a plus. Knowing that every hairstylist in London would either be booked or taking the day off and not wanting to have to answer questions about where she was going with a fancy updo on the evening of the royal wedding, Maddy had done her own hair, blowing it dry and setting it with hot rollers before pulling just a small section of hair back on one side and clipping it with a black sparkly barrette.

Happy with her hair, she turned to the black velvet box waiting on her dresser. It had arrived by courier two days earlier with a note from Alex, written in his own handwriting: *Hannah said these would look lovely with your dress. I can't wait to see you in them. But mostly I just can't wait to see you. XO, AW.* The signature had immediately reminded her of the card that had come with the flowers he'd sent her after martini-gate. Inside the box she'd found a pair of diamond and emerald drop earrings and a delicate diamond and emerald bracelet. Her jaw had dropped when she opened them, stunned by Alex's generosity.

Stunned and also slightly unsettled. Part of her brain was still insistent on the fact that this couldn't turn into a long-term relationship. She would eventually have to return to America, and he would eventually have to find a bride befitting a prince. But part of her heard Hannah making comments about how nice it would be to have another woman in the family. Saw Alex buying lavish gifts for her to wear to his brother's wedding reception. Noticed her thoughts idly shifting to what she wanted to get Alex for Christmas that year or what their own wedding could be like. And she felt her resolve melting. She and Alex had both been conspicuous and intentional in avoiding talking about anything beyond the immediate future. But she didn't think she was the only one who had started to let herself imagine a future beyond the next month.

The email from Georgetown was burning a hole in her inbox. Something else they hadn't talked about. She didn't have much longer before she needed to accept or decline their offer. She'd almost succumbed to the temptation to talk to Alex about it multiple times. But she knew that, as supportive he would certainly be, as clearly as she could hear him saying "I'll support you whatever you choose," this had to be her decision and her decision alone. This was her future, and she had to make a choice. And soon.

Given the bank holiday, most of the staff were off for the day, and Maddy knew that Pierre and Nadia had left leftovers for the Stewarts to eat for dinner, so she just had to be sure that she didn't accidentally cross paths with anyone as she slipped through the kitchen. As she crept to the top of the stairs out of her rooms and cracked the door open just slightly, she didn't hear anything and so, tiptoeing in her heels, a tan trench coat covering much of The Dress, Maddy slipped out into the temperate late spring evening.

Since it was getting late, most of the holiday picnickers who had filled the park that afternoon were gone, although a few revelers still lingered. They were all too engaged in their own celebrations, though, to pay any attention to Maddy as she darted across the road to the side street where she and Graham had agreed to meet. Alex had tried to insist on Graham picking her up at Winfield House, but Maddy was already concerned about how she was going to sneak out of the house in The Dress without being seen, let alone getting into a Range Rover with a driver at Winfield House, and Graham had actually been on her side, so Alex had relented.

Maddy's eyes looked for his standard Range Rover, but didn't see it, so she was surprised when she heard his quiet voice call, "Good evening, Miss Maddy." She turned and saw him emerging from a nondescript navy-blue hatchback.

"Hi, Graham," she said, walking toward him. "Is this your car?"

"Yes, miss. I thought it might be a little less conspicuous than the car I use with the prince."

"Great idea," she said, grinning, and remembering what Alex had told her about Graham's mystery-writing hobby. Alex hadn't seemed overly concerned about anyone noticing her arrival at the palace, but beneath the excitement and general pre-event anxiety she'd been feeling in the lead-up to the wedding, Maddy had also noticed herself worrying about being caught. She was glad Graham seemed to be on the same page.

"If you don't mind, miss," Graham was saying, leading her around to the back of the small Citroen, "I was thinking you might be less noticeable back here."

He opened the trunk to reveal a soft-looking plaid blanket carefully laid out across the back of the pristinely clean trunk. "If it won't ruin your dress to lay back here, we can pull the cargo cover over and you'll be completely hidden until we get to the back entrance where I'll let you in."

Maddy was already climbing in as she said, "Brilliant plan, Graham," over her shoulder. After she had arranged herself carefully to avoid being speared by one of the sequins on The Dress, Graham pulled the cargo cover carefully over her and shut the back hatch gently. It was completely dark, but that was fine with Maddy. It told her she was also completely hidden from view.

"Alright back there, Miss Maddy?" Graham called back. Maddy felt the car shift slightly as he sat down in the front seat and shut the driver's door.

"Just fine, Graham, thanks!" she called back.

The experience of riding in the back of a car without being able to see out at all was both entirely foreign and wrapped in a strangely comforting cocoon of nostalgia. Even though the circumstances were completely different (and the fit of her body in the trunk of a car was, as well), it reminded her of their trips to the Adirondacks during her childhood. When they all piled into Evan's family's station wagon, sometimes there weren't enough seatbelts for everyone, so she and Evan would wind up lying in the back of the wagon, their mothers' admonitions to stay low and not move so they wouldn't get hurt—or worse, caught by the police—ringing in their ears.

Maddy knew it would take roughly twenty minutes to get to Buckingham Palace, but her sense of time, like her sense of direction, was strangely muffled by her inability to see where they were. At first she'd tried to keep up with the turns, but she quickly realized that she didn't know the surface streets well enough and was soon completely disoriented. Graham was too far away to make easy conversation besides his occasional calls back to check on her, so she mostly lay in contemplative silence.

She and Alex hadn't seen each other in over a week and even finding time to text or FaceTime had been challenging with the mad dash leading up to the wedding, and so she realized that, despite the excitement of getting to attend the party, she was mostly just excited to see him. As she ruminated, she realized she didn't remember ever having been this excited to see anyone. Sure, she'd always been relieved and happy to see Evan when he came home from long trainings or deployments. But, she reflected, never this kind of "crawl out of your skin to get to them" level of anticipation she felt at the idea of finally being in Alex's arms again after just a week away. When she'd moved to England, it was supposed to be to start a new chapter in her life. Maddy 2.0. The dawn of a new era where she made decisions based on what *she* wanted and what was best for her, not anyone else. Especially not a man. And yet. She now found herself dangerously close to breaking rule number one of The Maddy 2.0 List.

Before she could pursue that tendril of thought further, she felt the car slowing and heard Graham roll his window down and mutter something to someone outside the car. Above the low murmur of their voices, she could hear cheers and realized this must be the gate outside Buckingham Palace, with folks still out and about celebrating the royal wedding and, perhaps, hoping to catch a glimpse of someone coming or going. Maddy felt the butterflies in her stomach whip themselves into a renewed frenzy. She was only a few moments away from Alex.

They hadn't discussed how they were going to act at this, their first time truly interacting in front of anyone besides Graham. At that moment, Maddy would have been willing to walk up to him and shove her tongue down his throat, she was so eager to see him.

The car rolled forward and she felt them making a broad turn. Maddy imagined passing the majestic facade of the king and queen's residence and looping around toward the back. Part of her wished she could see, but particularly with the knowledge that people were still congregating outside the fence, she was glad for her protective cover. A moment later the car came to a stop again. "Alright, Miss Maddy, we're here," she heard Graham say over the thudding of her heart, which was so loud it had to be clearly audible to anyone in the vicinity.

A moment later, the back hatch was opening and the cover was removed. Maddy blinked, her eyes readjusting to the lights illuminating what looked almost like a loading dock. Graham extended his hand and she took it as she swung her legs back over the hatch of the car and stood, smoothing The Dress. "Thanks, Graham," she said, offering him a smile. She hoped nobody else could tell that her hands were shaking.

"Absolutely, Miss Maddy. Have a smashing time." He winked at her and indicated a door that was opening outwards toward them. She saw Eric walking toward her, his tuxedo impeccably tailored, a hand extended to greet her.

"Maddy, lovely to see you again," he said, taking her hand and leading her toward the open door.

"You too," she said, her mouth going dry as she realized she was walking into Buckingham Palace. And this time she actually was an invited guest, not just The Help.

"Alex has been checking his watch obsessively and asking me if you're here yet," Eric said, glancing at her out of the corner of his eye, a smile on his face.

She felt herself relax infinitesimally, relief at the knowledge that he was as eager to see her as she was to see him coursing through her body. As they exited what was clearly a behind-the-scenes area and entered the more traditionally regal looking part of the Palace, Maddy felt her heart start to beat faster, if that was even possible. "Let me take your coat," he said, stopping to help her out of it before handing it to a liveried servant behind a desk. "I'll make sure it gets back to you," he said, taking the coat check and slipping into the inner pocket of his suit jacket.

"Thanks, Eric," she said, hoping that her voice didn't sound too breathless or nervous.

"You ready for this?" he asked as they approached a larger hallway where Maddy could start to hear the faint sounds of music coming from several sets of doors. "You look stunning, by the way," he said, with a smile. "Alex is going to lose his mind."

She felt her cheeks flush. "Thanks." She took a deep breath, adjusting The Dress and patting her hair. "And I don't think there's any way I could ever be ready for something like this, but I'm not going to get any more ready, so let's do this."

"Atta girl," he said, taking her arm gently and leading her toward the grand ballroom and Alex.

* * *

Alex looked at his watch again. It felt like half an hour since Eric had left to go meet Graham and Maddy, but he knew realistically it couldn't have been more than ten minutes. He tried to focus on the small circle of people standing around him: his cousin Elise, a friend of Ben's from Oxford and his wife, and a few other people that he definitely knew but couldn't be bothered to place. He'd intentionally positioned himself to have a clear view of the door he knew they'd be coming in, and he fought the urge to check every ten seconds for Maddy. It had, of course, been a magical day. Getting to see his brother marry the woman of his dreams and to stand next to him while he did it had been an honor, and finally getting to show his family once and for all that he could hold up under pressure at public events had been a side perk. But this, this moment, finally getting to see Maddy after days of only intermittent texting and fleeting calls, was going to be the highlight and he knew it.

He realized the people around him were laughing at something and he belatedly joined in, even though he had no idea what was funny, but his laugh died in his throat as he finally saw Eric standing in the doorway. He was suddenly slightly afraid he might pass out. He was pretty sure he excused himself as he moved away from the group and strode towards the door as Maddy appeared.

His breath caught in his throat and his purposeful stride faltered as he saw her. She was stunning. The sparkly green dress fit her like a glove, highlighting her breasts and the gentle curve of her hips before cascading to the floor in a sea of sparkles. The earrings he'd sent her glittered against the mahogany curtain of her hair. He realized they hadn't discussed how they were going to handle interacting in front of other people and desperately hoped she was okay with PDA because there was absolutely no way he was going to make it through the next several hours without touching her.

He finally came to a stop in front of her and she looked up at him, her eyes shining. "Hi," she said, her voice quiet and a bit breathy.

"Oh Maddy," he breathed, his eyes taking her in up close. Of course the dress and the jewels were lovely on her. But her smile. The shining chocolate pools of her eyes. The way he could see her chest rising and falling, as nervous and excited to see him as he was to see her; those were the things that made her exquisite. Unable to control himself, he leaned down to press a gentle kiss to the side of her face. "God, I've missed you," he whispered into her ear.

"Me too," she replied on an unsteady exhale. "So much."

There was a moment of slight awkwardness. After so long of not having seen each other and now to be reunited in such a public place it was like neither of them knew what to do besides stare at each other, grinning slightly goofily.

"You look jaw-droppingly beautiful," he finally said, wrenching his eyes from her to take in her appearance again.

She flushed slightly and smiled a bit self-consciously, "Thank you. So do you. I mean, you know I go crazy for you in a tux." He'd changed from the morning suit he'd worn for the wedding to a classic Tom Ford tuxedo. "And the jewelry is just… thanks, again."

"Hannah was right," he said, smiling. "It's perfect."

"She's something else," Maddie said with a rueful grin. "I thought a tornado had entered Harrod's when she showed up."

Alex chuckled, imagining his new sister-in-law taking over Maddie's shopping appointment. "I can only imagine." He suddenly realized that they were in the middle of a party. "Let's get you a drink, and then I want you to meet my brother."

"Okay," she said, taking his extended hand with a grin. A waiter cruised by the edge of the dance floor, and Alex grabbed two flutes of champagne from their tray, handing one to Maddy.

"To Ben and Hannah," Maddy said, her eyes still shining as they clinked their glasses together.

"I mean, okay," he said, smiling, "But also to you. You're amazing, and I'm so bloody happy you're here." She smiled back at him as they clinked glasses again, and he took her other hand as he started searching the dance floor for his brother.

It would be incorrect to say that his brother had never met any of the girls that Alex was seeing. There had been Imogen, after all. But they'd also often been together when Alex was in his slutty era, sleeping his way through every weekend in the country they were invited to. This felt really different, though. Most of the people he'd dated casually in the past had been mutual acquaintances, members of the tiny group of those deemed appropriate company for the sons of the king, women they'd known since they were children. There had never been someone he'd wanted to be sure his brother met. Who he wanted to show off—in a totally non-misogynist way—to his big brother as if to say, "See, I can find someone normal and appropriate to date." Much as he wanted to be perceived by his family as a real functional adult and a valuable member of the family business, he also found himself desperately seeking his brother's approval.

But in spite of his and Maddy's insistence that what they had was casual and short-term and their mutually resolute refusal to acknowledge or discuss the future, he'd finally started to admit to himself that, whether he wanted to or not, he had real feelings for the amazing woman weaving her way through the crowd next to him, and he hated the idea of letting her leave him to go back to America someday. He was terrified to ask about it, terrified of the rejection that was sure to come if he suggested anything less casual, but he also found himself growing more and more certain that he was going to have to bring it up. He was falling in love with her, and he couldn't carry on without telling her for much longer.

He finally found his brother and Hannah, dancing at the center of a crowd of sweaty socialites. His brother's bowtie was untied and hanging around his neck, the top button of his tuxedo shirt undone, and Hannah had changed from her massive wedding gown into a sleek white one-piece garment that he thought he'd heard someone call a "jumpsuit."

When Hannah caught sight of them her face lit up as she pushed past Alex to hug Maddie, who narrowly avoided sloshing her champagne onto Hannah from the force of the embrace. "You look *smashing*!" Hannah was almost screaming. "I *knew* that jewelry was going to be perfect. You look like a *snack*!" Anyone else might think that a bride at this point on her wedding day was a few glasses of champagne past her limit, but Alex knew Hannah well enough to know that this was just her over-the-top level of enthusiasm for things she cared about. "I'm *so* glad you're here," Hannah was gushing as she drew Maddy into their circle.

Ben came closer, clearly waiting for introductions to be made.

"Ben, I'd like to introduce Madeleine Cartwright." He realized that they hadn't really discussed labels in their secret relationship, so as much as he desperately wanted to call Maddy his girlfriend, he refrained. "Maddy, this is my brother, Benjamin."

Maddy dropped an adorable curtsey in his brother's direction, "Congratulations, Your Royal Highness," she said, just audible over the music.

"Oh my god, Alex, what have you told this poor girl about me?" Ben said, laughing and reaching for her hand. "Call me Ben. It's about time my idiot brother brought you around. I've heard a lot about you."

Maddy smiled shyly as she shook his hand, "You too," she said, looking as if she felt slightly out of her element shaking hands with the heir to the throne, but thankfully before she could retreat into her shell or Ben could start telling embarrassing stories, the Great Equalizer intervened as the unmistakable strings that signaled the beginning of "Come On Eileen" started blasting and everyone started jumping in synchronized absurdity. Maddy threw back the last of her champagne and Alex hastily found a corner in front of the stage to ditch their flutes before joining her and his brother and Hannah in an exuberant mass of flailing limbs and shaking hips. Alex took Maddy's hands, twirling her and laughing freely at the mirth on her face.

The evening flew by. Alex couldn't believe how easily Maddy fell into their circle of dancing madness. Despite her earlier protestations that she "couldn't dance," Maddy impressed with her ability to keep up with the seemingly unending key changes of Beyonce's "Love on Top," and delighted Hannah with her ability to recall every word and most of the dance moves to "Wannabe" by the Spice Girls.

After a number of consecutive upbeat bangers, the DJ slowed things down, and the mellow piano intro to "Come Away with Me" by Norah Jones began to waft over the crowd. Just as Alex started to pull Maddy into his arms, he found himself victim to something he'd only ever seen in movies—in one fluid motion his brother tugged Maddy into his own arms while simultaneously pushing Hannah into Alex's. Alex almost protested, but Hannah cut him off, "Don't waste your breath," she said with an affectionately cheeky smile. "Give him a chance to make the 'big brother' speech." Alex looked helplessly as his brother whisked *his* girl into an effortless slow waltz and finally, realizing that Hannah was right, refocused his attention on his new sister-in-law.

"Alex, she's great," Hannah said, as he rested a hand lightly on her back, taking her right hand in his left.

"She really is," he said, smiling fondly over her shoulder toward where Ben was leaning down slightly to hear something that Maddie was saying to him.

"Do you think she can hang?" Hannah asked. She didn't have to spell out what she meant: could Maddy make it in the royal family? Could she withstand the spotlight and the media attention? Alex knew she *could*—she would be brilliant at it—but *would* she was the real question. After everything she'd been through after Evan's death, he couldn't bring himself to think about asking. He wanted to, though. More than he'd ever wanted anything in his life before.

He sighed, refocusing on Hannah. "It's a lot to ask of someone," he said diplomatically.

"I mean, she's done the paparazzi thing before," she countered.

"So you know about that."

"I obviously Googled her immediately," Hannah said.

"Of course you did," he said, rolling her eyes as he pushed her out into a gentle spin. "But," he continued, pulling her back to him, "she moved to another continent to get away from it."

Hannah sighed. "I was hoping that wasn't why she was here."

"It's totally why she's here."

"Have you talked about it?"

"What, about how the paparazzi hounded her after her husband was tragically killed in action?"

"No, about what would happen if you went public. "

He huffed out a laugh. "We haven't even talked about whether we'll still be together next month, let alone whether it's going to be more serious than that."

"But you want it to be."

Alex sighed heavily. "I do."

"You need to tell her."

"I know." The song ended, ending their conversation, as well. Alex released Hannah as Ben and Maddy made their way back to them, but before he could ask Maddy what his brother had said to her, the inimitable '80s synthetic rhythms of the opening of "I Wanna Dance with Somebody" started and the whole crowd went wild, the cream of young English aristocracy all singing, as if with one voice, into imaginary microphones. Even as he enthusiastically joined in, Alex couldn't help but look at Maddy. He hadn't been entirely sure what to expect from her at an event like this. She'd initially been somewhat reluctant to come, claiming she wasn't sure that she really belonged, worrying that they'd be seen, that she'd be recognized, clearly just generally uncomfortable with the idea.

Yet, after the initial slight overwhelm and awkwardness he'd sensed when she arrived, she'd loosened up noticeably, seeming at ease with both Hannah and his brother, dancing, as it were, as if nobody was watching.

As Whitney Houston's unparalleled vocals faded away, the rich brass opening to Ray LaMontagne's "You Are the Best Thing" began, and Alex pulled her toward him, a lazy grin on his face as he pressed their hips together, swaying Maddy back and forth in his arms, singing quietly in her ear and realizing that the lyrics about feeling seen perfectly summed up the way he felt with Maddy. To her, he wasn't a prince, or a celebrity. He'd never been a cardboard cutout in her teenage bedroom. To her he was a real man—just Alex. She gazed up into his eyes, her eyes sparkling and, as the final chorus echoed the lyrics about being the best thing that ever happened to someone, it was like something moved through them. Some kind of tacit understanding. Alex felt absurd calling it a seismic shift even in his own mind, but it was as if their souls locked into place and some sense of mutual understanding flowed between them. Maddy's eyes grew soulful as he saw her feeling it too. She gave him a tiny, subtle nod, and his heart soared. No words had been spoken, but he knew what she was saying and suddenly, he knew that he might have a chance and he really couldn't wait any longer.

Chapter 24

Maddy had to shake herself slightly as the brassy chords of "You Are the Best Thing" segued into the soulful piano intro to Adele's "Make You Feel My Love." She was pretty sure he'd also felt whatever it was that had happened as they both heard Ray LaMontagne's lyrics. The way he held her tighter as Adele sang about the difficulty of making decisions made her sure. The way she felt about Alex was becoming undeniable, ungovernable. She wasn't going to be able to contain it for much longer and suddenly she wasn't sure how she could ever have imagined leaving him to go to Washington, DC. As they swayed gently to Adele's luscious voice, she couldn't imagine ever dancing with anyone ever again.

As the song ended, she looked up at him, and his lips came crashing down on hers. A small part of her wondered if they should really be kissing in public, but the rest of her immediately overrode the worry, relaxing into their kiss as if nobody else existed. After a moment, Alex pulled away. "What do you say we get out of here?" he whispered hotly into her ear.

"Yes, please," she responded immediately.

They quickly said goodbye to Ben and Hannah, who promised to have them over for dinner as soon as they were back from their honeymoon to an exclusive island in the Aegean, and Alex wove a path through the crowd toward the exit, stopping briefly to whisper something in Eric's ear along the way. Eric nodded and pulled out his phone, clearly following the instructions that Maddy hadn't been able to hear over the loud music.

As they exited the ballroom into the relative calm of the hallway outside, Alex wrapped an arm around her, pulling her closer. They descended the grand staircase, and Maddy had a surreal moment remembering the last time she'd made this descent. It was the night she and Alex had had their meet-disaster and she'd been shepherding the Stewart twins back to Winfield house, completely oblivious of the way that evening was going to shape the next eight months of her life. The passing memory must have shown on her face because Alex quietly asked, "What? What was that thought?"

"I was just remembering that the last time I walked down these stairs was the night of martini-gate."

"Martini-gate?" he asked, laughing.

"Yeah, you know, the night we met."

"You call it martini-gate?"

"What do you call it?"

There was a brief, self-conscious pause. "The night that changed my life."

Maddy's breath caught in her throat and blinked back the sudden tears that clouded her eyes. Even though she'd just been thinking about the event in similar terms, it was somehow different hearing Alex say that it had been life-changing for him, as well.

"I mean, it was that too," she replied quietly as they reached the bottom of the staircase. A liveried attendant pushed the door open for them, revealing one of the royal family's seemingly endless number of identical Range Rovers. The driver opened the back door for them, and Maddy quickly climbed in, sliding over so Alex could join her. As the car pulled away from the portico outside of Buckingham Palace, Alex reached over and took her hand. She squeezed, rubbing her thumb across the back of his hand and turning to look at him as they pulled out of the gates into the non-existent traffic of London at one a.m. There was the same look in his eyes as there had been when they danced. One that portended something ineffable but monumental. She found herself thinking that she couldn't imagine a life where she didn't get a chance to gaze into those eyes as often as possible. As if sensing her train of thought, Alex leaned over and kissed her. His kiss was gentle but searching, as if he was trying to tell her something and discern her answer all at once, without words.

They rode in near silence for the short drive from Buckingham to Alex's apartments. When they got there, however, after Alex had unlocked the front door to his apartment and led Maddy in, the mood shifted instantly. As the door closed behind them, Alex had her pressed up against it almost immediately, his lips crushing hers in a searing kiss, full of urgency and need. And Maddy gave it back in spades. Between their separation during the lead-up to the wedding and then the full day of activity and full night of being in near constant physical contact but unable to do more than steal a quick kiss, the tension had been simmering all evening and immediately erupted into a full boil.

Maddy reached up, raking her hands through Alex's hair as he invaded her personal space, cocking a knee between her thighs. Maddy immediately found herself grinding against it, ignoring the slight abrasion of the elaborate beading on The Dress in favor of the exquisite friction he was offering her.

"Fuck, Maddy," he hissed out as her hands moved to grasp

his butt firmly, pulling him closer to her. "I know it's not classy, but part of me kind of just wants to take you right here. I need you so much."

She huffed out a laugh that turned to half a moan as his lips found the sensitive spot on the side of her neck. "Well, the floor looks pretty cold and I don't think I can come standing up, so I'm voting for bed."

His eyes darkened. "That's not what you said in my shower on Christmas night, but for tonight, if you say bed, then bed it is."

He tugged on her hand, leading her quickly to the stairs and almost dragging her towards his bedroom.

"Where's Bertie?" she asked, suddenly realizing that they hadn't been greeted or interrupted by the adorable canine cockblock.

"Boarded him for the weekend," Alex replied, fully focused on his mission as he pulled her into his room.

Despite the urgency of a few moments before, he slowed down enough to reverently unzip The Dress, kissing his way across the backs of her shoulders and her neck as it fell to the floor.

"Gorgeous," he breathed, running the back of one of his fingers down the column of her spine to the waistband of the black lace thong, which was the last vestige of clothing on her body now that The Dress lay in an iridescent green pool around her feet. Cupping her left breast with one hand and pinching her already erect nipple, he tugged gently on the back of the thong with his other hand, exerting exquisite pressure.

"Alex," she gasped, nearly overwhelmed with sensation.

"You like that, hm?" he almost growled in her ear, slipping a knuckle beneath the thong to tease her gently where nobody had ever touched her before. The only response she could muster was an incoherent groan, her head lolling back onto his shoulder in pleasure as he continued driving her crazy with both hands.

When she finally managed to formulate a sentence, it was "You're wearing too much." She worked up the fortitude to turn in his arms, their lips meeting again as she started working at the studs of his tuxedo shirt. She thanked the menswear gods who had decided that the strangely small fastenings were the thing for tux shirts—it was much easier to undo them in a lusty haze than it was normal shirt buttons—and soon they were pressed together again, bare chest to bare chest. When he'd managed to toe out of his shoes and she'd shoved his pants and boxer briefs down in one go, she finally succumbed to the urge to climb him like an incredibly sexy English tree. He backed toward the bed, her legs locked around his lower back, their kisses growing more urgent, almost frantic.

When the back of Alex's legs hit the bed, he sat, pulling her with him. She could feel his rock-hard cock pushing against her lace-covered pussy and she gave into the urge to grind against him again. "Maddy," he moaned. "You're going to kill me."

"We haven't even started yet," she said, in the sultriest voice she could muster. She felt an unusual sense of confidence. One that she didn't usually feel in the bedroom, where she was usually quite happy for Alex to take the lead, almost to the point of dominance. Pushing him back onto the mattress, she backed up, standing in front of him with one thumb tucked into the hip of her thong. Alex had one arm bent behind his head, his other hand stroking himself lightly as she bit her lip and, never breaking eye contact, slid the thong down her legs, leaving her standing there in nothing but the black shoes she'd worn to the party. She stuck one foot out at an angle and started to bend over to unbuckle the ankle strap when he gasped out. "No, don't. Leave them on."

She cocked an eyebrow at him and said, "Well then,"

before stalking back towards the bed and crawling toward him. Planting her hands on either side of his head, she held herself up, leveling a smoldering gaze directly into his eyes. She lowered her head so that only their lips were touching in a tantalizingly gentle kiss. He moaned beneath her, and she felt the mattress shift as his hips writhed beneath her. She lowered herself a bit more so she could suck on his neck and she felt one of his fingers find her entrance.

"Fuck, Maddy. You're so wet." His moistened fingers found her clit, circling once, twice, before dipping down to slip into her again. "I need you, Mads," he rasped, his other hand gripping her ass tightly.

Maddy reached for the nightstand and pulled out a condom, ripping it open as he watched her, his gaze burning with heat. Leaning back, her thighs bracketing his, she sheathed him, breaking eye contact only to make sure the condom wasn't going on inside out. As she rolled it down his length, Alex hissed, flexing his hips. She kneeled back over him and lowered herself onto his cock, her eyes rolling back in her head as he filled her.

She didn't know quite where this was coming from, why tonight of all nights she wanted to be the one in charge, but it just felt right, and she loved that Alex was going along with it happily, unquestioningly. She started rolling her hips, testing out what felt good in the unfamiliar position. Finding her rhythm, she found his hands, pinning them on either side of his head on the pillow, using him for leverage as she moved on top of him.

Their eyes met and, for the third time that night, she found herself in some kind of magic bubble. From the look in his eyes, Maddy could tell that Alex felt it too. A new sense of energy flowed through her as they both climbed toward the peak. A new confidence, a new certainty. She suddenly knew that there was nowhere else she could be. She couldn't leave him to go back to the States. She was exactly where she needed to be.

"Maddy." Alex's voice was urgent. "I'm close."

She unclasped her right hand from his left to reach between them. She was so close that it only took a few seconds of touching herself before she felt her orgasm overtake her and Alex cried out almost immediately after. She continued moving slowly, wringing as much pleasure as she possibly could before she collapsed against his chest, both of them breathing hard. Alex wrapped his arms around her loosely, stroking up and down her back absently, his muscles clearly still recovering, and she almost purred.

"Alex," she whispered, a sudden moment of the strange confidence and clarity returning to her.

"Hmm?"

"I love you," she said. It happened so fast that she didn't really have time to be nervous about his response or second-guess herself—it just came out, and she somehow knew that it was the right thing.

His hands stilled on her back and a flicker of a doubt crossed Maddy's mind, but a moment later she felt his chest rise with a shaky inhale and his arms came around her more firmly. "I love you too." His voice was thick with emotion, but absolutely steady.

She levered herself up so she could look into his eyes, a feeling of almost giddiness washing over her, a grin splitting her face and found him gazing back at her. He had the same look in his eyes that she'd noticed a few times that day and suddenly realized that it was love. She kissed him exuberantly before snuggling down into his arms.

They talked for a little while coming down from the high of their shared professions and debriefing the day together.

When they started to drift off, Maddy found herself idly composing the email in her head telling Georgetown that she would not be accepting their offer of admission.

Chapter 25

When Maddy woke up the next morning, the first thing she felt was utter contentment. She was cocooned in Alex's arms, and even without opening her eyes, she could tell that sun was streaming through the window next to what had become her side of the bed. As her brain came fully online, she remembered the night before: the glittering party, dancing with Alex and his friends and family, and their professions of love.

But the utter contentment gradually turned to confusion as she realized that a faint but persistent banging sound was what had woken her. She rolled over and pushed herself up on one elbow, placing one hand on Alex's shoulder. "What's that noise?" she asked.

"Nothing, don't worry about it, we have nothing to do today except this," he mumbled blearily, pulling her back down into her arms and kissing her. The banging sound had stopped, so Maddy allowed herself to be drawn back into his embrace and tried to relax.

But a second later she heard someone calling and the muffled thumping of what was clearly someone coming up the carpeted stairs to the second floor of Alex's apartment. "Alex," she said with more urgency filling her voice, "someone's here."

"Hmm?" he murmured. He didn't have time to say anything else before someone was knocking on the bedroom door.

"Alex?" Eric's voice came through the door, and even though Maddy had only met him on a handful of occasions, she could tell by the tone of his voice that he wasn't there on a social call.

"Eric?" Alex called back, confusion creasing his face.

The door opened and Eric came in, dressed as casually as Maddy had ever seen him in chinos and a button-down shirt, one hand in front of his face, clearly hoping to avoid seeing more of his friend slash boss than he wanted to. "Alex, I'm terribly sorry, but this really couldn't wait. Are you decent?"

"Absolutely not," Alex said, his brain finally fully awake. He pushed himself to a seated position and glanced over his shoulder. Maddy had already hastily wrapped herself in the sheet, shielding her nakedness. Alex swung his legs over the side of the bed and quickly grabbed the boxer briefs he'd discarded the night before. "Okay, you can look now," he said, standing and striding towards the closet for his robe. "What the bloody hell is going on?"

It was only then that Maddy noticed the bundle of newspapers folded in half under Eric's arm. Her heart sank, somehow innately knowing what they'd contain, as he handed them to Alex.

"Fuck" was all Alex said, running a hand down his face before looking at Maddy.

She was fairly certain the blood had already completely rushed from her face, but if it hadn't already, it would have when Alex gently laid the array of tabloids on the bed next to her and she saw the headlines that only the British tabloid media could conceive and publish.

ALEX'S MERRY WIDOW
ALEX'S AMERICAN SECRET
DON'T SPARE US THE DETAILS, ALEX – WHO IS SHE?
THE SPARE'S SECRET AFFAIR!
HEIR'S SPARE: A PAIR?

The cover image was one taken with a long lens the night previously—*wow, they were fast*, she thought—of Alex's arm around her, ushering her out to the car as they left the reception. As she idly flipped through the stack, she realized that someone must have been working on this for weeks. There were pictures of her jogging in Regent's Park, of Alex entering a restaurant and her leaving the same restaurant hours later, and even one of the two of them leaving Winfield House to get into his car on Christmas night when he'd taken her back to his apartment.

Maddy found herself transported back to another time. Heard the unceasing vibration of her phone as texts, DMs, alerts flooded it with friends, acquaintances, total strangers asking for interviews. She remembered the feeling of struggling to get from her car to her parents' front door, so besieged by paparazzi that it made it hard to even leave the house. Remembered the feeling of seeing people she barely knew quoted in colorful insets in *People*, being interviewed on *Good Morning America*, talking about Maddy as if they talked every day when, in reality, she hadn't seen these people in years. A feeling of total numbness washed over her.

"Maddy?" She felt Alex's hand on her upper arm and, when she looked up and saw his and Eric's faces, realized it wasn't the first time he'd tried to get her attention.

Air finally forced itself into her body, her biological imperatives taking control as her brain short-circuited. "Sorry," she said faintly. "What were you saying?"

She saw Alex and Eric give each other A Look, and Alex

said, "Eric, let us get dressed. We'll meet you in the sitting room in a moment."

"Of course," he said, giving Maddy one more worried look and quietly leaving, closing the door behind him with a soft click that somehow managed to sound ominous.

"Mads," Alex said gently, turning to her and attempting to peer into her eyes, which were still focused, unseeing, on the abhorrent headlines. She shook herself and pushed her legs over the side of the bed, walking numbly toward the drawer that had a few of her clothes in it for when she stayed over. "Maddy, I—" Alex tried again.

"We shouldn't keep Eric waiting," she said, single-mindedly focused on trying to put on a pair of leggings that were half inside out and half right side out. She robotically slipped into a black-and-white-striped tunic sweatshirt and threw her sleep-mussed hair into a high bun. When she turned around Alex had donned a pair of gray sweatpants that normally sent her mind straight to the gutter, but today had no impact. He was shrugging into a worn Cambridge T-shirt, looking at her searchingly, but apparently having given up trying to get her to talk about it. "I'm just going to brush my teeth," she said. "I'll meet you in there."

Alex frowned, but he nodded as she turned towards the en suite.

She didn't register the taste of the toothpaste, the feel of the water she splashed on her face, even her own appearance in the mirror. She moved as if in a trance, so trapped in the emptiness of her own thoughts, forcing the memories out, not allowing the reality of the present to encroach, that she only registered having left Alex's bedroom when she walked into the lounge and found Eric leaning against the mantle and Alex pacing behind the couch.

"Eric, *how* did they get this?" Alex was saying, sounding quietly furious.

"Alex, I know you were careful, but you know the British press. You both have experience with this." Maddy wasn't surprised that Eric knew her entire backstory. "You had to know that it was only a matter of time before this got out."

Maddy sighed and nodded, studiously not making eye contact with either of the two men who she knew were watching her carefully, waiting for any sign of reaction, breakdown, basic emotion. And it wasn't that she was afraid to show emotion in front of them. But she also knew that it was going to be a long day. That there were many important conversations to be had. And that once she let herself actually feel the feelings that she was currently forcing down somewhere below her diaphragm, she wouldn't be able to stop feeling them and function normally for quite a while. And so she said, perfectly calmly and rationally, "Yes, we should have known. It was stupid to think that we'd be able to keep this under wraps. We were naive to think that we could have kept this secret for very long."

She saw Eric nod out of the corner of her eye. "So I don't know if either of you has checked your phone yet..."

Maddy shook her head and saw Alex do the same from where he was still pacing.

"So the most important thing is not to talk to any press. Don't answer calls or texts from any numbers you don't know, don't comment to anyone. Who else knew about you before this broke?"

"Besides you? My brother and Hannah. That's it."

"And Graham. And Hannah's personal shopper at Harrods," Maddy added. "And, of course, everyone at the reception last night."

"What about you, Maddy? Who did you tell?" Eric asked. "Those are all our people."

"No one," she said quietly. "My friend Nadia knows I'm seeing someone, but not who it is."

The hollow numbness in Maddy's chest started to give way to anxiety. A need to fix things. "What's next?" she asked, turning to Eric, a new sheen of resolve falling across her face. "We just made your week a lot harder. What do you need from us?"

Eric smiled. "Well, this is my job, so don't worry about me. But we do need to sort a few things out rather quickly," he began. "Their Royal Highnesses want to see you at one p.m. at Buckingham."

Alex's head fell, and a small part of Maddy cracked open. Not enough to let her actually feel things, but enough to realize that this was going to be much harder on Alex. He'd spent his entire adult life fighting back from a single misstep as a child, and she could see his brain convincing him that this was going to be a reason for his family to whisk him back into their cocoon again. She crossed to stand next to him and took his hand, putting her other hand on his upper arm. "It's going to be okay," she said quietly, not believing it for a second, but feeling compelled to offer him some kind of reassurance.

He smiled at her a bit wistfully and put his arm around her, kissing the top of her head tenderly. "I think I'm supposed to be telling you that."

"Okay, so you'll go to your parents'," she said, glancing at a clock on the mantle and sighing, "and I'll go back to Winfield House and do some damage control." The niggling concern that she was probably about to lose her job wormed its way into the hollow emptiness she was feeling.

She turned to go, but Eric stopped her. "Maddy, you'll need to wait for me to call a car. You won't be walking anywhere alone anytime soon."

Of course she wouldn't. She knew how this went. She'd done this before. "I'll just go pull a bag together if you'll call one for me, please, Eric," she said quietly.

"Mads, wait, I'll come with you," Alex started, but Maddy silenced him with a look.

"You shouldn't keep your parents waiting." It came out sharper than she'd intended, but she knew if she and Alex were alone together he'd try to comfort her and she'd lose control. The effort of forcing her emotions down was starting to weigh on her. "I'll talk to you later."

She walked swiftly out of the room before either of the two men had a chance to say anything. *Just keep moving.* It was the same mantra she'd used two years previously when she'd been in an almost identical situation. *Get your things and go. Face the Stewarts.* She wanted nothing more than to slip back under the comforting weight of Alex's duvet and go back to sleep. To wake up again in a few hours and find out this had all been a terrible nightmare. But she knew that it wasn't a dream, that she was repeating history, and that she had no choice but to face it. As she grabbed her phone from the nightstand she saw an eerily familiar shockingly large number of notifications. Missed calls from friends, strangers, Mrs. Stewart, her former sister-in-law. *Evan's family.* Her heart sank further. They never should have found out like this. A fresh wave of guilt washed over her, and she renewed her efforts to force her feelings as far down as she could.

As she turned to leave Alex appeared. "Darling," he said softly, his eyes full of emotion.

She took a deep breath and looked up at him. "Go talk to your parents. Let's talk tonight."

He nodded and she saw him swallow. Somehow the emotion she saw breaking through his facade of calm was what was going to break her, so she gently pushed past him. *Just keep moving. Just keep moving.*

Eric met them at the front door. "The car is outside," he said quietly, a sympathetic look on his face. "There are quite a lot of reporters at the gate," he continued. Maddy fished an old Vassar baseball cap out of the tote bag she'd found in Alex's room and pushed it onto her head, pulling her messy bun through the hole in the back. "Keep your head down, don't talk to any reporters."

She nodded tightly, forcing herself not to remember the last time.

"Someone from the Kensington press office will be in touch to coordinate some kind of statement."

She swallowed and nodded again, unable to form words. The warm sparkly feelings of the night before were gone. She'd forgotten how this felt. She realized belatedly and terribly that this was what it would be like if she picked Alex. This would be her everyday.

"Mads," Alex said, turning her toward him and taking her in his arms. She forced herself to meet his gaze and found his warm eyes searching her face, concern etched across his face. "We'll figure this out. I'll take care of you." She nodded silently. "I love you," he said, a heartbreaking earnestness in his voice.

"I love you too," she managed to get out. That hadn't changed. The way she felt about him hadn't changed. And that made what was about to happen even worse.

Chapter 26

Maddy tried to keep her mind blank as the Range Rover made its way through the throngs of photographers at the gates to Kensington Palace. She remembered what Eric said and kept her cap pulled low, her head down. Tried to force herself to think practically: she'd need to call her parents. Evan's family. Her college friends. She'd more or less stopped using social media after the last time this had happened, so she didn't need to worry about that. She kept the mental list running, trying to keep her mind off the reality of what was happening. Again.

The driver wasn't Graham, and Maddy was almost relieved that it was a silent stranger. She wasn't sure she could have abided Alex's normal driver's kindness and loyalty. It would have broken her. All too soon, the car approached Winfield House, and she calmly directed the driver to the side entrance that would take her to the kitchen. There were still photographers lining the sidewalk on either side of the less obtrusive gate, but at least the kitchen door was slightly more protected from prying eyes than the main entrance.

As they pulled up to the door, she gathered her things and

pulled down her hat again, as if the canvas might protect her further. "Please wait for me to let you out, Ms. Cartwright," the driver said, clearly sensing that she was planning to make a dash for it. She sighed and nodded, and allowed him to at least slightly block the view as she darted from the open door of the Range Rover into the Winfield House kitchen. She could hear the faint calls of the paparazzi as she went, but it was over in a second and then she was slamming the door behind her and leaning against it, trying to catch her breath.

When she opened her eyes, Pierre and one of his sous-chefs were staring at her with a mix of confusion and pity, but she gave them a small smile and breezed past them. She wanted nothing more than to turn down the stairs into her room, but knew putting off the inevitable wasn't going to make what she needed to do next any easier. She headed toward Ambassador Stewart's office.

Most of the staff were still observing the bank holidays given around the royal wedding, so when she approached the ambassador's office, his secretary wasn't there and the door was ajar. She could hear murmured voices inside and knocked with as much confidence as she could muster.

"Come in" came the ambassador's booming voice from the other side of the door.

Maddy took one more deep breath before straightening her shoulders and walking in. Ambassador Stewart was sitting behind his desk wearing a pale-blue button-down shirt, unbuttoned at the collar. Mrs. Stewart was mid-pace in front of his desk when Maddy entered. There was a moment of awkward silence before Maddy finally said, "Hi."

"Madeleine—" Mrs. Stewart began, and Maddy could tell from just the one word she got out that she was furious.

"Delia." Ambassador Stewart also only had to say one word, his voice kind, but stern, stopping his irritated wife both mid-sentence and mid-stride. "Can I have a moment with Maddy, please?"

"Andrew, I really think—" his wife began again, not one to be easily cowed.

"Delia, I'd like a word alone with Maddy first." His tone brooked no argument.

She sighed and nodded, glaring at Maddy as she walked past.

"Have a seat," he said, gesturing at one of the chairs across from his desk.

Maddy sat in the same seat she'd taken four months earlier when the Ambassador had called her in to ask her to reconsider going home for Christmas.

"Ambassador Stewart—" Maddy began, but he held his hand up.

"Maddygirl," he said, looking at her searchingly. "Are you okay?"

His question surprised her. So much so that it took a second for her to respond. Her instinct was to say that yes, of course, she was okay. But the look on his face told her that he wasn't interested in her stock answer. "I… I don't know," she said simply.

"Have you talked to your parents?" he asked.

"Not yet, sir."

"And what about the Grogans?"

Maddy blinked back tears as she shook her head no, remembering Evan's sweet parents who absolutely didn't deserve the renewed media attention their son's death was about to get.

"Is this a fling? Or is this real?" he asked. Maddy was, again, surprised by the genuine empathy in his voice. She'd expected to come in and be fired immediately, not to have a conversation about her relationship. "I know the prince has in the past had... a reputation," the ambassador went on tactfully.

"It's real," Maddy whispered. "Or at least, it was." She paused and then figured in for a penny, in for a pound. "I love him."

"Then it seems like you have a decision to make," he said. Maddy nodded silently. There was another pause. "You haven't asked for my opinion," the ambassador said, "but this feels an awful lot like the circumstances that brought you over here in the first place." Maddy nodded again, miserably. "And, much as I hate to say it, unlike the way they would have died down if you'd stayed back home, I don't think the interest will die down here. Prince Alex has been a topic of great interest to the British public for years, and especially now that that wedding is over, they're going to be gunning for something new to rip into."

Maddy sighed. "You're right."

"I don't envy you that decision, Maddygirl," he said. Another pause. "I wish you'd told me."

"I'm so sorry," she said, finally looking at him.

"Take some time for yourself. You've got a lot of thinking to do."

"Thank you," she said, standing and picking up the bag she'd brought home from Alex's.

She walked numbly back through the main wing of the embassy towards the kitchen and slipped down the stairs, grateful that she didn't run into anyone on the way. When she reached the bottom of the stairs, she dropped the bag and collapsed onto the couch.

Before she'd even had a chance to fully relax onto the couch there was a knock at the door, and without waiting for Maddy to answer, Nadia appeared at the top of the steps, a tea tray in hand. She pulled the door closed behind her and descended the steps. She set her tray down on the table and perched on the end of the sofa next to Maddy's legs. "Well, you've had one hell of a morning," she said matter-of-factly.

Maddy let out the first half of a watery laugh, but midway through it turned into a sob and before she knew it, Nadia had gathered her in her arms and was holding her as her whole body shook with the emotions she'd been valiantly holding in since Eric had woken them a few hours earlier. Nadia rubbed her back gently, murmuring comforting words as Maddy cried, letting out the feelings that had been choking her all day: guilt, shame, embarrassment, the trauma of the flashbacks to Evan's death, and, most of all, the utter devastation that she was going to lose the love of her life again. And this time he was the *real* love of her life.

She cried for what felt like hours, and when the tears had finally petered out, Nadia passed her a box of tissues from the end table. Maddy accepted them and set about cleaning up the metric ton of snot that had escaped her as she sobbed. "So Mr. Martini is Prince Alex, eh?" Nadia said wryly.

"I'm so sorry I didn't tell you," she said, her eyes welling up again.

"Don't apologize! I assume you've signed all kinds of things saying you won't blab about it."

"Actually, I haven't. At least not yet," she said, wiping at her nose. "But we promised to keep it secret. It wasn't supposed to be for real. It was supposed to be a casual fling."

"But it's more than a casual fling," Nadia said, filling in what Maddy had left unsaid.

Maddy nodded. "Nadia," she said, taking a deep breath. "There's something else I should have told you a long time ago."

"What else can there possibly be?" Nadia asked in astonishment.

"I was married," Maddy began. "Before I came. That's

actually why I came. He was a soldier. He was killed in action two years ago."

"Oh, I know all that!" Nadia said, her hands flapping in dismissal.

"You do?"

"Of course I do! You showing up out of nowhere all suddenly like that? I Googled you the day we met!"

Maddy gaped at her for a second and then burst out laughing. "I should have known," she finally said as her laughs subsided into misery again. "Why didn't you tell me you knew?"

"I knew you'd tell me when you were ready," Nadia said simply.

"Well, I'm sorry that I didn't tell you sooner," Maddy said. "I should have. You've been a good friend to me, and you deserve better than this."

"I have to imagine," Nadia said, pouring them each a cup of tea from the pot on the tray she'd brought down, "that going through what you went through would make it a bit hard to trust people."

Maddy nodded. "But still."

Nadia shrugged at her and sipped her tea in silence.

"There's more," Maddy said. She went on quickly before Nadia could respond or Maddy could lose her nerve. "I wasn't in love with him anymore. With Evan, my late husband, I mean. We were childhood sweethearts and he meant a lot to me, but I wasn't in love with him anymore. I was planning to ask him for a divorce and then he died," she blurted out.

Nadia let out a long breath. "That's... a lot" was all she said.

"Yeah."

"But you are in love with the prince?"

"I am." Her eyes welled up again.

"So what now?"

"I don't know," Maddy said, staring miserably into her tea. But as much as she hated to admit it, she did know. In her heart, she knew that the reason she came to London no longer made sense. She couldn't let herself lose agency again. The answer became clearer by the second. She had to leave. And the perfect reason was sitting in her inbox, waiting for her answer.

* * *

Alex took a deep breath and fidgeted with the button at the cuff of one of his sleeves before striding into his family's private sitting room at Buckingham Palace. Much as he didn't want to have this conversation, he couldn't put it off any longer. He pushed the door open and walked in.

His parents were sitting in matching armchairs watching news coverage of the royal wedding. "Alex, darling!" His mother said, sounding thrilled to see him as she muted the TV and stood to greet him. She enveloped him in a warm hug before relinquishing him to his father.

"Dad," Alex said, accepting his father's hug, quieter, but no less warm.

"Son," his father said with a smile.

Alex hadn't been entirely sure what to expect. He was fairly certain his parents wouldn't be furious about his relationship with Maddy, but he also didn't expect quite the warm welcome that he seemed to be receiving. His parents had never pried into his personal life. He'd been as discreet as possible about his... activities with romantic partners, but he couldn't be sure that they'd never heard whisperings. He wasn't naive enough to think that the gossip in their tiny social circle wouldn't have made it back to the king and queen. But either out of ignorance or out of respect for his personal life, they'd never said anything to him. He leaned toward the former since, as loving and caring as his family was, they were not inclined to mind their own business.

"So tell us about Madeleine!" His mother crowed as she and his father resumed their seats and Alex sat on the sofa, his mother's black cat Anne of Cleves opening one eye to glare at him from the other cushion before tucking her nose back under her tail and going back to her nap.

"I..." Alex paused for a second as his parents looked at him, expectantly. "Well, as I guess you probably know she's American." He began, unsure of what to say or how to tell them. "And well, I..." He tried to be self-assured, tried not to stumble over his words or give them any reason to doubt his capability, his confidence. "I think she might be the one."

"Really?" His mother sounded positively delighted. "That's wonderful, darling!"

His father looked skeptical. "What makes you think she's the one?"

"Because I love her. And she loves me. And she loves me for me, not for my family or my title. She's kind and smart and funny and I've never met anyone like her."

"From what I'm hearing, she's been married before."

"Yes," Alex said, "so I assume you also know that her husband was killed in action serving in the American Army."

"So terrible," his mother interjected.

"Do you think she's up to the job?" his father asked bluntly.

Alex sighed. He knew that Maddy *could* do the job. She'd be bloody fantastic at it. Her warmth, her empathy, her concern for others came through in everything she did. She was practically the perfect candidate to be a working royal. The question was *would* she do it. And he was afraid of what the answer to that question was.

When he didn't respond, his father went on. "My sources tell me that when her husband was killed she was hounded by the American press. That she moved to London to work for the embassy a year later." Alex nodded silently. "The British press aren't the American press."

"I know—" Alex started.

"They're much worse."

Alex sighed. "I know."

His father looked at him kindly. "I want you to be happy, son. And if Madeleine is the right person for you, we will back you absolutely. But you both have to be very clear on what she's getting into if you bring her into this family. She has to be okay with what happened this morning being her everyday normal level of scrutiny." The king glanced at the TV, and inset over a wide shot of the crowds outside his brother's wedding, Alex saw footage of a black Range Rover leaving the gates of Kensington Palace. He realized it was video of Maddy leaving his apartment that morning. Through the gap in the front seats, he saw her, head down, dark sunglasses on, baseball cap pulled low. And she looked like a shell of the woman he knew. The woman he loved. Could he ask her to endure this every day for the rest of her life? Especially knowing the memories it must trigger for her? Could he be that selfish?

When he looked up from the television he saw both of his parents looking at him carefully. He had a nearly impossible decision to make.

Chapter 27

Maddy had just hit "submit" on the fateful form for Georgetown when her phone rang. Again. She felt like she'd spent the entire day on the phone. Her parents (concerned, slightly hurt that they'd been kept in the dark, but cautiously happy for her), Evan's parents (weepy, but kinder than she'd had any right to expect), a four-way call with her closest friends from college who mostly just wanted the dirt on what it was like to date a prince. She'd ignored any number of other calls and texts from "friends" who had already ridden her coattails the first time her life fell apart on national television, well-meaning acquaintances that she just didn't have the bandwidth for, and countless unknown numbers that she was sure were journalists. After the late night the night before and the drama of the day that she'd capped off by making a huge decision about her future, she was completely emotionally and physically exhausted.

She almost didn't even turn her phone on the couch cushion next to her to see who she was ignoring, but after a second, she gave in. It was Alex. "Hi," she said, answering the phone and resting her head on the back of the sofa.

"Hello, darling" came the familiar warmth of his voice. He sounded about as exhausted as she felt. There was a brief pause. "Are you okay?"

"I'm..." She really wasn't sure how to answer that question. "I don't know? I'm exhausted."

He chuckled softly. "Same." Another pause. "I wish you were here with me."

Suddenly there was a lump in her throat again. She swallowed against it, not wanting him to know how overwrought she was. "Me too," she managed to get out. "How did it go with your parents?"

"Fine, really. Mum was overjoyed. Can't wait to have you over for tea. And Dad just wants me, us really, to be happy. He wants to be sure we know what we're doing."

Maddy sighed. "Yeah." She felt bad that she wasn't holding up her end of the conversation very well, but she was so worn out that it was hard to even formulate sentences.

"How did it go for you? Did you talk to your family? The Stewarts?"

"Yes. My parents are worried about me and I think a little hurt that I didn't tell them before the news showed up at their house, but they want me to be happy. Mrs. Stewart was... not thrilled to be caught off guard by a PR moment that she could have spun to work better for them if she'd had control over it." She'd had a difficult conversation with Delia Stewart that afternoon. She'd definitely be doing nothing but desk work for the foreseeable future. "But I still have a job. For now."

"Good." He paused again. "Did... did you talk to Evan's family?"

She welled up remembering the hardest conversation of the day. "I did," she said, trying not to let him hear her emotion over the phone. "They..." She sniffled and then forced herself to go on. "They were lovely. They told me Evan would have wanted me to be happy and to find love again. They were shocked, but very kind about it." A tear trickled down her cheek, and she knew Alex could hear it in her voice.

"Oh, Mads." He sounded anguished. "I hate that you had to do all that alone. Do you want me to come over?"

"I'm okay," she said, wiping her eyes and trying to pull herself together. "I'm honestly so tired that I'll probably pass out pretty soon."

"Okay," he said quietly. There was another beat of silence. Their calls weren't normally this fragmented. Maddy bit back the urge to tell him about the decision she'd made, but she couldn't make herself do it. Couldn't add more to the awful, long day. And she knew she owed it to him to at least tell him in person.

"Maddy, I'm worried about you." Alex's voice was laced with concern. "I don't like you being alone through all this. This has to be bringing up so much for you."

"I mean, yeah, it is," she said, swallowing another lump in her throat. "And I appreciate your concern. But really right now mostly what I am is just exhausted." And feeling guilty. Again. "Please know that of course I want you here, but if you were here, you'd just be drawing more attention to this, and all you'd be doing is watching me sleep."

"I love watching you sleep," he said affectionately. "And I love you," he added more strongly. "I need you to know that nothing about all of this changes how I feel about you."

"Me too," she said, her voice watery with yet more unshed tears. "I love you too." At least that statement was 100% true, even if she was leaving out some significant information.

"Go get some sleep," he said gently. "We'll need to talk more about how we're going to handle this going forward, but that can wait until tomorrow."

"Okay," she said, her lip starting to tremble, thinking about how the decision she'd made would probably make their future planning a lot easier. And a lot shorter. "Goodnight, Alex."

"Goodnight, Mads," he said.

She really did wish he was there to hold her and tell her everything was going to be okay. Even though she knew in her heart that the email she'd sent just before he called was likely to be the beginning of the end of their relationship.

* * *

As much as Alex had truly intended that he and Maddy would see each other the next day, it didn't happen. Nor the day after. It had been decided that, given the current significant uptick in interest in Alex he needed to travel with security, but that meant making sure security was available. And then security didn't want to let him go to Winfield House because they hadn't had a chance to do a sweep before he went, despite his increasingly frustrated assurances that the residence of the American ambassador to England clearly had ample security measures in place.

Similarly, he'd tried to arrange for Maddy to come to him, but the throngs of paparazzi at the gates to both Kensington and Winfield meant that it would be a visible departure that he hated to put her through, and thanks to the influx of family and outings surrounding the wedding, there weren't enough cars to send one for her. They'd texted and talked on the phone a bit more, but Alex wouldn't feel settled—he hesitated to use the word "better," since the entire thing was a cluster-fuck and he was constantly worried Maddy was going to call him up and tell him it wasn't worth the scrutiny—until he'd seen her again. Seen for himself that she was physically safe and not a full-on emotional trainwreck. He knew she wasn't okay. But he'd settle for a slight derailment.

Finally on Thursday they were able to arrange for him to

bring carryout to her at Winfield and have dinner. It felt a little odd to be going to dinner there for the first time since their relationship had become public. As the car carrying him and his new constant companion Cross—unclear whether that was his first name or last name—pulled up to the entrance, he ducked his head to avoid the worst of the paparazzi flashes and Graham navigated the crowds and pulled in. When they arrived at the side door that he'd always gone into, he leaned forward, "So I'll just text you when I'm ready to come home, then?"

"Actually, Your Royal Highness, we'll be staying here," Cross said in his monotone voice. Truly he was like a security guard out of the movies.

"Ookay... I mean, I'm sure you can come in, if you like. The kitchen's just through there?" Alex said awkwardly.

"Thank you, Your Royal Highness, but I'll be here surveying the premises, and Mr. McIntosh will stay with the vehicle in case we need to make a rapid exit." Alex raised his eyebrows at Graham in the rearview mirror. Graham just shrugged. Alex sighed.

"Okay, then. Well, I'll see you in a few hours then."

He stepped out of the car before Cross could try to open the door for him and strode to the door, pointedly ignoring the photographers calling his name from the other side of the fence at the end of the drive. As he walked into the warmth of the Winfield House kitchen, a few kitchen staff looked up in surprise, but before he could say anything, Mrs. Stewart came bustling in. "Your Royal Highness, what a pleasant surprise!" she chirped, a large smile on her face. "We were so delighted to hear that you and our Madeleine had become closer friends!" He plastered on a smile of his own and started attempting to conjure some kind of appropriate response when Maddy emerged from the door that led down to her rooms.

Immediately, she could have been the only one in the

room, for all that Alex registered anyone else's presence. He walked around Mrs. Stewart, straight to Maddy and put the arm that wasn't holding a bag of Indian food around her, drawing her head to his shoulder. She was pale and had dark circles under her eyes, and Alex hated knowing that he was the reason she was so exhausted and upset. With a polite and he hoped not-too-dismissive comment to Mrs. Stewart over his shoulder, he ushered Maddy back down to her rooms so they could finally talk.

Maddy's brown hair was in a slightly limp ponytail, and she had on leggings and a gray long-sleeved Vassar T-shirt. For once, though, he didn't register the way her ass looked in the leggings. He needed to be holding her, assessing for himself that he hadn't completely ruined her life, trying to convince her not to give up on him. On *them*.

Reaching the bottom of the steps, Alex set the bag of carryout on the coffee table, slipped out of his coat, and immediately pulled Maddy down next to him on the couch, cuddling her close, as if they could snuggle their way out of the situation they were in. She allowed herself to be held, resting her head on his chest and wrapping her arms around him. He relaxed infinitesimally. At least she wasn't pushing him away.

Dropping a kiss to her head, he said, "I want to ask if you're okay, but I know you're not... so how not okay are you?"

She huffed out a shadow of a laugh. "I'm surviving," she said. "I think I've managed to block the numbers for most of the major news outlets again, so my phone is ringing slightly less off the hook." She shifted to look up at him. "What about you? Your parents really weren't upset?"

He smiled down at her, even as concern washed over him at how tired she looked. "No, not at all. I think Mum's mostly just jealous that Ben and Hannah got to meet you before she did. And Dad's fine. He wants me to be happy. He wants the press to leave us alone."

"You and me both, Your Majesty," she said wryly.

"He was angry," Alex said, remembering the second conversation they'd had after the news had broken. "When he realized the degree to which they'd been following you and for how long, his lawyers had to talk him off a ledge."

"That's kind," Maddy said. "But we knew this was going to happen sooner or later." She sighed.

Alex found himself unsure of how to proceed. He was used to the Maddy who not only took care of everyone around her, took charge of most situations, and actively resisted being cared for unless he got pushy. He didn't know what to do with this Maddy. She was quiet, resigned... she seemed *empty*. And he hated both that he'd had a key role in making her that way and also that he didn't know how to fix it.

"Let's get some food in you," he said, leaning forward to start opening to-go containers of curry and unwrapping the foil from around several pieces of naan, dripping with garlic and butter.

"Yeah, good idea," Maddy said halfheartedly, walking to the kitchen and coming back with plates, utensils, and napkins. They dished out their plates in silence, and then Alex watched her pick at her food aimlessly for several minutes. Finally he couldn't stand it anymore.

"Maddy," he began, "I... I know this is hard, but I'm feeling like I don't know how to help, don't know how to fix this... I just—"

"I'm going to graduate school!" Maddy blurted out, interrupting him.

"You're... you're what?"

"I'm going to graduate school. It's something I'd been interested in pretty much since college, but with moving around so much with the military it just never seemed practical. So when I got here this fall I started thinking about it again and sent in an application, just to see what happened. I was applying when you first asked me out and it just never came up, so I never mentioned it and I honestly didn't know if I had a chance of getting in, but they emailed me a few weeks ago and I got in." She finally paused for a breath. "And I accepted the offer."

"Maddy! That's brilliant! I'm so proud of you!" Alex's heart soared with pride—pride that other people recognized how smart she was, pride that she was taking control of her life and doing something for herself for once. "Where are you going?"

"Georgetown."

His heart plummeted. He probably should have assumed that she'd be going back to the States, but for a moment he'd let himself imagine a scenario in which she enrolled at University College London or some other local school and they could live together. Him bringing her tea while she studied, sneaking into the back of tutorial sections and watching her work with undergraduates, then taking her home and acting out filthy fantasies about professors and students.

He saw her studying his reaction and forced himself to keep the smile on his face, even though he wanted to burst into tears. To beg her not to leave him. "That's such a good school. I'm so proud of you."

"You are?" she asked, sounding surprised.

"Of course I am! You're going after something you've wanted for years and doing it at one of the best schools in the country—that's huge." He meant it too. Even though it was breaking his heart.

He leaned across the coffee table to kiss her. "You're going to be brilliant at this," he said, looking into her eyes.

"Thanks," she said, her eyes getting a bit misty. "I'm really going to miss London. And you." Her voice broke, but she swallowed and kept going. "But the timing felt right." She took a deep breath. "I mean, I guess I'm not flying under the radar here anymore."

Alex smiled ruefully. "I guess not."

Out loud, Alex tried to ask the right questions, show interest in what she'd be doing and how she'd chosen her program, but inside, his brain was spinning. Saturday night she'd told him she loved him with so much conviction that he'd let himself believe that they would soon be taking their relationship to the next level, despite both of their repeated insistence that it was casual. Even as the media had gone feral over the news of their relationship and he worried about Maddy and how she was handling the unwelcome attention, he'd always told himself that the interest would die down eventually and they'd be able to forge on, finding a new path where they were still in the public eye from time to time as necessary, but mostly were able to figure out what the future of their relationship looked like in relative privacy. But now that Maddy would be moving to DC, all bets were off.

He wanted to think that their relationship, new as it was, was strong enough to survive long distance. He could visit her; she could fly over to see him on school breaks. But was that what Maddy would want? If he knew one thing about Maddy Cartwright, it was that she had basically never made a decision with her own best interests front and center before in her life. She had always been the dutiful daughter and then the dutiful wife, showing up for the people in her life who stood out front while she stood behind, quietly and cheerfully doing what was expected of her. But now she was finally doing something that she wanted to do, and that would be good for her. Alex was afraid to ask her to do anything that could risk her first big step towards doing something for herself.

"Alex... I think we need to end this." Her sudden declaration jolted him out of his thoughts.

"You..." he started to respond, but she barreled on.

"I love you. Honestly, I wish I didn't because this would be a lot easier that way. But I just don't see how this works. For one thing, we're a media circus. And for another thing, in three months I'm going to be five thousand miles away and you're going to be here. I've already done a long-distance relationship across an ocean for what felt like an unending amount of time, and I wouldn't wish it on my worst enemy. I couldn't ask you to do that. I just couldn't. And no amount of love changes the fact that your life is here and my life is there. This was supposed to be a fling. We were never supposed to be more than casual. Love was never supposed to enter this equation. Your future is dragging this monarchy into the twenty-first century. The work you and Eric are doing is important. But I don't fit into that plan, and I won't be the one keeping you from doing it. I think we both know I can't handle even a fraction of the media scrutiny you get. I'd just be holding you back. So we can drag this out through the summer, knowing that it's inevitably going to end with both of us having broken hearts, or we can do the smart thing and just end it now. Go back to just being friends." She somehow seemed to have said all of that in one breath, but when she finally paused for air she was still avoiding looking at him.

He started to respond, but his phone started buzzing. Turning it over on the couch cushion next to him, he glanced down and, seeing that it was his father, dismissed the call. He'd ring him later.

Refocusing on Maddy, he forced himself to pause. Every instinct in his body was telling him to fight for her. To beg her not to leave, to use all of the resources at his disposal to devise a way that they could still be together. That they could both have what they wanted and keep each other. But then he remembered how not ten minutes earlier he'd been so proud of her for making such a big decision on her own. For putting herself first for the first time, possibly ever. How important her independence was to her and the ways she'd pushed back against his attempts to manage her life. So he swallowed the lump in his throat and nodded. "I understand," he said simply. He was formulating his next thought, still trying to decide how he could fix this, could grasp at the grains of sand that were slipping through his fingers right in front of him when there was an abrupt knock at the door to the Winfield kitchen, and immediately after, it opened. Graham stood at the top of the stairs, and even from a distance, Alex could see that his face was ashen.

"Sir, the Palace just called." Alex immediately knew something was very wrong. "It's the queen. She's had a heart attack."

Chapter 28

Alex woke up to the sound of the door to the private waiting room opening. He sat up, expecting to see the doctor with an update on his mother. He was surprised to see his brother and Hannah, twin expressions of concern on their faces.

"Hey guys," he said, running a hand across his face, rubbing away the last hints of sleep. "How was the trip back?" He hugged them each, giving his brother an extra-long, extra-tight squeeze.

"Fine, we're fine. How's Mum?" Ben's hair showed clear evidence of having been ripped at the entire way back from Athens, a sure tell of his brother's anxiety.

"She's going to be okay," Alex said and watched his brother's body visibly relax as Ben sank into one of the chairs that lined the walls of the small room. He was certain it was more comfortable than the normal waiting room—which was obviously a crock, why would his DNA merit him a more comfortable hospital waiting room experience?—but it was one hell of a place to spend a day. He looked at his watch, realizing that it had been almost a full twenty-four hours since he left Maddy at Winfield. Possibly for good.

Everything that had happened in the past day felt like a blur. Graham's sudden appearance in Maddy's rooms. The anguished knowledge that he needed to leave Maddy immediately, but didn't know if he'd ever see her again. Their fleeting goodbyes that seemed woefully inadequate, especially if they were for forever. The ride to the hospital, which felt unending. Sitting in the waiting room with his father for hours—mostly in distraught silence—while his mother was in surgery. His father had been at her bedside since the surgery had ended in the early morning hours, and at some point Alex had managed to fall asleep in the fiendishly uncomfortable chairs, exhaustion and worry mercifully blotting out the agony that he knew was coming as soon as he had a chance to process it. It was like the moments after you scrape your knee when you look down, see the blood, and know it's going to hurt a lot, but the nerves haven't quite caught up to your eyes yet.

"They had to do a triple bypass. So she's going to be here for a while and then out of commission recovering at home after that, but she's going to be fine."

Hannah had sunk into the chair next to her new husband, her arms around him as he hid his face in his hands. "What a relief," she said, her eyes just as tired and worried as his brother's.

Ben looked up, his eyes watery with unshed tears and bloodshot from a sleepless travel day back from their remote honeymoon in the Aegean. "Where's Dad?" he asked, clearing his throat.

"He's with Mum. She's in the ICU. We're only allowed one person in there at a time."

"How long has he been back there? How do we get updates?"

At that moment, the door opened, and a statuesque

woman with box braids wearing green scrubs and a white coat walked in. "Ben, this is Dr. Price," Alex said. "Dr. Price, this is my brother Benjamin and his wife Hannah." It felt absurd making the introductions since there was no way in hell that Dr. Price didn't know exactly who they were, but to not make them also felt somehow weird.

"Your Royal Highness," the doctor began, but Ben interrupted her.

"It's Ben," he said, holding up a hand. "My mother's life is in your hands. I'm just Ben."

"Okay, Ben," she said with a small nod. "So, as you probably know your mother was in surgery for almost seven hours," she began. "It wasn't as straightforward as we would have hoped, but in the end we were successful and she seems to be tolerating the surgery well. She'll be in intensive care for several days and will need to stay in hospital for at least a week. After that she'll be convalescing at home for at least eight weeks."

"But she'll be okay?" Ben asked, looking at her urgently.

"I do believe she'll make a full recovery," Dr. Price said. "The king has been with her since we got her stabilized after the procedure," she went on. "I think it would be good if we could convince him to go get some rest, have one of you sit with her for a while. This recovery is going to be a marathon, not a sprint. He needs to pace himself."

"Yes, of course," Ben said. "I'll go."

"Ben," Alex interjected. "You two have been traveling for hours. You're exhausted. Why don't you go back to your place and grab a nap and a shower and then come back? I'll stay with her for now."

"But you've been up all night too," Hannah said, looking concerned.

"I was able to get a little rest," he fibbed, glancing at the offensive hospital chairs out of the corner of his eyes. "Go say hi, convince Dad to leave with you, and I'll take the next shift," Alex said, taking the lead in his family for what felt like the first time ever.

He saw Ben preparing to argue, but Hannah put a hand on his arm and silenced him with a look. Ben sighed and said, "Yeah, okay, you're right."

"Ben, why don't you come with me and we'll go get your father?" Dr. Price motioned to the door.

Ben nodded, dropped a quick kiss on Hannah's head, and followed the doctor out of the room.

Alex sighed and sank back into what had become "his" chair. Hannah dropped down next to him. "How are you?" Hannah asked. He could feel her gaze, even though he wasn't looking at her.

"Fine? I guess?" Alex said, raking a hand through his hair. The truth was he was exhausted, his eyes were gritty, and his mouth was dry. He'd barely eaten anything since lunch the day before, but he also couldn't imagine putting anything in his stomach.

"Uh-huh," she said knowingly.

"How is it out there?" he asked. "I assume the press is pouncing on this?" His father's press office had decided that they couldn't keep the story private any longer once the queen had made it through the surgery.

"About what you'd expect," she said.

"At least maybe now Maddy can leave the house again," he said ruefully.

"How is Maddy?" she asked.

Alex was saved from trying to figure out how to answer that question by the return of Ben and their father. Hannah stood and went to embrace her father-in-law. When Hannah released him, he looked up at Alex. "You'll call me if anything changes?"

"I promise, Dad. I won't leave her for a second." Alex looked his father squarely in the eye. "Trust me."

His father's eyes closed, hiding his emotion from his sons, and nodded. "I do, Alex."

"All of you go get some rest," Alex said, ushering them towards the door. "I don't want to see you before tomorrow morning."

They said their muted goodbyes, and then Hannah and Ben led the king towards the back entrance and Alex turned the other direction where an orderly was waiting to lead him to his mother's private room in the intensive care unit. He'd caught a brief glimpse of her when they'd brought her out from surgery, but taking a seat next to her bed was the first chance he'd really had to get a good look at her. She was still asleep, heavily sedated after the trauma her body had been through. Her face was starting to show the natural signs of aging, and there were dark circles under her eyes that he'd never seen before. When he reached down to take her hand gently, he was struck by the wrinkles that had started to form there, the way her rings were slightly loose. Even though he still spent the occasional weekend staying with his folks at Windsor and Sandringham, it had been years since the last time he saw her looking anything less than put together.

The realization that his parents were aging was a sucker punch. The doctors had reassured them repeatedly over the last day that, although her condition was serious, she was expected to make a full recovery. But it had been a shocking reminder of her mortality. That she and his father would probably start to slow down one of these days. That someday they would be gone and Ben would be king.

This fact was something he'd known for his whole life. Even though his parents had done their best to give them a "normal" upbringing, Alex had known for as long as he could remember that someday his brother would be king. That their family business was being the royal family. And his feelings on that had evolved significantly. As a younger child, in the aftermath of the humiliation at his father's coronation, Alex had wanted nothing to do with the institution. He'd wished on every birthday cake, every found penny, every first evening star that he'd wake up the next day and that his family would be normal. That he'd never be expected to be in the public eye. That he'd never have to make a speech. And then, somewhere along the way, things had changed. He'd started to feel coddled. Cocooned. *Too* protected. He worked so hard on himself to be someone who could be a productive member of the family business, but nobody noticed.

And now, finally, here was his opportunity. As much as he hated the reason, this was finally the chance for him to prove himself both to his family and to the nation. He could do this, he could be a leader, he could do the job. And yet, the thrill that he would have expected to come with this realization didn't thrill like he thought it would. He would do it, certainly. He would never let his family down. But the fact that this huge opportunity for him was simultaneously costing him the woman of his dreams poisoned it for him.

He spent the night by his mother's bedside, intermittently resting his head on the side of her mattress and dozing off, but mostly lost in thought. His brain bounced back and forth, unfocused in the way that brains get when you know the rest of the world is asleep and you're drifting between light sleep and the midnight melancholy of being awake and alone. He had vivid images of him opening hospitals, shaking hands, using his family's name to bring attention to the people in his country who needed it the most, being able to at least in some small way shape the royal family's plans and priorities. But then the scene would shift. He'd see himself cuddling Maddy, see them wandering through DC together, playing with Bertie, cooking together. It was disorienting to realize that the simplicity of the second set of visions was somehow more enticing to him than the grandeur of the dream he'd been working towards for years. To realize that he'd been fighting so long to get his family to notice him, to use him, to include him in their mission, and that now he wished he didn't have to. Would rather continue to live out of the public eye and take a back seat, if it meant being with Maddy. Two days ago he might have been trying to figure out a way to convince Maddy that she wanted him to join her in the States. Finding a way to beg her to let him come too. But not now. Now his family needed him, and as much as it was going to break him to watch Maddy walk away, he was going to have to do it.

Chapter 29

The weekend dragged like rubber cement on a cold day. After Alex had rushed out on Thursday night, Maddy had gone through the motions of wrapping up the remnants of their Indian food and putting it away before collapsing on the sofa in tears. There was no world in which she could ask Alex to come with her to DC, and no world in which she could handle walking six feet behind him for the rest of her life. She knew she'd done the right thing. But she hated that doing the right thing involved breaking her own heart.

She also deeply regretted the unfortunate timing of her declaration. She had been distracted by her own jumble of thoughts and emotions, by the guilt that was eating her alive from the inside, so she hadn't really registered the nuances of Alex's response to her announcement. She had no idea if he'd been relieved or about to make some kind of counteroffer or, less likely, argue with her. When Graham had suddenly appeared at the top of her stairs, Alex had immediately stood and, after giving her a fierce but distracted hug, followed his driver out of her room to go to the hospital. There had been no closure, no final declarations of love, no discussion of trying to be friends or what to say to the press. No goodbyes. She was pretty sure she had broken up with him, and couldn't imagine a world in which he'd fight for the opportunity to be in a long-distance relationship with her an ocean away. And at this point maybe she'd never know what his thoughts had been at that moment.

The next morning, the king had released a statement about his wife's health, and she'd watched the coverage, hoping futilely to catch a glimpse of Alex coming or going on the cameras that were stationed outside the London Clinic. Even though she knew it was almost impossible that they'd be entering and leaving through a public entrance. She'd been resisting the urge to text him all weekend. They'd broken up. She didn't get to expect updates that the public wasn't getting. She didn't get to check on him to see if he was taking care of himself. But she still worried. And wondered.

She'd made it halfway through Sunday before she'd finally caved and gone up to her office to go through emails. She couldn't bear just sitting and watching the commentators on TV talk endlessly without saying anything. If she didn't get to be useful to Alex, she could at least be useful to the embassy. And so she worked, all afternoon and into the evening on Sunday, going down to her rooms to sleep for a few hours, and then back at it Monday morning, hoping that if she busied her mind with work she could avoid thinking about Alex. Worrying about him.

She tried to force her brain back to the mundane office tasks that were the new normal at her job. But the further from Thursday night she got, the more she started to wonder if she'd made a mistake. She desperately wanted to think that she could have worked up the courage to try to convince him to come with her. But the more information that dripped out into the media about Queen Sarah's condition, the more she understood that it could never happen and that it would be unfair of her to ask. They said she'd be in the hospital for a week. That she'd be recovering at home for at least eight weeks. Triple bypass was major surgery, Maddy knew. There was no way the queen would be back to her normal pace of activities before the fall, and from what she knew of Alex's father, he wouldn't be going too far from her side until she was fully recovered. Which meant that the next generation would be stepping up. Ben and Hannah were ready. They'd known this moment would be coming for them. And Maddy knew that this was finally Alex's chance. His opportunity to prove to his family that he could do the job. That they'd been overlooking an amazing asset right in their laps for years. Even if she thought he would want to, she could never ask him to give up this chance. The goal that he'd been working toward for so long.

Thursday afternoon after lunch a text from an unfamiliar number popped up on her phone.

UNKNOWN NUMBER

Hey, it's Hannah.

Hannah Cromwell.

> Hannah, how are you? How's everything going?

HANNAH

Doing okay. Slow but steady improvement.
We're all tired.

> I'm sure. I can't imagine what you all are going through right now. Do you need anything?

HANNAH

No, but Alex does. Are you free this
afternoon? He's barely left the hospital
since the weekend. He needs to get out
and get some fresh air and think about
anything besides his mum.

Maddy's heart stopped. Alex clearly hadn't told anyone
that they'd broken up. She was momentarily unsure of how to
answer. Did she tell Hannah? Did she say she was busy? After
waffling for a few seconds, though, she knew what she had to
do. The way she felt about Alex hadn't changed. If he needed
her, there was no way she wasn't going to him.

Yes, of course. What's the best way to get
there?

HANNAH

Graham will pick you up in an hour and
then take you over to get Alex. We'll make
sure he actually leaves.

Ok, sounds good. Can I bring you
anything? Or anyone else?

HANNAH

Thanks, love, but we're all set here. We'll
just be glad to see Alex getting out. He's
starting to drive the rest of us a little bit
mental, tbqh. Just text me when you're on
your way and we'll have him ready for you.

When Graham arrived, she was ready. She'd changed from her
work clothes to jeans and a short-sleeved pink T-shirt with
some macrame detailing across the shoulders and carried a

small backpack containing a selection of the pastries Nadia had on hand, a thermos of coffee, and two bottles of water.

"Hello, Miss Maddy," Graham said, opening the back door for her.

"Graham, how are you?" she asked.

"Hanging in there, hanging in there," he said with a slightly melancholy smile.

They headed out the gates onto the ring road. Being outside of Winfield House still felt slightly odd to Maddy. For the first week after she and Alex had been exposed she hadn't left the grounds for any reason. Once the queen's health scare had pulled basically all of the media attention in the country, Maddy had started tentatively venturing out, still not doing public appearances for the embassy, but willing to chance going out to pick up Mrs. Stewart's dry cleaning or to grab a quick coffee from the cafe down the street. She hadn't braved her run around the park yet, but driving through the streets of London made her realize how small her life had been for the last two weeks. It was like when she'd first arrived the year previously, barely leaving the embassy, preferring to stay close to Winfield House to prevent being seen.

She hadn't realized how much her relationship with Alex had drawn her out of her cloistered bubble until she was suddenly confronted with the contrast and realized that she'd missed being out and about. The vibrant floral boxes attached to so many of the brick windowsills were starting to bloom, and there were still some buntings up from the royal wedding, which, amazingly, had been less than two weeks before. The grounds at Winfield were beautiful, but it was striking being out and about.

Maddy texted Hannah to let her know that they were on the way and got a response saying that Graham should go to the usual spot and they'd meet them there. Maddy relayed the message without fully understanding it, but Graham had just answered with a cheery "Very good, Miss Maddy," and continued driving.

"This route takes a bit longer, but it allows me to approach from the rear," Graham said, as Maddy realized they were nearing the hospital. "So far, nobody's been seen coming and going this way."

"Okay," Maddy said, anxiety creeping into her mind. But she pushed it down. Getting to Alex, getting him out and away from the hospital was the most important thing. She could conquer the slight gnawing in her stomach for Alex. If he needed her, she could endure the pain of seeing him and knowing she couldn't have him.

Graham pulled up to a guard station and was admitted to what seemed to be an underground parking garage. She could see signs for staff parking in the dim, fluorescent light. They turned a corner, and Graham stopped in front of an elevator. Maddy saw Ben and Hannah involved in what looked like a heated conversation with Alex. He looked exhausted. He was wearing jeans and a gray zip-up hoodie. His hair was mussed, his face stubbly, his eyes bloodshot. The knots in her stomach doubled back on themselves as competing emotions flooded her nervous system. Exuberance at seeing him, utter worry at his rundown appearance, and the gut punch of devastation as she remembered that Alex was no longer hers.

She could see Ben gesturing at the car and Alex shaking his head. But when Graham came around and opened the back door, Alex's body slumped in defeat and turned unenthusiastically to get in the car. "I'll be back soon," he said over his shoulder to his brother. It sounded more like a threat than anything else. He didn't even notice Maddy as he slumped into the seat and buckled his seatbelt.

"Hi," she said quietly.

His eyes shot open and he turned to look at her, disbelief on his face. "Maddy, what are you doing here?" he asked, sounding incredulous, exhausted, and, if Maddy was being honest with herself, not entirely happy to see her.

She forced herself not to dwell on the knowledge that he probably didn't want to see her. That she probably shouldn't be there. Hannah had made her mission perfectly clear: fresh air and space from the hospital. "I know you might not want to see me, but Hannah thought you could use a break," she said. She paused, uncertain for a moment, before reaching over to cover his hand with hers.

He sighed. "I mean, sure, but my family needs me," he said, blinking at the sudden change of light as they left the underground garage.

"They do," she said gently. "But they need you to be a functioning human being so that you can be of service to them. And never leaving the hospital does not a functional human make."

His chin hit his chest in defeat, and he scrubbed his face with the hand that wasn't nestled under hers. He hadn't moved the hand she was touching, she noted. That had to mean something. They rode in silence for a few moments. "I want to ask how you are, but I know you must feel terrible and exhausted and worried."

He finally looked at her again and his eyes were red and watery and empty. "Oh, Maddy," he said, his voice breaking and his face crumpling.

Going against every rule-abiding instinct in her body, ignoring the dull voice in her head reminding her that they'd broken up, she unbuckled her seatbelt and shifted closer so she could wrap her arms around him. Burying one hand in his hair and anchoring one on his back, she tried her best to provide a soft landing spot for the emotions he'd been holding in all week. His shoulders shook and she felt his tears trickling onto her neck, and she just held him tighter, hoping that just her physical presence could convey the words that were stuck behind the lump in her own throat. She forced herself to focus on the fact that Alex needed her comfort, not the fact that this might be the last time she ever got to hold him.

After a few long moments, he pulled away, wiping his eyes and taking a deep, shuddering inhale. He opened his mouth and Maddy cut him off. "If you try to apologize right now I will open that door and dropkick you into the middle of the M4, so help me god."

Alex managed a watery laugh. "I believe you'd do it too."

The city was getting less dense around them as they passed a sign for Kew. "We're still about thirty minutes away. Why don't you close your eyes for a little bit." She saw him instinctually go to reject her suggestion, but when she leveled him with a look, he sighed again and nodded. She rebuckled herself into the middle seat and, within a few moments, he was fast asleep, his head nodding gently onto her shoulder. She leaned her own head back and relaxed, hoping that her calm facade would be convincing and contagious. At least enough to allow him to get some real rest.

Alex woke just as they pulled through the gates into the private area of Windsor where he had taken Maddy to walk the previous winter, the day he'd kissed her for the first time. She'd remembered him saying that it was good for his mind to go there and walk, so when Graham had picked her up, she'd set that as their destination. They arrived just after three and she asked Graham to be back at five, in time for them to get back to the city to pick up Thai takeout for dinner. She was hoping to convince Alex to sleep at his own apartment that night, but if not, she'd at least be sure he got a square meal of non-hospital food before he went back.

When he realized where they were, Alex turned to her, surprise written across his face. "Windsor?"

"I thought a walk and a picnic might be good for you," she said with a shrug. Part of her was regretting coming back to a place where they'd been so happy, where their relationship had first blossomed. But it was too late now. She needed to just focus on Alex and what he needed in this moment, not on her own feelings, her own heartbreak, the past.

Graham stopped, and they climbed out of the car after confirming that he'd come back for them in two hours. They walked in silence that Maddy hoped was companionable. She desperately wanted to address the elephant in the room, but kept convincing herself that it wasn't the right time. She really wasn't sure what to say to him, but he didn't seem to mind the lack of conversation, so she just followed his lead, literally and figuratively, as they rambled through the private pathways of his family's estate.

After a while, Alex finally said, "I'm sorry that I had to rush out like that on Thursday night. That's not how that conversation should have ended."

"Oh, Alex. Why would you apologize for that?"

"No, I mean, obviously I had to go, but I'm just sorry we didn't get to talk about it. And honestly, I'm really not in the right headspace for it right now."

"Of course not," she said, squeezing his hand gently. "Don't think about that for now. You've got much more important things to worry about."

Alex stopped and turned to look down at her. "My mom's health is important, yes, but hear me when I say that you are important. *We* are important. And I am worrying about that because our relationship is important to me." Maddy tried not to latch onto his use of present tense. "It's impossible to know what the next few months are going to look like for me. They're just now trying to sort out how they're going to divide up all the things that are on my parents' schedules for the next few months, but I'm probably going to have to step up and play a bigger role in the family."

"Of course you are," Maddy said, "and I'm thrilled for

you. This is finally your chance to prove to them that you're not a shy little boy anymore."

They walked in silence for another moment before he said, "I hope this isn't too awkward for you. I mean, I know you ended things on Saturday, but I haven't really gotten around to telling anyone yet. I hope Hannah didn't bully you too much to get you to come."

She swallowed a lump in her throat. "Alex, I ended our relationship because our lives don't fit together. I don't belong here. But that doesn't change the fact that I love you and have been worrying about you and want to be here for you." She swallowed again, and changed the subject, knowing that if they kept talking about their breakup she'd cry, which wasn't at all what he needed. "What do you need?" she asked as they strolled on.

"What do I need?"

"Yes, you, Alex, a human who has spent the last week ignoring his own personal needs in the service of his family. What. Do. You. Need?"

He sighed. "Honestly, I don't even know."

"And that's okay. But I'm pretty sure I do know, so why don't you let me take over for a bit and you just sit back?"

"I'm supposed to be the one taking care of you—"

"You just spent days doing nothing but giving, giving, giving. Right now what I think you need is to do just a tiny bit of taking so that you don't lose the ability to keep giving. Your family isn't going to stop needing you anytime soon, but if you don't take even a little time to recharge your own batteries, you're not going to be able to be there when they need you."

His sigh told her he knew she was right. Without waiting for him to actually say it, she stopped and took off her backpack. "Good. So for right now, we're going to sit here and have a nice little picnic. I have coffee and some of Nadia's treats.

And when we finish up here, we're going to go back to your place and get some takeaway and then I'm going to put you in your own bed and you're going to get a good night's sleep before you go back to the hospital." She could tell he wanted to resist, but as she leveled a look at him, she could also see him realizing, again, that she was right. And so he nodded and helped her lay out the picnic blanket.

Maddy guided the conversation as they snacked, not expecting too much from Alex, who was clearly barely conscious. When they were done, she'd packed it all back up and they'd walked back to Graham and the waiting car.

"Where to, Miss Maddy?" he asked, opening the door.

"We're going to pick up Thai from Meekhun and then back to Alex's. Unless you'd prefer something else for dinner?" She looked to Alex and, when he shrugged, she said, "Yup, Thai and then home. Thanks, Graham."

They were quiet on the drive. Maddie put together a large order of assorted Thai food for them to pick up, enough that it would leave leftovers for Alex when he came home. When they got back to his place, she nudged him toward the shower and set up the Thai spread on the coffee table in his den.

When he came out, he collapsed on the sofa next to her and put his arms around her. "Thank you," he breathed into her hair. "You're right. I did need this."

She knew she shouldn't let him cuddle her like this, knew that the longer she let herself forget that Alex wasn't her boyfriend anymore, the worse it would be for her later. But if this was what he needed, she couldn't deny him, even if it was just going to compound the heartbreak when things went back to normal. "I'm glad I was right." They sat that way, holding each other for a moment before Maddy said, "Okay, so if we don't dig into this, my stomach might actually start eating itself and you might pass out right here on the couch, so we should probably eat." Alex barked out a laugh, grabbed a plate, and started dishing out steaming curries, noodles, and rice.

Maddy had turned on the TV before he came in, so they both sat back with their plates and spaced out watching the escapades of a time traveling nurse and her kilted Scottish Highlander. Midway through the second episode, Maddy looked over and realized that Alex was fast asleep. She debated just tucking him in on the couch, but realized he'd get better sleep in a bed, so she coaxed him awake and led him to bed.

"Are you going to be okay?" she asked, smoothing the covers over him and loitering awkwardly next to his bed.

"I'll be fine." He sighed deeply before looking up at her. "But Maddy? If you're really committed to ending this, I don't think we can keep spending time together. It's too hard for me to be around you and not have my hands all over you all the time. I kept forgetting all afternoon."

She nodded sadly, closing her eyes to prevent him from seeing the tears pooling there. Part of her wanted to take it all back, to beg him to take *her* back. Part of her yearned for him to sit up and fight for her, for *them*. But she also knew that, even if there was any way their relationship made sense in the long term—which it didn't—now wasn't the time. She couldn't ask him to focus on anything besides his mother and the family right now. So all she did was nod and swallow. "You're right," she whispered, through her unshed tears. Clearing her throat and trying to think of all the things she needed to say, somehow she landed on. "I know the family is focused on much more important things right now, but obviously if you want to put out a statement, I support whatever you want to say. Or we can just assume that people will forget about this quickly with everything else going on. Up to you." Nodding, she bent down to brush a chaste kiss across his forehead. "Goodbye, Alex."

She didn't wait to see if he'd say anything else. She was

barely holding it together and couldn't let Alex see. So she turned and left. Mercifully, Graham was in the area, and so she was able to make it into the back seat of his SUV before the sobs that had been threatening to bubble out of her throat overtook her. Folding herself in half in the backseat so there was no chance of anyone seeing her, she allowed the tears she'd been holding back all afternoon to flow as Graham maneuvered them out of the Kensington Palace grounds and into the dark.

Chapter 30

The next six weeks passed in a bizarre combination of whirlwind speed and unbearable torpor. But no matter what she did, the slow, inexorable fact remained: Maddy was leaving. She'd given Ambassador Stewart her notice, and he'd accepted the news with clearly mixed emotions. Nadia had cried when she'd told her, but had jumped at the excuse to make her first visit to the United States and promised to plan a trip.

The queen had been released from the hospital three days after Maddy had kidnapped Alex from the hospital. She was recovering in the relative privacy of Windsor, the king steadfastly at her side. As a result, Ben, Hannah, and Alex had all had to quickly step up to maintain even a facsimile of the royal family's normal slate of appearances. Among a busy schedule of more local appointments, Ben and Hannah had taken a week-long visit to the Caribbean on the king's behalf, and Alex had been sent to France, Germany, and Austria on a diplomatic whirlwind.

As much as she missed him, Maddy was happy for Alex. Yes, he'd been dumped into the deep end of life as a real working royal. And yes, the circumstances were far from good, but he was finally getting to show his family and the world that he could do this. And he was excelling. Maddy found herself waking up and checking tags on social media first thing to see clips from his appearances. He politely dodged questions about the end of their relationship while artfully turning the topic of conversation back to the cause he was supposed to be promoting. She assumed he'd undergone an intensive crash course on How to Royal before being deployed on the family's behalf in the queen's absence, but to Maddy, it seemed like he'd been doing this for years. As if he'd been born for it. Which he had.

Was keeping up with Alex and his career the best thing for her emotionally? Absolutely not. By two weeks after their last walk at Windsor, she could make it through a workday without having to duck into the bathroom to cry, but lying in bed at night, sometimes the ache overtook her. She knew it would be better to block all mentions of him from all of her various apps, but somehow she couldn't stop herself from checking. Just to make sure he looked okay, she told herself.

Maddy tried to remind herself that she was excited for her new adventure, that she was making the right choice for *her*. She was thrilled when she found a furnished apartment she could afford tucked into the side of a hill. It was small, but had been recently remodeled and would be big enough for what she needed. She tried to throw herself into thinking about what she might need, thinking about how her wardrobe might shift as she transitioned from working at the embassy to going to class. But a small part of her kept wondering if she was *actually* doing the right thing. Wondering what it would be like to stay and make a go of it with Alex. Wondering if the decision that was currently actively breaking her heart was really going to make her happier in the long run.

. . .

The end of June came, and so did Maddy's last week in London. She was going to visit her parents in Fort Leavenworth, Kansas, before flying to DC to move into her new apartment at the beginning of August. A few weeks earlier over cocoa in the kitchens, Nadia had asked, "So wait, your last day of work is June 23, but you aren't leaving until the first of July?"

"Yeah," Maddie had replied, feeling slightly despondent about the whole thing. "I figured I could use some time to pack and wrap up loose ends."

"Pack?" Nadia had exclaimed incredulously. "You have clothes and nothing else. Your rooms have fewer personal items in them than a university boy's dorm room. On what planet would it take you a week to pack?"

"That's... fair. Harsh, but fair," Maddy admitted.

Nadia looked thoughtful. "You got here, put your nose to the grindstone, and then before you had a chance to come up for air, started dating Alex. Did you ever really see any of London?"

"I mean... I went to Buckingham Palace. Twice!" Maddy was feeling a little defensive.

"Okay, but did you take the tour? Have you been to the Tower of London? Did you ride a double-decker bus? The London Eye?"

"Well no..." Maddy said, drawing out the vowels.

"Okay, so here's what we're going to do. I'm making a list, and you're going to pick one thing for each of those days and we're going to do them. I'm not letting you leave London without having actually experienced London."

"Don't you have to work?" Maddy asked, touched that Nadia was trying to give her a good send off.

"Don't worry about that," Nadia said, and immediately

pulled out her phone to start a list.

Which is how Maddy found herself sitting on the top level of one of the many ferry boats that traversed the Thames the day before her departure. The sun was warm on her face and arms, the wind ruffling her hair, and the sounds of other boats and seagulls echoed around her. Nadia sat next to her, snapping pictures like a proud mom. They'd taken the Tube out to Greenwich that morning and, after touring the observatory and posing for photos with their feet on either side of the Prime Meridian, had grabbed sandwiches to eat on the ferry on the way back down to the center of London.

"Thanks, Nadia," she said, opening her eyes and smiling at her friend. "You were right—I really did miss out on a lot about London."

Nadia shrugged, the corner of her headscarf wafting gently in the breeze. "You had a few other things on your mind."

"I did," Maddy said with a reluctant chuckle. "I hope you know how much I'm going to miss you."

"It's okay, you can say you're going to miss my food."

"I mean, that too." She giggled. "But mostly you. You've been a really good friend to me at a time when I really needed it and wasn't able to give much in return. I won't forget that."

"You better not, woman! I'll be coming to visit as soon as you get settled!"

"I'll hold you to that!"

"Has anyone else talked about coming to visit?" Nadia asked, looking at Maddy pointedly over her hot-pink-framed sunglasses.

Maddy sighed. "No. I haven't heard from him since the week we broke up."

"Remind me why you broke up again? Hadn't you just finished telling each other how in love you were?"

"I mean, yes, I love him. But we just don't make sense. His life is here, his job is here. His family needs him now more than ever. I came here to be out of the public eye. I was supposed to be living my independent woman era, not falling in love with a prince. Which is the opposite of staying out of the public eye. Plus, I owe it to myself to really follow my own dreams. I've wanted to go to grad school for years. This is finally my chance. I need to at least try it."

"And he didn't want to come?"

"Nadia, I can't ask the second in line to the British crown to move to another country! That's practically treason."

"Really? I think I must have missed that line in the Magna Carta..." Nadia's voice dripped with sarcasm. "Plus, you seem to be forgetting that he lived in New Zealand for like five years."

"Yes, well... that was different. For one thing, it was a Commonwealth country. He was practically doing diplomatic service." Nadia rolled her eyes, but Maddy went on. "Plus, with the queen's health the way it is, he and Ben and Hannah have been working like crazy. And he's working on this really important new initiative around reparations. He spent years trying to show his family that he wasn't a shy kid who needed to be protected. Now that he's finally proving himself, I could never ask him to leave. His work is too important, and his family needs him."

"But you don't think you're important to him?"

Maddy gazed at the row houses that backed up to the Thames as they glided past. "Well, for one thing, I think I might have broken his heart a little bit. But also, I could never ask someone to choose between me and their duty."

Nadia hummed skeptically, but their conversation came to an end as the boat pulled up to the dock.

Chapter 31

THREE MONTHS LATER

"Sorry, sir," Graham said, looking at Alex ruefully in the rearview mirror of the Range Rover. "I'm afraid this is really the only route back to the palace."

"Graham, you don't have to apologize for traffic," Alex said, glancing through the heavily tinted windows at the gridlock surrounding them. "You're good, but even you aren't *that* good."

"Right you are, sir," Graham said merrily, returning his focus to the road as they crept slowly forward.

Alex sighed. It had been almost four months since Maddy had walked out of his apartment for the last time, and he still thought about her every day. He'd had to force himself not to text her, not to ask when she was leaving. He knew by now she had to be gone, back in America, starting her new life. But he wondered. Wondered where she was living, whether her classes had started, if she'd made friends in DC, whether her new apartment was any less sparsely decorated than the rooms she'd inhabited at Winfield House.

He wondered at least three times weekly if he'd made a huge mistake not asking if he could come with her. He'd thought about calling her so many times, about begging her to take him back, to take him with her. But the knowledge that his family needed him, that he was being useful for once in his entire life, kept him from reaching out. Not to mention that Maddy hadn't asked him to come. And she had to have had a reason. He knew she'd felt very responsible for making the decision on her own, considering her own needs and priorities without bringing her feelings for him into it. And even if it stung a little, he also respected the hell out of her for it. She'd been a dutiful daughter and then wife for so many years that he glowed with pride when he thought about her confidently going after what *she* wanted. Making the best choice for herself and only herself. He'd convinced her to let him intrude into the London chapter of her burgeoning independence, but he'd be damned if he became the third man in her life whose public persona pushed her dreams into the background.

They finally arrived at Buckingham Palace an hour later, and Alex let himself in the side door, heading to the sitting room where his mother had taken to spending most of her time. As he let himself in, he narrowly avoided being tripped by Anne of Cleves, who was sinuously winding herself around his ankles the second he walked through the door. "God-damned cat," he muttered under his breath as he walked toward the couch.

The queen looked up from her iPad as he crossed the room toward her. "Hi, Mum," he said, leaning down to kiss her cheek.

"Hello, darling," she said, smiling warmly up at him. She looked normal now. Not ashen and frail the way she had after her surgery. It had been hard to be reminded of his mother's fallibility when she'd had the heart attack, but Alex was reassured by the way that she had bounced back. Almost four and a half months after the surgery, you almost couldn't tell that anything had been wrong. She still tired easily and she wouldn't be going back to her private Pilates sessions anytime soon, but the doctors were almost ready to clear her to return to a modified version of royal duties.

After convalescing at Windsor for a month, she and the king had returned to London, and the king had started easing back into work. At first he refused to leave central London, wanting to be close enough to rush back to his wife's side at a moment's notice. But as her strength returned, he had gradually started venturing further afield with the promise that at least one of his sons would be nearby. He had finally returned to more or less a normal schedule. Currently, Alex was pretty sure his father was in Switzerland at some kind of international economic summit. In order to convince him to go, he and Ben had had to promise that they would look in on their mother every day, and so one of them would stop by in the afternoon before an evening outing or after their last appearance of the day each day. It was an odd callback to the way their parents had carved out time to spend with the boys in their youth.

Alex was surprised to hear the door open again behind him, followed by both a high-pitched shriek and a frantic yowl as Ben entered and promptly stepped on Anne of Cleves.

"What are you doing here, mate? I thought tonight was my night?" Alex asked, as Ben regained his footing, muttering curses, and made his way over to kiss the Queen's cheek affectionately.

Offering Alex a fist bump as he sat down in an armchair across from the sofa, Ben replied, "What, I can't just stop by to see my mum and my brother?"

"I mean, of course you *can*," Alex sputtered.

"What do you mean it's your night?" their mother demanded in mock outrage. She knew that her sons were taking turns coming to check on her in her husband's absence. Alex and Ben knew that their mother knew. And yet the three of them continued operating under the thin fiction that the brothers were just casually dropping by to say hello each evening.

"How was the rugby match?" Queen Sarah asked, sliding over to make room for Alex to sit next to her as she put her iPad on the end table.

"Good," Alex said. "Cute kids. I think our side won." He had gone through the motions of the appearance, a charity game benefitting a youth rugby club in an impoverished area of London, shaking hands and cheering at the appropriate time when the brawny men used their shapely knees to bludgeon each other.

"You think?" his mother asked incredulously. "It was a rout!"

"Was it?" he asked distractedly.

"Alex," she said, putting a hand on his knee.

"Yeah, Mum?"

She didn't say anything, and finally he looked up at her from where he'd been picking at a loose thread on the brocade of the sofa. She was looking at him intently. In her eyes he saw concern and something that he couldn't pinpoint. It seemed eerily like conviction or knowledge. Like she knew something he didn't. He expected her to chide him for not paying close enough attention to the game. Instead she simply asked, "Are you happy?"

He blinked at her. "What do you mean, am I happy?"

"I mean: Are. You. Happy? You've been working your tail off all summer, but is it bringing you joy?" His mother had taken to reading popular titles during her convalescence. Clearly Marie Kondo had made the list.

"I'm..." Alex searched for words. "I think staying busy is good for me. And I thought I was being useful."

Ben jumped in. "Alex, you've been enormously useful. Not only am I just happy you're here because I missed you when you were away, but I can't imagine what we would have done without you here to pitch in this summer. But we can also do this without you. If this isn't what you're meant to be doing, we don't want you to feel like you have to be doing it."

It was at that moment that Alex realized he was in the middle of an intervention. "I mean, at the risk of overinflating my importance, I thought I was needed here." He tried—and definitely failed—to keep the defensiveness out of his voice.

"You were. You *are*. I always need my boys near me," his mother said, seeming to realize that he'd been slightly offended by the implication. "But the doctors are going to let me start going back to work next week. And Hannah is really stepping up. People love it when she turns up at events with your brother. I think she's ready to start going out on her own soon."

"She absolutely is," Ben added. "Honestly, I think most of the time the crowds are more interested in seeing her than they are to see me."

"Ah, I see," Alex said. A part of him had thought that now that he'd stepped up and shown that he could pull his weight in the family that there might be a permanent place for him. That he might have finally found some kind of purpose to his life. The thought had been the only thing really keeping him going since Maddy had left him. He'd thrown himself into work, taking on as many appearances as the Private Secretary's office would allow him to take, with the excuse that his father needed to spend as much time with the queen as possible and his brother and sister-in-law were still newlyweds who'd had to cut their honeymoon short and deserved to take it easy. But this conversation was making it seem like maybe that wasn't the case at all and that he'd been making a nuisance of himself.

"No, Alex," his mother said, firmly. "You're misunderstanding us. We all see how much you've stepped up. You've done an incredible job. You're a natural at this, and I feel badly that we didn't see it sooner. We should have noticed that you didn't need us to protect you quite as much as we had been." Alex shifted, slightly uncomfortable with the praise, even as much as he needed to hear it. "But," she went on, "it's also clear that you're throwing yourself into work to compensate for the fact that you're miserable since you and Maddy broke up."

"I also can't leave Eric in the lurch," Alex retorted, pointedly ignoring the last part of his mother's statement. "The reparations project is just now finally starting to get some traction. I won't abandon him."

"You're not the only one who cares about that, Alex," Ben said gently. "We all love Eric. We won't let him flounder. I think Hannah would actually be super keen to get in on that."

"Alex," his mother said, clearly unwilling to let the Maddy conversation drop, "what actually happened between you and Maddy?"

He sighed and leaned his elbows on his knees, his hands raking through his hair.

"Yeah," Ben added. "You seemed *so* happy and in love at the wedding. And then next thing we know you're not together anymore."

"She'd been hounded by the press in the States after her husband died and she couldn't take it anymore, so her father sent her to London to work for the ambassador. She literally came here to escape the press. We were never supposed to be anything besides casual. Once the media found out about us, it didn't make sense for her to keep hiding here. She got accepted to a grad program in foreign affairs at Georgetown, and it felt like the sign she needed to accept the offer. She had just broken things off the night that you..." It was still hard to say. "The night that you had your surgery." It felt good to get all of that off his chest. Other than a few hurried conversations with Eric about what had happened amongst all the drama around his mother's health, he really hadn't talked to anyone about it at all.

Recognition dawned in Ben's eyes. "So wait, the day that Hannah texted her to come get you out of the hospital…"

"We'd already broken up," Alex confirmed. "I just hadn't really processed any of it. She literally said she thought we should end things and then my phone was ringing and Graham came in and said I had to leave right away."

"Shit, mate," Ben said. "I had no idea."

"Of course you didn't. Way more important things were happening," Alex replied.

"But was it super awkward?"

"No." Alex sighed. "I mean, I was basically a husk of a human. I hadn't slept, hadn't left the hospital in days, I hadn't processed anything. She took me on a walk, and we pretty much just pretended it hadn't happened. But then at the end of the night, she was being so sweet, and I just kept forgetting… I told her I didn't think we could hang out if we weren't going to be together."

Their mother sighed. "I'm so sorry, darling."

"Gosh, Mum, how *dare* you have a medical emergency at such an inconvenient time!" Ben quipped sarcastically.

"I just, I knew it was hard on you boys, but between your honeymoon being ruined, and Alex also going through so much personally… I'm just sorry that there was extra hurt besides just me being sick."

"I mean, the bright side of all of it is that you did a great job of pulling focus," Alex said drily. "If that hadn't happened, Maddy wouldn't have been able to leave the house for weeks, and our breakup would have been a much bigger deal."

"Always happy to create a scene, darling," the queen said airily. "I just hope that next time it doesn't come with such an unsightly scar. I may never wear a bikini again!"

"Okay, but back to you, Alex," Ben said, blinking rapidly

in a way that told Alex he was trying to erase the mental image of their mother in a bikini. "Do you actually want to be doing this work? I know you don't have the stage fright you did when we were kids, but being a working royal isn't for the faint of heart. If this isn't what you want to be doing or where you want to be, that's okay, mate. We want you around, but only if this is where you truly want to be."

Alex sighed and let himself really think about it for the first time. He was definitely thriving on the feeling of being useful, of helping out the family cause, of being one of the drivers behind significant institutional change...in as much as someone whose heart had been thoroughly broken could be thriving, that is. But his mother wasn't wrong. He *had* thrown himself into work. It was the easiest way to keep himself from missing Maddy so much. But it was exhausting being "on" all the time. With the exception of the family Sunday night dinners and the occasional hangout with Hannah and Ben, he really hadn't had a social life since Maddy.

"I mean..." he started.

"Do you still love her?" his mother asked gently.

His head fell. "Yes," he breathed out. "I feel like my heart has been run over by a steamroller."

"Finally! He admits it!" One didn't get to be queen for decades without a flair for the dramatic, Alex was reminded.

"Okay, but what do you expect me to do about it?" he asked, exasperatedly, raking a hand through his hair.

"Go. To. Her." She said it as if he was very stupid.

"But you all need me here."

"We'll find a way to soldier on without you," Ben said matter-of-factly. "I mean, we'll miss you and you better come visit, but we want to hang out with happy Alex, not 'work myself to the bone to avoid my feelings' Alex."

"But I haven't been invited."

The queen leveled him with her own look of exasperation.

"Alex, for someone who purportedly shagged his way through the entire upper crust of British society for years, you know shockingly little about romance."

"I didn't—" She silenced him with a glance. "Okay, I might not have described it exactly that way."

"Alex, your relationship might not have been public knowledge, but the impact she had on you was crystal clear. We all noticed that you were happier than we'd seen you in years last spring. I don't think there's any way she could have been making you that happy if you weren't having a similar impact on her. If you still love her, I highly doubt, given the rationale you provided for the breakup, that she doesn't feel similarly."

Alex sighed again. "It's complicated."

"Try me."

"Her father is a three-star general. She spent her entire childhood being moved around at the whims of his job. And then she married Evan. And even though she'd wanted to go to graduate school for years, they kept having to move for his job. It took me weeks to convince her to even entertain the idea of a relationship with me because she was so opposed to the idea of losing control of her life right after she'd just taken the reins for the first time ever. We were never supposed to be more than just casually dating... and then we both let it get serious. She didn't even tell me she had gotten into George-town until she'd already sent in the paperwork to go because she needed it to be based only on what she wanted. So, yeah. I'm so proud of her for doing this, but I think it's something she needs to do for herself. I don't actually know that she wants me there."

His mother smiled at him sadly. "My darling, she's a military daughter and a military widow. You just said it yourself. Her sense of duty to family and service is on overdrive. Is it possible she didn't ask because she didn't want to put you in the position of having to choose between doing your duty to the family and going with her? That she's spent so much of her life doing her duty that it might not have even occurred to her that you might be willing to relocate for her?"

Alex blinked, stunned. It truly hadn't ever occurred to him. But as his mother's words sank in, he became increasingly sure that she had hit the nail on the head. Maddy had ended things with him only days after telling him she loved him. The way she felt hadn't changed. It was the realization that to get what she wanted – a relationship with him – *his* life would have been disrupted. And it was just like her to sacrifice something she wanted for fear of inconveniencing someone. He was suddenly certain of it. But now that he'd finally found a purpose in London, he was faced with a decision: did he stay and do his duty to his country and his family? Or did he take the leap of faith and hope Maddy would be happy to see him?

* * *

"Don't forget, your first essay is due at the end of next week and the second quiz is the week after. Have a good weekend, y'all." Maddy felt her energy level drain immediately as her students started shoving notebooks and computers into their backpacks and rushing for the door. The only thing worse than enrolling in a discussion section Friday afternoon at three p.m. was teaching one. She had landed a coveted spot as a TA for the international relations course required of all first-year students in Georgetown's government major, but as a first-year grad student, she had gotten last pick of the discussion sections and had wound up with two eight a.m. sections and the dreaded Friday afternoon slot. By the end of the week she was always exhausted.

Maddy had settled in well at Georgetown. After Nadia and Alex had each made a few joking comments about how little she'd put her own mark on her rooms in London, she'd made an effort to hang art on the walls and put out some framed photos of herself with her parents and college friends. She'd even hidden a photo of her and Alex that someone had taken the night of his brother's wedding in the drawer of her nightstand. She only let herself look at it in the really low moments. She'd thrown herself into classes and her TAship and finding the best Thai takeout and lattes in Georgetown. She'd even started to make friends with a few of the other students in her cohort. She tried to ignore the gaping hole in her chest, to focus on her gratitude for the new opportunities she was having and the agency and independence she'd gained. But a piece of her had still felt like it was missing.

She hadn't been able to make herself delete Alex's number from her phone. At least daily she had to force herself not to text him random things that made her think of him. How was it that, even with her newfound independence, she was constantly thinking about the one person whose presence in her life would undo all the work she'd done to become Maddy 2.0?

She plastered a smile back on her face as two students approached to ask questions. She answered them as kindly and quickly as she could, and as the two trailed out of the class-room, she repacked her own bag and, looking around to be sure she hadn't forgotten anything, headed out into the mostly deserted halls of the Intercultural Center. The bricked Red Square outside the building, too, was mostly empty, so she was surprised to be pulled out of her thoughts by someone calling, "Ms. Cartwright?"

She stopped, puzzled. None of her students had an English accent like that. And most of her students called her "Maddy." The only person she knew who sounded like that was...

She heard footsteps echoing as they neared her. She took a

deep breath and forced herself to turn around slowly, still not allowing herself to think that she might see who she thought she might see. When she opened her eyes, she still thought she might be dreaming. Alex stood there, a bouquet of dahlias in his hand, looking at her with an inscrutable expression. "Maddy?" he said, seeming more unsure than she'd ever seen him before.

Her hand went to her mouth, and then, almost as if on instinct, she was dropping her shoulder bag and launching herself into his arms. Later, she would reflect on the moment and be glad that almost no one had been there to see the graceless way she had wrapped herself around him, like a jellyfish climbing a tree, tears streaming down her face. She almost couldn't believe he was real, but he smelled just like he always did—like sandalwood and his expensive cologne—and his arms wrapped around her with the strength and familiarity of slipping into her favorite pair of jeans.

He clutched her to him, and she vaguely heard the sound of cellophane hitting the bricks below them as he dropped the flowers to pull her tighter. Later she'd be glad that very few people had been around to see their dramatic reunion, but in that moment, the president of the United States, the dean of the graduate school, and a full marching band could have walked by and she wouldn't have cared. Finally, realizing that the pencil skirt she was wearing might be nearing the limits of its structural integrity, she lowered her legs and he set her gently on the ground.

She looked up at him, stunned, and wiped a tear from her cheek. "Alex? What... what are you doing here?"

He looked uncertain again, as if he wasn't sure that she'd be happy to see him, which was obviously patently ludicrous. She'd never been happier in her entire life. "Well, I thought..." he said, rubbing the back of his neck awkwardly, "I guess... I just... missed you?" There was a short pause. "And I guess maybe I thought you might miss me too?" His total uncertainty was adorable if absurd.

Maddy reached up to take his cheeks in her hands. "Alex, I have never been happier to see anyone in my entire life." She kissed him fiercely, as if to drive her point home, and she felt him relax as his arms wrapped around her again. He tilted her head slightly to deepen the kiss and, again, later, she'd be glad that nobody had been around to see them borderline making out in the Red Square, but again, in that moment, she didn't care at all.

She pulled back, reluctantly, as he came up for air, and laughed a little as she reached up to wipe some of her lip gloss off his face. Smoothing her skirt down, she leaned down to pick up her bag as he leaned down to pick up the flowers, and they knocked heads. They both laughed as he put his arm around her waist and they started strolling in the direction of the Carroll Walk and the main gates.

She felt, rather than saw, him lean out a bit to look her over. "The TA look?" he said, "Works."

Her cheeks flushed as she glanced down at her outfit. Little did she know when she got dressed that morning in a blue chambray shirt tucked into a black and white polka dotted pencil skirt that she'd be seeing the man of her dreams again for the first time in months.

"Thanks," she said, feeling ridiculously shy in a way that was bizarre, considering Alex knew everything about her. He pulled her to him again and kissed the top of her head as they kept walking. "I still can't believe you're here," she said almost dazedly.

"You *are* happy to see me?" he asked, seeming almost shy himself.

"Alex, how can you even ask that?"

"I don't know," he said, pulling her onto a bench under a magisterial oak tree with fiery autumn leaves along Healy

Lawn. He took a deep breath. "I was so proud of you for making the choice for yourself, and then with everything with my mum I just... I wanted you to have the independence that you wanted. But it also broke me a little bit letting you go. You have no idea how much I thought about you this summer. Wondering if you were still in London, wondering how you were doing..."

"I think I can imagine, because I was doing the same. Wondering how your mom was, wondering how you felt about being thrust into such a big role in the family. I almost texted you *so* many times, but that night after Windsor, you asked me not to, so I wanted to respect that." Her voice was thick with tears. "But I wanted nothing more than to beg you to come with me, for you to pull one of your ridiculous over-the-top stunts and magically throw some money around so we could be together."

He smiled at her sadly. "If I'd had any idea that you felt that way, I would have bought a plane if it meant getting to you sooner."

She let out a watery laugh. "How *is* your mom, by the way?"

"She's fine. She's got her first few appearances next week. She's the one who told me to come here, actually."

"She did?"

"She and Ben basically staged an intervention. They told me that I was a fool for not following you in the first place and made me see that you probably did want me here, you just didn't want to ask. So I just decided to come and find out for myself."

She beamed and snuggled closer to him on the bench, watching the last few touring prospective students and their families heading toward the main gates. They sat in comfortable silence for a moment before Maddy suddenly sat up and looked at him incredulously. "Was that your stomach?"

"Possibly?" Alex said, looking sheepish. "To be fair, all I've had today is airplane food and my stomach thinks it's about ten p.m."

She stood and pulled him to his feet. "Okay. I found a place with killer burritos a few blocks from my apartment. Let's grab some food and get you home."

Later, when they'd finished their Mexican food and digested for a bit, Maddy had led him gently towards her small bedroom. "Are you sleepy?" she asked, looking up at him, with one thought in her mind.

"Never too sleepy for you," he said, his pupils dilating.

They undressed each other slowly, Alex reacquainting himself with Maddy's curves and Maddy refamiliarizing herself with the hard planes of his chest, which had, if anything, grown starker in her absence. When he sank into her a few minutes later, they both sighed in contentment. Maddy hadn't let herself really truly imagine what it would be like if they were ever together like this again, but she would have expected their reunion to be untethered and impassioned. Instead it was languid and tender, emotionally weighty; the familiarity of their bodies and movements erasing the months of distance and longing. Alex's gaze bored into Maddy's soul, maintaining the intense eye contact even when he lost control. Afterwards, Alex collapsed onto her heavily, and Maddy thought she'd never felt anything better.

$$Chapter\ 32$$

E arly afternoon light dappled the walkway next to the Tidal Basin, the light streaming through the blazing autumnal leaves of the cherry trees that lined the reservoir. Maddy hadn't spent a spring in Washington yet, but even though she knew the blossoms would be radiant in April, it was hard to imagine topping their October glory. She and Alex were strolling leisurely, hand-in-hand, his plainclothes security officer following them at an inconspicuous distance.

She glanced up at Alex's face, shaded partially by the Georgetown baseball cap he'd borrowed from her hall closet on their way out the door. After another languorous session of reunion sex that morning, they'd wandered over to Maddy's favorite brunch spot in the neighborhood, where Alex tucked into a huge plate of challah French toast and Maddy stuffed herself with eggs Benedict. The conversation had been easy— they fell right back into their old ways and had so much to catch up on after having not spoken in months. She told Alex about the relaxing few weeks she'd spent at her parents' before moving to Georgetown, about the orange-and-white-striped neighborhood cat who kept jumping the brick wall into the courtyard outside her bedroom window and scaring the crap out of her when she opened her blinds. Alex got her up to speed on his mother's recovery, the way he and Ben and Hannah had stepped up to fill in for his parents, and the slow but steady progress he and Eric were making on their reparations project.

Maddy found herself marveling that they could just pick back up where they'd left off. In her low moments, when she couldn't sleep and felt the absence of a warm body in the bed next to her, strong arms encircling her, she'd sometimes allowed herself to wonder what it would be like if she ever saw Alex again. Let herself dream about him surprising her by coming to Washington. Never in a million years had she actually thought it might happen.

And yet here he was. Walking next to her like it was the most natural thing in the world. Like she hadn't broken both of their hearts and left him just exactly at the moment he'd needed her most. Like they hadn't been apart for five months. But they had. And the facts of the situation hadn't changed. Maddy's life was here in DC, going to class, teaching her students, and figuring out, for the first time ever, what she really wanted to do with her life. Actually choosing a path forward, blazing her own trail. And Alex was doing amazing work in London. The way his face lit up when he talked about the team Eric was developing and the weekly Wednesday dinners he'd instituted with Ben and Hannah. How could she ask him to leave all of that? She couldn't.

And so, even though she was deliriously happy to find herself strolling past the elegant arched dome of the Thomas Jefferson Memorial, looking across the water at the Washington Monument, holding hands with Alex, she couldn't stop herself from asking, "Okay, so I have to know: what are we doing here? How long are you staying? We can't keep doing this without an actual plan to be together. It's not good for either of us."

Alex smiled down at her fondly. "My Mads, always thinking about the logistics."

He led her over to a bench and drew her down to sit next to him. After kissing the side of her head gently he turned, one bent leg on the bench, to face her.

"You're right," he said, inhaling deeply. "Well, to answer one of your questions…" He paused and bit his lip. "I bought a flexible ticket. I can leave tomorrow, or I can stay forever."

Her eyes went wide.

"I mean, if you want me to."

"I mean, you staying forever would be the absolute dream, but what about your family? Your patronages? Bertie?"

"Well, Bertie we'll have to get over here, one way or another," he said. "But really, my family has been doing just fine without me for years. Plus, now they've got Hannah. She's got the mind and complete intolerance for bullshit to keep Eric's reparations project on track day-to-day. And I'll go back for the big meetings, videoconference in when I can. That's really the only patronage I'd be really worried about. And realistically, with the way she and my brother can't stay away from each other, they'll start popping out heirs to replenish the ranks any day now. I have a degree in the history of art and architecture, and I have a little bit of experience and family history in international relations. I figured between the modernity you Americans consider 'old' buildings and this being the center of your government, I can probably find some way to earn my keep."

Maddy huffed out a laugh then sobered. "But what about your role there? You wanted them to take you seriously for so long. And you finally got there. You're doing this. You're amazing at it. Why would you walk away from that?"

"Well, you see, there's this girl," he said, reaching out to toy with a strand of hair that had come loose from her pony-tail. "And it turns out, I can't really live without her."

"Alex, be serious."

"I'm dead serious."

"But you'd just walk away from that role for me?"

"My role being 'the Spare'? Maddy, the fact that it took me this long to do it makes me a certifiable dumbass. I'm a prince. At the risk of sounding obnoxious, I could have twenty job offers tomorrow if I wanted them. All I want is to be here. With you. Making sure you finally get to do whatever you want." He smiled at her and then grew more serious. "What *is* it that you want to do? I never got the chance to ask about your program, to hear what you're dreaming up. It's been eating at me for months."

"What?" she said incredulously. "All those important things to figure out, and you're wondering what I'm doing for my master's?"

He leveled her with a serious gaze. "There was not a single day I didn't think about you. Wonder what you were doing. Wonder how you were. I regretted letting you walk out of my apartment that night as soon as I woke up the next morning and wasn't out of my mind with exhaustion. Hell, I think I regretted it that night too. But I never stopped wanting to fight for you. For us." Her eyes filled with tears, and she looked out over the water, blinking. "So yes, I want to know what you're doing. What is this amazing degree you're getting?"

"Well, the degree is called Democracy and Governance."

"And what does one do with a degree in democracy and governance?"

"Well, past graduates have worked for all kinds of American government agencies, international agencies, NGOs, political campaigns..."

Alex interrupted her. "Ok, let me rephrase that: what do

you want to do with a degree in democracy and governance, besides memorizing the brochure?"

She sighed. "Honestly? I'm not really sure. Which feels kind of stupid."

"Are you enjoying your classes? Do you feel like you're getting something out of it?"

"I mean, it's only been six weeks, but yeah, I love them. I'm learning so much. It's so hard but so fascinating. They're taking us on a trip to Slovakia in the spring to learn about establishing post-communist democracy."

Alex smiled at her warmly. "Then it's not stupid at all. It sounds like a great fit for you, Mads." She felt her cheeks flush, warming at his praise, his interest. "You don't have to know exactly what you want to do—as long as it feels like you're doing something that's the right thing for right now, I say that's more than good enough."

"Thanks," she said. "When I applied I thought I'd want to use the degree to go back and get another embassy job, something with a bit more policy and strategy and a bit less coffee fetching and craft projects, but now I'm not sure. There are so many opportunities here."

"Do you want to know what I think?" Alex asked, reaching over to put his hand over hers where it rested on the bench between them.

"Of course."

"You're doing this amazing thing, choosing your own adventure for the first time in your life. I don't think you have to decide exactly what you want to do. Let yourself explore. Let yourself try things and see what you like. You're finally doing this, finally figuring out what you want for yourself. You don't have to know exactly what that is on the first pass. You can take time to just enjoy the journey."

"I know," she said quietly. "I just... I don't want anyone to think I'm wasting time."

"Maddy, I'm so proud of you. In my book, nothing that you're choosing to do just for yourself could ever be a waste of time."

Maddy found her eyes filling again. "Thank you."

"And, if you'll let me, I'll be here cheering you on the whole way and finding anyone who says you're wasting your time and kicking them in the shins."

She let out a watery laugh, then leaned closer to kiss him, nuzzling her nose against his. "Are you sure?"

"Madeleine Cartwright, I've never been surer of anything in my life."

$$Chapter\ 33$$

ne morning a few weeks later, they woke up, curled around each other. "There's something I have to do today," Maddy said.

"Okay..." Alex said, kissing her naked shoulder. "What is it?"

"I need to go out to Arlington," she stumbled a bit, "to... to visit Evan. To go to his grave. It's his birthday." The words came out in a rush.

"Of course, sweetheart," Alex said, holding her closer. "Would it be okay with you if I came with you?"

She shifted, looking at him in surprise. "You'd want to do that?" she asked. "You really don't have to. I don't mind going alone."

"No, I'd actually really like to," Alex replied. "He was an important part of your life for a really long time. I'd like to join you." He paused. "Of course, if it's okay with you."

She looked at him, her eyes a little watery, "Of course you can come." She kissed him, sweetly, tenderly, and then snuggled up to him, her arms around his naked chest, her head tucked under his chin. He kissed the top of her head, and she sighed contentedly. A year ago, the idea of doing this, of going to Evan's grave, would have filled her with guilt and grief, but today she was different. Her heart still ached for Evan, for the waste of a young, promising life. For her best friend. But the guilt that had consumed her wasn't there anymore.

"Okay," she said, rolling over and sitting on the side of the bed. "I'm going to shower and get dressed, and then we can go."

An hour and a half later, they were driving through the main gates at the cemetery. Maddy pulled a card from her purse and showed it to the guard at the gate, who saluted and waved them through. Alex looked at her questioningly. "It's a pass. Family members get permanent parking passes so that we can come visit anytime we want."

He squeezed her hand, gently. "When was the last time you were here?"

"The day he was buried. About two and a half years ago," she said quietly. "Part of me wanted to come before I left for London, but between the media and the guilt and needing to get there, it didn't happen."

She directed their driver to the appropriate section and pointed him to the curb where they could park. She and Alex got out, and she led the way up a hill. Evan's final resting place was in a line with the others in his unit who had been killed in the same accident. Together in their ultimate sacrifice, together for eternity. As his headstone came into view, Alex stopped and said, "I'll be right here."

Maddy nodded, grateful both for his company and that he understood that this was something she needed to do alone. She took a steadying breath and then walked the last twenty feet or so on her own, noticing the familiar names as she passed. Michael, Cameron, Joaquin... a few had fresh flowers by their headstones, but not all, and she made a mental note to bring more bouquets on her next visit. At the small white headstone, she crouched to lay the small bunch of burgundy dahlias she'd brought down in front and ran her hand across the top, wiping away the small amount of dust and pollen that had settled.

"Hey, Ev," she said quietly, clearing her throat to try to dislodge the lump that had developed there. "It's me." She ran a finger over the inscription on the front of the stone, a simple outline of a cross with his name, followed by the insignia of the Medal of Honor he'd been awarded posthumously. Although they'd handed it to Maddy at the ceremony, she'd insisted that his mother take the medal itself afterwards. "I'm sorry it's been so long since I've been here," she went on, feeling slightly ridiculous talking to a marble slab. "I needed to get away for a bit. To clear my head, to figure out what to do next." She paused. "I feel like you either know all of this or can't hear me at all, but I guess I can just tell you," she said with a sad chuckle. "I went to London. I met someone. He's amazing. I think you'd really like him. His name is Alex. He understands what it means to be loyal almost to a fault. Like you." She choked up, again, surprised by her own emotion. "And he loves me. So much. He'll take care of me.

"Evan, I think we both knew that even though we loved each other, it wasn't the fireworks and stars kind of love. It kills me that you never got to experience that... but I do. Alex showed me what love can really be like. And I think I owe it to myself to let him love me. And to love him back. He can never change that you were my first kiss, my first everything. You'll always have a special part of my heart. Please know that." Her voice broke and as she closed her eyes, and took a steadying breath, a tear slipped down her cheek. "But I think Alex is my future, Ev. I'm pretty sure he's the one. He brought me back from such a terrible place. He held me. He forced me to let him take care of me, which you know isn't easy to do. You never could," she let out a watery laugh thinking of Evan's occasional half-hearted attempts to be the caretaker in their relationship, when they both knew that wasn't ever going to be his role.

"I'm going to grad school now," she said, unsure of what to say when there was so much to say. "I got into Georgetown, so I'm closer. I won't go so long between visits," she promised. "I hope you knew. How much I loved you. How much you meant to me. Even if you weren't The One, you were so important. And I miss you so damn much." She swallowed again, choking back the tears. "But I hope you can be happy for me. Maybe even proud of me. Because I'm so proud of you."

It was an unusually warm day for November in DC—blue skies, the last vibrant leaves of fall clinging to the trees nearby, completely calm. But at that moment a sudden gust of wind swirled past Maddy, rustling her hair where it lay on the shoulders of her coat and cooling her tear-streaked cheeks. She looked up in surprise. She wasn't one for superstition, but for just a second there, she believed that it almost could have been a sign.

A few more tears fell down her face and she pushed herself to standing, unable to keep going. She kissed her fingertips and pressed them to the top of the stone, her eyes closed, trying to convey her feelings without the words that she was struggling to form.

Brushing the grass clippings and a few leaves from her black pants and the hem of her coat, she turned and headed back to Alex. He opened his arms as she got closer and held her, silently stroking her hair as she cried into the front of his jacket. After a few minutes she pulled back, wiping her eyes, and nodded as she looked up at him. "Thanks," she said unsteadily with a small nod. "We can go now."

"Actually," he said, swallowing thickly, "I wanted to pay my respects too. If you're okay with that?"

She looked up in surprise, but nodded. "Of course. I'll wait right here." A pause. "Unless... you want me to make introductions?"

He chuckled and kissed the top of her head, "No, I think I can take it from here, thanks."

She squeezed his hand as he walked past her, stopping at Evan's headstone. He crouched, a hand balanced on the top of the stone. Wiping her eyes again, Maddy could see his lips moving, hear the low murmur of his voice, but she was too far away to hear the words he was saying. After a few minutes Alex stood and, after standing silently in front of the stone for a moment, touched the top of it again, as if in farewell, and walked back to Maddy.

He took her hand and they started walking down the hill to where the driver waited, leaning against the car, his hat under his arm. "Do you feel better?" Alex asked, looking down at her.

She nodded. "Yes. I got a few things off my chest that I think needed to be said."

"Good," he said, squeezing her hand.

"Do you mind if I ask what *you* said?" she asked.

"I just thought I owed him an introduction. To make sure he knew that you had someone looking after you. I suspect he and I have a few things in common, and if I were in his place, I'd want to know that someone was taking care of my woman. Especially if she was a woman who was so focused on taking care of others..." He left the "and not herself" unsaid, but they both knew it.

"Thank you," she whispered, wiping one last tear from her face.

"Let's go home," he said, putting his arm around her and guiding her into the back seat.

T *hree Years Later*

The black Range Rover glided to a stop in front of the turreted facade of Balmoral, the royal family's summer home in Aberdeenshire, Scotland. Maddy stepped out of the back seat, not waiting for Graham to open the door for her, and inhaled the fresh August air, redolent of pine, petrichor, and freshly cut grass. A broad smile spread across her face. In the three years since she and Alex had given up the farce that their relationship was only a fling, Balmoral had become one of her favorite places. She felt like she really got to know her in-laws as people there. Although they clearly adored her and made valiant efforts at normalcy in London, it was only at Balmoral where she saw the king in his cargo shorts with Birkenstock sandals and tall white socks. Only there where she occasionally saw the queen in leggings and a sweatshirt. And it was at Balmoral where she really saw Alex at his most comfortable.

They were cocooned in the rural Scottish countryside, the locals mostly left them alone, and unless something utterly unprecedented was happening, the press couldn't be bothered to travel that far into the wilds of Scotland. The two weeks they spent there with Alex's family each summer had quickly become the happiest, most relaxed weeks of her year every year.

"Miss Maddy," Graham's voice broke into her reverie. "Alex said you all would have drinks and dinner here and then stay with Ben and Miss Hannah and the children at Craigowen, so I'll just drive your luggage there and have it taken to your suite."

"That sounds perfect. Thank you so much, Graham. And thanks for picking me up. I know it's a long drive to Edinburgh."

"Not at all, Miss Maddy. We're just thrilled to have you back."

She smiled warmly at him, delighted to see their British driver. Although Alex had tried valiantly to entice him to join them in America, Graham had politely declined, stating that his mother needed him in the UK. He worked primarily for Hannah and Ben now, but was always on call for Alex and Maddy when they were in the UK several times a year. "It's good to be back."

Just then an odd mechanical sound greeted their ears. Maddy's brow furrowed as she struggled to identify the noise. "Graham," she began, "what's..." But their driver was already getting back into the Range Rover. She could have sworn she heard laughter coming from the open window as he headed toward the cottage on the grounds of Balmoral where they stayed with Ben and Hannah and their family when they came to Scotland. It almost seemed like he was driving faster than normal, as if to avoid her question... but that had to be her imagination.

Returning her attention to the vehicle on the horizon, she

was certain she had to be having a jet lag-induced hallucination. It couldn't be... But it was. As the absurd wheeled conveyance drew nearer, Maddy realized that it was a vintage dark-green motor bike with an attached sidecar. Alex was driving with Bertie riding in the sidecar, both of them wearing matching dark green helmets.

"Darling!" Alex cried, pulling the helmet off and throwing his leg over the side of the bike to stride in her direction. Maddy was overwhelmed by seemingly discordant reactions: amusement, horror, and, inexplicably, lust. There was something about the way Alex took off the helmet and strode toward her that did things to her. It had to be the jet lag. And the two weeks of being apart. There was no way that death trap could be sexy. Definitely not.

Rational thought ceased as Alex drew her into his arms and kissed her thoroughly. He'd had to come to the UK early to attend a board meeting for Eric's Royal Council on Reparations. When he'd moved to America mostly full-time three years earlier, he'd handed day-to-day mitigation of the toxic Caucasity in the room to Hannah, who was more than capable of deploying a stern look and a carefully chosen phrase to make sure everyone stayed focused and respectful as Eric and his small team led them steadfastly into the future. But Alex still came for significant board meetings, and this one was the most important. After several years of hard work, the meeting the previous week had been an opportunity for recipients of reparations to share the impacts that the financial support had made in their lives and for their analysts to share initial data regarding the success of their program.

Alex slipped his tongue into Maddy's mouth, his delectable groan vibrating against her sternum where their chests were pressed together. She sighed into him. Two weeks was really too long. They'd figured out a pretty good cadence for their trans-Atlantic relationship. They went to the UK together three or four times a year: Christmas, the king's ceremonial birthday in late spring, Balmoral in August, and sometimes for a quick trip during the fall if they could get away. Then Alex would come for the odd long weekend or week where necessary to support the family and show up for the patronages he'd remained involved with after he'd moved. It was, for the most part, a dream arrangement: they still saw Alex's family regularly, Alex still got to be involved with the family firm, and Maddy had limited press exposure and only on her terms. They'd established mutually agreed-upon boundaries with the media whereby they provided at least one opportunity to be seen and photographed during each visit home, and then the Royal Rota more or less left them alone the rest of the time, unless there was another family outing that generated press coverage.

The arrangement had, at first, been a challenging compromise for her. Worthwhile to get to be with Alex, for sure. But hard to willingly submit herself to that level of attention. But she'd soon found that it wasn't so bad. When they were in Washington, even though they still attracted the occasional stare from a passing tourist or drew glances when they took their seats at a restaurant, they weren't nearly as prominent as they were in London. They were constantly surrounded by the American political elite. And the denizens of DC took pride in being outwardly entirely disinterested in the prominent citizens in their midst.

A short yip reminded them that they weren't alone, and Maddy turned to greet Bertie who, she realized, was strapped securely into his sidecar by what appeared to be a custom five-point harness. As she greeted him, freeing him from the absurd doggy helmet, and unclasping the harness, she looked over her shoulder at Alex. "What the hell is this?"

Bertie leapt into her arms, licking her face jubilantly, his entire back half waving back and forth as if he had more than a stub of a tail to wag.

"Yes," she said in the voice that she knew sounded ridiculous, but that somehow always emerged from her mouth when she was talking to the dog. "Your daddy is so silly. What was he thinking? Huh? What did he think he was doing buying a motorcycle and letting you ride in it?"

Alex joined her on the grass next to the driveway. "It's only for use on the property, it's from the fifties, so it barely breaks fifty miles per hour, and it's just so fun!" He had a boyish grin on his face that caused Maddy's heart to overflow. In the years that they'd been together, Alex had honed his public work, assisting not only with his family's patronages, but also taking seats on a number of boards in DC to advocate for historical preservation and build more ties between the UK and the US. Maddy had watched him work up to doing more and more public work, saw the way it got easier for him and exhausted him less. But it was still hard work for him, being perceived by hundreds of people at a time, having assumptions made about him based on who his family was. And seeing him so light and free at Balmoral made her heart melt.

She gave him a begrudging smile as Bertie flopped over in the bowl of her crossed legs, presenting his belly for scritches. "Okay," she said with a fond smile and a sigh, "just be careful. You're carrying my two favorite creatures in that thing."

He leaned over to kiss the side of her head as he put an arm around her and looked lovingly down at the bundle of fur and energy in her lap. "Yes, dear."

* * *

Alex gazed across the dining room table at Maddy, her head thrown back in laughter at something Hannah had said. The two had become thick as thieves, despite the ocean between them most of the year, with weekly FaceTime dates and seemingly endless voice memos flying back and forth across the Atlantic. The low light from the sconces along the wall and the taper candles dotted down the long tartan-covered table brought out the auburn highlights in her dark hair and made the diamonds in the ring on her left hand sparkle. He allowed his mind to wander, remembering the day the previous autumn when he'd finally decided the moment was right to ask her the question he'd wanted to ask her since about two weeks after they'd met. He'd taken her on their favorite walk at Windsor, retracing the steps they'd taken the day he'd first kissed her there. At the overlook where Bertie had almost garroted them, he'd gotten down on one knee and asked her to marry him using a ring that had once belonged to his great-grandmother.

Waiting so long had been an excruciating test of his patience. He'd been positive that Maddy was the one for so long. So sure, in fact, that the day they'd first gone to Arlington together to visit Evan's grave, Alex had asked permission from her late husband's... spirit? Ghost? Alex wasn't sure what to call talking to a headstone. But he'd made his intentions clear on his first visit to the States and, given that the lawn hadn't opened up beneath him and lightning hadn't struck him down, he liked to think that Evan approved. But Alex had also known that, despite his total confidence in their relationship, Maddy needed more time. She'd come around to a relationship, had allowed herself to experience love, but he wasn't prepared to ask her to marry him until she was ready. Alex had watched her blossom through her graduate program and supported her toward a path to a future that was fully of her own design. And he wanted to be sure that his presence in her life didn't impede her dreams. That their relationship and eventual marriage didn't supersede the goals she'd finally been able to craft for herself.

When he looked at her now, leaning to her other side to listen to something their two-year-old niece Eliza was telling her, he was filled with pride. She'd graduated a year earlier with her master's degree. Alex had been careful not to push too hard, but after months of periodic late-night conversations where he encouraged her to dream about what was really important to her, about the types of change she wanted to be able to make in the world, she'd realized that there was important work to be done closer to home. Which is how she'd found herself working for the Department of Defense supporting Gold Star families whose service members had been killed in action. It had also led her to use the money she'd inherited upon Evan's death to start the Evan Grogan Memorial Fund to provide extra support to families with particular need.

She caught his eye from across the table and winked at him saucily. He was incredibly glad for the tartan napkin in his lap, which hid the rapidly growing erection from his family. Ben was still telling him something funny that their five-month-old daughter Erin had done, and his mother was sitting on her other side making googly eyes at his father, who sat across from her next to Hannah. It had been more than two weeks since he and Maddy had been alone together. There hadn't been any time between her arrival and dinner. He couldn't wait to get her back to Craigowen.

* * *

An hour and a half later, Maddy found herself being enthusiastically hoisted onto the granite countertop in Craigowen's kitchen. The king had gotten carried away wanting to talk more about one of the patronages Alex was still involved with, and while Ben and Hannah had managed to leave as soon as dinner was over with the excuse of having to get the girls to bed by a reasonable hour, Maddy and Alex had been stuck in horny jail, Alex smiling and nodding at what his father was saying, while Maddy tried to hold up her end of the conversation with Queen Sarah and surreptitiously looking at her watch. When a genuine yawn—she was exhausted after a busy week at work and the trans-Atlantic red-eye flight—overtook her, the king and queen had finally released them and Alex and Maddy had made a beeline to the "cottage" on the estate where they stayed with Ben and Hannah and their girls when they visited Balmoral.

Calling Craigmore a "cottage" was about as accurate as calling Alex's—now their—place in London an "apartment," but Maddy supposed, it was petite compared to the Victorian palace where the king and queen stayed. As comfortable as staying in the palace was, they enjoyed getting a little space, not having to worry about Bertie chewing quite as many valuable objects, and knowing they wouldn't bother Alex's parents. Maddy refused to let Alex drive her on the motorbike after dark, so they made the ten-minute walk quickly, mostly in silence, Bertie hurrying along in front of them on his leash.

When they finally arrived at the cottage, Alex shoved open the door to the kitchen with more force than was really necessary, and practically threw Maddy atop the countertop, quickly invading the space between her legs and gripping her ass firmly in his hands. Not that Maddy was complaining. After so long apart, feeling the already prominent bulge in his pants as he pressed firmly against her center made her almost feral with need. She cradled the back of his head, anchoring his mouth to hers as they devoured each other, making up for lost time.

Alex's hand snaked beneath the cotton sweater she'd worn on the plane, gliding up her ribcage to cup her breasts through her bra. "Alex," she groaned into his mouth, their connection never breaking. Her hips were writhing against him, desperately, naturally seeking pressure, friction, more.

They were racing towards third base when she heard a loud, pointed throat clearing over the sounds of their heavy breathing.

"Could you two get a room?" Ben drawled sardonically, bringing them slamming back to the present.

Alex pulled back, resting his forehead against Maddy's, both of them catching their breath.

When Maddy finally managed to force herself to turn around, Ben was standing next to the refrigerator, rifling through the open freezer with a baby bottle in one hand. As he pulled out a small plastic baggy of frozen milk, he turned to give them a wicked glance. "I know it's been two weeks, but really, man. There are children here!"

"And unless Hannah's on the fast track to sainthood, I also know how they got here!" Alex retorted good-naturedly, while sliding Maddy off the counter, twining their hands together, and making a hasty exit from the kitchen towards their wing of the seven-bedroom house.

"Night, Ben!" Maddy called over her shoulder as Alex practically dragged her to their room.

They got a late start the next day. Between the reunion lovemaking and the jet lag, which led to more, middle-of-the-night lovemaking, very little actually sleeping had occurred until the wee hours of the morning. When Maddy finally woke up, Alex was propped up against the ornately carved wooden headboard looking at something on his iPad.

"Good morning," she said, stretching and rolling over to face him.

"Well, good morning to you, sleepyhead," he said, his smile warming his slate-gray eyes.

"What time is it?"

"Almost eleven."

"Wow." She ran a hand blearily over her face. "That's like teenager-level sleeping in."

"You need the rest. You've been working so hard." Alex looked down at her fondly, smoothing her sleep-tousled hair.

"I mean, a lot of last night did not involve much sleeping, Your Royal Highness," she said, smirking at him.

"Hey, the best cure for jet lag is a solid orgasm. That's what I always say," he held his hands up in innocent protest. "I'm just doing my job as a public servant."

Maddy laughed and pulled him down to her. "Public service, my ass," she said between slow, sensual kisses.

When they finally came up for air again, Maddy levered herself up, slipping from beneath the sheets and fumbling around with her feet for the slippers she needed to counteract the Scottish chill, even in the summer. "So what are we doing today?" she asked, cinching her bathrobe around her waist.

"Well, my dad is dead set on teaching Eliza to ride a pony..." Alex began.

"Eliza's *two*!" Maddy shrieked. "Two-year-olds don't ride horses!"

"Mads, I know that. And you know that. But try telling that to His Majesty King Alfred."

"Oh god," she said, rolling her eyes and going to the armoire where one of the staff had unpacked her suitcase before she'd even arrived the day before. "I'm not sure I can watch that."

"Me neither. That's why I asked them to put together a picnic lunch for us. I thought we'd go down by the river," Alex replied, watching her slip into a pair of leggings and a lightweight oversized sweater.

"Sounds lovely," she said.

. . .

An hour later, they were stretched out on a tartan blanket along the banks of the River Dee. The kitchen staff at the main castle had packed an over-the-top picnic—cold salmon from the night before, a loaf of crusty bread, fresh sheep's cheese made on the estate, the crunchiest, sweetest grapes that Maddy had ever had, a packet of shortbread, and a delightfully refreshing bottle of dry Riesling.

"Ahh, this is the life," Maddy said, looking up through the leaves to the cerulean Scottish sky. "It's so beautiful."

"It is," Alex's voice was close to her ear and she flushed, realizing that he hadn't been looking at the sky.

He drew her towards him and kissed her, his lips and tongue cool from the chilled wine. As he invaded her mouth she moaned involuntarily, her libido springing to life as if they hadn't been making up for lost time for half the night. She ran her hands down his back stopping to knead the firm globes of his ass appreciatively. The groan that rumbled in his chest, coupled with the bulge that was increasingly noticeable beneath his joggers left her breathless. She kept wondering if sex with Alex would ever get old, but in more than three years it hadn't. He was seemingly insatiable with apparently unlim-ited sexual creativity, and between that and their periodic brief separations when Alex went to the UK or Maddy traveled for work, she was constantly hot for him. Before meeting Alex she'd certainly enjoyed sex, but it was never something she craved when she wasn't getting it. With Alex it seemed like one of them was constantly having an orgasm, recovering from an orgasm, or plotting out the next way one of them was going to have one.

And so, even though the old Maddy would have been absolutely horrified, the new Maddy—Maddy 2.0—barely batted an eye when Alex's hand slid between their bodies, massaging her firmly through her leggings. "Oh god," she panted.

"Yes?" Alex said, taking a break to look down at her with a wicked glint in his eye.

She scrunched her face at his absurd joke, but was almost immediately distracted as he started to gently work at the high waistband of her pants. "Can we?" he asked, his eyes dark with desire.

"Here?" she panted, lifting her head slightly to look around.

"Ben and Eliza are with my parents and Bertie at the castle, Hannah and the baby are napping at Craigmore, and if anyone else is out here, they're going to be smacked with such a big trespassing lawsuit that it won't even matter."

Allowing herself to think for only a second more, Maddy nodded quickly, reaching up to kiss and lick her way down Alex's neck as he disentangled her legs from the stretchy material. The fresh air against her center was a new sensation and slightly unsettling, but after a brief adjustment, Maddy was reveling in the slight summer breeze against her overheated core. Moments later, Alex's warm breath provided a delicious contrast as he angled her hips up to meet his mouth, his tongue reaching out to outline the shape of her sex. "Alex," she gasped, trying to keep her voice down.

He looked up at her, an eyebrow cocked in consternation. "If that's all you've got, I'm clearly out of practice." Giving her a playful nip on the inside of her thigh, he said, "The deer don't care what we're doing as long as it doesn't involve a shotgun and there's nothing else for miles. Let me hear you, Mads." This time when his thumbs coaxed her open and his tongue skated around her opening, she let herself moan in pleasure. And when his lips briefly sealed around her clit she was practically keening with need. "That's more like it," Alex growled, slipping two fingers inside her, urging her towards her release.

"Fuck," she hissed, as he pushed her closer and closer to the edge. "Fuck, *so good*" was practically becoming a mantra as she moved nearer to climax. Withdrawing his mouth slightly, Alex let go of her hip to smack her sex firmly, never slowing the pace of his fingers surging in and out of her. Returning his lips to suck at her most sensitive spot, she finally felt herself go flying over the cliff, stars bursting in front of her eyes.

She returned to awareness to find Alex sucking his fingers clean, looking down at her with a self-satisfied grin on his face. "Okay, so they might have heard that back at the castle..." he said sardonically. She felt her cheeks heat. "Just kidding," he said, rubbing the tip of his nose against hers and kissing her lightly. She laughed and then abruptly launched herself at him, pushing him down onto his back and gripping him through the soft fabric of his joggers.

"Madeleine Cartwright, what are you doing?" Alex cried, his voice shot through with mock outrage.

She reached for his waistband and rolled her eyes before turning her attention southward with only a sarcastic "Oh, spare me."

Acknowledgments

For as many times as I've eagerly read the acknowledgements of other books, actually sitting down to write them feels *incredibly* daunting. I have been enormously fortunate to have an unparalleled team of cheerleaders, helpers, advisors, and listeners as I went through the process of writing my first novel. Without any of them, this book wouldn't be what it is today.

First off, thank YOU, reader! Thank you so much for taking a chance on a debut author. To have anyone that I don't actually know reading my book is a complete win for me and I am truly grateful. I hope we meet some day so I can gush about how smart and talented you are and how cute your outfit is.

I also have to thank Sarah Pesce at Lopt and Cropt Editing, who has been with me almost since the very beginning. Her encouragement and thoughtful feedback made this book SO much better. Any mistakes are absolutely mine, not hers.

Kelsey Bowman at Let's Get Lit Studio did an absolutely phenomenal job with my cover. I gave them next to no useful direction and look at what the result was!? I cannot believe I'm so lucky to get to work with someone who is both an absolutely brilliant designer and artist and also a friend.

Erin Smith was both one of the earliest readers of *Spare Me* and has also been so helpful trying to teach me how to Instagram. This technologically illiterate elder millennial could definitely not have gotten this far without her. Getting a notification saying that she was crying while reading an early draft of *Spare Me* was one of the first things that really made me feel like a true indie author. Thank you so much, my friend.

To Erin Fasone and Maj. Joe Fasone, my sensitivity readers, I am so grateful for the time you took to provide such thoughtful and helpful feedback. Hearing your perspectives on this story, and having you find my mistakes was so valuable and I am so thankful both for this and for your many years of friendship. Any errors relating to the military lifestyle are fully mine.

To my alpha and beta readers, thank you for the hype, the love, and the excellent constructive criticism. This book would be a lot worse without each of you and the squealing comments helped keep me going when the editing slog was long and hard.

I think every modern author owes a big debt of gratitude to at least one group chat. To the combined membership of both the Crane Coven and the MacCoven: even though I've only met a few of you in person, your friendship and support over the years means the world to me. I am so grateful to each of you for your enthusiasm and love. To the members of MomCamp: the memes and reels get me through the days, but your friendship gets me through life. I treasure you all.

Lara Hodo was the first person to read an entire draft of this book and reassure me that it didn't suck, so I am particularly grateful to her not only for that, but for our weekly writing cave Zoom dates, the beautiful fan art, and for answering my long list of absurd questions about dog ownership. My friend, you're the best and I can't wait to return the favor.

Eliza MacArthur is actually the reason this book exists. If I hadn't tipsily confessed to her one night that I had an idea for a book and then told her what it was, this book would still be 1400 words in a document that hadn't been touched since

2018. She has been there for every single step of the way from squealing into a voice memo that I had to keep writing to helping me figure out all of the intricacies of being an independent author, to building my website, to listening to me yap for literal hours about this book. Basically every part of this book that isn't actual words on the page is thanks to her (and her feedback made a lot of the words on the page much better, too). I love you so much and cannot imagine my life without you.

To my IRL friends: Patty and Cody, Rob and Emmy, Joaquin and Jess, Lori, Joyce, Amy, Betty, Erin, Nicole, Monica, and all the ones who I know I'm missing. I know you have all been slightly baffled by what I've been up to, but you've gamely expressed interest and enthusiasm anyway and I am so grateful. If you need to know which pages to skip, just let me know.

To my parents: if you've gotten this far, you've successfully navigated several layers of carefully laid deception and I salute you. You raised me to be a smart, independent woman and I'm so grateful for that, but we can never talk about this book.

To my kids, if you're reading this and you also read all of the words before this, first of all: congratulations on learning to read! Second of all, please send the therapy bills my way.

And finally, to my real-life romance hero: John, you have been 1,000% supportive from the very first day of this process, even when it has meant additional parenting duties while I finished a draft, having less of my attention while I tried to figure out how to market a book, and unquestioningly spending a not insignificant amount of money on this passion project. I could not ask for a better partner, co-parent, husband. You are my rock and I love you HHHCK.

About the Author

Parker Blythe writes smart, steamy romance novels with healthy doses of both humor and heart. A classically-trained singer and musicologist, when she's not writing, she can be found working a day job in higher education, singing along to show tunes, playing word games, baking, or sipping on a cocktail. She lives on the Central Coast of California with her earth angel husband and two children.

www.parkerblythe.com

www.ingramcontent.com/pod-product-compliance
Lightning Source LLC
Chambersburg PA
CBHW070601300726
48975CB00006B/1671